# HEAVEN'S FALLEN

## BENJAMIN MEDRANO

Heaven's Fallen by Benjamin Medrano

Contact the author at BenjaminPMedrano@gmail.com

Visit the author's website at benjaminmedrano.com

Cover Art by Nguyen Uy Vu

*For my friends, my family, and my beloved.*

# FOREWORD

This book has surprised me at every turn. First, in getting as far as I did on it while working on my primary projects, then by taking twists and turns I didn't anticipate. *Heaven's Fallen* was spawned from several older story ideas I'd shelved, but which had some plot seeds which I wanted to use in the future. It appears that the future is coming sooner than I expected, though.

To be clear up front, *Heaven's Fallen* isn't completely self-contained. It's going to be part of a trilogy, and there are going to be many unanswered questions at the end of it. The story is also dark in some ways, which shouldn't be surprising when demons are major characters and it's set in the hells.

I hope any of you who choose to read this enjoy the book. I certainly enjoyed writing it!

*Benjamin Medrano*

# PROLOGUE

𝒶 gony seared through Isalla as the wind whipped by her face in a dull roar that suppressed all other sound. Pain radiated from the numerous wounds she'd received, most notably from her back, but also from a half-dozen other wounds and the virulent poison that seeped through her body like dull flames. Worst of all was the collar around her neck, its spikes buried in her flesh as it slowly pumped more of the poison into her.

If Isalla still had her wings, she might be able to redirect her course somewhat, or even get help, but Haral had taken pleasure in severing them with a flaming sword that cauterized the wounds. The poison steadily weakened Isalla as well, and with the tendons severed in her arms and legs, her limbs were worse than useless for trying to change her course as Isalla fell from the clouds.

The fall was long, and if she could have, Isalla would have cursed the traitors who'd ambushed her. As she fell through the towering clouds, the light abruptly shifted, growing duller and more muted as the clouds changed. She'd left the heavens, Isalla realized, trying and failing to swallow her saliva. The traitors obviously didn't want her dying in the heavens, as they'd dropped her in a location that connected to the mortal world.

Anger rushed through her in waves, but the anger was threaded with fear. Fear of what Haral might be planning.

Yet there was nothing Isalla could do as she watched the clouds of the mortal world around her pass by, until they opened before her to reveal the approaching vistas of the ground below, from towering, green-swathed mountains to rolling plains with the glittering ocean in the distance. It was as she looked directly below her that Isalla's fear grew yet again, for there wasn't ground beneath her.

Directly below her was the heart of the mountain range, and the vast, cavernous cone of a volcano yawned open before her... yet one without lava within. The smoke rising from it came through yet another portal, and at last Isalla realized what Haral's plan for her truly was. She'd fall through the gateway into the lower planes, into the very hells themselves, and there was *nothing* Isalla could do to stop it. If anyone used magic to look for her, it would appear as though she'd gone on a foolish crusade into the lands of their enemies.

Isalla struggled, trying to change her course, but her arms simply flapped uselessly at her sides as panic grew within her. She plunged into the sulfurous smoke, and she began to cough, agony spiking through her with every breath that passed. Unconsciousness would almost be a blessing, but it eluded her.

She fell into the volcano, helplessly watching as she closed on the portal, seeing the winding paths and roads which demons took into the mortal world pass by. She braced herself as best she could as she plunged through the ink-black portal, and into the sulfurous clouds of the hells.

The skies here were different than those of the heavens or the mortal world. The world was darker, with the skies a deeper crimson, while the clouds were nearly black. Below her, she could see the expanse of one of dozens of immense, magical mountains that pierced the sky of the hells and gave the demons access to most of the portals into the mortal world.

A magical gust of superheated air hit Isalla, and she grunted in pain as it caused her wounds to flare with agony again, her eyes watering as she was magically shunted away from the mountain and sent spiraling outward over the dark landscape.

At last, Isalla's fall was nearing its end, and she felt her stomach tightening as she descended toward the ground like a falling star. At least the end would be quick, she hoped, though the sheer length of the fall had almost been worse than being killed by a demon. As she descended toward a huge forest, Isalla closed her eyes and braced herself for the end, anguish rushing through her at the thought that she'd never have the chance to stop the psychotic zealots who were in the heavens.

The impact of a branch against her shoulder sent Isalla spinning, and she tried to scream in pain, only to have it cut short by the collar. Isalla's mind was swimming, the poison even hotter in her veins as she braced herself… then stopped.

"Now, just *what* do we have here?" a woman's sultry voice asked curiously.

Isalla opened her eyes, barely retaining consciousness, and found herself hanging motionless in the air just a few feet from the rocky ground, streamers of purple light wrapped around her. She was in the middle of a forest of black trees, and she looked up at the speaker… and if anything, her terror grew even greater. And with it, something inside her snapped.

A woman stood nearby, the purple light extending from her fingers. She was beautiful, with pale skin and deep violet eyes, but it was the narrow purple horns extending from her brow and the swaying tail behind her that truly terrified Isalla. The robes the woman was wearing were black and shrouded much of her figure, but her hair shimmered almost like obsidian in the light as she looked at Isalla curiously, her purple lips pursed.

And then, as despair overtook her, Isalla lost consciousness at last.

# CHAPTER 1

*I*t was almost a surprise to wake up. Even more surprising to Isalla was that the pain which had been afflicting her had receded, and she couldn't feel the venom at all. She was laying on something soft, and as she twitched a leg, she felt something silky over her. The somewhat rougher material around her neck and on her back concerned her, though, and she could smell something odd. It might be soup, but that seemed strange to her, so she opened her eyes just a crack.

The room she was in was small, so small that just opening her eyes she could see where each of the dark planks of wood on the ceiling reached the walls. Despite her natural ability to see in far less light than most people, Isalla had trouble making out the room, and she winced, opening her eyes fully as she shifted onto her side slowly, more surprised that she wasn't tied down or otherwise restrained. She felt incredibly weak, which worried Isalla, but she frowned as she looked at the rest of the room.

There was a small wooden stool next to the bed, along with an end table, while the bed itself was barely wide enough for a single person. Between the table and the bed, the room was almost completely full, and Isalla's gaze drifted to the door, and to the brass knob holding the door shut. The hinges were on the outside, and she couldn't see a keyhole, which concerned her.

She vaguely remembered seeing a demon just before she lost consciousness.

Just as she was debating whether to try standing up, the door suddenly opened, and the warm light from outside the room caused her to flinch back. Standing in the doorway, silhouetted by the light, was the same demoness. The woman's eyes were hard to see, and she was holding a steaming bowl in one hand and a basket in the other. The woman looked at Isalla and smiled, not showing her teeth. The demon was terrifying, especially considering Isalla's situation.

"I thought I sensed you waking. You're a most unusual guest, and I must say that you made quite the entrance. If I'd been a moment later, it would have been too late for you," the woman said, her voice oddly smooth and seductive as she set the basket on the table, along with the bowl. "I've never had an angel as a patient before, either."

"G-get away from me!" Isalla exclaimed, her voice breaking slightly as her throat barely cooperated, sending a spike of both pain and fear through her as she tried to force herself up and back against the wall. "If you don't, I'll—"

"You'll what? Drool on me?" the demoness asked mildly, folding her arms in front of her, an eyebrow arching curiously as she looked at Isalla, who flushed in embarrassment. "You're so weak I believe most children could overpower you, but even so, if you keep straining yourself, you're going to snap your ligaments again. With as difficult as it was to put them back together the *first* time, I might just leave them that way."

"W-what?" Isalla asked, feeling distinctly off-balance, then she glanced down to see obvious bandages on her arms and wrists. With trembling fingers, she slid one aside to see the swollen flesh below it, along with the angry red line where the blade Haral had wielded cut through her skin. It was partially closed, and she looked up at the demoness in disbelief as she asked. "You... you *healed* me?"

"Angels," the demoness muttered under her breath, shaking her head as she snagged the stool with her tail, pulling it into a better position, then sat down. "Yes, I healed you. I *also* kept you from making an enormous mess in the forest nearby when you

6

landed. Now, lay down, hm? I need to see how your back is healing. Those were the worst of your injuries, and there's nothing I could do to repair that much damage."

"B-but… but you're a *demon*. Why would you…" Isalla floundered, and her eyes widened as she thought of another possible motive. "You're just going to sell me to some demon that'll sacrifice me, won't you?!"

"You angels are just *so* bigoted, aren't you?" the woman replied, glowering at Isalla for a moment, then gestured at the door. "Fine. If you *really* want to accuse me of something like that, you can leave. I won't stop you, though I doubt you'll make it more than a few dozen feet or so in your condition. Never mind saving your life when I kept you from splattering across the forest floor, I also neutralized the toxin which was going to liquefy your muscles and heart before it could kill you, but I suppose this is the gratitude that I should *expect* from an angel."

Isalla stared at the woman for a long moment, disbelieving, and yet at the same time she felt herself begin to calm down. Finally, she asked hesitantly. "Then you… you *aren't* going to hurt me, or sell me? Why not? Isn't that what demons do?"

"No, demons *don't* do that. If we did, there wouldn't be any of us left. Those who go to war, maybe, but not the common demons who live here from day to day. Do your people do nothing but perform work for others selflessly?" The demoness demanded, her voice almost cracking like a whip and causing Isalla to flinch. "As for doing anything to you? I could do *anything* I wanted to you right now, and you couldn't stop me. You aren't strong enough, and you've been laying in that bed for three days. I could've done anything I wanted to you or drugged you so that you wouldn't be able to wake for as long as I liked. I chose to save your life because I'm the local healer, nothing more."

Looking into the woman's violet eyes, slowly Isalla began to realize the woman seemed to be telling the truth. The idea of a demon not wanting to hurt her or enslave her was… unbelievable. After the decades she'd spent fighting against demons, it was preposterous, and yet here she was, with one having rescued her from certain death and healed her. As much as Isalla's instincts screamed that she should take the offer to run, she also knew the woman was right. Isalla's muscles were trembling even after the threadbare effort she'd made to press against the wall. It was doubtful that she'd make it more than a few dozen paces out the door. Between that, her reactions, and everything else, Isalla's cheeks flushed as shame began to overwhelm her.

"I'm... I'm not entirely certain I can trust you. Everything I've experienced says that I shouldn't... but you're right. I *am* weak," Isalla admitted nervously, and slowly took a deep breath, then laid down carefully, her arms almost giving out beneath her. "It... you scare me. I'm sorry."

"As nervous as the angels who cut the wings from your back?" the demoness asked, not touching Isalla yet, her eyebrows raised as she sat back, tapping the table with a single, violet fingernail.

"W-what? Why do you think angels cut... cut my wings?" Isalla gasped, her eyes widening and a thread of pain going through her as she instinctively tried to flex her wings, prompting the injuries to throb and anguish to rip through her.

"Oh, *please*. Your wings were perfectly severed right where they joined your back, cauterized such that they left no stumps. Furthermore, most demons have claws or fangs," the demoness replied derisively, baring her teeth to reveal two sharp canines, though they weren't *that* prominent, and continued as Isalla winced at her biting tone. "None of your injuries were from either, and considering the number of injuries you sustained, that beggars belief. I know most demons would be curious about how you'd taste, especially a young, beautiful angelic woman. Now, the poison... that *is* of demonic origin, but the method of administering it was foolish. The poison weakens in contact with iron, and they used iron spikes in the collar. No demon would use it that way. No, that means that whoever did this to you was either an angel or a mortal. The precision indicates angel."

"You know a lot about this sort of thing," Isalla replied, swallowing hard. She did consider trying to conceal who'd attacked her for a moment, just to keep it from a demon, but abandoned the impulse after a moment. "But you're right, it was angels who hurt me."

"Of course I am. I've seen about any injury the hells can inflict on someone over the centuries, so I've gotten used to identifying where the damage came from. Yours are a bit more unusual, but not unheard of," the woman replied, carefully peeling one of the bandages on Isalla's back away. It must have been attached with some type of adhesive, Isalla realized, cringing as she felt the air wash against the injury. "Hmm… they're coming along fairly well, considering. I expect you'll have scars, despite my herbs and how cleanly angels are said to heal, but at least they're healing. The scars can always be dealt with later. I'm going to wash the wounds, then apply bandages again. Try not to move too much, or to try flexing your muscles. It could open the wounds again."

"I'll try, but it's difficult," Isalla replied hesitantly, watching the demon dip a cloth in the bowl, then gasping as the soft cloth ran over her back. It stung, but from the warmth she suspected the water in the bowl had been boiled recently. That was slightly reassuring, since it reminded her of what some angelic healers did.

"That which is good for you is rarely easy. Do try, though," the woman replied, continuing to work, her movements surprisingly gentle.

For a long minute, the room was silent, and the angel felt herself relax marginally. Eventually, Isalla asked, "What did you mean about the poison? I didn't really have a chance to know what it was doing…"

"That was a toxin called warrior's end. It's an extract of a particularly nasty plant from one of the jungles, and it causes the muscles of the victim to slowly atrophy and liquefy over the course of several hours," the demoness replied softly, her words causing Isalla to flinch in horror, but the woman continued speaking as she continued the treatment gently, then set aside the cloth and picked up another, along with a jar. "Some demon lords use it as a painful method of execution, as it leaves the victim looking wizened and old before their heart bursts. More commonly, it's used to weaken particularly violent or strong prisoners or enemies. It isn't easy to acquire, that much is for certain... it likely will take you months, at best, to regain your strength. You're fortunate that I had the antidote, at least if you like living."

"I am. That's just a *horrible* poison to inflict on anyone," Isalla said, cringing internally, then letting out a gasp of relief as the woman dabbed something cool onto the injuries, easing the discomfort radiating from them.

"It is. There's a reason why I *have* the antidote. I try to always keep some on hand, just in case," the woman agreed, spreading the liquid slowly. "I'm about done here, then we can get you something to eat, if you'd like."

"That... would be appreciated," Isalla admitted, feeling a little guilty about her suspicions. Even angels had to eat, and she hadn't been terribly polite. She hesitated, then offered softly, "I'm called Isalla. What about you?"

"You can call me Kanae," the demoness replied, pulling out some bandages. "Now, let's get this done, shall we?"

There was something odd about Kanae, Isalla thought, and it wasn't just that the demoness wasn't trying to hurt her. It was something that Isalla couldn't place, though, but for the moment she put it aside and tried to relax, even if her discomfort and fears made that difficult.

It wasn't as though she could do anything else, yet.

# CHAPTER 2

*I*salla found herself confined to bed for another two days, though she *did* make a single brief attempt to walk the next day. The results had made her unhappily aware of just how weak she was, and the attempt had been quite short, as her legs had given out within three steps and Kanae had barely caught Isalla before she hit the floor. So instead of trying again immediately, Isalla had given her body a bit more time to recover, despite how much a part of her mind was screaming not to just lay in bed.

It became readily apparent that Isalla could have escaped if her body was able to move properly, too. Kanae had informed Isalla that she was leaving the next day to gather herbs, and for hours the angel had found herself alone in the building. It was eerie, how a demon had saved her and was trusting her to stay in her home… but in the end, Isalla had decided that she *had* jumped to conclusions, as much as it pained her to admit that. The only demons she'd ever encountered were those who were involved in the war, and when Isalla considered most of her kindred who'd fought against the demons, she realized that, from another point of view, it might seem like all angels were violent warriors. It wasn't a pleasant thought.

Eventually Kanae had returned and put something on to cook before coming to check on Isalla and her injuries. Now that she'd stopped objecting at every turn and watched her hostess, Isalla found Kanae to be brisk and almost always on the move, but neither was the demoness inattentive. Yes, she scolded Isalla when she nearly injured herself, but at no point had she brought up any form of compensation for her treatment.

The second day was far better, though, because, under Kanae's watchful gaze, Isalla had managed to put on a thin shift and totter out into the main room of the small house. She might have almost immediately collapsed into a chair, but she *made* it, which was an achievement all on its own, and an immense relief for Isalla.

"Congratulations, you managed to get out of bed without completely collapsing. Would you like a mug of water?" Kanae asked, a faint smile flickering across her face. A tiny part of Isalla wanted to complain about the smile, but it wasn't really fair. Had their roles been reversed, Isalla probably would have laughed.

"Please. Heavens, I never thought that *walking* was so hard," Isalla complained, breathing quickly to try to still the trembling in her legs.

"I'd recommend trying to avoid oaths like that. They'll give your nature away if you aren't careful." Kanae said, stepping over to a cabinet and pulling out a ceramic mug. Next to the cabinet was a large copper barrel on the counter with a spigot at the bottom. Isalla watched in fascination as the demon turned the spigot, releasing a stream of water into the mug, then shut it off.

"I'll try to remember that. But... won't it be fairly obvious anyway?" Isalla asked, frowning as she considered the situation and growing less pleased as she did so. "I've heard plenty of demons can detect us by smell."

"That's quite true." Kanae agreed, setting the mug in front of Isalla. "In fact, I had a solution for that in mind. If you'll give me a moment, I'll go find it."

"Sure." Isalla said, a little surprise surging through her at the offer. She took a sip of the water and blinked. It had a faint coppery taste to it, but it was surprisingly good despite that.

Kanae stepped away and headed for a back room, and as she

did so, Isalla examined the room again, curious despite herself. She didn't feel nearly as awkward looking around without the demon there to see it.

The house was different than Isalla had expected. Most demon structures were all dark stone, skulls, and images of horrible things that Isalla shuddered to think on. This was dark, yes, because the smoothly planed wooden boards were almost pure black, but that was where the similarities ended. The room was reasonably large, with a table big enough to seat eight and four chairs at its heart, as well as a single, heavily stuffed leather chair near the fireplace that a part of Isalla longed to collapse into. Five doors pierced the walls, one obviously the exit, while one was to her own room and another that Isalla suspected led to an identical room, while Kanae had gone through a third into the back. The last door Isalla wasn't sure about, but she gave even odds that it led to a privy or a root cellar.

The wood by the fire was just as dark as that which made up the walls, while the bricks that made up the fireplace were a simple brown, which told Isalla that the planks were simply what had been available, not a deliberate attempt at making the house oppressive, though they succeeded at that anyway. A couple of cabinets adorned the walls, one crowded with books, and other with a variety of jars of different herbs and substances Isalla couldn't identify on its shelves. Considering that a couple of the items looked like they might be organs, Isalla didn't really *want* to know what they were. Conversely, the kitchen was much more heavily built, with several counters, including the one the copper keg was on, and a fireplace filled with what looked like burning coal to Isalla, with a wide grate over the flames. It was kept clean, and there were several washbasins about, ones that were ceramic, and she could see that they'd fit onto the grate. Most remarkable was the large mirror on one wall, though, the edges of it finely carved wood that shone with a gold luster, and with a dozen jewels that glittered with internal light set around the edges of it.

The room was fascinating to look at, but Isalla thought it'd get boring eventually. Taking another sip of water, she waited for

Kanae to return patiently. Or as patiently as she could, as she'd fallen into the hells, of all places.

Eventually Kanae opened the door and stepped through, holding a copper bracelet in one hand as she sighed. "Well, that took longer than expected. My apologies, this wasn't where I left it."

"What is *it*, exactly?" Isalla asked curiously, looking at the bracelet and tilting her head to try to get a better look. The outside was smooth, but she thought she could see some symbols on the interior.

"This bracelet is enchanted. I had a human brought to me for healing, but it was far too late to save him, unfortunately, and he didn't have any companions. With no one to claim his things, I kept them." Kanae explained, coming over to the table and sitting gracefully. "These bracelets are relatively common among merchants and other mortals who come to the hells. They adjust the wearer's scent so they seem like a demon, or at least a native of the hells. While it isn't made specifically for an angel, it should work well enough, since you don't have your wings."

Isalla winced at the reminder about her wings, her back muscles twitching painfully, but nodded, swallowing and looking at the bracelet as she did so. Kanae's offer sounded good, but she couldn't help a niggling feeling that there might be a catch.

"That does sound useful," she admitted, then hesitated before asking. "What about my appearance?"

"That? You're beautiful and unusual, but not *that* strange. If you had a halo, or the innate glow of a few angels, we might have issues, but not now." Kanae explained, frowning thoughtfully at Isalla. "Doubtless *someone* saw you fall from the sky, but I think I can keep you safe enough until you're ready to attempt your escape."

"Attempt my escape? Why do you assume I will? I had other angels cut my wings off. I *could* be a traitor," Isalla said, looking at the bracelet as Kanae set it on the table in front of her. She wanted to snatch it up, since it would make her a little safer, but she didn't want to appear too eager, no matter how helpful Kanae seemed to be.

Kanae simply laughed and shook her head, her reaction prompting Isalla to flush. "You, a traitor? One who was wearing the armor of the Order of the Phoenix? No, I don't think so. You won't be comfortable in the hells, Isalla. Your very nature will rebel at it, and eventually you *will* attempt to escape if you avoid capture. That won't be easy, even with a disguise and that bracelet, but I believe you'll have decent odds. For now, though, my goal is to make certain you're well enough to manage it."

"You recognized my armor?" Isalla asked, fighting back the heat in her cheeks, and a little surprised.

"Of course. How could I have realized how foolish the conflict between the heavens and hells was without seeing it in person? I've faced angels before, Isalla, and even slain them." Kanae's slight smile faded as a hint of sorrow crossed her face. "I regret that, at least in some cases. Some angels are brutal, and others… were simply in the wrong place at the wrong time."

"O-oh," Isalla said, a bit of her relaxation around Kanae fading away. The idea that the demon had killed other angels was… worrisome. Even so, Isalla didn't have a choice but to trust her, at least for the moment. That being the case, she took a breath and continued. "I… you said that you'd help me recover, but I don't really see how you could, at least not in a reasonable amount of time. I lost more strength than I can believe, and I think it'll take years or more to fully recover."

"True, if I was going to allow you to do it normally. I can't have patients staying indefinitely, not with so few rooms available. No, I have a few alchemical concoctions I can brew to help," Kanae said, her voice lightening as she smiled. "I don't have one of the ingredients just now, but I was planning to go looking for that in the next few days. It's a bit hard on the body, so we need you fully stable before I go stressing you even further. I expect it'll take a few months despite that, and it won't be the most pleasant sensation in the world, but it's possible."

"If you say so. It's a bit… strange, to me," Isalla said, reaching for the bracelet, then paused and admitted nervously, "You know I can't pay you for what you've done, don't you? I didn't have any money on me when I was attacked, and the only thing I had was my armor."

15

"Which, if you think I *want* your armor, you're crazy. That's dangerous to have around," Kanae said, sniffing. "No, that's going with you when you leave... or you can bury it or something. I hid it for the time being, just to be safe. I don't expect you to repay me, Isalla. You don't have anything that I'd value in that manner, and I'm not one to take advantage of my patients. Once you're well enough to walk around, you can help around the house, or even help me gather herbs and alchemical materials, but that's it. You don't have some huge debt hanging over your head, girl."

"That's a relief... and I'd be very willing to help with things around the house," Isalla said, smiling in relief as she picked up the bracelet. After a moment, she slipped it around a wrist, well away from one of the injuries. She felt the faintest tingle from it, but nothing more. Suddenly she stopped, though, and she asked, "Girl? I'm not *that* young."

"Perhaps not," Kanae agreed, standing and moving over to the cabinet, pulling out a pot. "I'm going to start on dinner, I think."

"Kanae... how old *are* you?" Isalla asked, growing more concerned as her sense that something was off about Kanae grew stronger.

"Older than you," the demon replied casually, and the confidence in her tone was startling as the demon smiled. "That's all the answer you're getting, Isalla. It's rude to ask a woman's age, you know."

Isalla let out a breath of annoyance, watching the graceful, practiced movements of the demon, and wondered. There was just something intriguing about Kanae, something she couldn't quite place.

# CHAPTER 3

*T*he sound of an axe splitting wood startled Isalla awake the next morning, and her abrupt movements nearly caused her to fall out of the narrow bed. After a few moments, she calmed down, and as the steady rhythm of the axe continued, Isalla dragged herself out of bed and moved into the main room. About half an hour later, the sound stopped and Kanae returned, this time not wearing the robes that Isalla had grown used to seeing her in. Instead, Kanae was wearing trousers and a simple tunic, and the sight was surprising enough to Isalla that her mouth hung slightly open in shock.

Isalla had thought that Kanae was pretty before this, but having not seen anyone else next to the demon, she hadn't realized just how large Kanae was. Kanae must have been close to six feet in height, but her shoulders were also broader than those of most women Isalla knew, while her hips were also wide and she had an almost unnaturally thin waist and large bust. The demon's arms revealed a surprising amount of muscle, though it was toned enough to not be overly obvious, and Isalla shut her mouth after a moment, trying to figure out why her heartbeat had quickened at the sight.

"Is something the matter?" Kanae asked, closing the door behind her as she stepped inside, taking a cloth by the door to wipe some sweat from her forehead. "You were acting like a landed fish."

"I just… I didn't realize how tall you were. Or… well, you don't look like any other variety of demon I've seen before. Your horns are fairly small, but you don't have even vestigial wings, and you're surprisingly… humanoid," Isalla said, flushing slightly in embarrassment. "What type of demon *are* you?"

"I'm a mutant. Oh, there are other demon-blooded creatures around who're similar to me—the children of demons and mortals, for instance—but in my case, I'm the offspring of an incubus and succubus, and their bloodlines mixed… oddly," Kanae replied bluntly, shrugging as she slipped off her heavy boots. "I'm most likely unique."

"Oh. That does explain why you're so unusual…" Isalla murmured, filing the information away, even if she wasn't sure what she'd do with it.

"Quite. Now, I'm going to take a bath and make breakfast and lunch for each of us. I'm going to be going into the forest to gather herbs, so you're going to have to fend for yourself for much of the day," Kanae told Isalla, heading for the door in the back.

"Okay…" Isalla replied, slightly taken aback by how brusque the woman was being. She hadn't thought she was being rude.

It did answer the question of what the rear door was for, though. Isalla waited patiently, and in relatively short order, Kanae returned, once again wearing robes that shrouded her figure as she dried her hair. Breakfast was a simple meal of porridge, and the demon's idea of lunch seemed to be a couple of slices of dense bread, hard cheese, sliced meat that looked much like ham, and a handful of berries.

Every attempt Isalla made to strike up a conversation was met with relatively short responses that cut Isalla off, and at last she stopped trying. Finally, the demon left, and Isalla found herself with only her own company while she wondered what she'd done.

～

THE EVENING WASN'T much different, though at least the food was better. Isalla barely spoke, afraid that she was going to upset her host. Eventually they went to bed, and the next morning started much the same, though instead of going into the forest, this time Kanae announced she was going to town. As she was about to leave, Isalla finally screwed up her courage and spoke.

"May I ask why you're so upset with me?" Isalla asked, bracing herself for a harsh response.

"Upset with you?" Kanae asked, pausing by the door as she looked at Isalla with just a trace of surprise in her voice. "Why would I be *upset* with you?"

"You're treating me… differently. Like you want to keep your distance, or like you dislike me," Isalla explained, growing confused at Kanae's response. It wasn't as though Kanae had been incredibly nice to begin with, but the change was obvious to Isalla.

"Ah, that. The issue isn't with you, Isalla. The problem is with me, and I'm attempting to minimize conversation to quell a rather *unwelcome* instinct," Kanae replied, her lips thinning slightly. "I anticipate this to last about a week, unfortunately."

"Uh, what kind of instinct?" Isalla asked, almost afraid to know, but her worry easing slightly at the information that she wasn't at fault for Kanae's reaction, and that Kanae wasn't upset with her. In fact, it was a bit surprising just how much of a relief it was.

"You're an angel, and you're so weak that anyone in the hells would have little issue defeating you. *I* am a demon descended from an incubus and succubus, creatures who have a nigh-legendary libido. What sort of instinct do you *think* it is?" Kanae asked, and without pausing, she took a basket and stepped through the door. The lock turned behind her as Isalla sat there, staring after Kanae in shock.

As she stared, Isalla slowly flushed bright red as she realized what the demon was talking about. She hadn't even thought about the possibility, though every angel had heard tales of demons taking advantage of captured angels. The thought that Kanae was deliberately suppressing any similar instincts was… strange. It wasn't as though Isalla was a virgin, but she hadn't even considered the demoness in that manner. At least, she hadn't *consciously* thought about Kanae that way, until now.

Her thoughts thrown into chaos for several hours, Isalla almost forgot to eat her lunch, distracted as she was by Kanae's revelation. Shortly after she ate, there was the sound of the key again, and Kanae returned. A part of Isalla was flustered, mostly because she hadn't figured out how to react yet.

"There, done. Finding them was a bit more difficult than I would've preferred, but…" Kanae said, closing the door behind her. The basket she was holding had several bundles in it, and Isalla frowned at them.

"What was more difficult than you'd prefer?" Isalla asked hesitantly, resisting the urge to fidget.

"Finding clothing which will fit you, as well as shoes," Kanae answered briskly. "I found two shirts and one pair of trousers, along with two skirts that will fit, and I also managed to get three sets of socks. Shoes were much harder, but they should work. I'll take them into your room, so you can try them on in private."

"You got me clothing?" Isalla asked, slightly stunned, considering the conversation earlier. "Why?"

"I can't have you wandering around naked, and as I said before, your previous clothing is *not* acceptable," Kanae replied, taking the basket into the small room. While she was gone, Isalla looked down at the thin gown she'd been wearing and blushed slightly, since it would've fit most humans, though not very well. Until now she hadn't thought about how poorly it fit her. At that point Kanae came out again, speaking quickly. "Now, try it on. I need to take it back to get adjustments if it doesn't fit."

"Um, alright, I suppose so," Isalla agreed, forcing herself to her feet, then headed for the room. She paused as she was about to enter, looking at Kanae as anxiety bubbled up inside her. "Do you want me to come out, or…?"

"No, I just need to know if it will fit. They should be a touch on the large size, since you lost quite a bit of muscle." Kanae replied. "There's a belt, so it shouldn't be too bad for you."

Nodding, Isalla stepped into the room and closed the door, pausing as she looked at the basket resting on the table in a bit of disbelief. She was relieved that Kanae didn't expect her to parade herself in front of the demon, but somehow Isalla felt like this was a strange dream or nightmare. Only a few days before, she'd been in the heavens, with fine clothing, immaculate housing, and had been surrounded by light. Now, though... she was in the hells, in a dark house that was oppressive, was subsisting on the charity of a demon, and had been weakened so much that she couldn't defend herself. The degree of change was startling and left her off-balance. Not to mention how much of a turmoil her uncertain emotions were in.

That didn't mean she shouldn't do as Kanae asked, though. Better clothing would be good, and that would help her rebuild her confidence.

Opening the top bundle, Isalla blinked at the sight of the deep red silk, her eyes widening as she murmured. "Silk? Why is *silk* available in an area that seems remote? Why for a patient like me?"

She hesitated, then pulled out the shirt, the other was relatively plain with a slightly off-white color to it, and each would reach her wrists, most likely. It was incredibly finely woven, which just made her even more confused. Hesitating, Isalla opened one of the other bundles to see more silk, this made into trousers. Frowning, she shrugged it off for the moment, resolving to ask Kanae about the clothing when she was done. She *did* like silk, after all, and it'd always helped her feel prettier.

It took longer to try the clothing on than she'd expected, and the only surprise was that the socks were wool, but every other piece of clothing was made of silk, including some underthings which Kanae hadn't mentioned. The shoes were leather, and didn't fit perfectly, but finally she put on a skirt and shirt before stepping out of her room, feeling strangely burdened by the clothing, but more comfortable. More... balanced, she supposed.

"Thank you for the clothing, but... I just have to ask..." Isalla began, then hesitated as she saw what Kanae had been doing.

"Hm? Have to ask what?" Kanae asked, looking away from sharpening a kitchen knife, then nodded. "It looks good on you, and I think you'll fit the clothing nicely once you've recovered."

"I just… why silk? You have wool socks, so… why would you use something so expensive for the rest of my clothing?" Isalla asked, her gaze still on the knife.

Kanae stared at Isalla for a long, long moment, then began to laugh as she set the knife aside. Isalla looked at her in confusion, then annoyance.

"What's so funny?" the angel demanded. "I was asking a simple question!"

"I'm *laughing* because the socks are more expensive than most of your other clothing." Kanae replied, mirth in her voice now. Her violet eyes were practically dancing as she explained, her face looking far more attractive in her amusement. "Wool and cotton have to be imported, along with most other thread, and importing it from through the portal is less expensive than from elsewhere in the hells, sadly. Silk, on the other hand… that we have in abundance. There are several spider demons in the area, and they herd a large group of giant spiders that supply the town's spider-silk. That's what you're wearing, Isalla, not the silly silk that comes from *worms*."

"Spider… ew." Isalla gasped, looking down at her clothing and wrinkling her nose. It didn't feel too bad, and considering things, there wasn't much choice, but the idea of giant spiders disturbed her. In fact, it disturbed her enough to distract her from the sight of Kanae.

"Oh? Are silkworms any better?" Kanae asked skeptically.

"I never said they were. I just said *ew* about spiders," Isalla said, shivering. "Thank you for the clothing."

"You're welcome. I think I can go get the last ingredient tomorrow, since you're looking about to the point I think the elixir will work," Kanae said thoughtfully, tapping the table gently. "Plus, it'll keep me gone most of the day, which would probably be for the best."

"If you say so," Isalla agreed, sitting in the chair again. She paused, then frowned as she asked, "You said that the concoction was alchemical, didn't you? Who's going to brew it?"

"Me, of course," Kanae answered, starting to sharpen the knife again. "I'm pretty sure I said that before."

"Oh. I didn't see an alchemy lab, though…" Isalla

murmured, her thoughts churning. Come to think of it, she thought Kanae had said something about performing alchemy before, but she'd mostly forgotten.

That prompted a chuckle from Kanae. "As if I'd want the lab in an attached building. No, it's a few dozen yards from the house. I don't want to lose my home if the lab explodes, after all."

That, Isalla reflected, was a *very* good point.

# CHAPTER 4

$\mathcal{B}$y the time Isalla woke the next day, Kanae was already gone. The only reason she knew that much was because she'd found breakfast and lunch set on the table, each of them covered and waiting for her. She couldn't have woken up too long after Kanae had left, though, since the breakfast sausage was still slightly warm. A small part of the angel felt guilty that she hadn't been awake when Kanae left, but she *was* still recovering.

Isalla hesitated, then decided to reheat the food over the fire, since the coals were still burning. Actually, once she thought about it, she'd never seen Kanae add *more* coal, which puzzled her. She shrugged it off, instead taking a pan off its hook, nearly dropping it on her toes due to its weight, then put it over the fire. She managed to avoid burning the food or hurting herself, but it was a near thing, and Isalla cursed her weakness under her breath, growing more frustrated than she already had been.

Once breakfast was done, she found herself alone once more, and Isalla found herself even more restless than she'd been before. Sitting around and doing nothing was starting to chafe, and finally she decided to do something to improve her situation.

First, she tried to exercise, hoping to build up her strength, but the experience was... disheartening, to say the least. She couldn't do push-ups at all, and aside from stretching, most of her exercise attempts got halfway at best. By the quarter-hour mark, Isalla found herself wheezing for breath on the floor as she tried to recover and decided that the best option was to stop exercising for the moment. As much as she hated to admit it, she simply couldn't exert herself for long.

Once she wasn't panting like an overworked dog, Isalla decided to explore the house. The building wasn't terribly large to begin with, but she was curious. She started with the door next to the room she'd been staying in and wasn't surprised to find that the room was identical to her own, save with the bed made and not having an occupant.

The back door went into a short hallway, followed by another door. Isalla hesitated before opening the door cautiously, only to be met by a wave of steam with the faint scent of sulfur. Inside the room, she found herself looking at what appeared to be a naturally formed pool, the surface of which was moving due to heat. A channel allowed the steaming, sulfurous water to exit the pool and flow out the wall, and it took Isalla a moment to realize that Kanae had built a small hut over a hot spring.

"I… suppose that works. Not what I expected, but it works," Isalla admitted, tempted to take a dip to soothe her aching muscles, but paused as she thought about it more. She didn't have any way to dry off, and if something happened, with as weak as she was… it probably wasn't a good idea. So she reluctantly left the room, closing the doors behind her with a last, longing glance at the pool of water. She'd have to ask Kanae if she could take a bath once she was back.

Kanae's room brought even more hesitation, but after a few minutes, Isalla's curiosity got the better of her. Kanae was a mystery and enigma to the angel, and anything that explained her further roused Isalla's curiosity. When she found the door was locked, though, Isalla sheepishly realized that her curiosity was doomed to disappointment. She debated on checking the front door, but remembered that Kanae had locked it after going out the previous day. That meant she likely wouldn't be able to look around.

With nothing else to do, Isalla examined some of the books

on the shelves, and was surprised to find that she could read most of the titles. Most of them appeared to be texts on medicine, herbalism, and even some on alchemy. With nothing else to do, she considered what was there, then took one of the medical tomes from the shelf. Maybe, just maybe, she could figure out how difficult her recovery would be.

Once she opened the book, Isalla quickly found herself out of her depth. While she could read most of the book, there were quite a few words that she couldn't understand. She persevered despite that, continuing to pore through the book intently, hoping she could find something of use. Some sections made more sense than others, but she had to admit that it was still far beyond her understanding.

The sound of a key in the lock startled Isalla, and she looked up from the book in relief as the door opened, about to welcome the woman back, then froze in surprise with her mouth open. Kanae wasn't exactly looking her best.

The demon was in a pair of trousers and a long-sleeved shirt, was wearing a cloak and had a sword at her belt, but she was absolutely filthy, and the stench coming off Kanae caused Isalla's nose to wrinkle. She thought there were shreds of fungus across the woman's pants and shirt, there was quite a bit of dirt and some sort of reddish-purple liquid, and Kanae looked... well, resigned, really.

"Um, are you alright, Kanae?" Isalla asked, swallowing hard and trying not to breathe through her nose. The slight surge of happiness she'd felt at the demoness's return was mostly buried by her shock.

"I'm fine. From the moment I decided to make the elixir in question, I knew that I was going to have to go into the mushroom groves, and it was just as unpleasant as I expected it to be," Kanae replied, closing the door, then leaning down to unlace her boots. They were also caked in muck, Isalla noticed, and she dearly wished she couldn't smell anything at the moment as the demon continued. "I did find the ingredients I needed, though, and that's the important thing. If I hadn't, I'd be rather angry that someone had hunted down all the growth

27

vines in the groves, and probably would've hunted *them* down to make my displeasure known."

"Okay. I just didn't think you were going to have *that* much difficulty." Isalla said, standing up as Kanae pulled off her boots, complete with the socks. At least the demoness's feet were clean, though it was a small blessing.

"As I said, it is what it is. Now, I'm going to go wash off before doing anything more. I'll get you your elixir tomorrow," Kanae said firmly, walking through the room and to the back door. Almost before Isalla could think of what to say, the demon had closed the door firmly behind her, boots in one hand.

"She's... strange," Isalla murmured, then took a seat again to wait. The stench wasn't gone with Kanae's absence, but it certainly wasn't as strong, which was a relief. Even so, Isalla felt relieved that she wasn't alone anymore.

It was about an hour before Kanae emerged, holding her wet clothing in front of her, draped over one arm. Kanae was wearing only the shirt, which was also wet, but the pale-skinned woman quickly vanished into her room. A couple of minutes later, she emerged in her usual robes and let out a sigh as she took a seat, glancing at the book in front of Isalla.

"Find anything useful?" Kanae asked, arching an eyebrow curiously.

"I'm afraid not. I'm not a trained healer, and a lot of this doesn't make much sense to me. I've figured out a few things, but most of it may as well be gibberish," Isalla admitted, her cheeks flushing slightly. She didn't like admitting ignorance.

"That would make sense. It took me years to learn enough to do what I do properly," Kanae said, smiling slightly. Isalla almost did a double-take since she thought she heard a bit of sympathy in Kanae's voice.

"I was going to ask... could I take a bath? I explored what I could of the house, but I didn't see any towels or the like," Isalla asked nervously. "I also was wondering why there weren't any windows, and only the one way out of the house."

"There's more than one way out, though I'm not sharing how just yet. As for windows... they're a weak point. I had numerous enchantments placed to defend the front door, and attempting to ward windows as well would be difficult at best, so I limited things so I could focus the home defenses on a single point," Kanae explained, studying Isalla for a few moments before she continued. "As for bathing, that's more questionable. I'd have to examine your wounds first. If they're healed enough that the water shouldn't aggravate them, I can allow it, but the water isn't as clean as what I've used to wash your injuries before."

"Oh, okay," Isalla said, smiling in relief as she understood why the demoness hadn't offered her a bath before. The explanation made far more sense, and it helped her understand Kanae a little more. "When could you do that?"

"While I'd *like* to wait a while, now would be fine," Kanae said, frowning as she stood. "It's been a long day, and if I don't do it now, I might forget later."

Isalla nodded in understanding, getting up and heading toward the room she thought of as hers. She did blush, as she realized that Kanae would have to look at her mostly naked, but it wasn't like the demoness hadn't had plenty of chances to see Isalla's entire body before this.

Undressing most of the way, Isalla laid down and waited nervously as Kanae followed her into the room. She sat on the edge of the bed and leaned over Isalla, examining her back closely. Isalla shivered at the touch of Kanae's fingers brushing against the injuries ever so gently, but didn't say anything. Neither did Kanae, as she checked the injuries that had been inflicted on each major joint of Isalla's arms and legs. Just as she was finishing, Kanae paused.

"You know, you're making this extremely difficult for me, Isalla," Kanae said mildly. "You can take a bath, just be careful not to scrape your wounds against the side of the pool. I'll get out a towel for you and leave it on the table, and you can wash at your leisure."

With that, the demoness pulled away, just as Isalla asked, "What? Umm…"

When she exited her room, Isalla only caught a glimpse of Kanae as she disappeared into her bedroom, a towel resting on the table.

"But…" Isalla began, flushing slightly as she realized what

the demoness had been meaning. The idea of a demon being attracted to her was... it *should* have been repulsive, and yet it wasn't, not entirely. Isalla tried to untangle her thoughts, and her blush grew brighter as she realized a part of her was pleased that a demon could see the beauty of an angel. Shaking her head to drive the thought from her head, Isalla took the towel and headed for the bathing room.

The bath itself was pure bliss, as the heat radiated through Isalla's body and felt like it was soothing every ache and pain she had. It wasn't perfect, but in short order she felt like she was almost melting in place. It took quite some time before she managed to drag herself out of the water to dry off.

Upon leaving the bath, she found a bowl of stew waiting for her. It was simple enough, though the stew had mushrooms this time. More surprisingly, Isalla didn't see any sign of Kanae. She tried to stay up and wait for the demoness, to apologize for any difficulties she was causing, but as time passed, there was no sign of Kanae. Finally, Isalla couldn't keep herself awake any longer, and she crept over to her room to lay down and pass out.

She did have to wonder why she felt so guilty, though.

# CHAPTER 5

"*A*ngels," Kanae muttered under her breath, trying to ignore her instincts. "The bracelet should be masking her scent, and *is*, yet I swear I can still smell her. Hellfire, it's frustrating."

It had been longer than Kanae cared to consider since she'd last been in the presence of an angel, and she'd forgotten how intoxicating their presence could be off the battlefield. It wouldn't have been as bad if it weren't for some of her previous experiences, but it weren't as though she could forget those.

"I blame Mother," Kanae announced to the room, unbottling the jar containing essence of life and dribbling a precise amount of the sap into the vial containing troll blood. The alchemical concoction in front of her didn't seem impressed by her announcement, instead continuing to bubble and churn.

Watching the sap and blood react for a moment, Kanae hooked it into the complex equipment and slid a heat stone under the vial. The alchemy she was performing wasn't terribly difficult but was rather time-consuming. She'd made the excuse to herself that it was the time which had made her start on the elixir tonight, but she knew better than that, and knew better than to truly lie to herself.

"An angel falling from the sky… and she just *had* to come

directly toward me. It's more than a bit ironic," Kanae mused, adjusting some of the beakers as she considered her situation. "Fortunate for her, really. I don't know that there's anyone else in the region who could have saved her, *would* have saved her, and wouldn't have immediately handed her over to the army or a local lord. That would've ended poorly."

It was nothing but the truth, too. All around Hellmount was a region that'd been ravaged by war with the angels on multiple occasions, though it'd been a long time since a full-scale invasion. It was said that the gateway it led through had been created by a war between angels and demons, and though Kanae had her doubts about that, it had led to a lot more distrust of angels than in many regions. Some parts of the hells were so remotely located that none of their inhabitants had ever seen the portals to the mortal world, and who considered the tales of war with the heavens as little more than rumors from far-off lands with little to no impact on them.

Visiting those lands had been educational and depressing in some ways. Kanae's personal belief that the war between the heavens and hells was pointless had only been reinforced by the trip, but upon returning, she'd realized how insurmountable the divide between the two factions truly was. So instead of throwing herself back into the horrific morass, she'd chosen to find someplace quiet to live. Somewhere that she could make a difference.

It had gone well, too. Until Hellmount had thrown a helpless, wingless angel at her.

"I wonder if the mountain is sentient? It would explain a few things... though that would cause other problems," Kanae muttered to herself, then sighed.

Regardless, it didn't solve the problem of an attractive woman who was in Kanae's home. If it weren't for Isalla's injuries, Kanae might have an even harder time controlling herself. As it was, the beautiful blonde-haired, blue-eyed angel looked almost doll-like, in an emaciated sort of way. Once she was fit again, though...

Kanae shuddered at the thought and firmly put it out of her mind. It wasn't something she was willing to consider, not right now. Instead, she continued working on the elixir. She'd be lying if she said she wasn't attracted to Isalla, but Kanae had enough self-control that she knew she wouldn't give in to her instincts. Maybe, just *maybe,* she'd approach Isalla when she was healed, though.

# CHAPTER 6

*W*hen Isalla woke, she was startled to see that Kanae was in the kitchen again, especially considering how long she'd waited the previous night. Kanae looked about how she usually did as she worked on the porridge, though there was also a large pot on the grate next to the one she was stirring.

"Your elixir is sitting on the table. One dose per month should help you recover quite quickly, but I should warn that it will taste *terrible*," Kanae said, lifting the spoon to taste the porridge. "I've yet to encounter an elixir of that type that didn't taste horrendous."

"Um, alright," Isalla replied, looking at the table to see a small vial of red fluid. It was somewhat transparent, which made it obvious that the substance wasn't blood, but she couldn't say that she was unconcerned. Approaching the table, Isalla slowly sat, hesitating before she spoke, still feeling a little guilty. "I… stayed up a while last night, waiting for you."

"You shouldn't have bothered. I was deliberately keeping my distance and decided that the safest thing to do was to start on the alchemy early," Kanae replied promptly. "It seemed like the logical thing to do, since the alchemy would take the entire night to finish."

"You stayed up all night?" Isalla asked, both surprised and feeling faintly ashamed, since she'd slept like the dead.

"No, only half the night. Once it was properly situated, I went to bed," Kanae explained, pulling the second pot off the grate. Finishing the porridge as well, she pulled it off and quickly filled two bowls, adding a spoon to each before bringing them over to the table.

"Thank you for doing that. Also, I wanted to apologize for... well, for making it necessary," Isalla said, picking up the vial and looking at it for a moment.

"It's fine, Isalla. I chose to do so of my own volition," Kanae replied, sliding a bowl in front of Isalla. "Here you are."

"Should I drink it before eating? I know some elixirs have requirements like that," Isalla asked, feeling even more nervous.

"I would. While it might partially ruin your appetite, at least the food will clean the taste from your mouth, and you won't risk throwing up your meal after drinking it," Kanae replied, causing Isalla to stare at her.

"Is it really *that* bad?" the angel asked hesitantly, her desire to drink the elixir fading along with her appetite, despite her wish to recover her strength.

"Unfortunately, yes. I've had to drink one once, and while it isn't the worst thing I've ever had, it'll turn your stomach," Kanae explained, beginning to eat her food slowly. "If it weren't for how useful the elixir was, I wouldn't even bother making it."

It wasn't a comforting confirmation, but Isalla didn't exactly see another choice. Grimacing, she uncorked the vial and did her best to avoid smelling it. Instead, she quickly drained the vial... and instantly regretted it.

The taste was indescribable, in her opinion. It wasn't quite as horrifically foul as some of the things she'd had the misfortune of smelling during the wars against demons, but it was bad enough that Isalla's stomach churned and revolted at the taste of it. She forced herself to swallow, her eyes watering as she did. Gasping as she forced the liquid down, the angel quickly grabbed a spoonful of porridge and swallowed it to try and remove the worst of the aftertaste from her mouth.

"That's... that's just... *ugh*, I thought you might have been exaggerating, but that was *horrible*," Isalla gasped, her stomach feeling like it was twisting inside her. She'd almost rather vomit than drink something like the elixir, though it was a near thing.

"That it is. Still, it'll have relatively fast results, especially with as weak as you currently are," Kanae agreed, smiling thinly. "I'm not certain exactly how long it will take, but I'm sure you'll manage until then."

"If you say so," Isalla said, eating more of her porridge to help cleanse her mouth. After a minute, she nodded at the other pot and asked, deliberately trying not to think about the subject of the previous night or the taste of the elixir. "What's that for?"

"Hmm? Oh, I boil my water before adding it to the tank for drinking water. It's a bit safer than drinking it directly," Kanae replied, waving her spoon at the copper keg as she added, "It'll require refilling a bit more often with company, but I regularly have guests like you. I'm not worried about it."

"I'll try to help," Isalla said quickly, relieved at the thought of *something* she could do. "It's the least I can do with everything you've done for me."

"Maybe once you're strong enough to hold more than an empty bowl as you cross the room." Kanae agreed, another smile flickering across her face. "As much as I appreciate the offer, until that point, you're not going to be much help."

"True," Isalla admitted, feeling slightly dismayed, despite herself. She did find herself happier now that Kanae wasn't outright ignoring her, though.

THE NEXT FEW days progressed more simply than the previous ones had. Isalla found that her strength began to improve rapidly, and by the third day, she was allowed to leave the house, though not without a warning to be prepared to get back inside quickly.

That said, the exterior of the building was a surprise, because Kanae's home was built inside a hill in the middle of a forest. The trees were the ones she'd seen in her fall, with black bark like ebony and with broad red leaves. Nearby, a few dozen yards away, were a couple of other buildings, each widely separated from one another, and there was a stream where the hot spring exited the hillside. A wood pile rested against one of the outbuildings, along with an axe and splitting wedge, giving an oddly normal feel to the clearing. A path led into the forest, winding among the trees, and it was surprisingly peaceful despite the looming black expanse of Hellmount in the near distance and the way the sky was lit by a red sun and shone through looming black clouds.

The grass was the same dark color of the bark, and Isalla simply looked around for a while before asking, her voice a bit soft due to the oppressive surroundings and how it made her mood less upbeat, "Is everything down here so dark? I've never thought to ask before, but…"

"For the most part. I've often wondered why myself, but for the most part, the plants and animals in the hells are much darker than in the mortal world," Kanae confirmed, standing nearby with her hands crossed in front of her, looking around calmly. "It's also more dangerous, but that's simply how it is. There are also more predators, including many plants."

"Plants are predators here?" Isalla asked, disbelief surging through her even as her eyes widened. "I'd heard some were dangerous in the hells, but…"

"Only some, and not many nearby. No coming outside without company until you're able to defend yourself, hm?" Kanae replied with a smile that warmed Isalla's heart. "Now, go ahead and look around. I'm going to take care of some weeding, then I'm going to have to go into town for a house call, and you'll need to stay inside while I'm away."

"There's no chance of me coming along, is there?" Isalla asked, letting out an unhappy sigh. "I'm hating being cooped up all the time."

"Maybe next week, once I'm sure you can make the trip, and after we figure out a good cover story for you," Kanae replied in a thoughtful tone. "We could always pretend you were a merchant, and that someone dosed you with warrior's end when robbing you, then abandoned you in the woods. It would make things relatively easy to explain and has the advantage of being at least somewhat true."

"That sounds decent to me," Isalla agreed, perking up at the thought. "Still, go ahead and do your, um, weeding. I'll just... walk around the house."

Kanae nodded and headed down toward a patch of vegetation that, now that Isalla looked at it, wasn't wild grass at all. It struck her as slightly funny, watching the demon doing weeding, but she tried to relax. The grove was pleasant enough, considering her circumstances, and she wanted to enjoy her time outdoors. Even if it was darker, fresh air was nice. She barely noticed the sulfur in the air, too.

# CHAPTER 7

*T*he next few days passed relatively calmly, which was a relief for Isalla. Her strength didn't come back nearly as easily as she hoped, but even in the few days since she'd taken the elixir, she'd noticeably improved.

The biggest thing that Isalla had learned was that when Kanae was feeling particularly uncomfortable, the demoness would wait until Isalla's back was turned, then simply vanish. It happened twice in the few days, which was somewhat eerie. Isalla may not have been quite as observant as some of the scouts in the legion, but it shouldn't have been *that* easy for a demon to escape her notice.

Regardless of how startling it was, Kanae had managed it several times and had worried Isalla by doing so, though she was slowly growing used to the demoness's habits. That morning, Isalla had been kept inside for about half an hour while Kanae had gone out with a sword, and when she'd finally been allowed out, Isalla had seen that there was a horse-sized, two-headed lizard with dark red scales lying dead on the hillside. Isalla had been even more startled when Kanae had started butchering the beast for meat, but she hadn't said anything as Kanae had taken several slabs of meat into the hut with the axe near it. It made her slightly uncomfortable, but she didn't really know what made good meat in the hells.

BENJAMIN MEDRANO

Eventually Kanae had hauled the remains of the lizard into the woods and returned to clean off the blood and offal, bringing Isalla inside with her just to be safe. Afterward, she'd gone back to the shed to treat the meat for preservation. It took several hours, but Isalla had noticed the look of happiness on Kanae's face, which helped assuage her fears.

It was after they'd started relaxing in the house for the evening that there was a sudden, quick knock on the door.

As Isalla jumped slightly, just about to attempt another sit-up despite her exhaustion, a man's voice echoed through the door. "Kanae! Are you in? Please, I hope to the lords of the Iron Circle you're here…"

"Enkax? What are you doing here at *this* time? It's almost dark, you old fool," Kanae said, quickly standing up and heading for the door. She opened it to reveal a man just as Isalla climbed to her feet.

The demon on the other side of the door stood on hooved feet, and a pair of ram's horns curled on either side of his face. With black skin, as well as a fringe of white hair around his skull and a ragged, thin beard, the golden-eyed demon was a bit startling to Isalla, especially since he was wringing a hat between his clawed hands. His clothing was relatively normal as well, Isalla noticed belatedly, almost looking like that of a common farmer… if a farmer wore silk, anyway. How anxious and… well, *normal* he looked startled Isalla, as well as making her relax a bit.

He caught sight of Isalla, and a startled expression crossed Enkax's face, but he spoke quickly. "I wouldn't be here if it wasn't an emergency, not *this* late! Qirress went into labor just a bit ago, and it's looking, um, worrisome."

"What, *already*?" Kanae demanded, paling slightly. "Damn it, I *told* her that a minotaur could lead to a premature birth, but… one moment, I'll get my things together and we can go."

"Yes, ma'am," Enkax replied, his worry appearing to ease slightly as Kanae almost ran for her room.

"Isalla, I'm likely going to be gone for the entire night, possibly longer. You're going to have to fend for yourself where food is concerned," Kanae called out from her room, the sound

42

of cloth rustling audible. "I'll leave a key by the door, but *don't* go far. As weak as you currently are, there are dozens of creatures in the woods that could and *would* eat you."

"Um, alright. I could always come help if you wanted," Isalla offered, frowning slightly. She didn't like the idea of being alone. Even if Kanae was a demon, Isalla liked having her nearby.

"No. You don't have the endurance for the trip and staying up yet," Kanae said firmly, looking up and smiling thinly as she stepped out of the bedroom with a satchel at her side and a sword hanging from her belt. "Besides, this… will likely be unpleasant. I don't think you'd enjoy coming along."

"Alright," Isalla conceded, a little surprised at how out of sorts she felt. "I suppose I'll see you when you're back, then."

"That's the hope. Come on, Enkax, let's get going. The sooner we go, the less likely something nasty will have woken up," Kanae said, and the man nodded, looking relieved.

"Of course, Kanae. Thank you so much!" he replied quickly, promptly putting his hat on and stepping outside. Isalla watched them, opening her mouth, but by the time she thought of what to say, it was too late.

Kanae dropped a key on the table, and then she was gone, the door closing firmly behind her, then locking.

Isalla watched her go, a bit dazed and uncertain of what had just happened. She blinked several times, then murmured, "That… was startling."

She also found herself oddly lonely, more so than when Kanae had chosen to up and vanish.

∾

"I HAVE TO… TO ASK…" Enkax puffed, his breathing heavy as it interrupted his words. "Who was… was that, Kanae? I haven't…"

"Save your breath, Enkax. Of *course* you haven't seen Isalla before," Kanae interrupted, jogging down the path with far more ease than the tanner did. Her own emotions were complex, since this wasn't how she'd have chosen to reveal Isalla's presence to the townsfolk.

They were heading back toward town, and while the trip was usually relatively safe, Kanae knew better than to assume that would be the case. The nearby Fungal Abyss was far too prone to spitting out monsters, and their proximity to Hellmount meant that occasionally soldiers would decide that they could raid the locals with impunity. They left the towns alone, but those traveling at night were vulnerable to ambush. Kanae wasn't worried about herself, but Enkax couldn't handle something like that.

"Where, then?" Enkax asked, keeping his inquiry short.

"She's a traveler from above," Kanae replied simply, ignoring her desires as they whispered in the back of her mind. "I'm not sure if she was ambushed by bandits or someone specifically trying to kill her, but they dosed her with warrior's end and left her naked and dying in the forest. I found her and have been nursing her back to health."

"Ah! Makes… sense." Enkax puffed, his gait heavy. "I was… just startled."

"I'm sure news will be across town by tomorrow. I'll bring her into town soon, I promise," Kanae replied, her eyes narrowing at a particular shadow, then relaxing as she realized it was one of the spiders Ikka kept for silk. The gigantic spider shuffled away from the path, and she passed, continuing in a calm tone, her anxiety heightening as she thought about what awaited her. "For now, we need to make sure Qirress survives. I *told* her a minotaur child would be too much for her!"

"She… loves him…" Enkax huffed, and she glanced back to see his helpless shrug.

"I know. No matter *how* bad of an idea it is, I know," Kanae replied quickly, then her thoughts grew a little more jumbled. Qirress's relationship was one thing, but it also brought to mind Isalla. Kanae shoved the thought of the angel aside as she shook her head. She didn't have *time* for that.

They turned the corner to see the town, and Kanae picked up the pace as she saw the gates were open. Obviously, they were expecting her, and *that* was a bad sign.

# CHAPTER 8

The night went by almost agonizingly slowly for Isalla. She wouldn't have thought that Kanae's absence would have that much of an effect on her, but it had. The house felt empty in many ways, and the angel had used the time to exercise and try to get into better shape, at least at first. It helped to mitigate the feeling of loneliness.

She'd grown used to the bandages on her back, while Kanae had removed the ones on her arms, legs, and neck the day before. There were still angry red lines where she'd been injured, but even those were fading now, and Isalla had to marvel at the amount of healing that the demoness's herbs could manage in such a short time.

Eventually she went to bed, then got up the next morning, fixing herself a simple breakfast. It struck Isalla as odd that Kanae could produce such potent healing elixirs, yet the food she kept on hand was so simple. It was just… strange.

Considering Kanae's warnings, Isalla chose not to go outside, at least for the morning. No matter how stuffy the air could get inside the house, the lizard the day before had proven that the demoness's warning wasn't without merit. No matter how much it ashamed her to admit it, Isalla knew she couldn't have fought the creature with her current strength, and she was too used to fighting while at least partially airborne to have done so easily even if she had most of her strength back. Instead, she continued exercising and waiting, wondering how long Kanae would be gone.

When the tumblers of the lock finally turned, Isalla sat up in her chair, her mood improving suddenly as the door opened, and she spoke brightly, happiness welling up inside her. "Welcome back, Kanae!"

As she stepped inside, Kanae smiled in return, nodding. "Thank you, Isalla. I hope your night went well."

"Well enough, I think. It was a bit boring, but that's to be expected." Isalla said, studying Kanae with concern as she added, standing up, "You look like you had a hard night."

The demoness certainly didn't look like she was at her best. Her skin was even paler than normal, and while she moved with her usual grace, Kanae stepped slightly more deliberately, as if she were having to think about each move in advance. Her clothing had a couple of dark spots on the sleeves as well, which was worrying.

"It was an… unpleasant experience, as I anticipated," Kanae said, setting her satchel on the table and letting out a soft sigh as she shook her head. "I had hoped that it would be easier, but I nearly lost both of them. Fortune smiled on me, though, and mother and child will live to see another day. Beyond that… who knows?"

"That seems oddly fatalistic," Isalla said, growing more concerned about how talkative Kanae was being, and the demoness sat down across from Isalla. Kanae looked tired, and her eyes looked a bit older than they had before.

"It's nothing but the truth. Death comes for everyone, from the lowliest insect to the most powerful deity, archangel, or archdemon," Kanae told her, shrugging. "Oh, perhaps not the *ephemeral* gods, but who knows if they truly exist? All the others… I've done my research, and every last one of them I've found information on has been slain at least once."

"I… I guess so?" Isalla replied, slightly taken aback by Kanae's words. She hesitated, thinking about the various archangels who'd fallen over the centuries, then shoved the thought aside, uncomfortable with the subject. Instead, she

46

asked about something else. "Why was the birth so dangerous? I thought I heard something about a minotaur, but you left so quickly..."

Kanae let out a heavy sigh, closing her eyes before speaking. "Qirress is a rather... *petite* minor demoness. She looks more like a half-human demon than anything else, to be honest. Enkax is her grandfather, but she doesn't have much in common with him aside from the hooves. However, she fell in love with a minotaur, and he's part of a group of guards that patrols the upper regions of Hellmount. This is one of his three-month periods away, unfortunately. The problem is that she's small, and minotaur children *aren't*. I warned them when they married that it would be extremely dangerous for her to bear him any children, but they insisted. Maybe they'll listen after this, but I have my doubts."

Isalla blushed as she listened, embarrassed that she'd even asked. Minotaurs were very large, so she could understand why they could be problematic. The thought that a couple of demons could fall in love surprised her somehow, but she kept that to herself. Kanae had already made her opinion about angels being biased against demons quite clear.

"Ah, well, hopefully they'll listen," Isalla replied, swallowing hard.

"Agreed. However, we have another issue we need to deal with, Isalla," Kanae said firmly, focusing on Isalla.

The demon's gaze had a weight to it that Isalla hadn't expected, and she froze, almost feeling like she was suffocating for a moment. Then the violet gaze shifted away, and the angel could breathe again. She swallowed before asking, even as she wondered what *that* had been, "What... what might that be?"

"Enkax saw you last night and asked about you. By this time, the entire town doubtlessly knows that you're here. I told him that you were a traveler from above, and that I suspected that you were attacked by either bandits or a deliberate assassination considering the poison which was used on you. I also told him you were abandoned in the woods without any of your things, which helps account for why they didn't see you before," Kanae explained, slowly tapping a finger on the table, her fingernail almost biting into the wood. "We need to figure out what story to tell them, as everything I told him was honest. Not the whole truth, but the best deceptions are ones that don't involve the whole truth."

"Oh. That does make sense, then," Isalla replied, relaxing ever so slightly as she realized that Kanae's concerns were fairly mundane. "I... well, what would you recommend? I haven't had to keep a secret like this before."

"That depends... but quite honestly, the goal will be to keep as much truth in the story as possible, since you *are* bad at lying," Kanae explained, watching Isalla with lidded eyes. "Tell me, was it an assassination attempt?"

"I'm not entirely sure. I think it was... I was investigating some rumors, and maybe I was getting too close?" Isalla hesitated, then admitted unhappily, "I thought that the woman I was meeting was a friend, actually."

"Obviously not. Well, no one will think of asking if you're an angel, or in the *extremely* unlikely event they do, it's best for you to laugh it off. We'll need to ensure you don't have the bandages on your back by that point, or it'll give things away, and unless you have me try to deal with the scars, you'll need to keep your back hidden. That shouldn't be a problem, though." Kanae replied, obviously musing aloud. "As for the story... you were trying to escape people who had a grudge against you, and they ambushed you near the base of Hellmount. I rescued you from the woods and began nursing you back to health. It's a simple story, and one which they'll believe."

"That sounds like it'd work. You're right, too... it's almost entirely true, and aside from where it happened, it isn't like I'd have to lie about things," Isalla agreed, rolling the story over in her mind. While it wasn't considered proper to lie to others among angels, she had to admit that survival took priority, and this wasn't much of a falsehood. It just was claiming that someone had attacked her near the *end* of her descent, rather than before throwing her out of the heavens. It also felt better to her.

"Good. Now, I'm rather tired, so I'm going to go sleep for a bit," Kanae said firmly. "Once I'm up, I'm going to give you a quick lesson on where we are and what you should know. Do you have much knowledge of the geography of the hells?"

"I'm afraid not. While I was in the Order of the Phoenix, we were never on the front lines while I was a member. We had a number of battles with demons, but nowhere near a gate," Isalla admitted.

"Not terribly surprising… angels haven't made many forays into the hells in the last couple of centuries," Kanae said, nodding firmly. "At least it means you won't have much knowledge to unlearn, and we can use the excuse that you didn't have much of a chance to learn about the region before coming down here."

"Very true," Isalla replied, a bit relieved that Kanae was being so proactive. It was better than doing nothing, too. If things kept going the way they had been, she was worried that she'd go mad from boredom.

"Well, I'm going to go collapse for a few hours," Kanae said, standing up and quickly heading for her room.

"Rest well," Isalla called after her, feeling a bit happier now that Kanae was back, even if she *was* going to be stuck inside for a bit longer.

# CHAPTER 9

*I*salla looked at Kanae in surprise as the woman poured herself a mug of water. It'd only been a few hours since the demoness had gone to bed, but when she'd gotten up again, Kanae looked like she'd fully recovered, though her hair wasn't *quite* as tidy as it usually was. Isalla suspected that'd be taken care of after Kanae took a bath, though.

"Alright, now that I'm awake, it's time for us to figure out a few things. First and foremost, let's get some basic geography out of the way," Kanae said in a brisk, no-nonsense tone. "I should have asked this before, but I neglected it. Do you know how territory is organized in the hells, Isalla?"

"Well, I know that the land is ruled by different demonic lords, whether called archdemons, archdukes, archdevils, demonic princes, or other names," Isalla said, racking her brain for additional information, but it was somewhat rusty, as she hadn't had to think about it recently. "I know each ruler tends to be something of a loner, and their armies are often… themed, for lack of a better term. I can't remember anything else. Oh, and they split the land between them, too, each ruling a section of the hells."

"Hm, not too inaccurate in most ways, though not quite right either. You're quite correct on the titles that demonic lords use, and it's *entirely* based on the whim of the demon in question,"

Kanae confirmed, smiling slightly. "However, plenty have alliances. The seven lords of the Iron Crown are one of the most powerful factions in the region, for instance. You're quite fortunate that they're more concerned with maintaining their power and stability than in invading the mortal world or the heavens. You're also incorrect on them ruling all the lands of the hells. Some realms don't have rulers with a mantle of power, some have died... and some are so far from the portals that most demon lords ignore them, and they remain independent."

"There're areas like that? I mean, where there aren't demon lords?" Isalla asked, honestly startled by the thought.

"Of course. At my best guess, the hells are at least ten times the size of the mortal world, if not larger. I'm not sure if the heavens are similar, but I wouldn't be surprised. Interestingly, the portals to the mortal world all seem to congregate in a space roughly equivalent to their separation *on* the mortal world, though it isn't precise," Kanae said, then hesitated before admitting, "I haven't found the edge of the hells, if I'm being honest, so I'm very much uncertain of its size. It's much larger than I was taught growing up."

"I... I see. I don't know on the heavens... I never thought about that part," Isalla admitted, considering the idea of a land over ten times the size of the mortal world. The continents were several thousand miles across, so the idea was incredibly stunning.

"Hm, interesting. Still, we're getting off track. You're somewhat correct about themes of different archdemons, though, as the vast majority of archdemons choose which of the seven sins they prefer," Kanae continued, her eyes contemplative as she took a sip of water and continued. "Envy, gluttony, greed, lust, pride, sloth, and wrath. Some choose to eschew these rough ideas, but it's... traditional, I suppose. Each realm is also classified in such a manner, which can give something of an idea of what you're getting into when you go into its heart."

"Ah, I remember hearing about that! I just didn't remember fully, I guess," Isalla said, suddenly remembering a fair amount. "There was a huge amount of variation, even so."

"There would be. Now, we're near the base of Hellmount.

Have you heard of it?" Kanae asked, tilting her head as she watched Isalla closely.

"No, I haven't. I know there are multiple demonic mountains that lead into the portals, but we didn't name them," Isalla told her. "We named the portals, but primarily based on whose order was assigned to guard the regions near the portal, if any. Some of them are too far into the Fallen Kingdoms to guard, though, and I never learned their names."

"The Fallen Kingdoms, is it? Well, I suppose it's better than the Alliance of Darkness, which is what I heard last time around," Kanae murmured, smiling slightly. "Well, have you heard of the Kingdom of Hragon?"

Isalla's eyes lit up with recognition. "I have! It's one of the oldest of the Fallen Kingdoms, and buried deep in the heart of Zintas, the southernmost continent of the mortal world."

"Well, that makes this easier. The portal you fell through is connected to Hragon, Isalla," Kanae explained, and as she did so, Isalla's happiness at being able to answer Kanae's question turned to confusion.

"But… but that doesn't make any sense," Isalla said, and it was Kanae's turn to look slightly surprised.

"What doesn't make sense about it? While it's a bit far, there *is* an outpost of the Order of the Phoenix not far off the coast, which they use to keep an eye on us," Kanae said, frowning. "Are you saying you aren't from there? I think it was named Firewatch…"

"No! I was investigating rumors in the heavens, and there isn't a portal from there anywhere *near* Hragon! They dropped me off one of the continents, and I fell directly into the mortal world, then through the portal to here!" Isalla explained, trembling a little. "I… it isn't *possible*!"

"Unless they had a portal they've kept secret, at least. That… is quite disturbing. I knew that you were attacked by angels, but considering that the nearest outpost is controlled by your order, I assumed that you were from there," Kanae said, a deep frown on her face. "I'd think we'd have heard if there was a portal to the heavens *above* Hellmount. It's rather unsettling to think about."

"I… I agree. I'm going to have to think about it… though

there's nothing I can *do* about it," Isalla said, almost feeling like she'd swallowed something foul.

"Indeed. Now, Hellmount is bordered by three realms. Estalia, Toflak, and Xanigar. We're in Estalia, one of the fourteen known realms of lust." Kanae explained shortly, her expression neutral again, though there was an odd note to her voice. "Estalia is... relatively safe, all things being considered. Queen Estalia likes having mortals visit, so it's not as hostile as its neighbors, but she's also known to focus on the core regions of the realm, so the borders are relatively wild. That's where we are, obviously. We're fortunate enough that most of the neighboring nations don't care to attack Estalia, so that's not an issue."

"Okay, that makes a bit more sense to me," Isalla agreed, though she did shiver slightly at the mention of it being a realm of lust. At least it meant she wasn't as liable to be murdered, and she internally resolved to stay as far from the core of the country as possible. She didn't want to be ensnared by those who might perpetuate the nation's reputation.

"I should hope so. As for our current location... well, we're a short distance outside of town. It isn't named, it's just town, as far as the locals are concerned. Those from farther away call it Fungustown, which you might imagine isn't popular among the locals," Kanae said, a smile flickering across her lips as she added, "In my time here, there have been at least eight attempts to give it another name, but none of them have stuck."

"I'll believe that," Isalla agreed, but her curiosity was piqued by the name. "Why's it called Fungustown, then? I imagine there must be a reason."

"There is. I'm not sure if the town existed before it formed, but nearby is an area called the Fungal Abyss. It's in the heart of the forest, and it's... unpleasant. There's a reason that the hells are called such, after all. In any case, the various abysses are dangerous. Useful, but dangerous despite that," Kanae said, a distinct note of distaste to her voice. "The ingredients I got for your elixir came from the outskirts around the entrance to the Abyss. Much like the portals that lead to the hells, the portal in the heart of the forest leads to the Abyss. It's immense and produces a great many monsters, many of them as types of animate fungi, and some of them occasionally come out in search of victims. It's the main reason I've told you to stay inside as much as possible. Everything outside can be replaced relatively easily, comparatively."

"Oh. Why would you live anywhere *near* someplace like that?" Isalla asked, more startled than she'd been before, and somewhat outraged. "Why would the town be here, either?"

"Because it's on the way to the mountain, the monsters aren't too dangerous when you have a town used to this sort of thing, and the herbs and alchemical reagents that can be acquired from the Abyss are useful," Kanae replied promptly, and raised an eyebrow at Isalla as she asked, "Are you telling me that the heavens are universally safe and pleasant?"

"Well… no, not entirely. There are some places that are more dangerous than others; I just…" Isalla's voice trailed off as she frowned, unable to figure out how to verbalize her unease. At last, she just sighed and shook her head. "Never mind. It just seems strange to deliberately live near someplace so dangerous."

"It's how people choose to live, and reasonably common among the mortal races as well," Kanae replied, shrugging slightly. "As for the rest… we'll leave you honestly ignorant of many things. It'll help with your cover, and I'm not willing to try to teach you *everything* a person native to the hells would know from growing up. I'd doubtlessly miss something even if I made the attempt."

"True enough. You also said something about the bandages on my back, though…" Isalla said, her anxiety growing again, rather suddenly this time.

"Ah, yes, of course. We do have to remove them," Kanae agreed, sitting back in her chair and staring at Isalla. "Before I do anything further, do you want me to leave the wounds alone so they scar, or use herbs to help them vanish? It's possible to make it so that most wouldn't be able to notice where they were at all."

"Um, well… how much effect would those have on eventually getting my wings regenerated?" Isalla asked hesitantly, her mind rebelling at the thought of losing her wings for good.

BENJAMIN MEDRANO

"Either way, it's not going to affect that. Once your injuries have healed, to regenerate your wings will require re-opening the wounds entirely," Kanae said bluntly, and Isalla flinched.

"It's that bad?" Isalla asked. "You're not just going off rumors, are you?"

"No, I've seen it happen, though not on an angel," the demoness confirmed, her gaze softening as she continued. "I can't help you with that, Isalla. I don't know of anyone capable of regeneration who wouldn't immediately hand you over to the queen or someone worse. If I did, I'd have already taken you to them."

"In that case... could you heal the scars? I don't think I'll be in a position where I have to show my back often, but it'd be suspicious if I refused," Isalla said, letting out a soft sigh of disappointment. A tiny part of her wondered if Kanae was being truthful, but she didn't dare say anything. Kanae didn't have any reason to lie, either.

"Mmhm. We may as well check your injuries and see if they're ready for the bandages to come off," Kanae said, setting her mug on the table, then climbing to her feet.

"As you like," Isalla conceded, rising as well, then leading the way to her room. She hesitated a moment, then laid on the bed facedown.

Kanae's footsteps were almost silent as she approached, and Isalla shivered at her light touch against the angel's waist as she took the hem of Isalla's shirt and slowly raised it. Isalla hadn't put on her chest-strap, as the back would've gone over the bandages, so Kanae was able to get to the bandages quite easily.

Kanae removed the bandages carefully, their adhesive not so strong as to hurt as they came off, and her touch was feather-light as she murmured. "Hmm... you're coming along quite well, Isalla. The scabs should start coming off any day now, and then I can start treating your scars. I'd guess that it'll take about half a month from now to make them mostly vanish."

"Okay, that's a relief. I was afraid it'd take a lot longer than that," Isalla said, relaxing slightly. "I'm impressed at what you've managed to do with herbs and alchemy."

"Thank you," Kanae said, and Isalla heard her depart, then

return. A few moments later, she applied new bandages as she continued. "I've spent quite a few years learning, so I'd hope I've improved. It's a pleasure to hear that it's the case."

"You're welcome. I'll be honest… I didn't know that alchemy *could* do this. Thank you," Isalla admitted, just as Kanae pulled her shirt back down.

"Mm, being honest, is it? Well, I suppose it's best," Kanae replied, and Isalla blinked as one of her hands appeared on the frame next to Isalla's head, and then the demoness was speaking softly in her ear. "I've been considering my reactions of the past few days, Isalla, and I think you should know that I find you *very* attractive. However, no matter how much I may feel this way, I realize that currently our situation is too… lopsided. You're in a position of weakness, and I'm in a position of power. Once the scales are closer to even, I will address this again, but for now I will leave things as they are."

With that, Kanae straightened and walked out of the room, leaving Isalla behind her, almost frozen on the bed. It wasn't as though Isalla hadn't known that Kanae was feeling something for her… but even so, it was startling. And Isalla couldn't help but wonder *why* her heart was suddenly racing. Kanae wasn't anything like Roselynn, after all, yet she could make Isalla's heart race like she was.

# CHAPTER 10

First Sword Roselynn frowned as she tapped her desk with one finger, slowly going through her dispatches. There were the usual reports on what was happening on other fronts, instructions from the Council on what the current goals were, and the usual requests for information on what was happening in Zintas. It was all as should be expected, which was what concerned her. She'd initially thought that Isalla's letter was a touch on the paranoid side, but now...

Roselynn set the sheets aside for the moment and stood, walking over to the window to look outside at the island. It wasn't a small island, but neither was it too large, extending just over ten miles from one side to the other, and as she watched, a group of mortals was harvesting fruit from some of the plantations just outside the fortress walls. Some of her lieutenants had suggested that they cut everything back for a hundred yards, but Roselynn didn't see the point, and kept it at a mere dozen feet or so. If the demons invaded, enough of them had wings that keeping the area around the fortress *that* clear wasn't likely to do much good.

"Isalla, what have you gotten yourself into?" Roselynn murmured softly, resisting the urge to tap her fingers on her vambrace. No matter how Isalla's actions had complicated her life, Roselynn still cared for the other woman, and the letter had indicated that Isalla felt similarly, despite the distance Roselynn had deliberately opened between them.

After a few more moments of staring at the immense clouds and the blue skies above, Roselynn turned back to her desk and opened a drawer, pulling out Isalla's letter again. The paper was still crisp, though the folds were a bit more pronounced after the half-dozen times Roselynn had read it. Opening it, the angel read through the letter yet again, trying to examine it more critically this time.

*First Sword,*

*I'll entirely understand if my letter irritates you, but I'm not certain who else to send this to. I originally thought my assignment to the outer tiers of the Evergardens was a complete waste of my time and skills, but I accepted my punishment. It still pains me to think about what my admission about our relationship did to your career, and I cannot express my apologies deeply enough. If you wish for me to cease contacting you, you have but to let me know and I will do so, no matter how much I would regret it.*

*However, something strange is happening in the Evergardens. At first, I didn't notice anything, as I was new to the area, but eventually I grew used to the peace of the region. It was then that I realized quite a few angels who I believed were highly ranking were coming to the area, and usually by night when they were least likely to be noticed. I was... confused, honestly. I thought that perhaps some of them were in a situation much like our own, but that makes no sense for the number of them I saw. So I began to investigate, and what I've heard worries me.*

*Whispers from the common folk through the Evergardens speak of someone new. Someone who glows with a brilliant golden light, and who they believe to be the destined deity of the heavens. Blasphemy, I know, but it's what they've heard and are slowly beginning to believe might be true. I fear that perhaps a faction might be trying to use an archangel's mantle, whether new or old, to make a play for control of the heavens. The problem is that I don't have proof, and since I'm not certain who I can trust... the only one I could think of sending a message to is you.*

*Soon I'll be meeting with a contact I trust, who indicated she can help me. Haral has been a friend since I arrived in the Evergardens, and she has more contacts here than I possess. Despite that, it's possible someone will learn of my investigation, and should they take drastic action... well, someone should know.*

*If I don't contact you by a week after this letter reaches you, I believe something will have happened to me. I don't know what you should do in that case, but please... know that I still care about you, Roselynn.*

*My Deepest Regards,*

*Isalla*

The message was simple enough, and at first Roselynn had believed that Isalla had been making a mountain out of a molehill, or possibly even been mistaken about others coming to visit. That had been before the week had passed and no additional letter had arrived, though. Isalla had never missed one of her own deadlines before, and despite Roselynn not having replied to her, her old lover had continued to send regular letters for the past several years.

"Haral, was it? Considering what she said..." Roselynn considered for a moment, then folded her letter again and slid it back into the drawer.

Retrieving a sheet of paper and an ink pen, Roselynn began to pen a letter of her own. It wouldn't be too unusual if she asked about Isalla, and asking about Haral at the same time would be easy. Her superiors would likely be mildly irritated after the scandal with Isalla, but under the circumstances they'd forgive her.

Besides, even if they didn't, it wasn't as though they could punish her much further. Not considering the weapon she bore.

# CHAPTER 11

"If I say to stop, do it. Similarly, if I tell you to run, *run*," Kanae said, half-unsheathing her sword and studying it for a moment before fully sheathing it again.

"Are you expecting trouble?" Isalla asked, feeling quite nervous at the warning.

"No more than usual. The path to town is safe three-quarters of the time, but there's no way to know when something deadly has camped out on the trail, at least not until you run into it," Kanae replied, smiling slightly as she did so. "It isn't the monsters that worry me, anyway. It's renegade soldiers that are more dangerous, particularly if they're from another domain. Many of those ones raid here because they believe there will be plenty of beautiful demonesses to bed, and that makes you and I prime targets."

"Ah. Why don't you *sound* worried, then?" Isalla asked, a little confused by Kanae's smile.

"Because I'm not. I served in the army for some time, and I practice every morning. I'm not afraid of any of the common raiders, and anyone stronger than that has better things to do than to come after a small town like this," Kanae explained calmly, picking up a basket. "I doubt it'll prove much comfort to you, though."

"Not really, no. I'll follow your directions, but simply *being* here makes me uncomfortable," Isalla replied, letting out a soft sigh.

They were going into town, and Isalla was bracing herself for a particularly unpleasant experience. It might not be, based on her interactions with Kanae so far, but she felt it was best to plan for the worst rather than the best.

"You'll be well enough in, oh... two months? Something like that. Then you can decide whether you're willing to risk the climb," Kanae said, nodding in the direction of the mountain, despite them being inside. She opened the door and checked on either side before stepping out. "It's not quite everyone for themselves on the way up, but it's close. Your best bet is to join a caravan, but those aren't too common and generally charge quite a bit."

"And since I don't have any money, that's not really an option," Isalla said sourly, following Kanae outside and watching as the demoness locked the door behind them.

"No, it isn't," Kanae agreed.

They started down the path, and as they walked, Isalla glanced around as she left the small clearing for the first time. The area was rocky and had numerous outcroppings that forced the path to wind through the trees. There were a few flowers here and there, but all of them were darker than she would've expected.

"One thing you should know is that the spider demons in town are the type which resemble spiders almost entirely, with a pair of arms that are similar to yours that allow them to manipulate objects. They'll likely keep their distance, as they're something of loners, but we may encounter them or their silk spiders," Kanae began speaking as they walked, her voice calm and direct. "Try not to overreact if you see them; I know that most people from above don't care for their appearances."

"That's fairly accurate... and I particularly don't like the idea of the webs they can spin. I've seen them before, actually. Some tried to infiltrate the fortress where I was stationed a few years back," Isalla said, her mood souring at the memory, and especially when she thought of Roselynn. She had to wonder what had happened with her letter, or whether Roselynn had even read it. The thought was… discouraging, really.

"Ah, well that makes things simpler. Those in town aren't nearly as combative as those who join in attacks in the mortal world, though they protect their livestock viciously," Kanae replied, leading the way around a tree at a sedate pace. "I'd not talk about where you've seen them before after this, though. We're getting close to town."

"Fine," Isalla said shortly, trying to be polite but failing. Kanae seemed to take it as a hint and didn't say anything more, heading down the path at the same easy pace.

Soon enough, they came over the top of a ridge and saw the town, and Isalla's eyes widened in a bit of surprise.

The town had a thick wooden palisade around it, along with heavier gates than she'd seen before on a town composed of no more than a hundred buildings. The buildings were largely wooden, and the planed boards must have come from the mill she could see by the river on the far side of town, and aside from the darkness of the building exteriors, it could've been most towns she'd seen in the mortal world. The strange aspect was how wide the streets were, and how she could see at least a dozen sheep-sized spiders in a field near the town.

Down near the gates, she could see a guard, the blue-skinned demon standing about seven feet tall, with long spikes extending from his shoulders and knees, while large horns rose from his head. He wore simple hide armor, likely from a type of lizard, and had a large crossbow in hand and a club sitting next to him. He looked up to see Kanae and smiled, revealing pointed teeth and slit-pupil eyes the same color as his skin.

"Kanae, it's good to see you!" he boomed, his voice a deep rumble. "And this must be the guest I've heard rumors about."

"Indeed. This is Isalla. Isalla, this is Deka, one of the town guards," Kanae said, smiling slightly more warmly as she did so. "Let me know if he's rude and I'll deal with him. We haven't had a sparring match for a while."

"Of course not. I didn't join the army. I'm just a town guard, and I have my pride," Deka retorted. He extended a hand which only had three fingers and a thumb, though all of them were larger than normal as he said. "It's a pleasure to meet you, Isalla. Don't cause trouble around town, and I won't cause trouble for you, no matter what Kanae might claim."

"Thank you, Deka. I'm happy she found me, and I have no intention of causing trouble. I've got quite enough problems as it is," Isalla replied, shaking his hand in surprise. She'd never met a *friendly* demon before. Kanae certainly didn't qualify when they first met.

"Glad to hear it! You'll be welcome around town, then, at least for the most part. Avoid Ms. Pix, she's just ornery," Deka said, giving her hand a firm shake before letting go. "Any idea what you plan to do in town?"

"I'm showing her around, getting a few sundries, and buying her a few things to keep her out of my hair," Kanae said, glancing at Isalla as she added, "Besides, as soon as Enkax saw her, I knew I'd be swarmed with questions and figured bringing her into town was the easiest way to deal with them."

"Hah! That sounds about right, especially with how much of a loner you usually are." Deka laughed, grinning broadly as he nodded. "Good luck with holding off the questions."

"I'm certainly going to need it," Kanae replied dryly, and walked into town at a more sedate pace, something Isalla's muscles appreciated.

"What sort of things are you planning to get me?" Isalla asked a few moments later, once they were out of easy earshot of Deka. "I didn't realize you were planning to buy me things."

"You need a practice sword at a minimum, since your calluses indicate you've used a sword quite a bit. One of the longer ones, I think," Kanae replied, glancing at Isalla skeptically. "I think a wooden one for practice until you can build up your strength, and a simple steel one for after that. Are you an archer?"

"No, I'm middling at best with them," Isalla admitted, a little surprised at the demon's suggestion. "Wouldn't a sword be expensive, though?"

"Not really. There are a few lava flows from Hellmount that produce large concentrations of iron, so metal weapons aren't too hard to come by," Kanae replied calmly as they approached the middle of town. "Not having to buy you a bow is useful, though not ideal from the standpoint of defending yourself. Beyond that, you need a comb, a few hair ties, and other bathing supplies. I can't have you using all of mine, and I don't have the ingredients to make decent soap."

"Oh, I'm sorry, I didn't even think of that," Isalla said, flushing slightly.

"Don't apologize," Kanae said, another smile flickering across her face. "I didn't tell you *not* to use them, after all. Now, try not to stare."

There weren't a huge number of people in the town square, Isalla realized, but there were enough to surprise her. A couple of demons much like Enkax were clustered around a cart full of some type of squash with dark rinds, arguing, while a demon-blooded woman with pale red skin sat in a booth weaving baskets.

The biggest building took up an entire side of the square, and the building must be an inn, the angel realized, looking at the sheer size of the stables. As she watched, a muscular, four-armed demon carried a pair of kegs out of the stables and toward the front doors, ducking his head to ensure his large horns didn't hit the doorframe.

Several of the demons in the square looked at Isalla curiously, most of them not bothering to hide what they were doing, and most of the others were glancing at her out of the corner of their eyes. Isalla tried to ignore them, but it was hard. Fortunately, Kanae didn't so much as pause at their looks, leading the way directly to a building with a broad front directly across from the inn.

A bell tinkled as Kanae opened the door, and as she stepped inside, Isalla's eyes brightened in recognition. Shelves lined the walls of the room they stepped into, and they were crowded with everything from a saddle and backpacks to pitons and rope. She could see vials of unguents, tins of what might be makeup or shoe polish, and belts hanging from the wall. She hadn't been in many stores like this in the mortal world, but she'd been in the heavenly ones before. The only difference was that the shelves were even more widely spaced in the heavens due to the wingspan of an angel, while mortals crowded the shelves even closer than these were.

"Hello, hello! How may I—ah, my darling Kanae!" A male voice broke the quiet of the store, and a man stepped out of the back, speaking with a more refined lilt than Deka had possessed. "How may I help you, my dear? I haven't seen you in an age!"

"I was here just a few days ago, Manog," Kanae replied, the smile that had been flickering across her face now sticking around. "Might I introduce my current patient and guest, Isalla?"

"Of course! It's a pleasure to meet you, Isalla," Manog replied, and it was all Isalla could do not to stare at him. In fact, she failed despite every attempt to the contrary.

Manog was a bone demon, and she'd only heard of them before. His face was like that of a doll, a sculpted mass of pale bone with enormous, faceted black eyes twice the size of a human's. He had a pair of horns that rose up and backward, while more bone ridges ran back along his head much like hair, and separated from his skull to dangle. Each of the spine-like 'hair' strands was split into inch-long segments that were held together by some form of red fiber within them. Beneath his clothing, it looked like the demon's arms and legs were almost identical, and it was eerie how his bone-like lips moved so easily. Bone demons were widely regarded as deadly combatants or assassins among angels, so seeing one running a store was stunning.

"Oh, my apologies, Mister Manog," Isalla said after a moment, as she realized she'd hesitated a bit too long. "I didn't mean to stare, it's just... I've never seen one of your particular species before. I've only heard rumors and was surprised. The pleasure is mine."

"Not a worry, Isalla! My people don't breed as quickly as most others, and our homeland is farther to the north, near the Pale Mountains, so I'm not surprised you haven't seen one of us before," Manog replied smoothly, his tone easygoing. "I'd *also* heard that you're from above, so it's even less surprising. Is there anything I might do for you lovely ladies?"

"Flatterer," Kanae said, smiling at Manog as she shook her

head. "Why am I not surprised that you'd already heard that much? Enkax must have been talking a lot since I talked to him."

"Well, any word regarding new people in town helps liven up the town. Perhaps it wouldn't have spread so quickly if we had travelers in town, but alas, it was not to be," Manog said, and Isalla found herself oddly fascinated by how expressive his face was. She hadn't realized that their bone could flex like it did.

"True, that would be more convenient. I can't control when I have patients, though, so I'll live with what I have," Kanae replied indulgently. "Now, I have a few things I'd like to purchase for Isalla, since she's lost everything and I'm getting tired of her using my things."

"Certainly! What do you need, my darling healer?" Manog asked, rubbing his hands together eagerly.

"To start, we need a comb, then some soap. Preferably something with a good scent…" Kanae began, and Isalla allowed her attention to wander as she walked between the shelves.

It was fascinating seeing what life was like in a normal town in the hells. It was nothing like she had imagined, which made Isalla wonder what else she might not have known about.

"There we are," Kanae said, sitting down and smiling at Isalla as the angel dropped into her own chair, surprised at how tired she was. Her endurance hadn't been impacted much, but her muscles wore out easily. After a bit of rest, she'd be good to go, but Isalla wasn't happy with how painful the experience could be.

The smith had been human, to Isalla's shock, and all the weapons had been so heavy that Kanae had been forced to check the balance of the weapons for the angel. Isalla had at least been able to find a decent practice sword, and Kanae had used that as the basis for purchasing a plain, serviceable steel blade. Kanae was carrying both weapons seemingly effortlessly, along with the other items they'd purchased.

They were in the inn now, and Isalla looked around curiously as she murmured, "Thank you. I don't think I could've gotten back to the house without resting."

"I thought as much, which is why lunch here seemed like a good idea," Kanae said, setting the purchases down, then leaning forward to rest her arms on the worn table.

The tavern area of the inn was large, and the variety of seats was startling to Isalla, as were the number of chairs. Some were obviously sized for smaller giants or larger demons, while others probably were for the more diminutive species. A few low-slung stools were probably for creatures like the spider demons, Isalla guessed, but she was relieved that few others were there, and no spider demons. In fact, the only person in the room was a lamia with bright pink scales and matching hair that was working behind the bar.

All the furnishings were pitted and worn with use, and glowing lanterns hung from the ceiling, while weapons and trophies from monstrous creatures hung from the walls. It was fascinating, and just as alien in some ways as the general store had been familiar.

"It's interesting to me how much like the surface this is," Isalla said suddenly, feeling the need to talk about it. "So many things are just like they are back home, but other things... the trophies, the chairs and that, are so different."

"Mm... I'm not surprised. Everyone has needs, whether demon or mortal, and they need to sate them," Kanae replied calmly, nodding to the lamia. "With those needs, it's always likely that some people will come up with similar solutions. Further than that... demons and mortals have been visiting the realms of one another for generations. Doubtlessly each side has been shamelessly stealing ideas from each other for the entire time."

"That *does* sound like something that would happen," Isalla said, and opened her mouth to continue, but bit it back before she could say something foolish. Fortunately, the lamia approached about that time, her snake-like lower body slithering its way across the room and with a bright smile on her face.

"Hello, ladies! How can I help you today?" the lamia asked, smiling broadly as she glanced at Kanae. "Your usual, dearie?"

"I have a name, Cyr," Kanae replied with a roll of her eyes. "But yes, I'll have my usual. If Isalla wants to figure something out for herself she can, but I'd recommend the same."

"What'll it be, Isalla?" Cyr asked, ignoring Kanae's protest. As Isalla watched, Kanae gently swatted the tip of the lamia's tail aside as it tried to run down her arm.

"I'll just go with her recommendation. I *am* still her patient and have no idea what you serve," Isalla said, not wanting to betray her ignorance too much, and also not wanting to hear if there were things that would turn her stomach on the menu. Heavens knew that was almost a certainty.

"Right away! Two portions of roast cave lizard and mashed potatoes with gravy, coming right up." Cyr replied easily, turning to slither away quickly.

"Cave lizard?" Isalla asked dubiously.

"It's not that different from beef and is better than most of the other meats down here," Kanae replied calmly. "I prefer it, and you need more meat to help your body heal."

"Alright, fair," Isalla conceded, letting out a soft sigh. "In that case… what's after this?"

"We eat, I take you back to the house, and since you're in decent shape and have something to do, I go do my rounds," Kanae explained. "I still need to check on Qirress again to make certain she doesn't overdo it."

"Oh, well… true, you do have a job to do," Isalla agreed, a little surprised with her own reluctance to let Kanae leave. "I suppose I'll just have to enjoy our time together."

Kanae's eyebrows rose, and as she realized what she'd said, Isalla blushed furiously. She opened her mouth to say something, then closed it again.

A few moments later, Kanae's comment was soft and faintly amused. "Indeed, that we shall."

# CHAPTER 12

*R*oselynn paused on opening the door to her room, looking down at the letter that had been slipped under it. The letter was something of a surprise, since most of the time when Roselynn got letters, they were simply delivered to her office. Beyond that, she only ever returned to her room when she needed to rest, so anyone wanting to contact her would know that this was possibly the least efficient way to go about it. Of course, Roselynn knew that could be intentional.

Stepping over the letter, the angel studied it carefully, a slight frown on her face. If it weren't for her letter from Isalla, she might have simply picked it up, but of late Roselynn had been feeling a touch more cautious. Pulling out a ring set with a moonstone, Roselynn put it on and leaned down to press the stone against the parchment, murmuring the word to activate the ring's magic. A moment passed, and Roselynn relaxed slightly as there wasn't a reaction. If the letter had been poisoned, she would have seen a black mist envelop the paper.

Picking up the sheet, Roselynn frowned again as she saw it'd been sealed with wax, though without a seal to identify it, and she murmured. "Curious… this is being a touch more mysterious than I like. I hope this isn't another love letter."

Her room was smaller than the one her predecessor had favored, though still finely appointed. She didn't pay it much attention most of the time, and today wasn't much different as she approached her desk. Pulling out a letter opener, she broke the seal and opened the letter to reveal a relatively hasty scrawl written in angelic.

*First Sword,*

*It's only by fortune that I learned of your inquiry into the fate of Isalla and myself, and I deeply hope you'll keep this letter to yourself. You won't be receiving a reply from your superiors regarding us, and doubtlessly someone is preparing to keep watch over you. I've attempted to outrun them here, and if we're to have any chance of speaking, we must do so quickly.*

*I dare not reveal myself openly or enclose much information, but I am willing to tell you what I know. If you wish to speak, come to the pier by Fisherman's Rock tomorrow night at midnight. If you aren't alone, I won't reveal myself. My apologies, I don't know who to trust.*

*I strongly suggest that you burn this letter, so no one else knows.*

*Sincerely,*

*H*

"Well, isn't *that* foreboding?" Roselynn said, unease welling up within her.

Even the implication that her letter wouldn't receive a reply was… unsettling. Yet the truth was that Roselynn had expected at least a preliminary response already, and she hadn't even gotten an acknowledgement that her inquiry had arrived. That lent a degree of legitimacy to the letter on its own, and based on what she knew, the writer likely was Haral.

Fisherman's Rock was a common name, but the location the other angel must be thinking of was located less than a mile from the fortress. The sightlines weren't perfect, with the rock between the pier and the fortress, but sending up a signal flare in the case of an ambush wouldn't be difficult. Roselynn tapped her lip as she considered what to do. She was tempted to tell one of her lieutenants, regardless of what the letter had said, but it was more of a risk than she was willing to take.

"As long as I'm careful…" Roselynn murmured, glancing down at her sword and armor. She wasn't going to go unarmed, regardless of what Haral might wish, so it wasn't like she could be overwhelmed easily, and she could always scout the area during the day. That would ensure that she had plenty of time for reinforcements to arrive if it turned out to be an ambush.

Satisfied with the thought, Roselynn nodded to herself and lit a candle. Once it was going properly, she lit the sheet of paper on fire and watched the flames slowly consume it, dropping the last corner as it was about to reach her fingers. Once the last embers went out, she pulled out a wastebasket and swept the ashes into it to be sure the document was gone, then blew out the candle.

"Alright, time for bed," Roselynn murmured, standing up again. Regardless of whether the letter was true or false, she needed her rest.

～

THE DAY HAD GONE AS WELL as most did, considering how quiet Roselynn's post was. None of her troops had noticed anything out of the ordinary, which was reassuring as well, and there'd only been mild concern when Roselynn had decided to perform an impromptu inspection of the island perimeter.

It had been easy to swing by the pier at Fisherman's Rock, and it was much as Roselynn had remembered it. The area in question was sandy, and despite the footprints of locals who went there to fish, it would be difficult for someone to lay a trap without being seen. Roselynn approved of the spot, as it was just far enough from any buildings to be an obscure meeting point, but it was still close enough to be relatively safe. She still wasn't happy to be meeting in private but was willing to play along for the moment.

Waiting until nightfall to leave had been a touch frustrating due to her impatience, but Roselynn controlled herself. Her explanation of wanting a quiet flight to help relax had calmed the nerves of the guards, and she'd done exactly as she'd said, flying along and relaxing before finally going to the rock to wait.

The sound of the waves softly crashing on the shore was soothing, and aside from the sounds of a few night birds and buzzing of insects, the evening was quiet as Roselynn waited. Of all the posts she could have been assigned, she supposed there could have been worse, as one of the frozen northern isles would have been unpleasant. Those would have also been a waste of her talents, though, which was likely why they'd chosen the site they had. There was no glory to be had at Firewatch, no matter how vital it might be.

It was all because she'd inherited Ember, Roselynn knew, glancing down at the sword. The magical weapon had been passed down through her family for generations, and no one else could wield it but those of her bloodline. It was unsurprising that the Council would be loathe to lose the threat of such a weapon, really. It was Isalla who had borne the brunt of their punishment, in all truth.

Roselynn had been a bit... naïve, she admitted. She'd thought that the punishment would be focused on herself, since she was Isalla's superior, and she hadn't argued with the accusations to help focus them on herself. She hadn't expected the Council to come down so hard on a promising young soldier. But they had, and she felt guilty about it, and even guiltier that she'd never responded to Isalla's letters. Never mind that it had been partially to prevent further retaliation against Isalla, Roselynn still regretted it.

That was a large part of why she was out here. Despite everything, Roselynn wasn't going to see Isalla abandoned again. It just wasn't right.

A flicker of movement caught Roselynn's eye, and she turned to see an angel slipping out from among a group of the nearby trees, wearing brown robes that would help her blend in better, and which partially obscured the blonde woman's white wings. She looked around before approaching, and as she did so, Roselynn was able to see the crystal blue of her eyes more easily, as well as the nervousness on her face. The woman was attractive, she realized, and looked slightly like Isalla, though her old lover had worn her hair shorter than this woman's.

"First Sword?" the woman asked, stopping a good thirty feet away.

"Yes. I assume that you're Haral?" Roselynn asked, watching the woman closely. Seeing the way her tension seemed to ease, it helped Roselynn's nerves settle a bit more.

"I am. I'm glad to see you didn't... well, let's just say that the past couple of weeks have been stressful." Haral said, letting out a breath and approaching until she was only a few feet away. "I'm fortunate to even be here, if I'm being honest."

"Yes, well, that's why we're both here, isn't it? The last I'd heard from Isalla, she said she was meeting with you, and then she never followed up. You claim that my inquiry won't be answered, so why don't you provide some answers?" Roselynn asked, folding her arms and pinning the woman in place with a glare. "I've chosen to listen to your suggestions despite not having any evidence that you're speaking the truth, but there's only so far I'm willing to go."

"Of course, I don't blame you. The situation is… complex, I'll admit," Haral said, playing with a curl of her hair nervously as she glanced around again. "I'd known Isalla ever since she arrived in the Evergardens, and we were good friends. When she confided in me about her suspicions about some of the activities in the area… well, I knew I could trust her, so I gathered some of my own information."

"Were? You seem to be implying that something happened to her," Roselynn interrupted, her eyes narrowing suddenly. She felt a flicker of anger surge to life at the thought, but she kept it from showing on her face.

"Something did. I don't know if she's alive or dead," Haral explained quickly.

"I need details," Roselynn insisted, that flicker of anger growing stronger.

"We met so I could give her the information I had on the… the *cult* that had been forming in the area. It was dangerous, and I knew that, but I didn't think anyone knew. Unfortunately, I was wrong." Haral's words were almost stumbling over one another at this point. "We were attacked just as we were leaving, though. There were dozens of cultists, and she began fighting them and told me to run! I did, and even so, I barely escaped, but when I went to try to find help, they tried to capture—"

A flash of light near the tree line caught Roselynn's eye, and suddenly the world around them rippled, as a huge sphere of distorted air suddenly snapped into existence for over thirty yards in every direction.

"Or *maybe* they just let you escape so they could track you to anyone you went to for help!" Roselynn interrupted, growling as she drew Ember and the ruby-bladed sword blazed to life, its runes glowing a bright scarlet. "Are you armed? Because *someone* just put up a powerful illusion to keep anyone from coming to our aid."

"I... I have a dagger," Haral said, snatching the dagger out of her robes. It was a stiletto, Roselynn noticed, so it wouldn't be much good against plate, but it might work well enough. "How did they—heavens help us! What are *demons* doing here?"

A group of a dozen demons had emerged from the trees, and Roselynn swore under her breath at the sight of them. Most of them were the typical demonic fare, brutes that weren't dangerous, but in the back was one that worried her. The pallid, eyeless upper body of a woman rested atop a scorpion's body, the latter with eyes, and with four arms weaving symbols for spells in the air. Hellweavers were *not* a good sign, and they were generally too rare to send against an outpost like this one.

"That is a very good question," Roselynn agreed, glancing over the group of demons. She wasn't worried about anyone but the hellweaver, but if she had to protect Haral, a fight would become problematic. Fortunately, the two of them had one major advantage. "We're going to fly directly up, Haral. Your only chance is if we signal the fortress that there's an attack."

"Okay... when?" Haral asked nervously, and the demons began loping forward, growling as they did so.

"Three... two... one... now!" Roselynn's voice was low, but she snapped out her wings with the last word and shot upward.

Or, to be more accurate, she attempted to fly upward. The instant Roselynn's wings beat for the first time, she felt something wrong as the muscles through her back twitched and cramped, and the beat had no power to it. Instead of taking flight, she went up only an inch or two before half-collapsing, all her muscles cramping suddenly. As she gasped in pain, her right arm was wrenched upward and a spike of pure pain lanced up through her shoulder.

"What—?" Roselynn gasped, looking over to see Ember fall from her nerveless grasp and Haral holding her arm, the stiletto buried in her shoulder through the thinner chain guarding Roselynn's armpit.

"A two-part poison to bypass any poison detection you might have, split between the letter and me. I couldn't have you flying away," Haral said, all her hesitation and fear gone as she smiled. "Coupled with the poison on this dagger, you won't be going anywhere."

"Why are you...?" Roselynn gasped, pain surging through her with every heartbeat, and a fuzzy sensation washing over her thoughts.

"As if I'd tell you. That would simply make this more difficult, and I can't have that," Haral replied idly. "Suffice to say that you were starting to stick your nose where it doesn't belong. I *do* need to find out what you knew, though, which is why I employed others."

"Speaking of which, Ms. Haral, the more you speak, the more difficult it will be to remove your words from her memories," the hellweaver spoke in a voice that had a faint buzz to it, almost like there were wasps within her pale throat. "I would suggest you cease."

"As you wish. How soon will you be able to get me the information I need?" Haral asked.

Roselynn felt her legs give way beneath her as her body began going numb. The demons had surrounded her, and she glared at them balefully, anger and frustration coiling within her, but her throat wasn't responding as she tried to speak. The numbness had killed much of her pain, but as her thoughts grew fuzzy, she also felt fear. Fear for her failure to avenge Isalla's death, and anger that she'd fallen into the trap Haral had set for her.

"The Flame of Ember is legendary for her stubborn nature, so you must expect as much as three months from now. The ladies of the spire require time to work," the hellweaver buzzed in return. "Now, I must work while the memories are still fresh."

"Very well," Haral conceded, stepping back. At least the annoyance on her face was satisfying, Roselynn thought. The problem was the approaching hellweaver.

"Hold still, Flame of Ember," the demon hissed at Roselynn. "The more you struggle, the more painful this will be."

Roselynn glared at her hatefully, but the demon simply began to cast a spell, glowing scarlet diagrams forming in each of her hands. Then it thrust them against her head, and pure agony radiated out from them as the magic slammed into Roselynn's mental shields.

She didn't relent, though, fighting back against the demon's magic with everything she had. Until she lost consciousness entirely, Roselynn fought against the spells trying to warp her recent memories.

But fail she did, and at long last Roselynn lost consciousness.

# CHAPTER 13

The axe bit into the wood solidly, though it didn't go quite as deep as Isalla would've liked. She'd never cut logs before this, and she was learning there was a certain amount of technique to it that she'd never realized before. When she did it right, the downward swing was almost effortless, as the weight of the axe would bring it down with sufficient force to split most log sections they had on hand. The problem was getting it right.

Lifting the axe and the log, Isalla brought it down again, which forced the axe blade the rest of the way through the wood. She still was fascinated by how easy Kanae made it look, a memory which made her pause to think. The previous week, she'd come out early in the morning, just after she'd heard the sound of splitting wood, and she'd stopped, stunned.

Kanae had stood there in simple trousers and a sleeveless shirt, her hair pulled back in a ponytail. While tall and broad-shouldered, Kanae wasn't rippling with muscles, but neither did she look like some wilting flower who'd never trained. Her muscles were toned and distinct as she smoothly placed a log onto the stump and swung the axe, which flashed in the morning light before splitting the log almost effortlessly. Kanae had kept going for almost fifteen minutes, until she had a faint sheen of sweat before stopping to collect the wood.

BENJAMIN MEDRANO

Isalla hadn't been afraid of staring, and having seen it, she'd asked if she could use the axe as part of her own recovery. Kanae hadn't objected, so Isalla had tried for herself... and almost immediately lost her grip on the axe. It had taken a couple of days before she could swing it properly, and then some instruction from Kanae after a few... less proficient attempts. She'd learned as best she could, though, and it was doing her upper body a world of good as she tried to rebuild her muscles, while she'd taken to jogging around the clearing in the mornings as well as her other exercises. She *had* wondered what Kanae used the wood for, since it was only used in her alchemical lab and the fireplace, but then a group of demons from town had come and traded some food for a large pile of wood.

Accompanying Kanae on a few of her house calls had been fascinating as well. The people she visited were all demons, save for a single family of humans that had startled Isalla, but their livelihoods were eclectic. Few of the farmhouses had large fields, which didn't surprise her after thinking about it. The land was too uneven and rocky for it to be easy to have large farms, but she'd been surprised at how verdant the fields they had were. Many kept a variety of animals, most of which were able to defend themselves, and all the families seemed reasonably well-armed. She found out later that a good number of the locals collected herbs or the hides of monsters to sell in the larger towns or to traveling merchants.

"Water?" Kanae asked, a flask in her hand as she stood a half-dozen paces back, well clear of the axe's reach.

"Please," Isalla replied, breathing heavily as she set down the axe.

Kanae stepped forward, and Isalla took the flask and half-drained it over several seconds. The water was cool and refreshing, and Isalla let out a sigh of relief as she lowered the flask again.

"Thank you, that is *very* much appreciated," Isalla said, capping the flask and handing it back. "I can't believe how easy you make this look."

"Lots of practice. At a certain point, you gain enough experience that you can make many things look simple," Kanae replied, shaking her head slightly as she took the flask. "After as many years of practice as I've had, it's no wonder I've grown rather proficient."

"I have to ask… you've talked a bit about your past, about fighting in the army and such, and it sounds like it was quite some time ago, especially with this stump looking so ancient," Isalla said, nodding at the stump, which was so weathered she was startled it hadn't split yet either. "How long have you been here, Kanae? For that matter, how old *are* you? I know demons don't age past their prime if they don't want to, much like angels, but…"

"That *is* prying a touch, Isalla," Kanae said, smiling and looking at the stump with a considering look. "Though you aren't wrong, either. I probably should replace the stump again, since it probably won't last more than a few more years."

Isalla didn't say anything more, as she could tell that Kanae was working her way around to answering, if she answered at all. It wouldn't be surprising if Kanae didn't answer in the end, since her past wasn't necessarily relevant, or possibly something she wasn't proud of.

"I'm not going to tell you precisely how old I am. Older than you by a large margin… and old enough to remember the last major war," Kanae finally said, looking at Isalla, her gaze revealing a surprising weariness. "Twelve centuries ago, I responded with excitement when the war began. A century and a half of brutal warfare… well, it cured me of any belief in *glory*, Isalla. I left the army afterward and went traveling, seeing what else there was to the hells and part of the mortal world. What I found didn't help, and about five hundred years ago I settled down here. I only knew the basics of healing at the time, but time taught me much."

"I…" Isalla found herself almost speechless.

Calling the War of Decimation just a major war would be putting it mildly. It had begun as a major offensive by the angelic legions and the Firetear Alliance to take back some of the lands of one of the Alliance's members. The Fallen Kingdoms had rallied, as had the demonic legions, and quickly the war had turned into one of the most horrifying incidents in the history of the wars between the heavens and hells. No war had resulted in the demonic forces coming closer to breaching a gate to the heavens, and it had even waged its way into the hells briefly. Heroes and villains had fallen, and all reports Isalla had seen indicated that nearly one-tenth of each generation that had fought in the war had died, proving that the name was accurate. That war was the reason that both sides had been on an uneasy, quiet footing for over a millennium. They clashed, but no one wished for such devastation to strike again.

"You survived the entire war?" Isalla asked, her horror growing at the thought.

"Yes," Kanae said simply, patting the stump gently.

"How? Were you stationed at the rear lines?" Isalla asked. "Everything I heard about the war... well, not many people were kept on the front lines, and I've never met anyone who survived *all* of it."

Kanae laughed, the sound bitter and sharp. "Well, you have now. I've met a few others who did, and I know a number of them did on the side of angels. Most people tried to get away after the first few battles, but my choices... well, they were limited. I was at the battle of Scarlet Peaks, as well as the siege of Rosken. Surviving them, though... that was pure fortune, from my perspective."

Isalla flinched. The battle of Scarlet Peaks had renamed the mountains where they were located, for the snow-capped peaks were said to have been stained red in blood by the sacrifices of those who'd fallen in breaking the demon assault driving toward the gates of the heavens. As for the siege of Rosken... it had been one of the most fought-over strategic fortresses, and three mortal gods, two archangels, and two demon lords had joined the fray in the end. Their clash of power had destroyed the citadel and left a wasteland of wild magic which had been abandoned ever since, and had been a telling blow in the war, as only one deity, archangel, and demon lord had survived the battle.

For a long minute, they were both silent. Isalla watched Kanae as she sat on the stump, staring at the sky for a long minute. She didn't look like a demon that had survived the War of Decimation. She looked... well, much like a succubus, if larger and without wings or as large of horns, which was unusual enough. Isalla tried to work through what it must have been like in the war, but her mind simply couldn't process it.

"I can't even imagine what that must have been like. I... I really can't blame you for choosing to abandon the war," Isalla said. She was going to continue, but Kanae interrupted.

"I didn't abandon the war." Kanae's tone was soft but precise. "I waited until it was over, then I left the army. I faked my own death to ensure that people would leave me alone, then chose to travel."

"That isn't what I meant, but you're the one who was in the war. What I *meant* was that I don't blame you for losing faith in the war between heavens and hells," Isalla corrected herself, toying with the axe handle, then taking it over to prop against the shed with a grunt. "I just have to ask... why here? Of all the realms of the mortal world and the hells... you're near the heart of where conflict might occur, with a gate from the mortal world only days away from you. Why here?"

"That is the question, isn't it? I have a couple of reasons... but all of them are shallow. I could have settled in many places in the hells without issue. I'm a skilled warrior, and those are useful almost anywhere. The mortal world... that wouldn't have been possible back then. There was too much death and destruction," Kanae murmured, letting out a soft sigh as she stood up again. "I'm not sure why I chose this place, Isalla. Perhaps I was simply tired of traveling... or perhaps this was just comfortable. I'm not entirely certain."

"I guess that's as good of a reason as any you might have had. I don't know... I just was thinking that the town and everything is a little bit odd for someone like you, and I was right. You're incredibly unusual for the area, and I had no idea how true that was," Isalla said, her voice hesitant as she paused, then put her hand on Kanae's shoulder with a bit of trepidation. "I'm sorry I brought it up, if it was painful for you. I'm more surprised you were willing to help me at all, considering how bad the war was."

"That was a long time ago, Isalla. I've had a lot of time to work through things, and you're hardly the first angel I've known," Kanae replied, glancing over her shoulder and smiling at the angel. "Not even the first wingless one, for that matter."

"What? But you said—" Isalla began, then stopped as Kanae stretched.

"I said I'd never *treated* an angel before. The army alone captured a good many angels, though many were abused and tormented," Kanae explained calmly. "I took up healing centuries after that, though."

"Oh. That's… well, it gives me mixed feelings," Isalla replied, her stomach tightening at the thought. "Did you…?"

"I never forced myself on anyone, and any angels I injured were in battle," Kanae said. "I might have, some days, but I never sought your kindred out for it. Time changed me, somewhat."

"Huh. Well, it makes me feel a little better," Isalla admitted, looking over at where the sun was ascending through the dark clouds on the horizon, the orb a deep red. After a moment, she asked, "Do you blame me for wondering?"

"Not at all. If you *didn't* wonder, I'd think you were suicidal. Or maybe masochistic, for that matter," Kanae said, grinning.

"Uh, what?" Isalla asked, slightly confused. She understood the first part, but… she couldn't help but ask, "What do you mean by masochistic? I haven't heard the term before."

"Oh? Well, hmm…" Kanae paused, looking slightly taken aback, and tapped her lips before shaking her head. "No, I think I'd best *not* address that just now."

"What? Why?" Isalla followed Kanae as she headed toward the house.

"I just think it might disturb you, and it's for the best not to do that," Kanae replied promptly.

"Oh, that's just… that's just making excuses. I'm a grown woman and have been for decades," Isalla said in exasperation. "I can handle finding out what a silly *word* means!"

"Really?" Kanae asked, turning to look at Isalla speculatively. "Are you sure about that?"

"Yes!" Isalla exclaimed, growing annoyed.

"Very well. Listen carefully, then," Kanae said, smiling slightly. Isalla nearly took a step backward but kept still as

Kanae came close to her ear and spoke softly. "Masochism is when one finds pleasure, usually *sexual* pleasure, from personal humiliation, pain, or both, Isalla. Does that apply to you?"

For a moment, what Kanae said didn't register, and then Isalla's curiosity turned to horrified mortification as heat rose in her cheeks. She'd never even considered the possibility, and she quickly stepped away, shaking her head vehemently as she exclaimed, "No, of course not! I've never even considered something like that, and… and how is that even possible?"

"Mm… like it or not, some people *do* feel like that, Isalla," Kanae replied, smiling as she took a step back. "Now, I'm going to take care of sorting some herbs, hm?"

Isalla couldn't bring herself to speak again, staring after her host in shock and with just a thread of curiosity. She didn't think she had any interest in what Kanae had said, but it was interesting, in a mortifying sort of way.

# CHAPTER 14

*K*anae took a deep breath of the air as she walked still deeper into the forest. The air was mostly clear, though she could smell just a hint of the Fungal Abyss in the breeze. She was closer to the Abyss than usual, though, so that much was natural.

Walking out to Odrak's home wasn't the most pleasant of trips, Kanae knew, which was the main reason that the elderly cyclops had built his home out this far from the main trade routes. He liked being left alone, but since he wasn't a demon, the man was starting to lose his strength. That was the main reason the town's mayor sent her to check on Odrak occasionally.

"Not that I really mind coming out here. It's peaceful enough, most of the time," Kanae murmured, looking upward for a moment. Her smile faded as she considered her guest and sighed. "Though it *is* somewhat complicated, with Isalla at home. She... makes things harder."

The forest didn't answer, of course. Still, Kanae couldn't help but think about her angelic guest. Isalla was interesting, and for the most part, Kanae liked her. That didn't mean that her presence was without its problems, though.

"She brings back memories. Ones I've spent centuries trying to leave behind," Kanae whispered, her mood growing still worse as she remembered some of the events of the war, and of the times even before that. There had been angels throughout her life, and she'd interacted with them more than she'd admitted to Isalla. That was part of the problem.

A flicker of light from one of the branches up above caught her attention, distracting Kanae. "Hm? What's…"

About twenty feet up one of the trees was something made of metal, and Kanae took a few steps back and to the side to get a better look at it. As she got a better angle, Kanae's lips pursed as she saw that a sword had been driven into the tree, and the blade was sticking out the opposite side of the trunk. The interesting thing was how the blade gleamed, and the gold cross guard shaped like bird wings. Even more intriguing to Kanae, it looked like the sword matched Isalla's sheath, and her sword *had* been missing when she found Isalla.

"Interesting. Her enemies must have thrown it through the portal as well… and the mountain threw it over here," Kanae said, a smile playing across her lips. "At least it answers the question of where it was. I suppose I'd best retrieve it… even if I need to leave it in the bushes until I'm on my way back. Isalla will probably want her sword back."

Approaching the tree, Kanae set down her basket and shrugged off her backpack, judging the best way to get up to the sword. The branches were thick enough to support her weight, and the tree didn't look diseased, though that might not last after the sword had pierced the trunk. It might be worth coming out and felling the tree later, in fact, but Kanae shrugged. That was a subject for later.

She jumped upward, grabbing onto one of the branches about halfway to her goal, then swung slightly to plant a foot on another branch. From there, it was a relatively quick climb up to the sword, and Kanae paused as she saw the sword from closer range, her opinion of it improving.

Several runes carved into the mithral blade showed that it was enchanted reasonably well, and it didn't take her much work to decipher them. Isalla's sword was enchanted to be sharper and strike more truly, though it wasn't heavily enchanted in either regard. If it were Kanae, she'd have tried to get something better, but she had no idea just how high of a position Isalla had possessed before her unfortunate encounter with her enemies.

"First, let's get this dislodged," Kanae murmured, adjusting her feet and wrapping her tail around the tree's trunk as a brace.

Kanae couldn't put all her strength into pulling the sword out, not without risking going flying out of the tree, and that would be quite painful. Instead, she had to carefully control her strength as she slowly wiggled the blade back and forth, working it out of the tree bit by bit. The sword was being stubborn, and as it began coming loose, Kanae realized why as she saw the congealed sap along the blade.

Eventually, she got past the worst of the sap, though, and as the blade narrowed it got still easier. Finally pulling the sword free, Kanae let out a soft sigh, examining the sword again. It was too obviously of angelic manufacture to show openly, except maybe as a trophy on a wall or the like. The only exception would be for the rare fallen angels, or even for the ashborn. Hells knew that Kanae had seen stranger things in her time.

"Alright, down we go," Kanae murmured, uncurling her tail from the trunk, gauging the distance, then jumping downward through the red leaves of the trees.

She hit the ground and rolled to break her fall, reducing the pain of the impact to almost nothing before springing to her feet, smiling as she did so. She hadn't done that in a while, and it was oddly refreshing... though it *did* mean she had dirt and leaves all over her clothing and hair.

Setting down the sword, Kanae began brushing herself off, sending bits of detritus back to the ground. After a moment, she noticed that there were also bits of bark on her tail, which prompted a little more time spent cleaning off. Only once she was done did Kanae look at the sword again. It was just a bit too distinct, and she debated on where to hide it, before finally simply finding a bush and burying it beneath some leaves.

"There we go. Now to go take care of errands and get back home," Kanae murmured, moving to pick up her things and to get moving.

The remainder of the trip didn't take too long, no more than a quarter of an hour, and then Kanae came into sight of Odrak's home. The cyclops lived in a rather large cave, but the front of it had been walled over with stone blocks that Odrak had quarried himself, and it was excellently constructed. Kanae didn't find that surprising, as in her experience the only ones who rivaled dwarves at forging and building fortifications were cyclops. More to the point, though, she also saw that the subject of her trip was already outside.

Odrak was a twelve-foot-tall, muscular man, with broad shoulders and bulging muscles, even though he was obviously growing old. He had a fringe of white hair around his head, and the cyclops was wearing simple furs as he examined one of the dozen fruit trees in front of his home with a single, discerning eye. A cyclops-sized battleaxe was near at hand, and Kanae knew from experience that Odrak knew how to use it.

"Why, is that Kanae? To what do I owe this surprise?" Odrak asked, looking up and smiling broadly at her. "I haven't seen you in, oh... two months?"

"Don't give me that, old man. You know as well as I do why I'm here," Kanae retorted, increasing her pace as she grinned at the cyclops. "The mayor sends his regards, as per normal."

"Ha, the youngster needs to learn not to pry too much. Some of us *like* our privacy," the cyclops said, his chuckle a deep rumble. He did give Kanae a pointed look as he added, "And here you are, calling *me* an old man? You've been living here for longer than I've been alive, Kanae."

"Yes, but *my* body has the good sense not to age. Yours seems to think that since everyone else does it, it should age, too," Kanae replied with a derisive sniff. "Hells know where it got *that* idea from, but someone has to try to keep it from going too far."

Odrak laughed at that, grinning broadly in return. "Is that so? Well, I suppose we'd best try to keep it in line. I'll admit that my knee *has* been giving me a few complaints, so having you look at it might not be a bad idea."

"Is that so? Well, let's have a look at it, then. We can't have it giving you problems," Kanae replied calmly, smiling back at the elderly cyclops. "Where would you like to take care of this?"

"Why don't you come inside and relax? I'll put on a pot of tea, then you can work your magic," Odrak suggested.

"It's hardly magic," Kanae disagreed but gestured for the house. "Lead the way, then."

The cyclops began leading the way to his home, and as he did so, Kanae followed. She imagined that this wouldn't take too long, but she could be wrong.

∾

As she approached the spot where she'd left the sword, Kanae paused, something about the silence making her uneasy. She glanced around and frowned as she didn't see anything immediately, which was worrisome. Most dangers in the forest tended to be on the obvious side of things, except for the plants which would lay in wait. The creatures that were patient were much more dangerous than she liked to deal with.

She glanced down at the basket of apples that Odrak had given her, debating for a moment, then carefully set it down. She hadn't expected the gift, but suspected that it'd make Isalla happy, since the angel wasn't used to the limited variety of food Kanae tended to eat. But first she had to get the food back to the house.

Nothing happened as Kanae set the basket down, then unsheathed her sword. Then she slowly stepped forward, her muscles coiling as the sense of danger grew stronger. She trusted her instincts, and her gaze drifted back and forth, then rose to look at the trees, then down at the ground. There wasn't any sign of an avian, which was good, and she didn't see the slight distortions of one of the rare chameleons that lived in the region, either. It might be—

As her boot came down on the ground, Kanae saw the dirt shiver and she had a split second to realize that the earth had recently risen before something almost exploded out of the earth at her. Kanae instantly dodged to the side, swearing under her breath.

"Crawlers. I *hate* crawlers," Kanae hissed, her sword lashing out to cut into the thick, worm-like creature's side. It's blunt, beak-like mouth snapped shut around the spot where Kanae had been standing, even as her sword left a wound on its side that dripped nearly black blood.

Kanae quickly danced backward as she felt the ground shiver, and the next moment five long, whip-like tendrils exploded from the ground as the crawler lashed out with its tails. The poisonous barbs punched through the bushes and into one of the trees, and Kanae sighed unhappily as she cut one of the tails off, leaving it oozing more black blood.

"This will take some killing," Kanae muttered, glaring balefully at the crawler as it began retreating underground, hissing in anger.

Just to be safe, she backed away from the basket of apples and where the angelic sword was hidden. She didn't want them getting caught in the mess. Fortunately, she was fast enough to avoid the attacks of crawlers, and they weren't very intelligent, just vicious and voracious.

KANAE ADJUSTED HER BASKETS, debating just how to handle them and the sword as she stood in front of the door. Eventually she sighed and set the sword down, leaning it against the frame so she could pull out the key she needed. She was tired and annoyed after the fight with the crawler, but at least she'd killed the beast, and managed to avoid getting more than a few drops of its poisonous blood on her skin. Fortunately, she was effectively immune to its poison.

Finally retrieving the key, Kanae unlocked the door and slipped it back into its pouch, then picked up the sword again. Opening the door, Kanae felt a faint warmth as Isalla spoke.

"Welcome back, Kanae!" the angel called out, sounding like she was out of breath and in her room, likely from exercising.

"Thank you, Isalla. I have some fruit, and something to show you," Kanae replied, closing the door behind her. She'd have to make certain to lock it a bit later, but her hands were full at the moment.

"Oh? What might..." Isalla asked, stepping out of her room,

and then the blonde angel's eyes went wide as she saw the sword. Her lips were slightly parted for a long moment, and then she asked hesitantly, "Is that... is that my *sword*?"

"If you say it is, yes. I was going out to Odrak's, and I found this buried in a tree twenty feet off the ground. It looked like it would fit the sheath I found on you, so I thought I'd see if it was yours," Kanae replied calmly. She pondered for a moment before adding, "If it *is* yours, we're going to have to hide it until you leave, much like the rest of your things."

"Heavens... I thought... well, I thought I'd never see it again," Isalla said, her eyes almost reverent, and she stepped over to take the sword from Kanae's hand. Kanae released the weapon as Isalla did so, and the angel nearly dropped the sword, gasping as she murmured, "Heavier than I remembered, but yes... this is my sword. Thank you so much, Kanae! This was a... a gift from a friend. Losing it would be terrible."

"Indeed? Well, I'm glad I was asked to go look in on Odrak, then. Someone else might've seen it instead," Kanae replied, smiling at Isalla's reaction and moving over to set the baskets on the table. "As I said, we *will* have to hide it, but once you leave, you can take it with you."

"Of course. That's fine... perfectly fine. I just don't want to lose it again," Isalla agreed.

"Now, Odrak also gave me some of his apples. They're a species native to the hells, and as I recall, their flavor is a bit different than those from the mortal world. Something along the lines of apple cider, though a bit spicier," Kanae said, looking over the red-skinned apples and taking off her backpack. "I was thinking of making a couple of pies, and having the rest with breakfast for the next few—"

The sound of quick footsteps made Kanae stiffen, but no pain lanced through her body, like she was half-expecting. Instead, one of Isalla's arms wrapped around Kanae and held her as tight as the angel could manage, her body pressing against Kanae's back. Kanae relaxed after a moment, glancing over her shoulder, but was barely able to see the angel's hair as Isalla pressed her face into the back of Kanae's neck.

"Thank you," Isalla whispered.

"You're welcome," Kanae replied simply. She waited for a few moments, then asked, "What do you think of my idea?"

"It sounds lovely to me," Isalla said, not moving. "But... could we just wait a bit? I'm just..."

"As you like, Isalla," Kanae replied patiently, her smile growing gentler as she stood there. "As you like."

# CHAPTER 15

*R*oselynn woke slowly, much more slowly than she was used to, but for some reason it didn't worry her. It was as though waking up gradually while sitting in a chair was normal, and the faint fog shrouding her thoughts didn't bother her either.

The angel didn't recognize where she was, but that didn't bother Roselynn as she looked around the room. Directly in front of her was a vanity with a large mirror at its back, the mirror perfectly placed to show Roselynn to herself, while dozens of jars and tools laid on the vanity's surface. Roselynn didn't recognize most of the tools, but she did recognize several paintbrushes, the hairbrushes and combs, and the nail clippers and files. There were also a pair of candles filling the room with the gentle scent of vanilla.

The rest of the room was interesting enough to hold Roselynn's attention for at least a few moments. There was a door in one wall, the dark wood polished and bearing a carving that looked vaguely like an angel's wings to her, though there was something odd about them, not the least of which was how the carving was painted gold. The floor was covered by a thick, warm carpet with white, gold, and silver patterns that drew Roselynn's eyes along their curves and whorls. It was a pleasing

BENJAMIN MEDRANO

pattern, and it took her a long minute before she looked at the walls and ceiling.

A dozen sconces along the walls contained crystals that produced a warm light not unlike that of the sun, and they were set into gold-veined white marble, complete with periodic pillars, and crimson curtains helped soften the imposing sight. The ceiling wasn't much different, though it was shallowly vaulted above her head. But without anything there to hold her attention, Roselynn's gaze drifted back to the mirror to examine herself.

The chair she was in was the same dark wood as the door, though it was exquisitely carved and comfortable, allowing her wings to rest easily, and the back and seat had soft cushions to make it easier to sit in. The only strange thing were the padded metal braces on the arms holding down her wrists, and the two holding her ankles to the legs. The true oddity was Roselynn herself, though.

In contrast to the beautiful room, Roselynn looked like she didn't belong there. She wore a simple white shift and skirt, revealing her arms and legs, with the dozens of faded white scars across them. Her face was slightly heart-shaped and pretty enough, despite the scars she bore there as well. Roselynn's eyes were a pale blue, and shadows surrounded them, while her lips looked thin to her gaze. Even her curly hair, so reminiscent of flames, was disheveled. It was a strange contrast, and Roselynn studied herself for a minute, that fog still over her thoughts.

"What are you doing here, Roselynn? You don't belong here," she murmured to herself, idly tugging at the band holding her right hand. It was quite secure, though, and after a moment she gave up. She didn't feel like doing much of anything anyway.

"Ah, you've awakened!" A woman's cheerful voice broke the quiet of the room. "How do you feel? You were injured when you arrived, so I've been quite concerned."

The woman who stepped through the door matched the beauty of the surroundings, and despite herself, Roselynn found herself unable to look away from her. The angel had beautiful white wings, though the gold rings through the upper joint where the wings folded startled her, considering how painful it would be to get a piercing like that. Her hair was like spun gold that fell to the middle of her back in a glittering wave, and she had a beautiful, wide smile with ruby lips and bright blue eyes that reminded Roselynn of her beloved Isalla. The woman was wearing a flattering white dress that revealed a generous amount of cleavage, and a white corset helped accentuate her narrow waist, its surface covered in golden patterns. The woman wore gold bracelets as well, but Roselynn found her gaze drawn to the delicate-looking tattoo on her upper chest. It looked like a black cross emerging from her cleavage, but with a budding rose atop it. The entire tattoo was only an inch or two tall, but it felt like Roselynn should recognize it.

"I... I'm not sure. I feel like I'm well enough," Roselynn replied, her throat slightly dry, and she licked her lips and swallowed before continuing. "Where am I? My mind feels... foggy."

"You're at the Spire of Confession, dear. You were injured in an attack by demons and were brought to us to help you recover. As for your mind, that would be from the medicine we've been giving you," the angel said, approaching quickly and setting a gentle hand on Roselynn's shoulder. "You sustained an immense shock, and it's designed to blunt that and help you recover. We'll wean you off it over the next week, though."

"Oh. That... makes sense. I vaguely remember demons... one ambushed me," Roselynn said, trying to remember the attack, but it was mostly a blur. She didn't remember ever hearing about the Spire of Confession, but there were plenty of places she'd never been to. "What about Ember?"

"Your sword is safe," the angel replied quickly, stepping in front of Roselynn and smiling as she continued. "Now, my name is Anna. What's yours? To be sure you're truly back with us."

"I'm First Sword Roselynn Emberborn," Roselynn replied simply, taking comfort in the fact she could remember. "I'm glad to meet you, Anna."

"Roselynn Emberborn... a beautiful name. Do you mind if I call you Rose?" Anna asked, her smile growing gentle as she held one of Roselynn's hands.

"That's fine. I... usually don't like informality, though,"

Roselynn admitted. Looking at her wrists, she asked, "Why am I restrained?"

"We need to have a serious discussion, Rose, one which has occasionally caused patients here to react poorly. That's why you're restrained," Anna explained, her smile fading slightly as she continued. "It regards your position."

"What kind of discussion? I wouldn't think I'd react badly…" Roselynn replied, growing confused. A part of her was whispering that she should be more upset about being restrained, but that part was tiny and buried.

"We'll see. Once I'm sure you're not going to overreact, we'll let you out, I promise," Anna assured Roselynn, then asked, "How long have you been in the army?"

"Um, about… two and a half centuries?" Roselynn said, slightly hesitant as she tried to remember exactly how long it had been, but unable to pin down the exact length of time. "Close to that. I don't keep that close of track."

"Hm, and you've never considered retiring?" Anna asked gently.

"Not really… the military is a family tradition. I'm needed there," Roselynn replied, feeling like she was on much firmer ground now. "I wield Ember, after all."

"I see. I was afraid of that," Anna said, her eyes darkening as she looked at Roselynn sadly.

"Is something wrong?" Roselynn asked, growing a little concerned. "You seem… sad."

"Our task here in the spire is to help those who've been fighting for too long to… find themselves again. That's why you were sent here, Rose," Anna explained.

"What do you mean, find myself? I enjoy my position… well, mostly," Roselynn said, her voice growing uncertain again. She didn't really understand what Anna was saying fully, but the worry in the back of her mind had grown a little.

"Rose, how long has it been since you weren't subject to the regulations of the army? Since you could do whatever it was you desired without fear of repercussions?" Anna asked, her voice slow and smooth. "How long has it been since you could truly relax and not have to *worry*?"

"I… I don't know," Roselynn replied, the questions causing her mind to reel in uncertainty, as if she couldn't quite find her footing. "It's just what I do."

"*That* is why you're here, Rose. You've lost balance in your life. Here in the spire, we help warriors rest, recover, and find the joy that they've been missing for so very long," Anna said, smiling slowly as she spoke, her face radiant. "Your time here is meant to bring you beauty, joy, and peace. If, once your time here is done, you feel the need to return to the battlefield again, you may do so. But until we're certain that you've regained balance, we cannot allow that."

"I… but…" Roselynn began, then hesitated for a long moment. "But what about my post? I can't just abandon it."

"Someone else has taken your place, don't worry. All you need to worry about is your recovery," Anna assured Roselynn.

"Very well," Roselynn conceded, a large part of her mind feeling relieved to let go of the worries that had been plaguing her for a while. "I just don't know what to do."

"Of course not, Rose. You've lost your balance, and that's why you need teachers to guide you onto the correct path," Anna said, smiling as she reached down and unhooked the restraints with a touch. "You're a beautiful woman, Rose, and you deserve a better life."

The compliment brought a flush to Roselynn's face, and as she rubbed her wrists she glanced into the mirror, looking at herself for a moment before shaking her head. "No I'm not. Not in comparison to you, Anna."

"Ah, but that can be fixed, Rose. Would you like me to show you?" Anna asked, gesturing at the vanity and the items across its surface.

"Um, yes? It's part of what I'm here for, isn't it?" Roselynn replied, the tiny resistance she'd been feeling slowly dying.

"Very true. Tina! Come in and help me, would you?" Anna called out, picking up a jar and uncapping it, then picking up a paintbrush. She dipped the tip into the jar and it came out a deep red that matched her own lips.

The door opened and another woman stepped in, but at the sight of her, Roselynn's eyes went wide. A part of her mind cried out in shock, but the fog and Anna's presence kept Roselynn from doing anything sudden aside from grabbing the armrests.

A succubus entered the room, her hair raven dark and her skin with a deep pink tinge, as opposed to Anna's pale skin. The succubus had bat-like wings and a fleshy tail that swayed behind her, and her eyes were like smoldering coals. Coals that caused Roselynn's heartbeat to quicken, much to her surprise. Even more surprising was that the succubus was wearing clothing that was nearly identical to Anna's, and she bore the same tattoo, though hers was on her lower right arm.

"What's... what's a succubus doing here?" Roselynn asked, staring as the succubus approached, smiling at Roselynn.

"Oh, Tina? She and a number of her sisters gained enlightenment and joined the spire's numbers years ago," Anna said, giving a comforting smile. "I promise, they won't hurt you unless that's what you desire."

"It's true. All we desire is to help you, Ms. Roselynn," Tina said, a faint, smoky accent to her voice.

Part of Roselynn wanted to run... but a larger part of her thought that Anna's words were reasonable. Stranger things had happened, though to her knowledge the angelic legions had never accepted a demon into their numbers. Perhaps the Spire of Confession simply wasn't part of the legions, and the demons had joined it.

"Okay... I'm going to watch you, though," Roselynn warned, and the gorgeous succubus smiled as Roselynn's hands relaxed.

"Of course, Ms. Roselynn. Whatever makes you feel better," Tina replied, her voice growing even more... interesting, somehow. Before Roselynn could put her finger on *how* it had grown more interesting, Anna spoke.

"Call her Rose, Tina. She seems to like it," the angel directed. "Now, purse your lips, Rose. Tina is going to be trimming your nails to start with, so hold still."

Despite her fading misgivings, Roselynn nodded, letting her mind drift in the fog as she followed their instructions. Maybe they were right... maybe she *did* just need some time to relax away from the frustrations of the Council's directives.

# CHAPTER 16

*A*nother peaceful day had mostly passed by, and Isalla found herself surprisingly happy with how things had been going. It'd been a week since Kanae had returned with her sword, and despite how it had been covered with congealed sap, Isalla had been thankful beyond words. The sword had been a gift from Roselynn and was one of the few things she owned that served as a reminder of her former beloved. It had taken hours to fully clean the sword, but Isalla had spent the time without hesitation, and only reluctantly had she allowed Kanae to hide it with the rest of her equipment.

Despite the excitement the sword had prompted, Isalla had quickly found things returning to their routine. She was growing stronger day by day, and Kanae continued to perform her usual visits to patients most days. They visited town together once during the week, which gave Isalla mixed feelings, since she'd met a few new demons, including one of the spider demons. The spider demon had left her shaking slightly, since the sight of the demon had caused near-primal terror.

Today, though, they were inside. Isalla was trying to read a book, though the handwriting was nearly indecipherable, while Kanae prepared herbs to be dried in her alchemical lab. It wasn't too different from their normal routine… at least until there was an abrupt banging at the door.

"Kanae! Lords of fire and earth, I hope you're there!" a man exclaimed, panic obvious in his voice. It took Isalla a moment to recognize the voice of Deka, the town guard.

"Deka, one moment and I'll be there." Kanae called out, wiping her hands on her robes to dry them as she moved toward the door.

The door opened to reveal Deka, the guard looking winded and slightly frazzled. He let out a deep breath as he saw Kanae, speaking rapidly. "Fires of Eternity, it's good to see you! We need your help, Kanae, I don't know what got into them, but—"

"Deka!" Kanae interrupted sternly, scowling as she continued. "Shut up, take a deep breath, and tell me what's going on."

"Yes, ma'am," Deka said, flushing slightly as he took a moment, then spoke more clearly, his eyes darting back and forth. "It's Vokal, Urek, and Brialla. They went into the Fungal Abyss this morning."

"They *what*?" Kanae demanded, her voice sharper than Isalla had ever heard it, and the angel saw the guard cringe.

"Uban told us. He was going to go with them but backed out at the last minute. He said he saw them go in near the eastern marker," Deka explained, swallowing hard as he continued. "We've sent a few of the hunters into that area, but since they're not back already, they probably went deeper, and—"

"And none of the hunters are strong enough to survive that deep. Heaven's *blast* the young idiots!" Kanae snarled, somewhat to Isalla's shock. The demoness spun and flat-out ran for her room, vanishing inside it.

"Is… is it really that bad?" Isalla asked, looking at Deka in surprise. "She told me the Abyss is dangerous, but I've never seen her react this way before."

"I don't dare go beyond the rim of the Abyss," Deka said simply, rubbing his head in agitation. "Consuming Fires… I don't know *any* hunters who go beyond the first tier of the Abyss, for that matter. The only one currently living and in the area who we know can go deeper is Kanae. That's why we came to her, because anyone else would just be throwing themselves into the meat grinder after them. Young, overconfident *idiots*."

"Oh," Isalla said, swallowing hard. "Well, maybe I could help somehow."

"Not a chance," Kanae said, her voice flat. "You're barely recovered enough to practice with your sword, you wouldn't last an hour in the Abyss."

Isalla looked over at the healer and gawked, surprise rippling through her. Kanae looked nothing like her usual self, as she wasn't wearing her robes, or the trousers and tunic she used when she needed more mobility. Instead, she was wearing black scale armor, the surface reflecting light dully, yet oddly silent despite its construction. The armor covered her from the neck down, with matching gauntlets and boots, and as Isalla watched, Kanae seated a black helm over her head. Even Kanae's tail was armored, and the tip was razor-sharp. With a sword at her side, Kanae looked deadly, despite the backpack she wore.

"But what if you're attacked or injured?" Isalla protested weakly, because she knew Kanae was right.

"If something that can take me down comes up out of the depths, the entire *town* would be in danger, not just me. If they've gone that deep, the three imbeciles are dead and we won't even recover their bodies," Kanae replied grimly, adjusting her sword-belt and pack. "You can *start* worrying if I'm not back in three days. As it stands, I won't be surprised if I'm too late as it is."

"I... I guess so. I hope you're going to be safe, though," Isalla replied, giving up the argument for the moment. She wanted to help, but she wasn't sure how, and it was obvious that Kanae was in a hurry.

"As safe as I can be. Deka, lead the way," Kanae said, and flashed Isalla a smile as she said, "Lock up behind me, please. This is going to be a long day. Or two, for that matter."

"Sure," Isalla replied, but by the time she'd taken to stand, the two were gone, both moving at a run.

She shut the door behind them and locked it, shocked at how suddenly the day had changed.

"I need my strength back," Isalla muttered, her determination hardening. She was tired of being viewed as helpless.

~

"STUPID *IDIOTS*," Kanae muttered, her sword leaving its sheath in a flash as the gigantic mushroom opened its maw and tried to bite her. The blade cut straight through the creature's mouth and caused the cap to topple backward as crimson liquid began spraying upward from the fanged stump she left behind.

The Fungal Abyss wasn't pleasant at the best of times, and Kanae had followed the youthful imbeciles into the second tier before losing their trail. It'd been obvious that they'd been chased into the deeper tier, but that didn't stop her from cursing as she looked around the foul place.

The air was filled with a foul stench, not unlike that of a rotting carcass, and the only light was sickly greens and reds shed by different types of fungi. Water slowly dripped from the upper tiers of the Abyss to the lower tiers, turning into a strange, thick sludge that gave the impression of a swamp. The different types of mushrooms and fungi all around her reduced the range of her vision, and Kanae scowled as she saw one of the bulging protrusions begin to ripple.

A mottled red and white fungus erupted in a spray of ichor and fungal flesh, and the creature that emerged let out a warbling cry that hurt Kanae's ears. It was alien, with three clawed front limbs and a dozen strange, filament-like rear limbs, along with a wide maw with what looked like a tongue lolling out of it. From the look of the interior, Kanae was fairly certain that being swallowed by the creature would be unpleasant and not unlike being run through a grater.

"I hate this place." Kanae muttered, her sword out as she watched the creature point at her, somehow seeing her despite not having eyes, then it charged.

Kanae waited just a moment, watching the creature come, then dodged to the side. As she anticipated, some of its rear 'legs' grabbed on to nearby vegetation to swing it around toward her, its maw wide open. Instead, Kanae ducked and rolled forward through the muck, her blade lashing out to sever one of the clawed legs and nearly half of the rear filaments, while her tail blade cut a long gash down its side.

The creature crashed to the ground with another warbling cry, struggling to turn toward Kanae, and her nose wrinkled at the stench as she almost instinctively lashed out to cut off part of the tongue that'd come after her, the end glistening with a sticky substance. Without waiting for it to attack any further, Kanae gripped the hilt of her sword in both hands and brought it down with a grunt, cutting the foul beast clean in half.

As it twitched behind her, Kanae continued onward, dripping muck and in a foul mood. "If they're alive, I'm going to give them one *hell* of a tongue-lashing."

Another howl of a monster split the air, this time accompanied by a scream. Cursing, Kanae broke into a run. Of *course* it was on the edge of the third tier.

~

ISALLA WOKE to the sound of the door slamming open and sobs, curses, and frantic conversation. She rolled out of her bed, wondering what was going on, just as Kanae's voice cut through the commotion clearly.

"Everyone but Manog, *out*. You're just going to be in the way. Deka, go to the alchemy shed and get me the red jar," Kanae ordered, and before the protests could begin, she spoke even more firmly. "I said *out*! I barely got to them in time, and I'm not going to let all of you get them killed!"

The commotion died down, and Isalla hesitated before carefully moving to the door and opening it slightly. It took her several moments to make sense of what she was seeing, but what she did see made her wince.

Kanae was in her armor, though she'd removed her gauntlets and helmet, and the grim-looking demoness was caked in layers of what looked like mud and slime that was mottled with red and green. She was washing her hands, and Manog was beside her, the clothing of the bone demon spattered with blood.

On the table were a pair of demons, and what she could see

horrified Isalla. One was a young woman, a half-demon human from the look of her, and her skin was unnaturally pale, with a bandage stained red across her stomach and her tail ending halfway down, the stump covered by another red-stained bandage.

The other was a male demon who looked a lot like Deka, save with pinkish-red skin, what she could see of it. His skin was inflamed in several spots, and bandages covered at least three-quarters of his upper body. As Isalla looked at him, the demon groaned, shuddering.

"What do you need me to do, Kanae?" Manog asked, looking concerned. "I'm not versed in injuries this bad."

"That's fortunate for you. I need you to help hold Brialla down while I open her stomach. She's got a gut-wound that needs to be stitched and sealed, that's why I had Deka get the jar. Keep an eye out for any debris lodged in the wound, because we *really* don't want her to get infected," Kanae ordered. "Other than that, I simply need you to be a spare set of hands. Besides, I might not always be here, Manog, and you might need an idea of how to do this."

"That idea terrifies me, but I'll do my best," Manog said, his face grim.

A moment later, Deka burst into the room, panting as he held up a red jar. "Here it is, Kanae!"

"Set it on the table and get outside. Keep anyone from disturbing us," Kanae ordered, finishing up her washing.

"Right," Deka said, looking relieved as he set the jar on the table, then stepped out.

Isalla hesitated, then opened the door more and asked, "Is there something I can do, Kanae?"

"Ah, Isalla. I wondered if you'd wake," Kanae said, smiling thinly and nodding as she pulled out a pair of short, long-handled knives. It took Isalla a moment to recognize them as something humans used, called scalpels, and she winced. "Yes, actually. Put more water on to boil and pull out the spare washcloths. I'm afraid I'm going to need them."

"Alright," Isalla said and winced as she saw the two get to work, prompting a soft cry of pain from the young woman.

She quickly grabbed a pot and went to fill it with water, glad that she wasn't going to have to help directly. A part of her wondered if Kanae had been forced to do that to her, and Isalla's stomach lurched at the thought.

Isalla imagined that the chances of the young woman were far worse than she might hope.

# CHAPTER 17

The house finally grew quiet as the last of the visitors left, and Kanae sighed loudly as she began removing her armor. Isalla winced at the sounds the armor was making, afraid of what cleaning it would be like. The muck covering it had mostly dried, but that wasn't necessarily a good thing.

"Thank you for being willing to give up your room, Isalla. While I think that Urek could have been safely taken home, Brialla is in a far more questionable state." Kanae said, setting a bracer on the table. "I'm surprised that I got to them in time... a creature had driven them into an alcove right on the edge of the third tier of the Abyss."

"It's not a problem. You saved me, and they need your treatment far more than I do right now," Isalla said, watching in idle curiosity as Kanae removed the armor.

"I still appreciate it. Those *idiots*... I can't believe they let themselves be driven deeper rather than running for the exit." Kanae sighed.

"What *are* the tiers of the Abyss that you keep talking about?" Isalla asked, looking away for the moment. "You've mentioned them a few times, but..."

"They're like... like levels of a vast strip mine, for lack of a better term. Each tier is deeper into the earth, but the entire Fungal Abyss is a wound in reality where space warps and mana

causes strange mutations," Kanae explained, shrugging
unhappily as she did so. "It's hardly the only Abyss in the hells,
but it's the only one nearby, and legend has it that it's where
angels and demons clashed in excessive force, much like the
siege of Rosken."

"Oh. That does explain some of what I heard... what
happened to them, then?" Isalla asked, shivering as she looked
at the bowl filled with what looked like bloody beads or rocks.

"Vokal, wonder of wonders, managed to get through things
with little more than a scratch or two. The other two, though...
they got ambushed by a number of fungal beasts. Don't ask what
they were, they're rarely the same in the Abyss," Kanae
explained, shaking her head. "Brialla lost most of her tail to the
ambush, which is going to be quite uncomfortable for her, I'll
imagine. She's probably going to have to save funds for a few
years then go to the capital to get it regenerated. They fled, and
mid-way, another ambush got her in the side. Urek and Vokal
managed to kill the creature there, but then Urek ran into a
pustule that exploded in his face, embedding dozens of spores
across the front of his body. I didn't dare leave any of them
inside, since they'd doubtlessly start consuming him as they
grew. With both of them down, Vokal managed to hole up in a
small alcove where he could hold off any attackers. It's still not
*good*, but he was luckier than he had any right to be."

"Ow, that's... well, they're alive. That has to count for
something, right?" Isalla asked, flinching at the idea of
something exploding in front of the young man. She'd seen how
deep the spores had been embedded, and the idea was
somewhat terrifying.

"Quite. I'm going to take a bath, then get some sleep," Kanae
said, sounding oddly tired to Isalla. "You can use my bed, I have
a bedroll that I can use."

"I could use the bedroll. It isn't like I haven't used them
before," Isalla quickly offered, flushing slightly at the thought of
using Kanae's bed.

"No, no... you're a guest. I'll be fine, Isalla, and you're still
healing," Kanae said firmly, now down to the padded gambeson
and her stockings, both of which had some of the same muck on

them, though not nearly as much as the armor had been caked in. Mostly it looked like they'd been hit by what had come through the joints of Kanae's armor.

"But—" Isalla began, but Kanae ignored her, heading for the bathing room quickly. A moment later, Isalla murmured, "But you *deserve* to have some comfort after all that."

She hesitated for a long moment, debating what to do, then slowly, curiously approached Kanae's room. She hadn't been in it before, but now that she had an invitation, Isalla couldn't help herself. The door creaked open at her touch, and she blinked as she looked around the room.

Unlike the rest of the house, Kanae's room was crowded with boxes, chests, a bookshelf, a wardrobe, and a bed, just to begin with. An empty armor rack was in the corner, with a weapon rack next to it on which hung a crossbow and a quiver of bolts. A set of nearby shelves held several towels, along with a nightgown that Isalla had never seen Kanae wear. The room was surprisingly cluttered, but in a way, it was reassuring.

Kanae had often struck Isalla as distant and, in a lot of ways… too perfect in what she was doing. Some of that could be ascribed to centuries of practice and personal poise, but that didn't mean that it was easy for Isalla to feel comfortable with the demoness.

The demoness's room, though… it was the look of a room that was lived in. Someplace private, where Kanae doubtlessly relaxed more fully. That was part of why Isalla was surprised that the other woman was offering her bed, because it *was* her private space.

"Actually… she didn't take a towel with her this time, either. I should take her one," Isalla murmured, looking at the towels and hesitating.

Part of her was uncertain how good the idea was, but it felt like the right thing to do. It had nothing to do with wondering what Kanae looked like beneath her clothing, Isalla told herself firmly as she took the top towel off the shelf. She knew she was lying to herself, but Isalla felt a little better when she told herself that.

Stepping out of Kanae's room, Isalla slowly approached the

door to the baths, trying to decide what she'd say. Eventually she decided on something simple, and opened the door as she spoke. "Kanae, I thought you might want a towel, and…"

Isalla's voice trailed off and she blinked owlishly, freezing in place as she looked at Kanae, who was just stepping into the pool. The demoness's clothing was piled nearby, and while there was steam in the room, it hardly hid Kanae, and the sight caused heat to rise in Isalla's cheeks.

Kanae's skin was flawless, without the slightest scar or other mark that Isalla could see on it. She had the same slight purple tinge to her skin that Isalla had noticed initially, and the darker parts of her skin were a more obvious purple as well. More interesting in its own way were her toned curves, and the demoness's beauty made Isalla envious. Kanae's tail swayed as she slipped into the water, which was cloudy enough that Isalla finally tore her gaze away, blushing furiously.

"Thank you, Isalla; that's appreciated. I forgot to grab one again, which could have proven a bit unfortunate," Kanae replied, her voice unhurried. It took Isalla a moment to realize the demoness didn't seem even slightly bothered or embarrassed by Isalla's intrusion.

"W-well, that is why I brought it in. Even if I appear to have intruded at an improper time," Isalla replied, her gaze still averted as she studied the wall.

"Mm… perhaps so. I *am* the child of an incubus and succubus, so let's just say that I'm used to people walking around unclothed, even if it's been a while," Kanae said, now sounding amused. "I'm not going to be upset about you walking in right then. If you had a sword, maybe, but you don't."

"I guess that's true," Isalla said, hesitating a moment before leaning over to set the towel down. "Anyway, I'll just set this here. I hope your bath goes well."

With that, Isalla all but bolted from the room, feeling as though her face was about to burst into flames, she was so embarrassed. Worse still was the faint laugh that she just *barely* caught as she left the room.

"Heavens, what made me think that was a good idea?" Isalla muttered under her breath, rubbing her eyes as she tried to drive the sight of Kanae out of her mind. That wasn't happening, though, as it seemed like the image was almost seared into her mind.

Opening her eyes again, Isalla hesitated for a long moment, trying to think of what to do. Her mind was racing in circles, and she didn't think she could sleep easily. Looking at the table and the mess on it, Isalla came to a sudden decision, and one that relieved her a lot.

"Oh, I can clean that up," Isalla said, letting out a breath and smiling to herself. "Something to get my mind off her."

With that, she quickly grabbed a washcloth and bucket, filling the latter with water that hadn't been boiled. She tried to clean off the muck first so that it wouldn't dirty the towel, then got to work wiping down the table. It didn't take too long, and Isalla hesitated before wiping off the bulk of the gunk on Kanae's armor as well.

It took Isalla nearly half an hour and left her exhausted, but at last she was done. Her cleaning wasn't perfect but took care of most of the debris. Since Kanae hadn't come out yet, Isalla decided that it was time for her to go to sleep again, despite how guilty she felt about taking Kanae's bed. She did take the time to wash up again, and then padded off to the bedroom.

Slipping into the bed was a surprise, and Isalla let out a soft gasp as she sank a couple of inches into its soft surface. The silk sheets were cool, and it was softer than any bed she'd ever slept on before, which was stunning. The pillows were made of the same material too, and Isalla slowly relaxed, luxuriating in the feeling as her exhaustion started taking its toll, and a faint, familiar scent surrounded her.

Isalla was mostly asleep when the door opened again, and she barely stirred. A minute later, she heard a soft voice near her ear, gentle and attractive. "Thank you for cleaning up, Isalla."

"You're... welcome," Isalla murmured, rolling over sleepily. "Was... right thing to do."

"It's still appreciated. Rest well. I'll go get my bedroll," Kanae said softly, and in the dim light Isalla saw her turn to leave.

Before she could, Isalla reached out clumsily, only barely

managing to catch the hem of Kanae's shirt as she murmured, "No. Your bed… it's big enough."

Kanae paused, and Isalla could barely see the woman's eyes glittering as she turned to study Isalla. After a few moments, she asked, "Are you sure?"

"Yes," Isalla said, smiling a little herself as she added insistently. "Is *right*."

"As you wish. Thank you, Isalla," Kanae said, and moved over to close the door.

As she felt the bed shifting, Isalla felt sleep finally claim her.

# CHAPTER 18

"*I*salla."

The soft voice didn't quite manage to stir Isalla from her sleep, though it came close. She was warm and comfortable, more comfortable than she'd been in ages, and she felt incredibly content as well. She did drift up out of the depths of sleep and closer to consciousness, but not all the way.

"Isalla!" Kanae's tone was firmer this time, but her voice still didn't fully register. "I need to get up, so let go."

Isalla let out a murmur of protest, her arms tightening as she hunkered forward, her fingers sinking into something warm and soft. That was what drew her closer to consciousness, though, as she blinked slowly, then she focused on what was in front of her.

She was in Kanae's bed still, the sheets soft and warm around her. More pertinently, Isalla was staring at the back of a neck, with floral-scented black hair almost tickling at her nose. It was the back of Kanae's head, she realized. *Then* she realized that her arms were wrapped around Kanae, and just what her fingers were sinking into as her grip tightened. The surge of embarrassment that blasted through her was incredibly potent, and for a moment Isalla was afraid that she'd spontaneously combust.

"Oh! S-sorry, Kanae! I was asleep and didn't realize what I was... I mean..." Isalla stammered, flushing deeply as she released the other woman as quickly as she could, recoiling so quickly she nearly hit the wall. Her cheeks felt like she was on fire, and she quickly looked at the ceiling.

"I'd rather guessed as much. Thank you for letting go," Kanae said patiently, the demoness slipping out of the bed and standing.

Kanae looked more amused than anything else, Isalla realized, her humiliation growing more pronounced. The demoness wasn't quite naked, as she was at least wearing her underthings, but that didn't mean that it made the situation easier on Isalla. Despite her attempts to put it out of her mind, holding onto Kanae had felt wonderful.

"I'm so sorry... H-how long was I, um..." Isalla asked, closing her eyes as she tried to gather the tatters of her composure again. It wasn't going well, and Kanae's response embarrassed the angel even more.

"About, oh... an hour ago? I woke up when you grabbed me," Kanae replied. The demoness turned away and approached the wardrobe, opening it as she continued. "I thought about saying something then, but you seemed to relax afterward, so I decided to wait until I needed to get up."

"I'm so sorry. I can't believe that I did that." Isalla repeated her apology, trying to resist the urge to hide, especially since there was an enormous part of her that would love nothing more than to crawl into a hole and fill it in behind her. At least then the demoness wouldn't look so entertained.

"It's alright, Isalla. I probably shouldn't have taken your offer last night, since you were mostly asleep," Kanae said, pulling out a change of her underwear as well as a pair of trousers and a tunic. She turned away to slip them on as she continued. "That said, I'm going to finish cleaning in the dining room, then I'm going to check on my patients and exercise. Feel free to rest a bit more, Isalla; it was a long night."

"But—" Isalla began, managing to overcome her embarrassment after a moment, but her protest came just as the door closed behind Kanae. Isalla blinked at the door, then continued, her voice softer now as embarrassment was forced back by concern, and even worry. "But you were the one who was up for so long, not me. *You* should be the one resting."

The empty room had no response for Isalla, and she rolled over to face the wall. She didn't need to sleep, in all honesty. She probably could have for an hour or so more, but the way she'd woken had rather firmly kicked her thoughts into motion, and there was no undoing that now. Still, she didn't want to get out of bed, not after the incredible embarrassment she'd been through.

Almost worse was that Isalla could still feel the warmth of where Kanae had been laying, as well as where she'd been touching the angel. The feeling of pressing against her… Isalla shivered at the memory, closing her eyes and breathing in again as her heartbeat quickened. Kanae's scent was that of a type of flower, but not one which Isalla had ever encountered before. It wasn't powerful, a somewhat subtler scent, but attractive anyway.

"What is *wrong* with me? Is it just having lost my wings?" Isalla muttered, feeling slightly frustrated as her confusion heightened along with her libido. "She's a demon. I shouldn't be… be *attracted* to her. And yet I am."

It was something that had been frustrating Isalla ever since Kanae had mentioned her attraction to Isalla. She'd never considered how beautiful or not a demon might be, not in the rare instances she'd fought them in her previous stations. It was a bit silly that she hadn't, since a succubus had managed to lure off and kill three men at one fort before being spotted and dealt with.

"Dealt with. That's a term for it," Isalla said, rolling onto her back and thinking harder as her mood soured a little. As she thought, suspicion began to grow inside her. "I was taught to hate them, wasn't I? It's easier to fight and kill someone when you think of them as a *thing*, rather than a person. Yet at least some demons are… people. Most of them, possibly, though plenty are as bad as we were taught they were. Heavens… what a *mess*."

Isalla had enough problems to worry about when she was back

in the Evergardens, though life had been fairly simple. Her position had been... well, as the only member of the Order of the Phoenix in the city, she'd been overworked and most people found her annoying, as she'd taken the place of an experienced investigator who was supposed to take care of figuring out the rare crimes. Not many people had trusted her when she'd abruptly replaced someone they'd known so well. Still, she'd done her best, even if the position was obviously a deliberate punishment. Her failures were being held against her at the time, she knew, which would limit her ability to ever rise in the ranks afterward.

"Not that it matters. They've probably reported me as dead. Even if I get my wings back, once they hear where I ended up, I'll be under so much suspicion I'll *never* get back into the order. They might even execute me," Isalla murmured, staring at the ceiling as she worked through the likely chain of events. She'd been ignoring her possible fate for a while now, but when she thought about it in more detail, it was depressing. Not depressing enough to disable her, but it didn't make her happy.

In the end, Isalla had to figure out what to do. Her primary focus had been on recovering, and she *still* had a long way to go, but... now she needed to decide on her future and what it entailed. The thought brought to mind the length of Kanae's tail as it flicked through the air, and Isalla giggled in sudden amusement.

"Oh, I'm an idiot..." Isalla murmured, stretching an arm toward the ceiling and debating for a long moment as she looked at her hand against the dark backdrop, the thought of Kanae improving her mood inordinately. Finally, she nodded to herself. "Fine, then. I'll let things progress how they will and considering where we are... once I'm well enough, I'll go warn Roselynn about what I learned. After that... well, we'll see how things have gone. My past isn't dead, but it's close to it."

Almost on cue, Isalla heard the muffled sound of an axe hitting wood. She had to marvel at Kanae's dedication. The woman had delved into what she'd admitted was a horrifically dangerous region the previous day to rescue a trio of young men and women, then had performed an intricate, bloody operation to save two of their lives before finally going to bed. Now here she was, getting up at a time that Isalla guessed was about normal, and going out to exercise and cut firewood like nothing had happened.

"Yet here I am in bed. I can't have her completely overshadowing me, can I?" Isalla murmured, gathering her motivation as she forced herself to push the covers aside. The bed was sinfully comfortable, but she couldn't let it stop her, not when she had a role model like Kanae. "Alright, up I go."

It took more effort than Isalla wanted, but she managed to escape the bed's clutches. She just had to get dressed, and she'd be ready for the day. Or somewhat ready, at least.

～

"Kanae, I brought out some water," Isalla called out, and Kanae looked up as she easily freed the axe from the stump. She was a bit surprised to see Isalla already, but wasn't going to argue.

The angel was looking a bit tired, but not too much. She certainly looked more poised than she had that morning, when her cheeks had been such a deep crimson that Kanae had been worried Isalla might faint. The chances of that weren't good, but it was always possible. Now she was just a *little* flushed, and the angel had taken the time to take a quick bath from the look of her hair. The outstretched hand holding the flask of water was a pleasant surprise, though, and Kanae smiled.

"Ah, thank you, Isalla. I imagine there isn't much left after last night," Kanae said, setting the axe aside and stepping away to take the flask. As she uncorked it, Isalla smiled in return.

"Very true. Fortunately you have the spring, or it would be more difficult to fill the keg," Isalla agreed, shrugging nervously. "I did put some water on to boil, so we can replace it before long."

"Ah, that's very kind of you, Isalla. I was planning to do that a bit later, but it saves me some time," Kanae said, taking a drink of the water. It wasn't the best water ever, but it was clean and should be disease-free, which was the important thing to her. After taking a few swallows, she lowered the flask and continued, feeling more upbeat at the angel's help. "I'm used to dealing with this sort of thing on my own, frankly. I didn't thank you for your help last night, either, and I want to apologize for that. It was a little chaotic."

"I'll definitely agree with that. I didn't expect anything so… strenuous, I suppose. I thought you'd be a healer, not a rescuer," Isalla said, looking like she was somewhat relaxed, but also pensive, somehow. That worried Kanae a little.

"Mm… well, when not many people in the area have the skill to go to that depth, you just end up helping out where you can in towns like this," Kanae said, capping the flask and handing it back. "Thank you again."

"Right, that does make sense," Isalla said, hesitating for a long moment as she took the flask, holding it in both hands. It was obvious that she was debating on saying something, so Kanae paused, studying the attractive angel. The question was whether Kanae should encourage her or not.

"Was there something you wanted to talk about?" Kanae finally prompted, knowing that many people would find an opening easier to take advantage of, and she *was* curious what Isalla wanted to say.

"Well, yes," Isalla admitted, taking a deep breath and looking Kanae in the eyes. Her voice was slightly unsteady, but she looked more confident to Kanae. "It's about your comment a while back. About you being attracted to me."

"Ah," Kanae said, letting out a breath of disappointment as she looked at the angel, faintly wistful, since she thought she knew what was coming. Isalla was just so… enticing. "I had intended to leave that for later on, actually. I'm not surprised that you're… skeptical of such, though."

"No, that isn't it at all! I'm just…" Isalla said quickly, surprising Kanae. "I'm not opposed to it, Kanae. A little confused, and cautiously curious… but not opposed."

"Oh. I… well, I'm a bit surprised to hear that. I expected you to not want anything to do with me," Kanae replied, a hint of warmth spreading through her, and she felt a smile growing on her face at the pleasant surprise.

"Even if I said that, this morning would prove it was a lie,"

Isalla said, blushing slightly as she looked to the side, and Kanae's amusement grew stronger. "Still, I wanted to talk about something else. About, well… why I'm *down* here."

"Oh," Kanae said, her amusement fading as she considered Isalla seriously, then continuing before the angel could say anything more. "Not while I have other patients, Isalla. I don't want any chance of others overhearing your explanation. Not that it necessarily would be dangerous, but I'd rather ensure that it isn't, alright?"

"Oh, right. That does make sense." Isalla nodded, looking sheepish as she ran a hand through her damp hair. "Do you mind if I ask something else, though?"

"Go ahead," Kanae told her, taking a step over to the axe again. She'd had enough of a break, and she wanted to keep in shape. Besides, it was a good excuse to keep her gaze off Isalla.

"I didn't see *any* scars, and you were in the army. How is that *possible*?" Isalla demanded.

Kanae laughed, grinning at the incredulous tone in Isalla's voice. Kanae gently replied in amusement. "Incubus and succubus parents, remember? I don't scar or develop calluses. Not that there aren't other methods of dealing with scars, mind you. Remember, I *have* been giving you that salve to help your own fade."

"Oh, well… right, that would work," Isalla said, sounding a little chagrined as her gaze drifted down across Kanae, lingering several times before settling on the axe next to her.

"Shouldn't you go check on the water? I don't want you burning down the house. I have patients in there," Kanae suggested, having trouble suppressing her smile.

"Oh no! I'll be back in a bit!" Isalla's eyes went wide and she turned to run toward the house.

Laughing under her breath, Kanae picked up the axe again. Another cord of wood, then she'd go in to check on her patients. Suddenly she found herself looking forward to them going home even more. She had something pleasant to look forward to.

# CHAPTER 19

*B*rialla and Urek were both quiet for the first couple of days, aside from the occasional groans of pain. Isalla didn't interact with them much, since Kanae was the healer. Despite her distance, as far as Isalla could tell, they seemed to be recovering at a good pace.

Their presence had drawn a lot of traffic to the house, though. Isalla found herself opening the door for the parents of the pair fairly often, as well as for their friends. Vokal was a lot like Brialla, and the young man had looked incredibly guilty as he asked about them. Kanae had been... firm with him, Isalla thought, and far gentler than the angel would have been. Kanae had answered his questions politely, but after a short while she'd interrogated him on just what he'd thought they were doing.

In short, he *hadn't* been thinking, from Isalla's perspective. The young man had been wanting to make money to buy better food and clothing, and none of the jobs around town had been profitable enough for him. Since some of the alchemical reagents that could be found in the Fungal Abyss sold for quite a bit, he'd hatched the plan with some of his friends to collect them and make a solid profit.

The plan hadn't gone well, and Kanae had been quite pointed about how close they'd come to death. It hadn't been a pleasant

BENJAMIN MEDRANO

conversation, that was for certain. Even if it *had* been a little satisfying to hear Kanae politely tear a strip off Vokal verbally.

Despite the regular visitors, Kanae had kept herself busy for a lot of the time, even going to town to buy supplies and check on other patients. It startled Isalla at first, but she supposed it made sense. It wasn't as though having two patients, three if she included herself, would stop anyone else from needing help.

Urek had been moved home after the third day, since his injuries were relatively minor when compared to Brialla, and the young man had guiltily limped home while accompanied by his parents. The looks on their faces had amused Isalla, since they looked much like any other parents she'd seen after their children did something stupid and survived. She preferred not to think about the times she'd prompted similar expressions.

It was the fifth day before Brialla had joined them for breakfast, the young woman pale and quiet. She had a green tinge to her skin, but looked different than Kanae, despite both of them having similar bodies. The woman had slightly pointed ears, a pair of short, back-swept horns, scales around her wrists, and a thicker tail, though at a guess it was missing nearly half its length.

"Thank you for the food," Brialla said softly, stirring the porridge slowly with her spoon.

"You're welcome," Kanae said, taking a seat herself, her voice calm.

"How are you feeling, Brialla?" Isalla ventured after a few moments, concerned about the young woman. She knew what it was like to lose part of her body, and she tried to flex her wings again, wishing they were back. The scars were fading quickly due to Kanae's salve, which fascinated her in a horrible sort of way. It was definitely a mixed blessing, since the idea of being unable to fly permanently horrified Isalla.

"I hurt a lot, but I'm okay," Brialla said, smiling nervously at Isalla, then looking down again. "It's... it's fine. I guess. I shouldn't have gone into the Abyss."

"Why did you go, then?" Kanae asked softly, an uncharacteristic note of compassion in her voice.

"Well…" Brialla hesitated, and Isalla grew more curious, setting down her spoon.

"I'm not your parents. I'm not going to get upset about whatever it is you had in mind. I'm just curious what nearly cost you your life," Kanae added, sitting back in her chair.

"I heard that some of the academies in the capital allow anyone to join, if you have enough for tuition," Brialla admitted, staring into her porridge intently. "I was hoping to earn enough for a year or two. I didn't think it was a good idea, but Vokal… he seemed so *certain* that we could manage it. I thought he must know something that I didn't."

"Ah. At least you had a goal that was worth something… though instead it appears that you've set yourself back. At least, assuming you want to get your tail back," Kanae said, sighing and nodding at the bandaged stump behind the young woman. "That will run you two or three years of tuition to get healed on its own."

"Brimstone… I screwed up so *badly*, didn't I? I lost most of my tail, and I'm going to take weeks to get back to normal. Am I ever going to make enough to get training in something important?" Brialla asked, her voice faintly plaintive. The protest sparked even more compassion in Isalla, since a large part of her identified with the young woman. Isalla had been a commoner to begin with, after all.

"That's entirely up to you," Kanae replied, not even flinching as she looked at the young woman. Her apparent lack of pity startled Isalla for a moment, but Kanae continued before the angel's worry could grow. "Look, Brialla, you tried to take a shortcut. Shortcuts are risky by their very nature, because, otherwise, everyone would use them. Your parents aren't wealthy, and though they're going to do their best to pay me back, I *know* they can't afford to. I'm going to be taking what they can give me, and it isn't much. So you're going to have to solve your problems for yourself, which *isn't* going to be easy. In my view, you have many options, but which you choose is up to you."

"What would you do, then?" Brialla asked, and Kanae fell silent, sitting back in her chair and examining the young woman for a moment or two. Isalla considered, then took a spoonful of porridge as she listened closely. This was the first time she'd heard someone ask Kanae for advice, and she wondered what the attractive woman would tell Brialla.

"You aren't unique, Brialla, at least in appearance, and your talents are decent but not exceptional. Attempting to find a sponsor would be difficult. In your situation, I'd avoid the army like the plague, because going with the army is far too likely to end in your death. You have three realistic choices, from my perspective," Kanae replied, her gaze and tone unflinching. "First, join the queen's priesthood. You'd likely be healed free of charge, but their indoctrination… you'd likely be with them for life, by the time your probationary period was done. You'd learn a lot, you'd still be *you*, but I'm not sure you want to be one of her devotees. Second, you can try becoming a merchant. While risky, if you can join a caravan going between the surface and here, you can likely earn coin more quickly in a relatively safe manner than you could in one of the cities of the hells. Last, you can stay in town and try to earn funds the slow, safe way. That would take you years, but it's possible to manage."

Isalla could almost see Brialla wilting under the explanation and couldn't help but wince sympathetically. She imagined that none of them were as glamorous as the young woman dreamed and glanced over at Kanae as she asked hopefully, taking another spoonful of food, "There really aren't other good solutions, Kanae?"

"Not ones which would be any easier. She could apprentice with a healer, though certainly not with me. I don't have the time or patience for that. She's moderately exotic and could attempt to earn money as a courtesan in Hragon, but her injuries are severe enough that I'm uncertain she could do well. Besides, I don't care to *recommend* that to anyone, outside of a few rare exceptions," Kanae replied, frowning thoughtfully. "All the other options I see are risky or incredibly time-consuming. What I'm suggesting are relatively fast, easy, or safe."

"But which would *you* choose?" Brialla asked, looking at Kanae pleadingly.

Kanae sighed and rubbed her eyes, then looked at Brialla

intensely. "Brialla... it's *your* life. I... care for the queen. If I *had* to choose, I'd probably join her priesthood. However, that's based on personal feelings, and without that, it'd be a difficult choice between it and trying to become a merchant."

Isalla blinked in surprise at that, opening her mouth, then shutting it as a thread of curiosity and envy coursed through her. The thought of Kanae having feelings for Queen... Estalia, she thought that was her name. She was rather surprised, considering how scathing Kanae had been about the war. It was odd, but Isalla wasn't going to ask about it in front of Brialla. Especially since Brialla was looking at Kanae so curiously, and a bit hopefully.

"You have feelings for Her Majesty? Have you *met* her?" Brialla asked eagerly, her depression seeming to fade. "I haven't met anyone who's seen her before! At least, not that admitted it, I guess."

"A few times, back when I was in the army," Kanae replied after a moment, her gaze distant. "She only visited the front a handful of times, but I saw her, and met her. I remember the experience vividly, even though it's been centuries."

"What was she like?" Isalla couldn't keep the words from coming out, curious despite herself. She shouldn't be interested in an archdemon, but any information was better than none.

"I'm not sure it's a good idea to tell you," Kanae replied, frowning slightly. There was a note of worry in her voice, Isalla noticed, which concerned her. Not enough to retract her question, though.

"Please?" Brialla almost begged. "I've heard legends, of course, but it's never very detailed. Mother and Father say that the descriptions get garbled in time."

"I... I suppose it won't do any more harm," Kanae said, sighing heavily and taking a spoonful of her food, though she barely seemed to see it. After swallowing, she added, "Just so you're aware, no words can do Her Majesty justice. She's everything I can tell you, yet so much *more*. Nothing can prepare you for meeting her the first time, no matter who you are."

"She's really that impressive?" Isalla asked curiously, even more intrigued now.

"Yes. If you haven't met her before and braced yourself, the moment you see Queen Estalia, it's like the world stops and everything else goes dim. You lose track of everything around you, because she becomes the center of the world. If she's distracted, you'll recover quickly, but if she pays attention to you... she's the center of *everything*. You'll do almost anything for her because she makes you feel *perfect*. Because you feel she's utter perfection," Kanae said, her voice still distant as she smiled sadly. "I'm not saying she isn't, though. When she talks to you, she pays *total* attention to you. You're the center of the universe, as far as she's concerned. It's hard to keep your composure, and harder still to dislike her, let alone hate her."

"Wow..." Brialla said, her eyes wide and voice eager. "What does she look like? I've heard she has blue skin and lights up the room when she enters."

"Her Majesty is a succubus, Brialla, but nearly unique despite that. Yes, she has blue skin, but that's a pale word for it. It's the blue of brilliant sapphires, glowing under white light, rich and bright. Brighter still because her skin is quite literally illuminated from within, bright enough to easily light this room via her mere presence," Kanae explained gently, smiling at Brialla. "She's beautiful, with swept-back horns that glitter like diamonds, and blue-black hair that nearly reaches the ground. Her voice is airy and beautiful, capable of singing the highest notes you can imagine, and she moves with an easy grace while a crown formed of five thumb-sized sapphires and a ring of mithral hovers over her head, slowly spinning. I'd go on, but how else can you describe the indescribable? She's... she's Queen Estalia. The Azure Lady, the Queen of Desire."

Even the description of Queen Estalia was amazing, and Kanae's tone made Isalla worried, even if she was more interested in the archdemon now. She sounded incredible, though Isalla was also a little jealous of the effect she had on Kanae.

"Wow. I can hardly imagine her," Brialla said, her voice almost dreamy. "She sounds wonderful to me."

"Perhaps. She, like most archdemons, is powerful and has her own desires. I suppose its unsurprising that they can be quite selfish," Kanae replied, letting out a soft sigh. "Even so, I would not blame you for choosing to serve her. She's… magnificent."

"I'm surprised you left the army, if you felt that strongly about her," Isalla said, a little worried by the thought of a demoness who could have such an immense impact.

She'd only heard of one archangel with the same sort of presence, and Amdieth the Enchanter was fairly private, rarely emerging from his citadel. The one time he'd taken the field of battle, only archdemons had been able to act close to normally in his presence, and *that* concerned Isalla.

"It was before the siege of Rosken. My near-death left me… spent. I just couldn't handle things anymore, and while Queen Estalia is incredible, she hadn't been there, and I didn't see her in the aftermath. If I had, things might have been different," Kanae admitted, pausing for a long moment before shaking her head. "What might have happened doesn't truly matter, though. Only what did. The choice is yours, Brialla, so think carefully before coming to a decision. No matter what comes, the choice is yours."

"I guess so. I'm going to have to think about it," Brialla said, looking thoughtful.

"Good. But before you do that, I'd suggest eating. You can't heal properly if you don't eat," Kanae said firmly.

"Alright," Brialla said, her tone resigned enough to prompt a giggle of amusement from Isalla.

Isalla smiled as the young half-demon began to eat. She finished her own food, watching Kanae thoughtfully as she did so. There were so many questions she had for Kanae, and she wasn't certain if she would get answers.

"I DIDN'T REALIZE you'd met the queen of the domain," Isalla said, her voice soft as the two of them cleaned the living room much later. She was surprised at how comfortable she was in the house, which she'd originally thought rather oppressive.

Kanae had gotten much of her work done earlier in the day,

BENJAMIN MEDRANO

while Isalla had been exercising and doing strength training. Now, while Brialla rested, Isalla finally had a chance to talk to the demoness about the discussion earlier.

"Mm, I wouldn't have mentioned it unless specifically asked about it. I'm surprised Brialla did so, and word will likely spread across the town within a day or two," Kanae replied, shaking her head. "I'll probably refuse to say more to them. It's not a subject I like remembering, really."

"But I thought you cared for her," Isalla protested, looking up from the broom. "That's what you said, at least."

"I did say that, and I do. However, just because I *care* for her doesn't mean that I think her rule is incredibly *wise*," Kanae explained patiently, dipping her rag into the bucket and wiping down one of the chairs. "If she arrived this evening and demanded my service... I'm not certain I could tell her no, Isalla. Her power is that intense, even after a millennium away from her."

"That's... terrifying," Isalla said, a shiver running down her spine.

"I agree. I agree, and yet... I cannot help but care for her. Love her. There's a reason I chose to stay this far from the capital," Kanae said, continuing to clean at a steady pace, yet her words just heightened Isalla's worry.

"Then why did you suggest her church?" Isalla asked, growing more concerned with every passing moment.

"Because she asked my honest opinion," Kanae said simply, stopping and looking at Isalla directly, seeming to consider for a long moment before speaking again. "Isalla, look at me."

"Hm?" Isalla asked, looking at Kanae and stopping at the serious look in her eyes. There was an odd gravity to them, one which made her nervous.

"The church of Estalia is the single most reliable way to get healing from nearly *anything* in this domain, at least if you're capable of meeting their standards of beauty and they like you. They're wealthy, many of them have shards of Estalia's power bestowed upon them, and as a whole, they are *powerful*," Kanae said gravely. "They'd accept you in a heartbeat, or me, and most likely Brialla. They could regenerate any damage any of us had

132

taken and help us refine our physical bodies. The price, though… they teach their members. Man, woman, or other, they're taught in-depth about the church's beliefs… and few have ever chosen to leave. It's a place of safety, and a place where you can lose yourself if you've lost your way. Remember that."

"Alright. I'll… I'll try. Why do you tell me this, though?" Isalla asked, feeling both shaken and confused.

Kanae looked back to the table, wiping it down slowly. After a minute, she finally explained gently. "From what I can tell, it sounds like you may not have a place above anymore. It's a last resort, in my opinion, but an option for you."

"Oh." Isalla digested the explanation, not entirely comfortable with it, but got back to sweeping. After a few minutes, she asked, "How do you know all this?"

"I'd rather not say, Isalla. Not unless I have to," Kanae said simply, but just that explanation made Isalla pause.

She started sweeping again a moment later. No matter how curious she might be, it wouldn't be polite to keep prying. Besides, Isalla suspected that knowing that few chose to leave was something that Kanae knew from experience. As hard as she'd described it being, Isalla couldn't help feeling a little more pity for the demon.

And so they continued cleaning in a companionable silence.

# CHAPTER 20

Roselynn examined her hands closely, flexing her fingers experimentally. She'd been slightly hesitant to try the hand creams that Anna and Tina had suggested initially, but eventually she'd decided that there was no harm in testing them. Not only were her calluses gone now, but her skin was smoother and softer than Roselynn could remember it being, and she thought that a few aches and pains from deeper inside were gone as well.

The angel wasn't certain how long she'd been in the Spire of Confession at this point. No more than a few days, she was sure, but her confusion was gone as well, as a lot of questions that she'd been unable to ask had been answered.

Roselynn's roughest revelation hadn't been that she wasn't in the mortal world anymore, but that she'd been captured and brought to the hells where the priesthood who ran the spire had taken Roselynn in. If it hadn't been for Anna's gentle, soothing presence, Roselynn might have attempted to escape, and *that* would have been a mistake, she'd come to realize. No matter that this was the hells, she'd never felt so accepted for who she was before. She'd never felt so comfortable or relaxed.

"How do your hands feel?" Tina asked curiously, the demon's hands resting gently on Roselynn's shoulders. They were incredibly smooth and soft despite the succubus's strength,

135

and it was that which had led Roselynn to try out the cream at last.

"They feel good. Almost as good as your hands do," Roselynn said, smiling and letting her eyes shut as she leaned back into Tina's touch happily. "I think they did a bit more than you said, though. I could have sworn that there was some pain inside that it eased, too."

"Pain, was it? Is there any in your wrists or arms?" Tina asked curiously, her thumbs and fingers gently kneading the angel's shoulders, helping her muscles relax still more.

Roselynn let out a sigh of pleasure as she nodded, murmuring. "Yes... not much, but just a bit."

"I told you that you've been working yourself too hard," Tina said, her voice gently teasing as she continued her massage. "I'll talk with Anna and we'll get some other salves to help you heal properly."

"That sounds wonderful," Roselynn said, opening her eyes and looking in the mirror at the succubus, who was smiling at her gently, a smile which Roselynn returned. "You're right. I didn't realize just how hard I'd been working until you made me slow down and think about it."

"I'm glad to hear that. Now, I'm going to go see Anna about that. You wait here, hm? Try out some of the other cosmetics if you'd like," Tina promised, pulling her hands away, prompting a small, almost unconscious, murmur of protest from Roselynn. The shoulder rub just felt so *good*.

"Okay," Roselynn replied softly, and watched the succubus go, following the gentle sway of her hips and tail, a sight that was almost mesmerizing. Once Tina was gone, though, Roselynn sighed and focused on the mirror again.

She'd been uncomfortable after Anna's revelation, but the fellow angel had managed to soothe Roselynn's fears, and she'd promised, with every binding oath Roselynn could imagine, that if she wanted to return to the heavens after three months that Roselynn would be allowed to go. That had helped significantly, but it was what had come afterward which had truly surprised Roselynn, for she hadn't been mistreated or pressured in any way.

A second succubus had been introduced, named Coral, likely for her light blue hair and lips. Between Anna, Coral, and Tina, they were waiting on Roselynn attentively. She was given luxurious baths and her hair was carefully brushed out and treated with oils so that it gleamed even more brightly. Her clothing was far softer and more comfortable as well, and the food that Roselynn was given was sumptuous and filling.

When Roselynn had requested sparring practice, Anna had accompanied her to a small salle and they'd exchanged blows with practice swords, at which point Roselynn had learned that the beautiful, gentle-looking woman was even more skilled than Roselynn was. By the time they were done, Anna's gentle banter had left Roselynn laughing and more at ease than she'd been before. While Roselynn knew she could request more bouts, she'd only asked once more so far, and she was loathe to take Anna away from her duties. Besides, Roselynn could always practice later.

A small part of Roselynn was starting to wonder if this was really so bad, though. When Roselynn had told Anna about what had happened when her relationship with Isalla had been discovered, the angel had been outraged. Even now, Roselynn remembered what the angel had said.

"How dare they? You've spent the bulk of your life serving in the army, putting *everything* on the line for them, and they did what?" Anna had demanded, her eyes flashing with uncharacteristic anger. "They exiled you to a far-off post and your beloved to a place she could rot for the simple crime of daring to love! I can hardly believe it, and I'm stunned that you accepted it, Rose. Even more, to hear what happened to your Isalla… you have my deepest sympathies, and I promise to see if we can't learn more of what happened to her."

The sympathy had been welcome, Roselynn knew. It helped that Anna reminded her of Isalla, as both of them were likely descended of the same choir. So, as she thought about things, Roselynn had started to wonder… what did she have that was worth going back to? Did she really want to return to the heavens?

The endless wars, watching the front lines for demons, and

administering over the mortals who venerated her as an agent of the archangels, and year after year of watching subordinates die? Living with the knowledge that at least one woman she'd cared for had her life and career ruined because Roselynn had loved her?

Worse, what would come in the future? It wasn't a subject that made Roselynn feel better, because with the cloud she'd been under, her reputation might never recover from being captured and released by demons. No, it was all too likely that she'd be dismissed from the order and sent back home, where her parents would arrange a marriage and she'd be expected to hand over Ember for its next wielder.

"That's not what I want," Roselynn murmured, and paused as she realized she'd spoken aloud, blinking at her reflection in surprise. Her pale reflection, with the faint scars on her face. Finally, she smiled at herself and took a breath before continuing. "But what *do* you want, Roselynn? What is it that you truly desire to do?"

Her reflection didn't reply, of course. But even so, there was a tiny part of her that thought again about Isalla, and wished for her presence. She didn't *know* that her former lover was dead, and if she wasn't... Roselynn closed her eyes and thought about Isalla, imagining her as though she was Anna. The image was... striking, and warmth spread through Roselynn's heart. So she slowly opened her eyes and smiled at herself.

"You want to be true to your feelings, don't you? If given a chance, you want to tell Isalla how you really feel," Roselynn murmured, reaching out to gently touch her reflection as she admitted the truth. Her gaze slowly lowered to the various cosmetics, most of them imbued with magic, and her smile widened as she added. "You also want to be as beautiful as possible for if that happens. So... just do it, Roselynn. Anna showed you how."

Roselynn reached down and picked up the brush for the lip paint and opened the jar, looking down at the deep crimson liquid within. Smiling, she dipped the brush into the jar, then paused.

Looking at herself, Roselynn whispered, "No. Not Roselynn, Rose. Anna's right; it *does* make you feel better."

Without another word, Rose began carefully using the lip paint. She knew the enchantments within it would change her lips to match it permanently, or at least until she used a different color, but for now she wanted to try it out. Soon, she'd use the salve Anna had said would eliminate scars within a few days.

She might try a few other things in the coming days as well. There was no harm in trying, so long as the effects could be reversed.

❧

"How DO you think she's doing?" Tina asked as she peeked through the mirror projecting an image of the room Rose was in. "You've been helping our guests for longer than I have, after all, and she's the highest-ranking angel I've met."

The succubus looked a bit tired, Anna thought, which only made sense. The process of helping a new resident of the spire come to terms with what had happened was exhausting. It would be better if they had others to share the duties with, but experience had proven that having more than a handful of people attending to guests slowed down the process instead of speeding it up.

Anna looked closely at the mirror and smiled as she saw Rose continue using the cosmetics, the angel's movements slow and precise. She was obviously doing what Anna had shown her by rote rather than using artistry, but that was to be expected. Skill would come with time, and it was obvious that Rose would do well in the end.

"Rose is coming along *very* well, Tina." Anna spoke at last, her voice gentle as she watched the angel in the mirror with a sympathetic smile, still feeling pity for the young woman. "She's been abused by the angelic legions and pushed to her limits for too long, and what likely happened to her beloved… that alone might have caused her to lose faith with them eventually. Such poor treatment means that she was ready to accept our suggestions, much as I was when Lady Estalia found me."

"Truly? It's been most of a week, and I thought that it was taking too long," Tina said, her eyes brightening and back straightening. "Most of the others have accepted things more quickly than she has."

"The difference is that Rose has had many more issues to work through, Tina. Her life has been more tumultuous, and she's fought demons for far longer than most angels you've met," Anna explained. "I've taken care not to push her too hard, because to do that might cause her to break entirely. With what I'm seeing, though, that's about to change. She's going to start eagerly *exploring* the options we can offer her in the near future instead of holding back. I look forward to seeing her truly accept herself."

"That will be an incredible sight to see," Tina agreed, smiling in return. She seemed to debate for a long moment, then asked cautiously, "Do you think she'll *fully* accept Lady Estalia, though?"

The succubus picked up the jar of salve which would help Rose's muscles recover, as well as helping her body grow a touch more sensitive in the process. It would help Rose significantly, but Anna couldn't do much but shrug at the question.

"I don't know. I have my doubts, because few angels truly *believe* in her in that manner, Tina," Anna replied seriously, thinking longingly of her beloved lady. "I suspect that we'll find out soon enough."

"Oh?" Tina asked curiously. "Is there a particular reason for that?"

"Yes, of course. Lady Estalia is coming here to check on us and look Rose over herself," Anna said, smiling broadly as Tina's eyes lit up, continuing. "She's also picking up Rose's gear to take to the palace, but she'd never come in person for such an errand. No, she wishes to see us and our guests, and *that* will have a marked effect, believe me."

"I believe it," Tina said, reaching over to stroke the holy symbol tattooed on her arm and smiling broadly. "I'll have to tell Damael. He's going to be delighted to hear it."

"I'm certain he will be. Now, why don't you go back to Rose? She looks like she needs help with something," Anna suggested, nodding at the mirror. "Once you're done in there, I'll come relieve you so you can rest. There's no reason for you to exhaust yourself."

"Right away!" Tina said, seeming reinvigorated by the knowledge that Lady Estalia was coming. The succubus quickly headed back for Rose's room and Anna smiled, admiring the mirror again.

A handful of the angels she'd encountered over the centuries had believed that Anna was being controlled by magic, or that she'd been forced to serve for so long that she'd become twisted, but that was far from the truth. Anna knew the truth, and she saw a significant part of herself in Rose, as young as the angel might be in comparison.

"Who needs magic when all it takes to convince someone is kindness?" Anna murmured, tilting her head to the side as Tina entered the room with Rose. "When you've been pushed to the breaking point over and over again... is it any surprise that someone showing that they love you as you are and truly *value* you is enough to change your perspective, and leave your attitude so malleable?"

No one answered, but Anna hadn't expected them to. Instead, she turned her attention away and smiled as she added, "Not that many angels are willing to listen at first, but that's why we only drug them for a couple of days. Oh, Rose... how I look forward to seeing you bloom."

≈

"I've got a salve which will help with your muscles, Rose!" Tina exclaimed, smiling broadly. "Anna says that it works practically overnight, so it should help a lot."

"Oh, that's wonderful," Rose replied, turning and smiling at the succubus happily. "I didn't think you'd be quite that fast, but it's good that you're back. I could use some help."

"Anna suspected that you might have overworked yourself, so she got some just in case," Tina explained, still grinning. "Now, what did you need help with?"

"Ah, that does explain it. As for me..." Rose hesitated, then admitted, "I just realized that I don't think I can apply the eye shadow correctly. Since this creates a long-term color, I'd rather not smudge it and waste any, so I was hoping that you'd be able to help apply it."

"Of course! Using the red to match your hair, is it?" Tina asked, looking at the makeup and nodding in understanding. "How dark were you wanting it? Barely visible or heavier?"

"Well, I'm thinking somewhere in the middle... would you mind starting light and slowly darkening it until we get to where I want it?" Rose asked hesitantly.

"Sure. We can start with one of your eyes, then do the other once we've got things perfect." Tina said confidently, picking up the applicator. "I think this will be a beautiful color for you, Rose."

As Tina was preparing the applicator, Rose considered the woman. She was a lot happier now, which was confusing. Tina had seemed happy enough before she'd left the room, but now she was practically giddy. Finally, Rose decided to say something.

"Tina? Is something going on? You've seemed incredibly happy about something ever since you got back," Rose asked, unable to suppress her curiosity.

"Oh, of course there is! Anna told me that Queen Estalia is coming to visit the spire soon, and I'm *incredibly* excited to see her again!" Tina said, her enthusiasm only seeming to increase as she spoke, practically bouncing in place. "She's the most beautiful, kind, and powerful woman I've ever known!"

"Queen Estalia?" Rose asked, dredging her memory for details.

She knew there was a region by that name in the hells, and that was where they were, but details on the domain hadn't been very important. If she remembered right, the archdemon in charge of the domain had never fought on the front lines, and while some demons from the realm occasionally were encountered, they didn't appear in huge numbers. What she remembered also implied that it was a domain more focused on recreation and trade, too.

"That's right! She's the patron of our order, our goddess made flesh!" Tina said, flashing another brilliant smile.

The praise made Rose worried, and she asked nervously, "Will… will I meet her?"

"Almost certainly. She likes to visit everyone when she's here, to be certain they're well-treated." Tina's voice held no doubt, prompting mixed feelings in Rose for a moment. "You'll love her, I'm sure of it! There's no one else like her in the world."

"In that case, I'm looking forward to seeing Queen Estalia," Rose said, pushing her worries to the back of her mind. But it also brought something else to mind, as she realized that if she was going to meet an archdemon, she'd best make certain that the woman wouldn't smite her out of hand. It added a bit of impetus to her desire to make herself beautiful, so she smiled and said, "Now, what do you need me to do?"

"Just close your eyes and hold still," Tina said, her tail swishing happily. "I'll tell you when I'm ready for you to check the colors."

"That sounds good to me," Rose agreed, closing her eyes readily.

She'd never imagined the hells could be so restful.

# CHAPTER 21

*A*fter another two days, Brialla finally was well enough to go back home, and if Isalla was being honest, she was amazed that the young woman was able to leave so quickly. She'd seen what Kanae had been forced to do to keep the young woman alive, after all, so seeing her able to walk around so quickly was startling. Certainly, she wasn't able to walk *easily*, but that she was mobile at all was impressive.

Still, her departure had, at least initially, led Isalla to believe they'd be left alone again, but that was when the townsfolk had descended on Kanae in force. For almost a full day, they'd shown up with food, offers to sharpen Kanae's axe, and other gifts. It took Isalla a while to realize it was their way of repaying the healer, but she figured it out in the end. Kanae didn't refuse anything except for the most extravagant of gifts, but even so, by the end of the day the table was piled with food, additional clothing, and a handful of tools.

"What is this? It looks like it's just a bracelet, but the wood is odd," Isalla asked, examining a bracelet and frowning curiously at it. The wood looked nice, but the strange thing was how there were hundreds of tiny holes in its surface.

"Hm? Oh, the whisperwood bracelet? You haven't seen one before?" Kanae asked, looking up from a basket of vegetables, then paused before continuing. "Come to think of it, the tree doesn't grow outside the hells, does it... that would explain why."

"What's whisperwood? You're right that I haven't seen it before," Isalla agreed, looking at the bracelet and turning it over in her hands.

"Whisperwood has an odd property which allows it to store sound that's released when the wood is burned," Kanae explained, stretching for a moment, her back popping audibly as she did so. "The trees tend to howl like the wind when they catch fire because of it. If you harvest wood from a whisperwood tree, though, you can cause it to record something by immersing it in warm water for about five minutes, then pulling it out and speaking to it. So long as no one repeats the process, when burned, the wood will *speak* whatever was said. It's usually prized when someone is trying to send a message that they don't want overheard, since even if you have magic that restores the wood from ashes, it doesn't reclaim the message."

"Oh, that's neat! Why would they give one to you, then?" Isalla asked, examining the bracelet with renewed curiosity. If she thought Roselynn knew how to use one, she might consider trying to send her a message using whisperwood. Unfortunately, she doubted that Roselynn knew, so it wouldn't be very useful.

"I have no idea, but it might be useful in the future. Stranger things have happened. As it is, the vegetables are far more useful," Kanae said, nodding in satisfaction. "I think a good soup is in order."

"That's something I wanted to ask, actually. If the townsfolk give you gifts like this rather than paying for your help, how *do* you make money?" Isalla asked, looking down at herself guiltily as she examined her clothing. "You paid for my clothing and sword, so I know you have money, but..."

"Ah, that's not a problem. I mainly make money by selling healing salves and other alchemical elixirs to caravans heading up Hellmount, and they pay well for them. What they don't use, they sell there, since many of the things I make require ingredients that are far less common in the mortal world." Kanae said, smiling as she looked at the next basket. "I also get paid by some of the townsfolk, since they can afford to do so. Everyone knows that if they need help, I'll do it, but none of them want to abuse my generosity. Since I don't like relying on just those who can pay, I invest some of my income into the trade house in town, and whenever a consignment of goods to the capital or the mortal world makes money, I get a portion of it. Between those, I've made a healthy sum over the years that I've lived here. It may not be much when you consider my expenses from month to month, but it adds up over time."

"Oh, that would do it, I guess. I thought… well, I'm not sure what I thought, exactly," Isalla said, relaxing slightly as she considered what she wanted to say, relieved that Kanae was doing well. "I was just afraid I was being a significant drain."

"Not really, no. A minor one, perhaps, but you're much better than many of the guests I've had over the years," Kanae replied, her tone light and almost amused now. "It's ironic, considering our situation. Most angels probably would have tried to kill me by now."

"Yes, well… most angels haven't been betrayed by their own before," Isalla said, bile rising in her throat, and she swallowed hard before continuing, watching Kanae's gaze sharpen. "We did decide to discuss this after everyone else was gone, right?"

"True, but based on what you just said, let me take a moment to ensure no one is nearby," Kanae told her, standing up with a grim look on her face. Isalla opened her mouth but shut it again and decided to wait instead.

Kanae slipped out of the house for a couple of minutes, then returned, nodding in satisfaction as she looked at Isalla. "No one's near the house, and it's growing dark, so we should be safe from eavesdroppers. The house is warded against most common scrying, so we should be safe from anyone overhearing that way as well."

"Ah, is it really that dangerous to talk about?" Isalla asked, her worry growing. "I mean, it's not like it's *that* big of a deal, is it?"

"You told me you fell directly from the heavens over Hellmount and into the hells. That means that you were somehow dropped here, likely from a portal they *opened* to the mortal world," Kanae said, taking her seat again, a pensive look on her face. "I don't know how, but obviously they did it. You also spoke of being betrayed, and that... well, I could easily see someone deciding that they need a pretext to start another war and throwing you down here. The last major war started with something similar, from what I've heard, including some backstabbing by both factions. That worries me."

"Really? I never heard about that. I'm not sure, though..." Isalla said, frowning as she debated on what to do or say. Most angels would think that telling Kanae *anything* was a betrayal, but Isalla also didn't want to hide how bad the situation was from her host. Besides, she *liked* Kanae.

"Mm, that's what I heard. One of the archangels died suddenly, and the new archangel of war blamed the demons and started a war. Now, I'm not saying some archdemon *didn't* try to have the archangel of war assassinated, but the chances of success seem slim, as does an archdemon not taking into account the likelihood of the mantle being passed on," Kanae said, shrugging. "I've never heard a certain explanation of what else helped start the war, but that's one of the major suspicions."

"I... hadn't heard about that before. I don't think this is the same, though," Isalla said, blinking and thinking about what Kanae had said. She'd never heard just what led to the War of Decimation, but for the moment she put it aside, instead taking a deep breath and continuing. "I was assigned to the Evergardens, as the head investigator of crimes there. I shouldn't say head, since I was the *only* investigator and I didn't have training, but that's what my title was."

"The Evergardens? I've never heard of them," Kanae murmured, and Isalla grimaced.

"You wouldn't have. The Evergardens are on one of the most remote continents in the heavens, farthest from anything worthwhile. They're not *worthless*, mind you, but... producing most of the food common folk eat isn't exactly glamorous," Isalla said, swallowing hard and admitting unhappily, "Being assigned there is something of a punishment, and not being trained for it, I've long thought that I was being set up to fail. I don't want to talk about *why* I was assigned there, though. It really isn't applicable."

"Everyone has their secrets, Isalla. It isn't as though I've told you everything about me, you know," Kanae replied calmly, sitting back in her chair and watching Isalla thoughtfully. "I suspect that the Evergardens are a bit more important than you thought, though. Why else would you have been betrayed there?"

"You may be right. It took a while after I was assigned there, but I started hearing odd whispers, about things that are blasphemy among angels," Isalla explained, hesitating for a long moment, then continuing reluctantly. She really didn't like talking about this, but she had to. "Whispers of an angelic *god*, who glowed with a brilliant gold light. The whispers seemed to indicate that the deity would rebalance the heavens, allowing those of the weaker choirs to rise, and the angelic orders to be humbled. It's the sort of thing that can cause harsh reactions from above, and the whispers were widespread enough that if I came to the Council without proof, I'd be punished for my failings. So I began to investigate."

Kanae nodded, and there was something in her eyes that made Isalla fall silent. Eventually she shrugged and continued. "I realized then that several *members* of the Council were appearing in the Evergardens without being announced, then returning to the High Halls. They certainly weren't telling me about their presence, which was worrying. Fortunately, I had a friend I'd made, a woman named Haral. She confessed to me that she knew something, but wanted to speak to me in private, because it was dangerous."

"I imagine that didn't go well for you," Kanae murmured, and as Isalla blinked at her in surprise, the demoness smiled and pointed out, "You *did* say betrayal before."

"Well, yes. I didn't think of that, but you're right. I took the time to send a letter to my old commander to be safe, but I went to meet with Haral, and walked right into a trap," Isalla admitted sourly, feeling slightly sick again. "I gave a good accounting of myself, but Haral backstabbed me, so I barely dealt with one of them. They're the ones who did... well, everything that you'd seen done to me. They threw me off the continent, too, likely in the hopes that others would think I'd rushed into the hells to try and regain my honor. I still don't know *why*, though."

"That's interesting. Dangerous, but interesting," Kanae murmured, sitting back in her chair, looking thoughtful.

"Agreed. I was just… well, I was hoping to get to the outpost north of Zintas, the one you mentioned. Firewatch is commanded by Roselynn, my old commander," Isalla explained nervously, her emotions tangled. Roselynn hadn't replied to any of Isalla's letters, but Isalla still had feelings for her that were as strong or stronger than her growing attraction to Kanae. "She's the one I sent the letter to. Heck, even getting her a *message* would be good, since I told her I was going to contact her again afterward, and obviously I didn't."

"Truly? That *is* interesting, and quite the coincidence that it's so close. I'm going to have to ask a few questions and see what I can find out. Getting you there might be… difficult, considering how finicky the kingdoms are about spies, but I'm sure there are smugglers," Kanae said, smiling slightly. "A message might be easier."

"I agree. I'm hoping she can make use of the information I have, but…" Isalla shrugged, feeling slightly helpless in addition to her discomfort.

Kanae didn't answer, sitting back and staring at the ceiling. Isalla didn't say anything either, looking at the things on the table. Part of her thought that a few of the shirts there were sized for her, which was odd. Unless a few people were grateful to her, which seemed unlikely.

"Do you know what the difference between archangels, archdemons, and mortal gods is?" Kanae asked suddenly, looking at Isalla.

"Um, I know that the mantle of each can only be passed to one of their own… faction, for lack of a better term. Only an angel can become an archangel, only a demon can become an archdemon, and only a mortal can become a mortal god," Isalla replied, blinking at the seeming non sequitur comment. "Also, the mantle can't be destroyed, though the remains of the predecessor can be hidden to keep the mantle from being claimed."

"True enough, though incomplete. One of the things that neither angels nor demons like to discuss is that mortal gods are more powerful than archangels or archdemons. Not only do they gain immortality, the mortals gain powers that are subtly more potent than their counterparts," Kanae said, stunning Isalla, who opened her mouth. Kanae wasn't done, though, and continued. "The issue is that angels and demons are innately slightly more powerful than mortals are, so the difference doesn't appear until they reach the same level of skill. That being said, if an angel gained a mantle equal to that of a mortal god, or somehow managed to convert a deific mantle... they might not be unstoppable, but it would shake the foundations of the heavens and hells."

"That... well, I haven't heard that, but assuming you're right... could they really *do* that?" Isalla asked nervously. "I've never heard of something like that before."

"Just because something hasn't been done doesn't mean it's impossible," Kanae said, her voice calm. "I don't know that it's what they're trying for, but it's something to keep in mind, even if we can't do anything at the moment. Thank you for trusting me, Isalla. As it stands... well, we'll just have to wait. I'll see what I can find out about getting you to Roselynn."

"Thank you," Isalla replied, feeling relief slowly work its way through her.

Kanae didn't reply, but Isalla hadn't expected her to, not with how distant Kanae's eyes were. No, not distant, the angel realized. She could see tears in the demon's eyes, suppressed but present, and Isalla suddenly couldn't help feeling guilty. She didn't know what exactly she'd done, but she'd obviously hurt Kanae somehow.

She hesitated for a moment, then stood. Kanae focused suddenly, tilting her head as she watched Isalla, but she didn't speak.

Isalla didn't allow herself to hesitate or second-guess herself, and she simply leaned down and gave Kanae a kiss. The demoness stiffened slightly, then relaxed, her lips warm and smooth, with the same scent that Isalla had noticed before, and a slight taste that was similar to the apples she'd had before. It was almost intoxicating, and Isalla held the kiss for a moment, then broke it off.

"Isalla?" Kanae asked, sounding slightly dubious, and Isalla smiled at her.

"Would you care to join me in the bath?" Isalla asked nervously.

At that, Kanae smiled as well, and happiness surged through Isalla.

# CHAPTER 22

*K*anae was having trouble sleeping. She stared at the ceiling above her, slowly counting to herself, but it wasn't helping with sleep. It wasn't what had happened over the last few hours… no, her time with Isalla had been pleasant, and the demoness smiled as she looked over to see the angel's back in the darkness, feeling the warmth radiating from her. It was… comforting, that someone might care about her.

Isalla's back was healing well, Kanae saw, though she felt both shame and pride when she saw the scars where Isalla's wings had been. Soon there would be no sign of the wings, which was a testament to her skill, but also was a sign that she couldn't undo what had been done to the angel. Not many people would be able to tell Isalla apart from a human anymore, though some could. The musculature of an angel's back was unusual enough to be distinctive if compared to a human's back.

But even the knowledge of what had happened, how Isalla had nervously tried to seduce Kanae… all of it paled before the revelations which Isalla had unveiled.

"I hope I'm wrong," Kanae murmured, her worry growing stronger. Isalla stirred slightly at her voice, and Kanae made herself still, not wanting to wake the angel. She didn't want to worry her, either, so it was a delicate balance, talking to Isalla.

She knew more than she'd admitted to Isalla. Kanae didn't

exactly try to forget what she knew, but she didn't like admitting it, either. The amount of misinformation that both demons and angels claimed was the truth was staggering, and that was an enormous part of why she'd abandoned the war in the end. But now, if the conflict was truly waking once more... Kanae shivered at the thought of what might be coming.

Kanae hoped that she was wrong, but more than that, she hoped that Isalla wouldn't be drawn into a conflict like the ones she remembered. There was a reason why there'd been peace for so long, after all.

Looking at Isalla's profile again and listening to her slow, deep breathing, Kanae gently leaned over and kissed the angel's back. She did enjoy Isalla's company, even if she knew it'd probably never last. Then she closed her eyes and tried to sleep. She imagined it would be a long time in coming.

MORNING CAME TOO QUICKLY, and Kanae had already gotten to work by the time Isalla woke, preparing breakfast and getting ready for her day. It was fortunate that she'd inherited the reduced need for sleep that both of her parents had possessed, or Kanae might be almost dead on her feet.

"Good morning, Isalla. Did you sleep well?" Kanae asked warmly, taking a moment to dribble a bit of honey into the oatmeal she'd prepared. Both the oatmeal and honey were rare in the hells, but after the night they'd had, she thought it was worth a treat for both of them.

Isalla blinked, rubbing the sleep from her eyes, and then the angel slowly blushed. It was adorable, and the blush deepened as Kanae smiled. The angel fidgeted, then cleared her throat and headed for her usual chair.

"I did. Very well, as a matter of fact," Isalla replied, watching Kanae intently. "What about you?"

"Not as well as I'd like. I enjoyed our time together, Isalla," Kanae quickly said, trying to head off the angel's disappointment, and it looked like she succeeded as the angel smiled shyly. "It's more that I'm worried about what you told me. I was in the last major war, so the thought has me concerned."

"Ah, of course," Isalla replied, blushing a bit more. "I... I enjoyed myself, too."

"I'm glad to hear that," Kanae replied, pulling out a pair of spoons and taking their breakfast over to the table. "Here you go. A bit of a treat today, at least for the hells. I suspect you've had food like this plenty of times, though."

"Um, maybe so, but it's certainly a change from porridge," Isalla said, taking a bite, then smiling happily. "Are oatmeal and honey really that rare, here?"

"Not exactly," Kanae said, shaking her head. "Oh, oats don't grow down here, so that's imported. The problem is that most grains in the hells are poisonous, and even those that are edible don't taste as good as what grows in the mortal world. As for honey... well, trying to harvest it from the swarms we have down here is taking your life into your hands, and even if you survive, it's probably not worth it. Our bees are closer to wasps the size of my hand. Sure, they make a *lot* of honey, but you have to get it out afterward."

"Eek, that... would be unpleasant," Isalla said, blanching visibly. "Are there many things that are... well, I hate to say *better*, but you said that most grains don't taste as good as what comes from the mortal world."

"Mm... I think some of our fruit is better, and particularly some of the wines we make sell for remarkable sums above. I wouldn't claim it's *that* much better, but it's different," Kanae said, sitting back and considering as she savored her food. "Meat from some of our animals is also prized... but for the most part, I'd say that the food from above is better. I wouldn't be surprised if that's an enormous part of why so many demons want to go up to Hragon."

"Huh, that's an interesting thought. I'd never considered that *food* might be a large part of why demons are so involved in the mortal world. If that's the case, why don't you just trade for it? You said that metal is easy to come by down here," Isalla said, looking speculative. Kanae envied her comparative optimism, though she'd thought the same once upon a time.

"We might have, in the beginning. However, the hells are immensely larger than the mortal world, and at some point, war broke out between the heavens and hells, and the mortal kingdoms got embroiled in it. I'm not certain how it started, Isalla, but neither side is willing to give up an inch of ground anymore," Kanae said gently. "As it is, we still import as much food as we reasonably can. The journey is difficult enough that it's less than even the nearby domains would prefer, unfortunately."

"I suppose you're right. It was just a hopeful thought," Isalla admitted, shaking her head slowly, looking a little disappointed. "Well, there's nothing to do about that, I guess. So, what're you planning to do today?"

"Well, since you discussed what happened above, I figure I'll go to the trade house and see if I can't figure out if there's any recent news that's particularly relevant. I'm also going to see if it's possible to get a message to your friend, but I'm not holding out a lot of hope there," Kanae explained, smiling at Isalla in encouragement. "Smuggling is a *bit* too much to ask for directly. Now, asking if someone is able to smuggle some of the produce from the northern continents to Hragon, and then having it brought down through the portal... that'll tell us if anyone is able to get there or not."

"True!" Isalla's expression brightened, then she laughed as she added, "You know, I've never had to *hope* that there were smugglers managing to get back and forth before! I was always trying to stop things like that, since they could be spies."

"I can't say that I blame you. It isn't something I put a lot of thought into, either. I'll see what I can find out, I promise," Kanae told the angel as her mood improved.

"Thank you. I guess I'll keep up the exercising... I'm almost back to what I'd consider normal. Weaker than I was, still, but at least fit enough to practice with a real sword," Isalla said, nodding at the sword in the corner.

"A good idea. Just be sure to not stray too far from the house. You've seen the damage that some of the creatures in the woods can do," Kanae cautioned, though she was confident that Isalla didn't need the warning.

"That I have. I'd tell you to be careful, but I suspect you'd be safer than me if you were in the middle of the forest, and I was here," Isalla said, her tone teasing.

Kanae shrugged and smiled. Isalla was right, but there was no need to brag. Instead, she continued to eat her oatmeal and enjoyed her company.

∽

SAMANTHA JOY SAT in the back of the hall, wondering what the summons was for. There hadn't been a general summons in the assassin's guild since she joined nearly a decade before, making this one of the most unusual events she'd seen. Nearly fifty other assassins were present, at least half of which she'd never seen before. More interesting was that none of the trainees were present, which told her a bit more.

The room they were in was large enough to contain nearly double the numbers within, and there were plenty of exits. If there weren't, Samantha suspected that most of the others wouldn't have come. She certainly wouldn't have, and she doubted Thomas, who was at her table, would have either.

It amused her how open Hragon was about there being an assassin's guild. The building was in the open, and they took jobs of anyone who could pay their fees, though the kingdom did regulate who they could take marks *on*. The guild didn't force the assassins to come out publicly, though, which was fortunate, considering how many people would likely try to kill them in turn.

"Hello everyone, thank you for coming." An echoing voice broke through the conversations throughout the hall, drawing attention to a raised platform in the front of the room. The voice was magically augmented so everyone could hear it clearly without being heard outside the room, Samantha knew, which had been frustrating when she'd been a trainee.

Standing in front of the hall was the Minister, as the one who ran the guildhall was called. Wearing a set of voluminous tan robes and a mask, the name and gender of the Minister was purposely obscured, and they took a step forward.

"What's this all about, Minister? It isn't like these meetings happen often," one of the men near the front called out, and Samantha nodded as a rumble of agreement echoed through the room.

"The guild has received an open request, one which is believed to be moderately dangerous," the Minister said, looking around the room through their mask. "The request is unusual in that it has a significant reward for not only the target's death, but also for confirmed information on where the target is. A servant will be handing out a copy of the request momentarily."

Samantha could see a couple of servants passing out sheets of paper, but they were taking their time to get to her. She was intrigued, but since she was near the back, she chose to let one of the people who was closer ask the question she was thinking.

"How significant of a reward are we talking about?" a female assassin asked, someone that Samantha didn't recognize.

"The client is offering one thousand gold for the target's head, and fifty for their location and associates," the Minister said simply, and Samantha whistled softly.

"I've taken jobs for less than the information on their location," Samantha said, and Thomas nodded.

"Agreed. Makes me wonder what the reason for the price is," he murmured, smirking at her.

One of the servants reached them and offered a pair of paper sheets, which each of them took. Samantha took it and her eyebrows rose as she read quickly. "Around Hellmount, through the portal? I guess that *would* explain part of it. Let's see…"

The description was of a blonde woman who'd appeared from nowhere, was quite beautiful, and who might be unusually weak. The information was simple, and there was a sketch of her appearance, which would help.

"Before you ask, there is a bit more information which might assist you in finding the target, should you choose to seek her out," the Minister spoke again, their voice calm. "It is known that the target is an angel, but she has lost her wings. It's believed that she's a spy, which would explain much, but the client insists that the target be silenced. While information on her location will be rewarded separately, it will only be granted up to ten times, once per individual reporting. If she is moving from location to location, the payment will be granted beyond ten times, but only if an assassin swears they are not deliberately allowing her to move in order to get additional funds. I will repeat, this task is not being assigned to a single assassin, as the location of the target is unknown. Should you decide to take the job, good hunting."

The Minister stepped down from the platform, and Thomas looked at Samantha in interest. "An angel spy? That's interesting, and not a strategy I've heard of them employing before."

"That just might be why they're paying so much to eliminate the target," Samantha murmured, then smiled. "What do you think, should we team up to search for her?"

"Sure. I've never hunted an angel before," Thomas replied, grinning and looking at the paper. "It might be worth taking a detour and getting some better weapons, too. I've heard that some of the smiths around Hellmount are damned good."

"True! Anyway, let's go. I'll bet that we're not the only ones interested," Samantha agreed, standing up and nodding at the crowd of other assassins. Several had already vanished, which was telling. "It isn't like they're going to wait for us."

"Yeah," Thomas agreed, looking his paper over again before standing up. "Neither is this Isalla, assuming she's still using the same name."

"Agreed," Samantha said, folding her paper and slipping it into a pouch.

She'd never killed an angel before, but there was a first time for everything. Samantha knew she was smiling broadly, but that was alright. That was the reason most of the others called her Smiles sometimes. Well, that and her favored way of killing people.

# CHAPTER 23

*I*salla looked up from doing sit-ups as the door unlocked and Kanae stepped inside. The near-giddy smile that appeared on Isalla's face was a surprise, but not a huge one. The previous night had been incredible, and Isalla felt both guilty and ecstatic about the experience. Heavens knew how badly most angels would react if they knew she'd bedded a demon, but as far as Isalla was concerned, they had no business sticking their noses where they didn't belong.

The look on Kanae's face did give Isalla pause, though. It wasn't that Kanae looked upset, more that she was disappointed. That was still a strong term for it, but it was the best description Isalla had.

"Welcome back, Kanae! How'd things go?" Isalla asked, sitting up as she drew in a deep breath, mingled worry and anticipation warring inside her.

"About how I expected, I'm afraid. There wasn't much information to be had, though there were plenty of rumors. I asked about the smuggling, and Rekkal said that he'd have to make come inquiries," Kanae replied, closing the door and locking it, then setting a basket on the table. "Fortunately, there's a trade caravan coming back through sometime next week or so, but until then I'm afraid we won't be able to find out much about what's going on. I wouldn't get your hopes up, though."

"Drat. Well at least there's a chance of finding out things relatively soon," Isalla said, letting out a soft sigh as some of her pleasure faded. It didn't fade much, but it didn't make the day better either.

"Exactly. I can't promise a lot, but at least that much I can manage," Kanae said, starting to pull several jars out of the basket. Most of it was earthenware, Isalla realized, but then she blinked as she saw a small wheel of cheese, or what looked like cheese to her.

"Um, what did you bring back, Kanae? Is that cheese?" Isalla asked curiously.

"It is. Since I was at the trading house, I decided to pick up a few luxuries," Kanae said, smiling as she touched the cheese gently. "This wasn't the most expensive thing I got, but it's close. I have jarred tomatoes, pears, and some pickles as well. I also got some flour, enough to make some pasta and a few other things... I figured a few nicer meals are in order."

"Really? I suppose that would be nice, down here," Isalla agreed, returning Kanae's smile. In all truth, she had no idea how much it might have cost Kanae for things like that, but considering their previous conversation about food, she suspected that they were far more valuable than she'd think, coming from the heavens. The idea that Kanae had gotten them specifically to share with Isalla improved her mood immensely, and she resisted the urge to kiss the demoness.

"It is. I've considered trying to move to the mortal world many times, but I've never felt like it was a good idea. Maybe I'm just afraid of change... that's something I've heard of many older demons running into," Kanae agreed, looking at Isalla contemplatively. "Unlike me, even if you decide not to go back to the heavens, you could live there without drawing too much attention. Your species isn't quite as obvious as mine."

The comment made Isalla blink, then she flushed slightly, shaking her head as she replied softly, not happy about the idea. "I... I don't know about that. I might be able to fit in, but losing the ability to fly permanently? That would be horrible, and I don't know that I could stand it."

"I understand, at least as much as someone who hasn't ever

had the ability to fly can," Kanae replied, nodding in sympathy. "I've flown a few times in my life, sometimes with magic, and a few on the back of a drake, but those aren't the same as what you've experienced."

"No, they wouldn't be. There's nothing in the world like the wind against your face as it rustles through your wings on a morning flight..." Isalla said, her voice trailing off slightly as she remembered what it was like. The memory was a bit bitter, though, and she shook her head as she continued. "Never mind that. While I can't express how wonderful it was, now it's somewhat... depressing to think about. What did you have in mind for the evening? I think I'm getting my strength back where I want it to be."

Kanae allowed her to change the subject, fortunately, and the demoness smiled as she replied. "Oh? That's good, at least. I was wondering how long it might take you. Heavy injuries can take a lot out of someone, even without the poison that you were dosed with."

"I believe it. I haven't seen many injuries like this and haven't had much to do with recovery afterward... that was the responsibility of other people. It's strange to think about, but our legions separated duties heavily," Isalla explained, considering the idea for a long moment, then smiled warmly as she added, "That said... I think that I could use help with my recovery, if you wouldn't mind."

"Oh? How so?" Kanae asked, an eyebrow arching curiously.

"It's hard to get my skill with a blade back when I'm practicing entirely on my own," Isalla explained. "I know you're more experienced than I am, so it's also an opportunity to potentially improve."

Kanae's other eyebrow rose and she blinked, then asked, "Are you sure? I haven't sparred with someone else in years and may forget to hold back."

"Of course I am! It's a bit lonely practicing on my own, too," Isalla said, smiling confidently. "Besides, I might surprise you."

"A fair point. Let me put these away and I'll find my own practice sword," Kanae agreed. Her amusement was obvious, but she didn't object any further, to Isalla's relief.

"That sounds excellent," Isalla replied and waited as Kanae began putting her purchases away, all but bouncing on the tips of her toes.

She was looking forward to seeing how well she could do when she went up against Kanae. Isalla had learned a lot from Roselynn, after all.

❧

KANAE'S PRACTICE sword was a blur as it flashed by Isalla's to hit the angel's leg, almost causing her knee to buckle as her block came just a moment too late. Isalla yelped, wishing she had a shield, since she might've been able to defend herself better that way. Kanae bounced away from Isalla, looking all too at ease as she held her practice sword in one hand, still in a combat stance.

"You aren't bad, Isalla, but you lack experience with those who're significantly faster or stronger than you," Kanae said, pausing for a moment before adding, "I think you're also used to being able to move upward or backward as part of dodging… I could've sworn you tried to jump into the air that time."

"That's because I did. Ow," Isalla said, wincing as she reached down to rub her leg. She could hardly believe how fast Kanae was. "I think I may need to pick up a shield in the future. It isn't my preference, but it might help block *some* of your attacks."

"Maybe so, but I'd just switch targets. Fully armored, you're going to be slower than you are now, and you aren't paying enough attention to what's around you," Kanae advised gently. "You don't want to be too predictable, Isalla. That's a good way to end up dead."

"Have you come close to that before?" Isalla asked, raising her sword and tapping Kanae's, though part of her just wanted to give up now. On the other hand, if she was sore, she might be able to convince Kanae to help her in the bath, which would be rather pleasant.

Kanae didn't attack seriously this time, instead making slower attacks for Isalla to block. The vibration of their impact caused Isalla's arms to shiver, but it was good practice, and she fell back step by step. Kanae seemed able to keep up her side of the conversation with little effort, something Isalla envied.

"I'm not dead, so not quite. I've come close a few times, though," Kanae replied calmly.

"Like what?" Isalla asked, slightly breathless.

"A ballista bolt severed my spine once. I really should've paid more attention to where I was fighting," Kanae said, and the response spoiled Isalla's concentration, allowing another blow to hit her in the ribs, causing the angel to gasp in pain.

"You... you *what*?" Isalla asked in disbelief, her eyes huge as she fell back and Kanae stopped attacking, reaching up to rub her side.

"I was fighting on a wall and didn't see a ballista to the side," Kanae explained, gesturing down at her lower body. "It went in one side and out through my back and spine. I was quite fortunate to survive and to be assisted in recovering."

"That's just horrible!" Isalla exclaimed, blanching at the thought. She'd seen ballista before, and the giant crossbows weren't really intended for single targets. The idea of one hitting someone in the side almost made her stomach lurch. She'd seen some bloodshed before, but something like that happening to someone she knew was quite different. In fact, it was pretty horrifying.

"It certainly wasn't a high point of my experiences in the war," Kanae agreed, shaking her head slowly. "The recovery was unpleasant, to say the least."

"I can only imagine what that'd be like," Isalla replied, shivering slightly. She didn't understand why Kanae could talk about something so horrible *calmly*.

"I hope you never have to do more than imagine it," Kanae said dryly, then raised her practice blade. "That's enough of a rest, though."

"Um, why are *you* pushing me so hard now?" Isalla asked, taking a step back as she quickly raised her sword.

"You asked me to help you. Enemies aren't going to go easy on you, so why should I?" Kanae asked, then she attacked.

Trying to fight back, Isalla had to admit that much was true. Even if she didn't exactly like it.

# CHAPTER 24

*R*ekkal brushed off one pair of hands while setting some of the jars onto the shelves carefully. He prided himself on keeping the trade house well organized, but the days that a caravan came to town were much harder on him than most days. Pausing, he stretched all four arms as best he could and rolled his neck, feeling two joints pop as he did so and sighed happily.

"Almost done, at least. Did people have to order quite this much from the caravan? I swear, this was nearly triple the usual amount," Rekkal said, shaking his head and looking at the remaining two crates, along with the one he'd just emptied. "Pays well, though."

The silk they'd shipped off had brought in a tidy profit, and Rekkal knew that the spices and other supplies his agent in Hragon had purchased would bring in even more in the capital, once the caravan reached there. Not that it brought in quite as much money as Kanae's alchemical supplies did, when he compared the volume each took. It was really too bad that the healer couldn't produce more, but the day Kanae had offered to let him help with her alchemy had been educational. He'd never realized just how much time it took to brew some of her salves and other supplies. That likely had been the entire reason she'd let him help, since he'd also stopped asking her for more to trade, he reflected.

"She should be in town a bit later, though. She always shows up when a caravan comes through," Rekkal muttered under his breath, growing a bit more excited since he had some news that the healer had been asking about. "No wonder the news has been spreading so quick up there... I can't believe we didn't hear about any of this before."

He was looking forward to seeing Kanae. He thought that she'd be stunned, and just maybe she'd be more receptive to his advances.

❧

"WHAT WAS THAT?" Kanae asked, looking up from the scroll abruptly, all thought of going over her accounts gone.

Rekkal was grinning at her, the four-armed, lizard-like man looking far too entertained. His amusement wasn't surprising, considering what he'd just said. Even more, she knew that not many things surprised her anymore, but this certainly did.

"I said that apparently the Flame of Ember was on that island you were talking about, and she was captured in a raid a few weeks ago," Rekkal said, sounding amused. "Stunning, isn't it?"

"Just a bit. The family is legendary in the army, and that sword is brutally powerful if the wielder can harness its full potential," Kanae said, trying to calm herself. "Do you have any idea who the current wielder is?"

"Um, yeah, they did use her name. Roselynn, or something along those lines," Rekkal said, not noticing as Kanae felt her heart sink slightly. "I'm surprised someone like that was on the island, honestly."

"It's a bit of a shock, yes. More surprising is that she was captured at all. I'd have expected any attack to be repelled, unless it was in overwhelming force," Kanae told him, keeping her dismay hidden as best she could. This would probably upset Isalla, and for good reason.

"I don't know about anything like that, but what I *can* tell you is that while there were smugglers that went there before

168

this, they're avoiding the island like the plague at the moment," Rekkal said seriously. "The place is like a kicked firebeetle nest."

"Of course it is. So much for getting some raspberry cordial smuggled in," Kanae said, sighing and shaking her head.

"It sounds like a fascinating drink, so it's really too bad. Maybe things will calm down by next year," Rekkal agreed, shrugging comfortably.

"Possibly," Kanae admitted, looking back down to the scroll that recorded her profits so far that year. They were doing pretty well on the whole, if not quite as well as the year before. She waited for several moments before asking the question she really wanted answered, though she didn't really want to know in some ways. There were three demonic domains that bordered Hellmount, and chances weren't in her favor. "Do you have any idea what happened to the Flame of Ember, then? If they captured her, I doubt they'd just kill her or something."

"Oh, that's the part that stunned me! Apparently, they brought her here!" Rekkal exclaimed, grinning.

"Impossible," Kanae said flatly, looking up. "I'd have heard something if they brought her into town."

"Not *here* here, but into Estalia," Rekkal corrected quickly. "I heard that they took her to the Spire of Confession."

Kanae's surprise turned to dread quite abruptly. The Spire of Confession wasn't the last place she'd hoped to hear about in the conversation, but it certainly wasn't near the top of the list either. She took a deep breath and shook her head. "Oh. That's... well, that's going to be interesting for her, I'm sure. They must have flown her, since we didn't hear about any of this until now."

"That seems pretty likely to me," Rekkal replied, leaning forward and grinning. "Now, since I've made you a good profit and found some of the information you're looking for, is there any chance of convincing you to have dinner with me?"

"No, Rekkal," Kanae replied promptly, finally nodding and rolling up the scroll to hand back to him. He looked a bit hurt, she noticed, but not surprised.

"No? You won't even give me a chance?" he asked in a wheedling tone. The man was certainly persistent.

"No," Kanae confirmed gently. "You're a nice enough young

man, but we wouldn't get along romantically, Rekkal. It's best to avoid relationships which are doomed to failure, in my opinion."

"Ah, dammit. Well, I'm going to keep trying," Rekkal said, barely looking dismayed and straightening slightly.

"You and half the town. Have a good evening, Rekkal," Kanae replied, shaking her head as she left, glancing down to make sure the jars of reagents she'd picked up were in her basket.

"See you later!" he called after her, then the door shut.

Kanae smiled at the others as she calmly walked out of town, but as she moved, her mind was considering the unwelcome news she'd learned.

Isalla wasn't going to like it, but she wouldn't have any idea how bad it actually was. The question was how to break the information to her without bringing Isalla to tears.

THE SOUND of the door opening caused Isalla to perk up. She'd been feeling restless since Kanae had left that morning, as she knew that Kanae had been planning to ask about events in Hragon. She hadn't even done much in the way of exercising, she was so nervous about things. Part of her hoped that she could make it to Roselynn, while another large part of her didn't want to leave.

"I'm back, Isalla," Kanae called out, her voice steady.

"Welcome back!" Isalla said, stepping out of the bedroom to greet the demoness, a warm smile on her face. Her enthusiasm faded slightly as she noticed the look on Kanae's face, one of worry. That was both startling and made Isalla nervous. "Is something wrong?"

"Take a seat if you would? I got some news, and I'm afraid it isn't good," Kanae said, gesturing to the table. She walked over and set her basket on the table, then slipped into a chair herself. "I half wish I didn't have to tell you, in fact. It's not what I wanted to share."

Dread washed through Isalla, and she moved to her chair,

pulling it out and carefully slipping into the seat. She licked her lips, then asked nervously, "Is it really that bad? I mean…"

"That depends on a few things. You called your friend Roselynn… is she the wielder of Ember? The fiery sword of the north?" Kanae asked carefully.

"Ah, yes. She didn't really like talking about that aspect of her life, as she found the fame it brought her a bit suffocating at times. The sword is part of her duty, from what she told me," Isalla confirmed, her worry growing stronger. "Why do you ask?"

"Hellscour," Kanae whispered, rubbing her eyes. For a long moment she was quiet, then she sighed, sitting back in her chair. "Her island was attacked by a raiding party of demons a few weeks ago, never mind that I have no idea why they'd be there. Worse, they *captured* the Flame of Ember, as she's called. The rumors of her name weren't reliable, which is why I wanted to ask you. Confirming it… well, I'm sorry, Isalla."

All the blood drained from Isalla's face at Kanae's words. For a long moment she couldn't say anything, and her pleasure at how things had been going vanished. Isalla couldn't really think about anything, except for the fact her friend had been captured. That was just so *ridiculous*, though.

"Are you certain? That doesn't seem right… Roselynn was always so *careful*. She would fight to the bitter end, and I imagine the entire island would be in flames before they took her down!" Isalla protested, worry flooding through her.

"I don't know. All we have to work off of is rumor, Isalla, but on something like this… I don't see why they'd lie. Apparently, all the smugglers are avoiding the place because the island is swarming with upset angels and the like," Kanae replied with a helpless shrug. "It's possible that they managed to catch her while she was out of the fortress and retreated before they could be stopped. I suspect it'd have to be a powerful force to do that, though."

"I… I just…" Isalla swallowed hard, trying to breathe through her fears. As the possibility of it being true settled in, she asked softly, "Is she… is she alive? You said captured, but I've heard of horrible rituals…"

"That's the part that's both good and the one which horrifies me more than anything else," Kanae told her in a grim voice. "She was brought to Estalia, then was taken to the Spire of Confession. The people there… they terrify me, Isalla."

"Torture?" Isalla asked, her voice trembling now, but with a bit of hope to her voice. If Roselynn was alive, she could be rescued or escape. "I don't think they'd break her will easily, but if she's alive…"

"Oh, I wish it was torture. Torture would be positively… simple. It's easier to resist than what they do, Isalla," Kanae replied, letting out a soft, unhappy laugh.

"What are you talking about?" Isalla asked, her worry growing sharply. Kanae's reaction wasn't helping at all. "You're making me worry even more than I was before."

"That's for the best," Kanae replied, standing up and walking over to the fireplace to stare into the flames. She was quiet, but after a moment, Isalla realized that her fingers were trembling slightly. Isalla opened her mouth to say something, then closed it again, not sure what to say or do. Her worry about Roselynn faded as she grew more concerned for Kanae. Fortunately, Kanae spoke again at last.

"We spoke briefly about the church of Estalia before, and how those who join their priesthood become indoctrinated far too easily. Well, the Spire of Confession is one of their… strongholds, for lack of a better term. The most devoted true believers go there, as do those who they wish to *twist*." Kanae's steady voice was at odds with the way she was trembling. "Some nobles have difficult children, and they donate heavily to get the spire to adjust their attitudes to something more… acceptable."

"Heavens…" Isalla swallowed hard, her terror for Roselynn growing. "They use magic to change people? That's really bad, but—"

"No, they don't use magic. That would be too easy to fix. Oh no, Isalla… they don't use something so simple as magic," Kanae interrupted, turning to smile at Isalla bitterly. "They're kind."

"What?" Isalla asked, taken aback and confused.

"They're kind to you. Oh, they drug those who come there for a few days, with something that makes the victim more accepting of their situation, but that's over soon enough. Instead, the most empathetic, kind, flattering men and women you can imagine pamper you. They make you feel like you're the most important person in the world, they become your friends." Kanae paused, taking a deep breath and shivering slightly. "They don't twist you personally, Isalla. No, they so wholeheartedly believe in what they're doing that they find it easy to convince you to change *yourself*. You willingly ask for magical changes to your body so that you're more attractive or change yourself to make yourself feel more beautiful. Worse still, the changes to your mentality and outlook on the world are the result of you coming to truly *believe* in them, so changing them back is nigh impossible."

"That's… that's terrifying, but Roselynn is so *strong*, she's always been determined and has refused to change simply because other people have different opinions," Isalla protested, trying to hide how shaken she was by the explanation. It was somewhat terrifying, but she refused to let herself show her worry.

"I'm sure she is… but it doesn't matter how powerful of a will she has," Kanae said simply, looking back to the fire again. "They're true believers. She won't detect anything but perfect sincerity from them, which will make it harder for her to resist in some ways. Oh, she might last a while… but eventually anyone will begin to fail in front of them. Demon generals have fallen under their sway before, Isalla, and come out completely changed. Worse still, in the vast majority of cases, those in the spire need a mere week to achieve those results."

Isalla's protests died suddenly and she swallowed hard, staring at Kanae for a long moment, then asked with her voice trembling, "A week? But you said that she's been in their hands for a couple of weeks, possibly more."

"I know. That means that they're either done and word hasn't spread, she's more difficult to deal with than normal, or that they're plumbing her for as much information as possible," Kanae replied softly, letting out a soft sigh. "No matter which it is, I don't have high hopes that your friend will be able to resist for long."

"I have to help her, then! If I can get her free before they can make her change too much, then—" Isalla began, only to be interrupted again.

"The only thing that would happen if you intrude would be for you to join her, Isalla. If I went with you, the exact same thing would happen," Kanae said flatly, turning to look at Isalla, worry in her eyes. "You don't understand just how dangerous they are, not really. There are very few things in this world that scare me, but they're among them. Perhaps scare isn't the right word, but they certainly worry me."

"Kanae…" Isalla began, then paused, studying the demoness for a long moment, and grew more concerned. Then she spoke softly. "How do you know this? It almost sounds like you're speaking from experience."

"That's because I am," Kanae replied simply, shivering as she looked away again. "It was a long time ago, but I was one of those stubborn young women I told you about. My mother… well, she sent me there. What happened to me was relatively mild compared to what others undergo, but my feelings haven't changed since then. Do you understand what I'm saying, Isalla? In a *thousand years* what they've convinced me of hasn't changed, despite me knowing what they did."

Isalla froze in place, her mouth half-open, then she closed it and swallowed. She hadn't considered that, not until Kanae had mentioned it. The thought was both terrifying and shocking, since she couldn't imagine someone being changed that thoroughly. If Roselynn had something like that happen to her… the thought made Isalla shiver in fear. It also made her internally curse herself for flirting with Kanae when her old lover might be fighting for her sense of self. It wasn't Kanae's fault, but even so…

"I… what can I do, then? I can't abandon her, Kanae. I just can't," Isalla said helplessly, her emotions in turmoil. "I believe you when you're warning me that we won't come out again if we go there, but I don't know what else to do."

"I'm not certain myself. I don't see there being any options to rescue her, to be perfectly honest with you. The only thing I can recommend is that we might be able to rescue her when they bring her out of the spire," Kanae explained. After a few moments of hesitation, she continued. "I don't know what condition she'd be in, Isalla, but it's the best chance we have of not being captured ourselves."

"But doesn't that mean they'll have completed whatever it is they're doing?" Isalla protested, her worry growing still stronger, and a hint of rage sparking at the demoness.

Kanae let out a soft sigh and nodded slowly. "Yes, it does. I'm sorry, but most likely it's already too late, Isalla. I wish I had a good answer for you, but I don't."

"I see," Isalla said, her mood sinking slightly. "I'm… going to go outside. I need to think about this for a bit."

"As you like," Kanae agreed, sighing softly.

With that, Isalla took her sword and belted it on before heading outside. She wanted some fresh air while she thought. The choices she had weren't something that made her happy, which was unfortunate after her hopes that morning.

"Well, damn," Thomas breathed. "I thought the lead had to be a red herring, but it looks like we just got lucky."

Watching the blonde woman slowly meandering down the hillside, Samantha nodded in agreement, a smile slowly blossoming on her face. "The others won't believe it when we tell them. I mean, this is our first lead after coming through the portal."

The trip through the portal had taken longer than Samantha had hoped, and once through the gate they'd had to choose which demonic domain to go to. Most of the others had chosen other domains, reasoning that someone seeking to hide would go to the less likely regions. Samantha and Thomas had chosen to go to Estalia, and they'd heard gossip about the healer's guest while at the tavern. She could hardly believe that the woman they were after was just standing there in the open, almost like she didn't have a care in the world.

"Their loss, our gain," Thomas replied with a grin. "How do you want to handle this?"

"You head back and ensure that a message is delivered. I'm going to take a shot at her and see if I can't take her out. Either way, I'm going to take off afterward. Meet you at the rendezvous point tonight?" Samantha suggested.

"Sounds good. Good luck, and give me a minute to make sure I've got a clean getaway?" Thomas asked.

Samantha nodded, pulling out her bow and stringing it. Thomas patted her on the shoulder as he left, and Samantha waited, watching the wingless angel carefully. Her position would make it difficult to sneak up behind her, which was a shame. Samantha preferred to use her daggers to eliminate targets, but she'd still use whatever weapon worked.

The angel didn't seem quite as carefree as Samantha had thought initially, and the assassin considered the woman as she paced pensively, wondering what had her so concerned. In the end, it didn't really matter, though, and Samantha drew back an arrow, taking aim at her target.

# CHAPTER 25

*P*acing through the grass around Kanae's home was calming. It didn't help Isalla figure out what she wanted to do about Roselynn, but it at least was enough to keep her from panicking or breaking down in tears.

It was that same calm that helped her notice how quiet the woods were, and to spot the hint of movement among the trees from the corner of her eye. Perhaps she hadn't noticed consciously, but the second the arrow hissed out of the trees, Isalla ducked. Cursing, Isalla glanced over to see the arrow buried in the hillside. In the same moment, she drew her sword and her thoughts grew calm, the same way they always did when she was participating in a real battle.

"Kanae!" Isalla called out, and at the same time, she began racing toward the spot where the arrow had come from. A flash of movement among the trees allowed her to barely see the shadow of someone darting away, and the angel swallowed a curse. It was better than being shot at again, but it made things more difficult for her.

"Isalla? What—" Kanae began, stepping out of the house.

"I was shot at!" Isalla exclaimed, then raced into the woods after the shadow, a tiny part of her relieved at the distraction. A larger part of her was upset, though.

Behind her, she heard Kanae curse, and then she was among

the trees, chasing after the shadowy figure darting through the forest.

Once again, Isalla missed her wings, since if she had them, she'd be able to catch up quickly. As it was, it felt like she was losing ground.

~

SAMANTHA CURSED INTERNALLY AS she moved through the forest, frustration rushing through her. She hadn't thought that the angel would react that quickly, and she really hadn't expected to fail. Worse, somehow the angel could see her in the shadows of the forest even when Samantha magically blended into the shadows. That was an unpleasant shock, as was the demon following her.

Glancing back, the assassin could see the pale-skinned demoness moving through the trees almost like a ghost, silent and faster than the angel was. If it weren't for magic speeding Samantha up, she'd be losing ground incredibly quickly rather than slowly. Which really meant that Samantha needed to focus on running and hiding, not on her pursuers.

With that in mind, Samantha hopped over a fallen tree and dodged behind several bushes as she kept going, trying to shake off the women behind her as she redoubled her pace and channeled more mana into the magical techniques she'd learned.

~

ISALLA SWORE under her breath as the person who'd tried to kill her started to open the gap slightly. She'd caught a glimpse of Kanae passing her, which would have startled Isalla if it hadn't been for some of the things she'd seen the other woman do before.

Jumping over a log, Isalla nearly stumbled as she hit a patch of uneven ground, but she managed to regain her balance quickly enough, and she saw Kanae stoop slightly. An instant later, a pair of stones flew after the shadowy figure, one of which missed, and the other just barely clipping a shoulder, causing the figure to change course.

At least Kanae wasn't losing the attacker, and despite the way her muscles were complaining, Isalla hadn't lost her endurance yet, so she could keep going for a while. Longer than her legs would be able to handle, in fact, which was frustrating.

Kanae tried to hit the figure a few more times, but the speed they were moving at made that difficult, and eventually she gave up, instead settling for closing the gap between them, as the two slowly began to leave Isalla behind. Only by putting everything she had into running was Isalla able to keep them in sight, and—

Kanae stopped quite suddenly as the other figure darted past a couple of the dark trees and into a patch of head-high bushes that bore scarlet thorns. Isalla blinked in surprise, but as she approached, Kanae spoke.

"Stop," the demoness said, her breath coming quickly but evenly. "You don't want to follow her in there."

"What? But they might get away!" Isalla gasped incredulously, slowing and panting.

"No, she won't," Kanae said, her lips pressed together tightly. "Going in there was the worst decision she could've made. I'll be able to get her remains, but we're not going to be getting anything out of her."

"Huh?" Isalla asked, growing perplexed.

The next moment, she heard the branches ahead of them hiss.

SAMANTHA'S SPIRITS rose as she lost the two pursuers. She'd decided that going through the bushes was a risk, since there might not be an exit and she could be forced to go through the thorns, but obviously it had been worth it. There were other exits as well, which would make escaping easy.

As she took another step, Samantha heard a rattling sound from below as her foot rocked, and she looked down for an instant as her eyes went wide. Below her, she saw bones buried in the dirt, almost all of them from animals, but they were piled on top of each other, some of them yellowed with age.

"Shit," Samantha murmured, her instincts screaming to get out of there, and she bolted for one of the exits.

The branches of the bushes rustled at that moment, and an instant later, the crimson thorns seemed to explode off the branches, trailing thin tendrils that connected them to the bushes behind them.

Samantha managed to dodge a few of them, but there were hundreds, and as they struck home in her flesh, she screamed.

∼

ISALLA FLINCHED as she heard a woman scream, recoiling slightly as she asked, "What was that?"

"Those are vampire bushes. A particularly nasty plant, they gain most nutrients from a creature's blood. The thorns build up a gas, and when the bush senses prey nearby, it launches the thorns at them, where they lodge in the victim's flesh and drain the blood from it. Once there isn't any more fluid to drain, it draws the thorns back and prepares for a new victim," Kanae explained, her voice grim. "The foolish woman, and it was a human woman, ran straight into the *middle* of the bushes. She might have survived skirting the edges and getting hit by a few thorns, but that was all but suicide."

The blood drained from Isalla's face at the description, and she looked at the bushes in horror, taking a few careful steps away as she said, "That's *horrible*! Why are they even this close to town, then?"

"They're a nasty weed, and it isn't like we have time to root out every weed in the forest," Kanae chided, frowning. "Children are taught to look for dangers, and if they get too close to town, they're dealt with. As it is, once you know what to look for, they're pretty much harmless."

"I... I suppose," Isalla said, swallowing a hint of bile as she looked at the plants. She'd have died like the other woman if Kanae hadn't stopped her. "You said you would be able to get her remains, but *how*? Those are terrifying!"

"There's another plant that is highly toxic to the bushes. If it scents the plant on a creature, it won't target them," Kanae said, wrinkling her nose. "I have some of its sap in the lab, so I can heat that and smear it on my skin. It's unpleasant, but I'll be able to get to her body. For now, there's nothing to be done."

"Alright, if you say so," Isalla said, still in a bit of shock. She shivered, then asked, "Do you have any idea why she tried to kill me?"

"Nothing for certain, and I don't feel like guessing, not when we might be able to find evidence soon enough," Kanae replied and nodded back the way they'd come from. "Come on, let's go get that sap heating, and then we can see whether we need to guess or not."

Isalla nodded, taking a deep breath to help steady her nerves, then started back toward the house. "Okay. That seems reasonable. I'm just... it's been a crazy day."

"I know. If I could have made it easier, I would have, but I never expected that someone might try to kill you," Kanae said, and her eyes went cold as she added, "Considering that the caravan just got to town today, I suspect some pointed questions might be in order."

"That... is a very good point," Isalla agreed, shivering as she realized how much of a coincidence it had been. And at the same time, her blood chilled as well.

She really hoped they'd be able to figure out why the woman had come after her. As for Roselynn... her decision would have to wait for a little while.

# CHAPTER 26

*I*salla waited impatiently as Kanae washed, wanting to look over the things the woman who'd tried to kill her had carried, but also unwilling to do so without the demoness. The sap had smelled somewhat foul, Isalla admitted, but seeing the corpse of the woman had been sobering.

Hundreds of holes had pierced the clothing and skin of the woman, leaving her drained of virtually all fluid. Her skin had been drawn taut against the bones, and Isalla had felt queasy at the sight, as she wouldn't have known the figure was a woman if Kanae hadn't told her it was, and she hadn't heard the woman scream. She'd also seared the appearance of the vampire bushes into her mind, because Isalla really didn't want to run into them by accident.

The body had been left in the woods after Kanae had looked it over and determined that there wasn't much to identify it. Most of the clothing had also been abandoned, though Kanae had removed the leather armor which had survived mostly intact, even if enough thorns had gotten around it to render the armor useless.

All the items they'd taken were sitting on the table, and Isalla glanced over at them again, still stunned. The short sword and four daggers the woman had worn were all enchanted, mostly to keep their edges, and the sheaths bore enchantments that made it so a weapon could be drawn silently. Similarly, the composite bow was enchanted not to make a twang when fired, and it seemed to have a stronger draw than it should. The arrows in her quiver were a mix of enchanted ones and mundane arrows, while the armor was also enchanted to be silent and to resist damage more readily. Those were just the runes that Isalla knew, and additional ones that Kanae had picked out as well, it was entirely possible that more of the woman's gear was enchanted, and that was moderately terrifying to Isalla. Weak as the enchantments might be individually, they added up to an enormous value, and the question of why someone like that might be after her was concerning.

The sound of the bath door proved a welcome distraction, and Isalla turned to face the second door as Kanae stepped out, her hair glistening and damp. Kanae let out a sigh and smiled at Isalla as she spoke. "There we are. Sorry it took so long, but the sap is hard to get off."

"No, no... thank you. We wouldn't have been able to get her things if you hadn't known how to get to her, anyway," Isalla replied quickly and frowned. "I'm just a bit worried. A lot worried, really, considering how many enchanted weapons she had."

"I don't blame you. The weapons she has, and the enchantments they bear... I think they have all the indications of her being an assassin, and if that's the case, we've got more problems than I thought we had," Kanae said, frowning. "I don't know if you noticed, but she didn't leave much of a trail, either. I suspect she was using a spell to conceal it, and that's yet another clue."

"I hadn't, but it doesn't surprise me. If you're right... well, it doesn't bear thinking on," Isalla replied, shaking her head as she approached the table. A tiny part of her wondered if this might be Haral trying to ensure that Isalla had died. It was entirely possible that the woman had been able to use a divination to figure out that Isalla wasn't dead.

"Indeed. I had a few ideas while I was bathing, but I'd prefer to go through what we have before voicing them," Kanae said steadily, approaching the table and draping the towel over the chair to dry, then taking another seat. "Let's look this over, shall we?"

"Sure," Isalla agreed, taking another seat to go through the things, even though the only real thing of interest was the woman's belt pouch.

Kanae started going through the items calmly, starting with the pouch. There was mostly coin inside, along with an eating knife, a touchstone, a few ceramic pellets, and a folded note. Kanae opened it, looked the paper over, then handed it over wordlessly. Isalla flinched on seeing the description of her inside, including her name and a rough sketch of Isalla, along with mention of an unspecified reward. It didn't mention she was an angel, but what she was reading was quite bad enough. Meanwhile, Kanae went through the other items.

"This is bad. If they know my name, I figure they *have* to know I'm an angel, yet there's no mention of it here, or of the reward amount," Isalla said, biting her lip nervously.

"Almost certainly. I'm thinking that your old acquaintance, Haral, has a long reach," Kanae said calmly, her words causing Isalla to flinch. The demoness was examining one of the daggers and shook her head. "At a guess, the woman was from Hragon. All her gear is the same style I've seen from there over the years, so that isn't too surprising. As well-used as it is, she's probably experienced, too. In fact, I'm wondering..."

Isalla's head rose, dread rising inside her as Kanae's voice trailed off. It took a moment, but eventually she spoke, her voice soft. "Are you thinking that she might be behind Roselynn getting captured?"

"That's right. I see you had the same thought, though it doesn't make you happy," Kanae said, looking back at Isalla worriedly. "Influence like this isn't impossible, but the chances of it coming about without there being support in the highest echelons of the angelic hierarchy seem slim."

"You're right. Even if only half the high-ranking angels I knew of visiting were involved, that makes up one in twenty of the ruling class of the heavens," Isalla replied grimly, tapping her fingers against the table as she felt that sinking sensation in her stomach. "I could entirely see someone of that power deciding that it was worth sacrificing Roselynn and being able to do so. If they could reach *this* far, though…"

"It's concerning, yes," Kanae said, frowning heavily at the equipment on the table. She was silent for a long minute, then she shrugged. "Still, we wouldn't realize just how bad it was without the attack on you, so I suppose we should be thankful she made the attempt."

Blinking, Isalla opened her mouth, then shut it, considering carefully. Then she asked cautiously, "Are you not going to ask me to leave or something? There could be more people where she came from, and I don't want to put you in danger."

"I truly hope you don't think that little of me, Isalla," Kanae said, smiling widely, just widely enough that it revealed the demoness's fangs. "I took you in, and we need to figure things out further. It would be best if I went into town and asked around about your attacker; she almost had to have come with the caravan. The question is, have you decided what you're going to do about Roselynn?"

"Um, well… your ideas had merit, and if you're so certain that trying to recover her would end poorly, I was thinking there wasn't any choice but to try to rescue her when she leaves," Isalla admitted, a little thrown off by the change of subject. "I'd *like* to recover her before that, but if there isn't any other choice… well, I do hope she isn't as vulnerable as you suspect she was."

"I see. Well, I'm going to tell the townsfolk what happened, and explain that I'm going to escort you deeper into Estalia to find somewhere you'll be safe from assassins," Kanae said, smiling slightly more. "That should keep the town safer, and it's nothing more than the truth. Recovering Roselynn is likely to be tricky, but we're going to have to move quickly. The terrain between us and the spire is bad, so it will take us a couple of weeks to get there, at a minimum."

"Wait, really? And you're going to help?" Isalla asked, her dismal mood improving suddenly, and her heart leapt with joy as she smiled. "I didn't think you would."

"If you go on your own, your chances of success are miserable at best. At least I know how most of those who've been into the spire are likely to act, and between the two of us we have a decent chance of success. On your own... I'd feel deeply guilty if you ended up being taken into the tower," Kanae said and shivered slightly as she added, "As much as you might enjoy it in the end, that isn't a fate I'd like to see you suffer."

"I... well, I can agree with that. Thank you, Kanae. I wouldn't have expected you to do that," Isalla said, flushing slightly. The thought of Kanae meeting Roselynn confused her emotions, but after a moment she lowered her gaze.

"Don't mention it," Kanae replied gently, sliding her chair back as she stood, adjusting her robe. "I'd best get dressed so I can go into town."

Isalla stood as well, then paused, looking at the equipment for a moment before asking, "What are we going to do with all this?"

"Hm? Well, why don't you clean it, and if the armor fits, it might be worth keeping. That and anything else you'd like," Kanae said, glancing down at it. "It'd be a shame to waste enchanted items, after all. The rest... well, we can sell it in a larger town on our way to the spire. It might help throw them off our trail when we change routes."

"Alright," Isalla agreed, looking at the armor skeptically. Even if she didn't have qualms about wearing a dead woman's armor, she sincerely doubted it would fit, since the human had been a good deal more slender than Isalla was.

Still, she did need to clean it up, so Isalla reluctantly picked up the armor's pieces.

# CHAPTER 27

"*H*m, I think I want it a little tighter," Rose said, looking into the mirror. The corset she was wearing was slightly uncomfortable as it forced her to take somewhat shallower breaths, but at least that was a temporary thing. Her waist was much narrower than before, but she wasn't quite happy with how she looked.

Tina hesitated, then the succubus asked in concern, "Are you sure? Unlike most of the other changes you could make, this sort of transmutation is much, *much* harder to undo. I think you might be underestimating how much this would change you, Rose, since you're wearing the corset right now, and it adds addition bulk."

Rose blinked, then frowned. It was rare that Tina gave warnings like this, but she'd learned that the succubus was usually right. Tina had already kept Rose from making mistakes that would have been quite awkward to live with. As it was, she was glad that she hadn't made her chest grow quite as much as she'd originally intended.

"Are you sure?" Rose asked, running her fingers over the corset slowly. It was relatively ornate, as the gold sigils stood out from the blue velvet starkly. She hesitated, then continued. "I just thought my waist could do to be slightly narrower…"

"Much narrower and I'm worried that you'd snap in half.

You're not a small woman, Rose, and you can't safely have as narrow of a waist as Coral has," Tina explained, shaking her head. "It just isn't safe for you. Think about Anna, since she's closer to your height and figure."

Considering the other angel, Rose nodded reluctantly, ignoring the persistent, quiet voice which occasionally tried to object to everything she'd done, no matter how much she'd enjoyed her time here. "I suppose you have a point. I just thought that if the queen is coming, like you said she was…"

"Oh, Rose…" Tina smiled warmly, her voice gentle as she hugged Rose from behind, her chin barely able to go over the angel's shoulder. Rose patted her hand and smiled as the succubus continued. "Queen Estalia will like you *just* as you are, I promise. She would have loved you as you originally were, or she'd love you if you made yourself into a copy of Anna. Just make yourself happy, and that's more than enough for her, alright?"

"If you say so," Rose agreed, running her fingers over the fabric of the corset once more. She wasn't wearing much more than her underthings and a skirt to make the project easier, and a tiny part of her still worried about being with a succubus in so little clothing, though she'd long since realized the woman wouldn't touch her that way, not without an invitation. Taking a breath, though it wasn't too deep due to the corset, she nodded and asked, "Do it, please?"

Smiling, Tina pulled away and reached down to touch the back of the corset. If Rose had more skill with magic, she would've been confident doing this herself, but she didn't, so Tina was helping her. Which, in all honesty, was likely for the best.

There was a tingle from the corset's magic, and Rose forced down the impulse to resist the effect, since she didn't want to ruin it. As the magic took effect, she felt her bones almost pop as they reshaped, while her entire waist slowly lost that tight sensation, feeling instead almost normal. Rose could finally take deep breaths again, and she inhaled as she felt the magic come to an end.

"I think it's done," Rose said, looking down and frowning. "I don't feel like I'm being squeezed, at least."

"Then it's done," Tina agreed, her hands going to the corset's laces. "Let's get this off you and see how you like the results."

Rose nodded, and held her arms out so that the succubus would have an easier time removing the corset once she was done. It took a little time, but at last the corset parted enough and Tina began sliding it off. The absence caused Rose to sigh softly, but not quite soft enough as Tina paused.

"Is something wrong? I think the enchantment worked perfectly, but if it didn't, we can see about getting it fixed," Tina said, sounding concerned.

Rose's waist was much narrower than it had been, but the skin was smooth and perfectly formed, while the divot of her navel was eye-catching. A tiny part of Rose liked the idea of a piercing with a gem down there, like she'd seen Tina wearing, but she hadn't quite decided one way or another yet. She flushed as she looked to the side, away from the mirror.

"No, no… that's not it at all," Rose reassured her. "It's just…"

Tina waited for a long moment, then asked gently, "Just what, Rose? You can tell me; I promise I won't laugh or criticize you."

"Well, I just find a corset oddly comfortable," Rose replied, resisting the urge to squirm. "Not when it's tightened, but when it just… fits. It helps me stand up properly, and it also feels just more… secure. Almost like armor, I guess."

"Really?" Tina said, her eyebrows rising. "That's interesting."

"Is it? I just feel that it's a little strange," Rose admitted, looking to the side toward the closet full of dresses, most of which wouldn't fit right anymore.

"Mm, I don't think so. If it makes you comfortable, that's just the way it is," Tina said, her voice calm. "I'll let Anna know, and maybe we can find you one that fits properly and that you'd enjoy wearing more. How does that sound?"

"That sounds wonderful," Rose replied, smiling warmly in return. "Thank you, Tina."

"You're most welcome. Now, I'm going to take this back to storage, and I'll be back soon. Why don't you find what you'd like to wear, and we can get it resized for you, hm?" Tina said, holding the corset.

"I can do that," Rose said happily. "I'll see you in a bit."

"Of course," Tina said, reaching out and squeezing Rose's shoulder gently, then turned and headed for the door.

For her part, Rose turned to the closet. Finding something that suited her wouldn't be too hard, though the fit *was* a concern. At least Anna had a few enchanted items to help resize clothing.

~

ANNA CURTSEYED DEEPLY, lowering her head as she smiled and spoke, happiness rushing through her. "Welcome back, Milady! It's been too long since your last visit."

"Rise, Anna. There's no need for formalities, not between you and I," Queen Estalia replied, her warm voice sending a thrill of pleasure through Anna, the intimacy within impossible to fully describe. "Alas, I must keep my visits few and far between, else others realize just how much I value your work here."

Rising, Anna smiled in return as she met the gaze of her beloved goddess, a gaze which few could meet as easily as she could. Even so, it sent a shiver down her spine, and Anna felt her mood improving still more.

"I'm glad to hear that you value us so much, Milady... many think we're less than we are, and don't give us much respect," Anna replied simply. "Still, no one will be surprised that you came out, not if they've heard just who was brought here."

"Oh, they've heard. Believe me, they've *all* heard by this point," Estalia said, letting out a faintly exasperated sigh as she stepped forward and reached up to embrace Anna.

Anna leaned down into the queen's embrace, gently kissing her goddess deeply and with unmasked passion. No one could compare to Estalia in her mind, and she was looking forward to seeing Rose's reaction to meeting Estalia. After a few long moments, she broke the kiss reluctantly and asked, "Oh?"

"Someone got word up in Hragon, and magic was employed to share the information. I do believe that every noble in the capital had word of the Flame of Ember's capture before the word reached the bottom of Hellmount," Estalia explained, still holding Anna, who felt happier with every passing moment. "I've received at least fifty inquiries asking if she'll become a courtesan so far, along with others asking if she'll have broken entirely and be available for purchase. Such *rude* inquiries, don't you think?"

"Very," Anna said, frowning in displeasure at the descriptions, though they only slightly dampened her mood at seeing Estalia again. "I don't know why they think that we in the spire only train courtesans. We help those who come here find their true desires and show them your glory. It's a trifle frustrating that so many misinterpret our purpose."

"I know it is, but if they knew how important you truly were, they'd stop at nothing to acquire you and your brothers and sisters here, Anna. I'd far rather they not understand you than that come to pass," Estalia said, smiling and letting go at last. "That said… how *is* the Glorious Flame doing?"

"Roselynn, who enjoys going by Rose, is coming along very well," Anna said, her mood improving slightly as she straightened. "Alas, she was heavily abused by the Heavenly Host, and was in a similar state to my own when you found me, Milady."

Estalia winced visibly at that, her voice ever so slightly plaintive. "That bad? Why is it that they tend to abuse those who're their greatest support, I wonder… well, no matter. That does mean she's likely adapting nicely, since you can understand where she's coming from."

"To some extent, but I've noticed that she still has the tiniest bit of resistance and doubt about everything," Anna replied, shaking her head. "It's going to take a delicate touch to remove that, I think. As to what she plans… that I don't know. She's a different person than I am, even if we are similar in some ways."

"Ah, interesting. However, even you had your doubts, Anna," Estalia murmured, shaking her head. "You came around in the end, though."

"I also changed my name to something more innocuous. Otherwise we'd still have angelic *rescuers* showing up," Anna pointed out dryly. "I think your intervention is the most likely method to help her, however."

"We'll see what I can do," Estalia agreed, her smile warming Anna's heart. "Now, before we do that, what of Ember and her armor?"

"This way, Milady," Anna said, gesturing to a nearby door. She'd known her goddess would want to examine both before taking them back to the capital with her, so she'd had them on hand.

Estalia followed her into the room, and she murmured softly, "Magnificent. It's unfortunate I didn't see her in this before... but there's still time."

The armor was an intricate suit of mithral plate which would've hugged the figure of the wearer without being too form-fitting. Anna had seen many angels who wore armor that was more decorative than functional, relying on magic to help defend themselves, but this suit formed a good balance between practicality and appearance. The emblem of a golden phoenix was emblazoned across the chest of the armor, and other gold, orange, and red adornments added to the armor's beauty. It was heavily enchanted, Anna knew, and she admired it as well.

Beside the armor was a sword in its sheath, one which could easily be wielded one- or two-handed. The sheath was red leather with gold reinforcements and had flame-like gold patterns across the surface, while the elegant hilt was wrapped in red leather and had a ruby in the pommel. It was a beautiful weapon, and Anna could feel the powerful magic rippling off it.

"While I agree there, I'm afraid the armor wouldn't fit Rose anymore," Anna said, reaching out and laying a hand on the armor gently. "She's adjusted her figure a fair amount, and it would be too tight across the chest, and too loose around the waist."

"Is that so? Well, at least the armor can be adjusted," Estalia murmured, smiling and running a finger across it slowly. "I've a few other ideas, but they'll have to wait until after I've met Rose. I'm curious to see what she'll do in the end... there are a great many possibilities."

"I take it you want to see her now, then?" Anna asked, growing more amused.

"That's right," Estalia said, her smile widening.

"I'll show you where her rooms are, then," Anna said, opening the door again. She paused, then asked, "Do you mind if I watch via scrying mirror? I do love seeing the expression on someone's face when they first meet you."

Estalia's laughter was music to Anna's ears, and the angel smiled as the queen replied, her tone teasing. "You *do* have odd ideas of enjoyment, Anna, but go ahead. I'm not going to object to something like that. Be nice though, hm? I don't want you using it against her."

"I won't, it's just for my personal enjoyment," Anna said, smiling even more.

Estalia nodded slightly, looking perfectly relaxed, yet eager as well.

Anna led the way to Rose's rooms, unable to keep the grin from her face. This would be entertaining.

# CHAPTER 28

*R*ose raised her gaze as she heard her door open and smiled, adjusting her clothing. She'd found a green top and a skirt which fit well, and she liked how they matched her eyes. "Back already, Tina? I think I found an outfit that fits, and which looks good as well."

"I'm afraid that I'm not Tina, but I must agree that it looks good on you."

The voice that replied was higher pitched but had a hint of a purr to it at the same time, while having an ethereal quality to it that sent a thrill up Rose's spine. It also wasn't a voice she'd heard before, and Rose spun around, opening her mouth to speak, but on seeing the speaker she forgot how to breathe.

There was a woman standing in the doorway, but calling her a woman was such a pale word for her that Rose hated that she couldn't think of a better one. Calling her a vision of perfection would be a better term.

The woman wasn't tall, standing barely over five and a half feet, and she had a heart-shaped, beautiful face with features better than any sculptor could carve. She had a petite but full figure that felt like utter perfection to watch as she moved, and Rose's eyes were drawn to the clothing she wore. The bodice was more a couple of lengths of glittering royal blue fabric attached to a collar of sapphires and mithral, almost a halter top, while she wore a similar sarong topped by a belt from which hung a beautifully crafted rapier in its sheath. Mithral and blue leather sandals adorned her feet, and matching earrings dangled from her ears, each of them pointed almost like an elf's, but closer to horizontal than an elf's might be. She had midnight blue hair that was long and straight, held back in a single ponytail behind her head by a mithral clasp, and it fell to her ankles.

Her skin was a pale blue, almost as brilliant as the sapphires in her jewelry, and a luminous glow radiated from beneath it, making her shine like a star in the room, from the tips of her fingers or toes to the end of her tail, while her bat-like wings shone more like a deeper blue velvet. There was even a mithral and diamond piercing in her navel that glowed brightly, drawing the eye. Delicate horns rose only a few inches from her brow, swept back and shimmering like jewels themselves in the light, almost touching the crown floating above her head, itself a circle with five equally spaced points and accompanying inset sapphires. But it was her eyes that caught Rose's gaze and held it. The woman's deep blue eyes felt enormous, and it was like they could swallow Rose entirely, as though she was ignoring everything else in the world and was *only* paying attention to Rose. Looking into her eyes, at such a vision of beauty, Rose couldn't help but yearn for the woman, as a part of her heart she'd thought locked away began to wake, and the voice of caution in her mind weakened.

Rose's lungs almost felt like they were burning, and it took a few moments before she remembered to breathe again, exhaling suddenly, then drawing a breath and gasping. "W-who...?"

"Who am I? I'm Estalia," the woman replied gently, still focused on Rose as she stepped into the room. "The realm you're in bears my name, and Anna and the others here are among my most trusted friends. Have they been treating you well?"

"Yes, of course they have, but... but you're the queen?" Rose began, floundering under that all-consuming gaze. "I thought you'd be... be..."

"Yes, I'm queen of these lands, Rose... may I call you that? Anna said you preferred it," Estalia said, approaching at a slow, almost delicate pace as she smiled warmly, a smile that could have melted a heart of stone. "Still, you are not one of my subjects, so you need not speak to me as such. Unless you wish to be one of my subjects, but even so, it would be a shame to have one so beautiful be formal with me."

"Of course you may," Rose replied, flushing bright red under the demon queen's regard, and feeling some of her panic ease. "I just… I expected more formality to your visit. I didn't expect you here, not now."

"Formality is good for keeping your distance, but that isn't what I want. I want to get to know *you*, Rose, not the legendary Flame of Ember," Estalia said, the sincerity in her voice soothing beyond measure, and Rose felt herself relaxing still more, blushing at the idea that such a beautiful woman wanted to get to know her. Estalia offered her arm and asked, "Would you walk with me? I'd enjoy your company."

"I… I suppose so. I'm just…" Rose paused, then slipped her hand through Estalia's arm and followed her sedate pace toward the door. Finally, she managed to continue. "I'm just startled, I suppose. I thought you'd be more distant, or maybe even cruel. I had my doubts about that, as kind as Anna and the others have been, but my background…"

"Cruelty and distance can be useful tools for some things, but those who wield them drive others away," Estalia said, her voice almost sad as she pushed the door open, holding it for Rose and stepping out, looking at Rose as she spoke sincerely. "If one wishes for true allies and friends, they must take other approaches. I have chosen to take those paths, and thus my realm is different. Not as different as I'd like, but the hells are a dangerous place. Some days there is no path to avoid conflict, and still other times it is necessary to fight."

"I see. That sounds accurate… and I think some angels could learn from you," Rose murmured, thinking back to the many situations which she thought could have been solved with a little kindness or sympathy from those in more powerful positions. No matter what, she couldn't quite pull her attention away from Estalia, though, and the woman continued down the hall sedately.

"Perhaps so. However, with that in mind, how has your time here been? I do hope it's been restful for you, Rose," Estalia asked, trailing a couple of fingers over Rose's arm, sending a thrill of happiness through her, and Rose felt her heartbeat quickening.

"It's been wonderful. I never realized just how tired I was getting, and how much I wanted to just *rest*. Anna has been amazing at helping me come to terms with everything, while Coral and Tina have been lovely at showing me how to use the magical tools here," Rose said, then flushed as she realized something, and cleared her throat before continuing. "I suppose I should thank *you* for this, though. If it weren't for you, I wouldn't have had the chance to rest or to meet them to begin with."

"You're most welcome, Rose. It's the least I can do for you," Estalia replied, her smile warming Rose's heart still more.

Rose didn't know what else to say, and they were just passing the doors that Rose knew went to the baths when Estalia spoke again. This time her voice had a bit more concern to it. "Rose... Anna sent me word that you'd been separated from an old lover of yours, a younger angel named Isalla. She vanished, and you were concerned about her, is that correct?"

"That's right," Rose agreed, her mood darkening at the reminder of her missing friend. "I was trying to gather information about what might have happened to her when I was ambushed, I think. My memory is fuzzy, unfortunately. I worry about her immensely, as I never told her how I really felt."

"I understand, Rose, truly. My daughter has been missing for years, and I worry for her even now," Estalia quickly assured Rose, her gaze helping ease the angel's unhappiness. "I was asking because I've received information that *may* be about your Isalla."

"Really?" Rose asked, her eyes brightening again. "What sort of information?"

"It isn't anything certain, I'll warn, and the reason I've heard word isn't good," Estalia said, but she was smiling as she said it, warming Rose's heart again. "Apparently a bounty was presented to Hragon's Assassin Guild, one for a blonde woman with delicate features and who is named Isalla. I've gathered a few more details that claim that she's an angelic spy who lost her wings, but no more than that."

"She's lost her wings?" Rose asked, her stomach clenching hard at the thought, bile rising in her throat as well. "And she has a bounty on her head? It... it sounds like her, even if it isn't much of a description, but—"

"Calmly, Rose, calmly," Estalia quickly said, reaching up to place a warm finger against Rose's lips to silence her. "They've put a bounty on her head, but that means she's *alive*. The assassins have also come into the hells, which means that they believe that she's in Estalia or one of its neighbors. No matter what information they might have, their ability to gather information here cannot match mine."

"But..." Rose began, only to fall silent as Estalia smiled warmly, taking Rose's breath away as she spoke.

"I'll find her, Rose. I'll find your Isalla, and the magic available to my priesthood is more than enough to heal her of any harm that has been inflicted upon her," Estalia said gently, her mesmerizing gaze meeting Rose's own. "I promise to rescue her, even from the gates of death itself. Then, once that is done... you can choose, whether to leave or to stay here in Estalia. You have my word."

The promise took Rose's breath away, because the sincerity in Estalia's voice was impossible for her to doubt. For a long moment, Rose couldn't reply and couldn't think. And then she felt the hot tears begin to spill down her cheeks as she murmured, "Thank you... thank you *so* much."

"You're welcome, Rose," Estalia replied, her voice gentle and her smile warm.

Then, ever so slowly, Estalia drew Rose downward toward her. Warm, silky lips met Rose's, and the angel melted into the gentle, passionate kiss. All thought slowly melted away, and as it did, the tiny, resistant voice went quiet for the first time in weeks.

Rose didn't care, though, instead wrapping her arms and wings around Estalia.

~

SHE WAS warm and comfortable when she woke, and Rose couldn't remember the last time she was so relaxed. She'd slept deeply, and she couldn't remember any dreams. It was so peaceful, and she didn't really want to get up.

It took a minute before she realized just why she was so warm, though, and the realization that something soft and warm was behind her, and another was in front of her made Rose start emerging from the depths of her slumber. She stirred and slowly let her eyes crack open, confused as she realized that her bedroom was illuminated by an additional soft radiance rather than the usual dim red light. That was unusual, and she blinked as she began sitting up, then looked down at the soft murmur of protest, freezing in place.

Cradled in her arms was Estalia, her hair like a dark wave over her luminous body, and her naked figure was breathtaking. More startling was how the succubus queen slowly opened her eyes and looked up at Rose, blinking slowly as she did so.

"Mm... awake already?" Anna's voice came from behind Rose, and it was only then that Rose realized that the other angel's arms and wings were wrapped around her and Estalia like a comfortable cocoon.

"I... I just woke up..." Rose said, her pulse quickening, and Estalia smiled warmly, meeting Rose's gaze.

"Is that so? Did you want to get up, or..." Estalia began, and leaned up to give Rose a long, deep kiss, a hand running down her side gently before she broke it off and asked, her voice breathy, "Or would you like more time together?"

The warm kiss and touch against her brought back Rose's memories of how things had developed the previous night, and she blushed slowly as she remembered them. The idea of what had happened... well, it would have mortified her even a week before. Even now it was embarrassing, but that was alright. Estalia and Anna had both accepted Rose as she was and wouldn't criticize her.

"More time, please," Rose said shyly.

Estalia laughed, her voice music in the angel's ears, and then she kissed Rose again, pulling her close. It was somewhat astounding to Rose how strong Estalia was, considering her size.

～

"WILL I SEE YOU AGAIN?" Rose asked, managing not to blush as she asked the question, despite how desperately she hoped that the answer was yes.

"Not here, I'm afraid," Estalia said gently, adjusting her belt as she looked at Rose with a smile that improved the angel's mood and blunted her disappointment, then continued. "If I travel here too often, it will make others wonder what is so important here, and it might draw undue attention down on everyone."

"I see. I wouldn't want that to happen, even if I'd love to see you again," Rose agreed, looking to the side as her cheeks warmed. She couldn't say just how much she'd enjoyed the previous night, and it was terribly embarrassing.

"I never said we wouldn't meet. I said we couldn't meet *here*, Rose," Estalia corrected her, drawing Rose's gaze back to hers again as she smiled.

"Really?" Rose asked, her heartbeat quickening. "When, then?"

"Once Anna and the others are sure that you've fully recovered, you can come meet me in the capital," Estalia said, smiling. "I'll be taking your armor to have it refitted to fit your new figure, and you'll have an escort to make it safely. Then you'll be able to decide what you want to do."

Rose's hopes surged, then were checked as she frowned and shook her head. "I... I don't know that I want to have my armor back. Fighting... I'm just so *tired* of that, especially after getting to know you, Coral, and Tina. It's been so restful here, and I'm not sure I want to go back to that."

"If that's what you decide, so be it. However, remember what I said, Rose. Sometimes conflict can't be avoided, and sometimes it's necessary. Better to have weapons and armor should it be necessary than not to be able to defend yourself or those you love," Estalia replied, smiling as she gestured to the rapier at her side. "I do the same, after all. As to your choices, though… if you choose to rejoin the heavens, that's one choice, or you could choose to remain here with me, or to try something else. Regardless, I promised to find your Isalla, and I'll do so."

"Thank you, Estalia. I can't say how much that means to me," Rose replied, tears forming in her eyes, and she brushed them away quickly, sniffling. "And… I'll think about what I want, I promise. Now, before I start to cry… I'll see you again. Hopefully soon."

"Of course. I'll see you soon, Rose," Estalia agreed, and she rose on the tips of her toes to give Rose a brief, passionate kiss. Then, leaving the taste of her lips on Rose's, she turned to leave.

Rose watched the door close behind Estalia, and her hand slowly rose to her lips. As she tried to fix the memory of the queen in her mind, Rose began to cry. She'd spent less than a day with the demon queen, yet why did she feel so *hollow* with her gone?

She never noticed how that voice of caution that she'd had before had vanished entirely.

~

"I'M ALWAYS amazed at how easily you can put others at ease, Milady," Anna said, admiration in her tone as she glanced toward the scrying mirror, where Rose was slowly dancing with a blue dress. "Even if your power assists you, you're truly skilled."

Anna's goddess was putting on her armor, a suit of plate that glittered like sapphires and diamonds, ranging between dark and light blues and with intricate silver runes and patterns carved into its surface. Estalia looked up from a greave and smiled in return.

"That's because far too many people underestimate how much good a little sincerity can do," Estalia replied gently, nodding to the mirror. "I didn't lie to Rose. I had no need to do so, after all. I believe the chances of her returning to the heavens are about as close to nonexistent as can be, especially if I find Isalla."

"That was true, then? I'm startled by the idea of a bounty being put on the head of an angel, or that one could survive in the hells without protection," Anna said, her smile fading slightly. "If she has, she might not be in the best situation."

"I'm well aware of that, but I did not lie. I will find her if it's possible, and if she's been injured in such a way... well, I will send her to you to be healed," Estalia said, her smile fading slightly and her gaze hardening. "I am beginning to worry about the motives of those who sent Rose here, but shall bide my time. Should they overstep themselves, though..."

"If they attempt to violate the sanctity of the spire, they will not succeed. On *that* you have my word, Milady," Anna replied, her voice turning steely as her back straightened. "And should that come to pass, I will bring them to Your Light. Then they will tell us everything."

"Of course they won't succeed. You're here," Estalia said simply, standing again and smiling warmly at Anna. "You're the only reason I can trust that the spire will hold, my dear, and I cannot thank you enough for what you do."

"As you say, Milady," Anna said, leaning down to exchange kisses with her goddess again, warmth flooding her at Estalia's reassurance. As she pulled away, she smiled broadly and added, "I believe that Rose will be ready in no more than three weeks."

"Excellent. That will give plenty of time for not only her armor to be adjusted, but for a new suit to be forged, one more appropriate for her if she joins us," Estalia said, smiling warmly. "I think I have an idea in mind. She truly *has* chosen a beautiful form, hasn't she?"

Anna nodded in agreement, then curtseyed deeply. "We are glad for your visit, Milady, and I wish you safe travels back to the palace."

"Thank you, dear," Estalia replied gently, and then she turned to leave.

Anna sighed as she did so, as Estalia's departure left the spire feeling, as always, just a little bit darker and colder.

# CHAPTER 29

"*A*re you sure you're going to leave for a while, lovely Kanae? We could always just not tell any other visitors about your guest, or could tell them that you're gone," Manog said, sounding quite anxious as he looked around the room. "With you gone, we're not going to be nearly as comfortable. What if someone gets hurt? We *need* you!"

"That's why I've been teaching you the basics for years," Kanae replied calmly, stirring the pot of soup. "I've told you plenty of times that I'm not going to be here forever. Yes, I've settled down for several centuries, but you can't count on that being the case forever."

"The woman who attacked Isalla is dead, though," Manog protested weakly, pacing back and forth quickly. "Sure, the other human who was with her vanished, but that doesn't mean that he knew what she was up to."

"And I'm an archangel in disguise," Kanae replied tartly, looking up at Manog, putting a hand on her hip as she scowled at him. "You know as well as I do that him vanishing makes it all but certain that he's involved, especially since the caravan master said the two of them joined together. I'm not going to risk Isalla's safety so readily, not right now."

"She'll be back in a few weeks anyway, right?" Isalla chimed in, feeling a little uncomfortable about the situation. She hated to take away the town's healer, but she didn't trust that she could make her way across Estalia safely on her own, not yet. Besides, she didn't want to be separated from Kanae. "It isn't like she's going to be gone for good."

"True, but it still makes me worried. Our incredible Kanae of many charms has been a staple of the region for decades, and everyone will worry if she leaves," Manog replied, sounding a little calmer. "My reaction is a mild one, not like those of so many others."

"They'll just have to live with it," Kanae said, stirring the soup again, and Isalla saw her tail give a slightly annoyed-looking lash. "I've spent longer elsewhere in my life than I have here. Perhaps not longer in one place, but I've never made a secret of the fact I've chosen to settle down here temporarily."

"Five centuries is temporary?" Isalla muttered under her breath, but neither of them seemed to notice. It was just as well, since she felt guilty as soon as she'd spoken.

"Very well. I see that I'm going to have to acquiesce to the reality of our situation," Manog admitted, sighing before he asked, "May I at least know when you expect to leave?"

"Tomorrow morning," Kanae said, and Manog stopped dead in place, looking stunned, but Kanae didn't pause as she continued calmly. "That being the case, we need to pack once dinner is done, so I'd appreciate some privacy."

"If... if you say so, Kanae. I will bid you good eve, and hope to see you on the morrow," Manog replied, bowing deeply, then headed for the door. Isalla's sense of guilt grew stronger as she watched him go. Kanae's explanation had obviously shocked the man.

Once Manog was through the door, Kanae spoke again. "Would you mind locking the door, Isalla?"

"Sure," Isalla replied, levering herself out of the chair and walking over to the door to lock it. She hesitated for a moment, then asked cautiously, "Did you have to be so harsh with him? Aren't you coming back?"

"Most likely, but I only told him the truth," Kanae said, sighing and shaking her head as she looked up at Isalla. "What we're doing is dangerous, Isalla. If we're caught, I *won't* be back.

Yes, the attack on you means that we had less of a choice in what to do than we would have otherwise, but…"

The demoness tapped her spoon on the edge of the pot to mostly drain it, then set it aside, shaking her head, and a thread of worry made its way through Isalla as she saw the concern on Kanae's face. The look was so rare that it just… startled her. And made her worry.

"I told you I was taught in the Spire of Confession before," Kanae said at last, breathing out slowly. "What worries me most is that we might encounter one of those who taught me. There were several of them, and I doubt they've passed on, no matter how long it has been. If they are there, I'll be in danger. No, I'll *be* the danger, Isalla, because they'll likely be able to influence me."

"Oh," Isalla said, swallowing hard as she frowned in worry. She hesitated for several long moments before walking over to Kanae, asking in concern, "Is it really that dangerous for you?"

"Probably not. I intend to take measures, but if we do, if they recognize me… it will cause problems," Kanae said, looking Isalla in the eyes seriously. "We'll have little choice but to rush at that point. They'll come for me, Isalla, I have no doubt about that. If that happens, we'll come here, yes, but we'll have to rush to get you up Hellmount to have any hope of you escaping."

Blinking, Isalla frowned deeply, then asked. "Kanae? You seem awfully certain about their reactions, and it makes me wonder *why*. It's been more than a millennium, hasn't it? Why would they remember you?"

Kanae hesitated, and the angel could practically see her struggling to decide what to say. A moment later, Isalla felt a rush of guilt, and added gently, "You don't have to tell me, Kanae. I can see you're struggling, and—"

"Wait," Kanae interrupted, cutting Isalla off. Isalla fell silent and saw Kanae place her hands on the counter for a long moment. Finally, the demoness spoke. "I'm going to tell you, but not now. Not everything, anyway. I'm far more important than I made out, or *was* more important, at any rate. I've changed my appearance and name to avoid being found, and I've not even spoken my original name in centuries for fear that they'd track me down magically. You may not remember, but have you ever wondered how I rescued you from your fall? If you'd hit the ground, it would have killed you instantly."

"I..." Isalla paused, blinking in surprise as her thoughts raced, speculating on who Kanae might be. Kanae being more important than a common soldier made a certain amount of sense, but her question dredged up a few memories of Isalla's descent. They were fuzzy, and she'd begun to think she'd imagined them. After a moment, Isalla spoke cautiously. "I vaguely remember just... *stopping*. I thought I might have been hallucinating, since I haven't seen you do anything similar, but I thought I saw you using magic. It could've been a magic item, I suppose, but..."

"That would make sense, wouldn't it? It was the excuse I had in mind, actually. That this ring was enchanted," Kanae said, smiling and showing a silver ring on the middle finger of her right hand, then continued. "No, I'm a mage. I'm out of practice, having not used magic much over the years, but I'm primarily skilled in personal defense magic and telekinesis. That's how I stopped you from hitting the ground."

"Oh, I see," Isalla said, relaxing slightly as she nodded, feeling happier that Kanae trusted her as much as she obviously did. She considered, then frowned. "Why would that be important, though? There are plenty of magi on both sides of the war."

"It's just an example of how wary I was, Isalla. I'm not going to tell you who I truly am unless they recognize me, or until you're about to leave the hells. It's just too much of a risk, in my mind," Kanae said and smiled thinly as she added. "I may be a touch paranoid about this, but it's because I don't want to bring down a disaster on our heads."

Isalla looked at her for a long moment, blinking. She racked her brain, trying to figure out why Kanae would be that worried about being discovered, but she couldn't quite understand it. She didn't think Kanae was an archdemon, and the idea of her being an older general flitted through her mind, but even that didn't quite explain it. But in the end, she nodded slowly, deciding to trust that Kanae knew what she was doing.

"Alright, Kanae. I don't quite get why, but I understand,"

Isalla said, nodding, then smiled as she added, "I'll hold you to explaining later, though."

"I'm sure you will. Now, let's get some food and pack," Kanae said, her tone turning brisk. "It's a long trip to the spire, and we're not going to be taking the most direct route, since neither of us can fly."

Isalla laughed and nodded, then headed to the cabinet to pull out a pair of bowls. At least it *did* feel like Kanae was starting to trust her.

She just wished the woman hadn't piqued her curiosity. Now she was going to be speculating for the entire trip, and Kanae had already been an enormous distraction.

# CHAPTER 30

*T*hey set out early the next morning, just as Kanae had said they would. Isalla had woken up to see Kanae methodically strapping on her armor, checking how each piece fit before moving to the next, an odd look of concentration on her face. It had been fascinating, and Isalla had watched from the bed as Kanae slowly prepared for the trip, transforming from the brisk doctor who lived in the outskirts to a trained warrior. Watching her, Isalla quickly realized that she didn't doubt that Kanae was more important than she pretended to be, not when she looked like that. It also made Isalla even more confident about following Kanae's guidance.

Eventually, Isalla had dragged herself out of bed to get ready, which hadn't taken her nearly as long, since she didn't have armor like Kanae did, and she'd packed most of her things the night before. It was slightly disappointing, but not so much that Isalla couldn't deal with it. Instead, she put on the new cloak and hat Kanae had gotten for her the previous day, and in short order she was ready to go.

"Do you think it'll be safe to leave my armor and sword hidden?" Isalla asked, glancing at the floor in the corner. The previous night she'd been shown the hidden compartment where Kanae had hidden her equipment. She'd been told there was a password to be spoken before opening it, but she was still nervous about leaving her gear behind.

"Yes. If they don't know the password, it'll set off a minor ice spray trap, which will make them think that's the enchantment, and they'll open it to find a lockbox with a modest amount of money in it," Kanae said, smiling slightly as she adjusted her cloak. "Your armor is in a folded space, along with a few more valuable items, so it'll be fine."

"Ah, that helps," Isalla said, letting out a breath of relief. She knew the password already, so if necessary, she could get in without Kanae, which reassured her.

"Indeed. If anyone manages to break in, I'll be surprised. I spent a *lot* of money hiring magi to ward the house, and more time adding my own additions," Kanae said, rolling her shoulders, then nodded firmly. "There. Time to go. You have your key?"

"I do," Isalla said, feeling like a few butterflies had taken up residence in her midsection. As much as she wanted to find Roselynn, she was nervous about going out into the hells. The world down here was just so dark that she always felt out of sorts. Sure, rain was rather common in the heavens, making it even odds about whether they'd have sunlight on a given day, but at least it was usually brighter. Only Kanae's company reassured Isalla.

Kanae headed for the door, interrupting Isalla's thoughts, and the woman paused by the kitchen hearth, murmuring a word to extinguish the magical flame there. Isalla briefly wondered how well the food they were leaving behind would hold up, but since most of it was jarred, she didn't think it would spoil quickly. Instead, Kanae took the wrapped food she'd prepared for their trip from the table and headed for the door, opening it cautiously, then letting Isalla out. When she locked the door, the click felt oddly final, which sent a shiver down Isalla's spine.

"There we are," Kanae murmured, putting the key away and taking a breath, then smiling. "Now it's time to go. We're going to skirt around the town, Isalla, which could cause us to encounter something predatory, but it isn't likely."

Isalla blinked, then asked, "Why avoid the town? I thought that you might say goodbye to Manog. He said he wanted to see you today before we left."

Kanae started toward the trail, and Isalla followed quickly. Kanae's pace wasn't quick, but it wasn't slow, either. It was the sort of pace that was ideal for long distances, Isalla thought, though she had to smile at the sight of Kanae's tail swaying in its own segmented armor. After a moment the demoness spoke, her tone slightly disapproving.

"Yes, he did. And if I thought it would lead to a good result, I'd visit town," Kanae said, her head turning from side to side to keep watch. "The thing is, if we go there, he'll have gathered other people to plead with us to stay, to ask us to do something for them when we leave, or even for us to escort Brialla to the capital, since that's where they think we're going. We'd be lucky to get out of town before noon, and with what we're going to be doing it just isn't a good idea to let them interfere."

"Oh. You know them better than I do, but… you're probably right," Isalla admitted, frowning as she thought about the townsfolk. They were mostly good people, but at the same time, they were people. She knew enough of them from the heavens to know that if you gave too much, some people would take advantage of you. It was sad but true. So she sighed and shook her head. "I do feel bad for Brialla, though."

"She'll be fine. If they want to take her to the capital to join the queen's priesthood, they can pay the minor amount the caravan would charge to take her there," Kanae replied absently. "It really isn't that much, and we're not going there, so—"

Isalla caught a flicker of movement from their right, and she quickly jumped back, her hand going to her sword. She had her blade halfway out when Kanae's sword cleared its sheath and there was the sound of a blade hitting meat. Isalla blinked as she held her sword, looking at the writhing lower body of a snake nearly five feet long, the head having been cut clean off.

"Good job, Isalla. You're fast enough you could've killed it before it hit you," Kanae said approvingly, smiling as she cleaned the blood from her sword and sheathed it.

"Thanks, but I'm still not as fast as you," Isalla replied,

sheathing her sword again and shaking her head. She was a little depressed about how much better Kanae was, but the compliment did improve her mood.

"Yet. You're not as fast as me *yet*," Kanae replied, a hint of laughter in her voice. "Never say never, and all that."

"True enough," Isalla admitted, the correction bringing a smile to her face. Kanae was supportive, that was for certain. She couldn't imagine how much practice the woman had put in, but at least she thought Isalla could catch up with her eventually.

~

THOMAS LET OUT his breath slowly, hiding behind the tree as the patrol of demons passed. They weren't terribly strong as far as he could tell, and he'd likely be able to kill them without trouble if he tried, but that would risk giving away his location. It was fortunate that he'd been able to learn that Samantha had been killed the previous night, as it'd given him time to get out of the immediate area.

"I can't believe she was caught. That angel must be stronger than any of our leads suggested," Thomas murmured, his voice barely audible to himself, let alone the guards as they ambled along toward the town again.

He was a little frustrated at the thought of Samantha dying, but despite that, Thomas wasn't about to lose his cool. While he'd liked Samantha pretty well, he'd never had illusions of true trust where she was concerned. Each of them looked out for themselves, and while he'd take the chance at vengeance if it fell into his lap, he also wouldn't put himself in danger for her memory.

For now, he just had to get back to report in on Isalla's whereabouts. Sure, she'd likely move soon, but Thomas considered fifty gold to be better than nothing. He valued his life more highly than the reward the employer was offering.

Once the demons were far enough away, Thomas allowed himself to breathe more easily and started toward Hellmount, glancing up at the huge mountain as he moved through the trees. The mountain was truly immense, and he wasn't looking forward to climbing it, but it wasn't as though he had another choice.

"Don't worry, Smiles... I'm sure one of the others will manage to get her for you. For now, it'll just have to wait, though," Thomas murmured, and he settled in for the long trip.

As dangerous as the trip up the mountain might be, Thomas was confident he could get past the creatures living on Hellmount without too much trouble, especially since he'd kept close attention to the route they'd taken on the way down. The monsters might be bolder, but he was skilled enough as it was.

# CHAPTER 31

$\mathcal{I}$salla slipped back so the sword missed, then took advantage of the demon's opening to counterattack. She really wished that she had a shield, but she worked with what she had, not with what she wanted. Besides, Kanae had promised to buy her a shield in the next city.

The female demon hissed in pain as she fell back bleeding, a deep wound in her side. The woman's wings beat quickly to try to keep her upright, but Isalla didn't give her a chance to recover, instead darting after her. The woman tried to parry Isalla's flurry of attacks, but she wasn't as good as Kanae, and she only blocked two blows before the third struck home and the demoness crumpled to the ground.

With her opponent dealt with, Isalla spun around to help Kanae, who'd been facing two more bandits herself, then froze for a moment, blinking as she saw Kanae pull her sword free of the one whose skin was covered in hundreds of needles. The other one was already on the ground bleeding out, and Kanae flicked her sword, then cleaned it off on the armor of the other demon, glancing over at Isalla as she smiled.

"Well done, Isalla. Flying opponents are always tricky when you're not capable of flight yourself, but you dealt with her handily," Kanae said, sheathing her sword. "Are you hurt?"

"Um, no, I'm fine," Isalla said, her breath still coming heavily

BENJAMIN MEDRANO

as she looked over the two that Kanae had defeated. Despite the other woman's praise, Isalla was shocked at how quickly Kanae had defeated two opponents, then looked back at the winged woman and added, "I nearly got hit initially, but she was more aggressive than skilled. I don't think she trained with a rapier... she kept acting like it was a longsword or something like that."

"I wouldn't be surprised if she simply didn't have one, or she did and it broke. While these three were reasonably skilled, they had to be desperate to attack us," Kanae said, shaking her head as she crouched next to one of them, frowning. "With me in armor, and both of us armed, they had to have known their chances of defeating us were poor, and none of them tried to retreat."

"Do you think that they were assassins, too?" Isalla asked, cleaning her sword after a moment, then sheathing it. She tried not to look at the body of her victim, since she really didn't want to think of her as a person at the moment.

"Hm, doubtful. They focused a lot on me, and I think they'd have teamed up against you if they were trying to kill you," Kanae said, and Isalla felt faintly squeamish as she saw the other woman open one of their belt pouches, then the next, pulling out a handful of coins and nodding. "I thought as much... they're *very* poor. Likely desperate, then."

"Ah. I... well, we had to defend ourselves," Isalla replied, taking a deep breath as she tried to settle her stomach. "Not how I wanted my first real fight since coming here to be, but there wasn't much of a choice."

"I prefer fights like this to those which can become far more complicated, but I do understand why you might feel that way," Kanae said, looking up from the two and sighing, then she stood and gestured around her. "The hells are a dangerous, brutal place, Isalla. Unless you have someplace or someone to shelter you, conflict is something that is always on the cusp of breaking out. There's a reason why I told you that your very nature would rebel at being here, and that eventually you'd try to make your escape."

Isalla paused, then looked around again, and as she did, her heart sank slightly. It was early in the day, with the red sun not far above the horizon, and she could see what Kanae was getting at, in her own way. The far western sky, what could be seen through the dark clouds that reminded her of smoke, was a deep purple, not the blue she was used to. Behind them to the north was the immense, dark expanse of Hellmount, with other reddish mountains extending to either side of it. Far to their east, she could see what looked like pale white mountains, almost looking like the spine of some ancient beast that had been unearthed, and the sight made her shiver at the thought.

The rough landscape they'd crossed over the past several days had also brought the differences between the hells and even the mortal world home for Isalla, let alone comparing it to the heavens. The ground was rocky, and most of the vegetation was dark, many of the plants with numerous thorns and poisons, according to Kanae. They'd crossed several rushing rivers via bridges, and she'd seen fanged fish in them, as well as two lava flows that had been far below other bridges, yet the smell of sulfur had nearly turned Isalla's stomach. If the landscape wasn't alien enough, they'd also been attacked by wildlife at least twice a day since leaving, showing just how bad things could be.

Yes, they'd easily fought off the wildlife, but that didn't change how much it weighed on Isalla, both the darkness and the attacks. It brought home the differences in the world in a way that living in Kanae's home had never quite managed. So Isalla sighed and nodded reluctantly, a part of her feeling terrible about her longing for the heavens or mortal world when Kanae had been so kind to her.

"You're right. I didn't really think you were when we were at your house, but something about the land here… it's oppressive. When I compare it to where I grew up… the differences are indescribable," Isalla admitted at last, glancing toward the sun again. "I wish they weren't, but there's no way to really deny it."

"I'm not surprised. There are places where you'd be able to rest and relax, but most of the hells are relatively inhospitable. Not as bad if you grew up here, but it's a shock for those who come from Hragon or farther afield," Kanae replied, leaning down to take the coins from the demon Isalla had defeated as well. "I'm sorry that it is, but there's not much to be done about it."

"It's alright; I don't blame you, Kanae. All of this is… illuminating, really," Isalla said, smiling at Kanae quickly, worried that her comments hadn't come across right. "I don't want you to think I'm complaining."

"That isn't what I thought you were doing, I promise," Kanae assured Isalla, smiling as she straightened. "We may as well go, though. Scavengers won't take too long to arrive."

"Alright," Isalla conceded, and followed as they started along the path again, leaving behind the three fallen. Isalla didn't like abandoning their corpses, but Kanae had explained that there was no point to burying bodies in the hells, as scavengers would just unearth them. After a few moments, she asked, "Where are we stopping tonight? Another cavern?"

"No, this time we're going to reach a proper city. Silken Veils, the first city in Estalia most visitors reach," Kanae said, glancing back and smiling. "Stay close, though. Some visitors don't have a good grasp of the rules yet when they reach Silken Veils, and some of the locals are a bit more predatory than they should be."

"Predatory?" Isalla asked, growing a little more worried. She thought Kanae had said that Estalia was fairly safe for visitors.

Kanae laughed in response, the sound disconcertingly bright considering the landscape around them, but despite that, it was heartwarming. Kanae slowed and pulled Isalla into a half-hug.

"Not the type where you're in danger of being eaten, Isalla," Kanae assured her, letting go as she continued down the path at a steady pace. "Silken Veils is a merchant city at its core, and it's dedicated to providing the most tantalizing delights the locals can come up with. Merchants will look for any weakness they can exploit to take your coin, as will guides, companions, mercenaries… the only ones who likely won't are the priesthood of Estalia, and their motive is simpler, the goal of converting others to the worship of Queen Estalia. It's a chaotic place, unless it's changed in the last three years. That's when I most recently visited."

"Ah, that does reassure me," Isalla said, hugging Kanae in return as she relaxed. The description reminded her of a couple of cities she'd visited in the mortal world, both of them major ports. As an angel, she hadn't been bothered nearly as much by the merchants, but the atmosphere had been markedly different than anything she'd encountered in the heavens, as the cities there were kept much quieter and more orderly. After a moment, she continued. "I've seen a few places like it, but after our discussion about how the hells differed from the mortal world, I was concerned."

"I don't blame you, it *was* a reasonable assumption. It's going to be interesting to see what you make of it, considering the oddities of the locals, comparatively," Kanae replied, letting go and continuing forward at a brisk pace. "I'll admit to looking forward to seeing your reaction to seeing the city. It should be entertaining."

"Thanks a lot," Isalla replied, her relief turning to just a hint of affectionate annoyance. She might not like the idea of Kanae enjoying watching her gape like a landed fish, but the angel had to admit that the thought of how the demoness would react to the sight of Skyhaven made her want to see it.

Kanae laughed again, but continued on her way at that same, quick pace. It pushed Isalla to keep up, but that was fine. It was good for her, after all.

# CHAPTER 32

*S*ilken Veils was larger than Isalla had expected. The city was built on the edge of a large river, and part of the dark waters had been diverted to fill a moat that circled the city's walls. The walls themselves looked largely ornamental, as they were relatively thin and were only ten feet tall, but the regular towers each were crowned by deadly-looking ballista.

The city itself was large, stretching at least a mile across, and the buildings were far more varied than those Isalla had seen elsewhere in the hells, though she had no idea how most cities looked down here. None of the looming, oppressive architecture could be seen as they approached, and the city was instead more like a human city, with shingle roofs and stonework. She could see several temple-like buildings within the city, including a ziggurat made of pale gold stone and illuminated by dozens of lanterns at the center. The city streets were swathed with brightly covered awnings and veils that fluttered in the wind and gave the city its name.

Isalla felt her surprise grow as they crossed the drawbridge and entered the city, passing well-armed guards along the way, along with more than a little growing fear. The city streets were lined with lampposts, each glowing with a pale light that helped illuminate the streets as it grew dark out. The number of enchanted items the lampposts suggested existed in the city made her nervous, but she was immediately distracted by the residents swirling through the streets, and for the first time she understood why Kanae had said she wouldn't stand out that much in the hells without her wings.

Nearly one in five people she saw were human or partially human, and several she saw in the first few seconds had skin and hair as pale as Isalla's was. Many of them looked reasonably well-off, and the variety of demons in the streets was almost overwhelming, causing Isalla to move closer to Kanae.

"Hm? Is something the matter?" Kanae asked, glancing over at Isalla as they started down the street, entering the swirl of demons and mortals.

"How wealthy *is* Estalia? I can't imagine a border city being able to leave out enchanted lamp posts like that!" Isalla said, gesturing at one, and her protest prompted a soft laugh from Kanae.

"That? It isn't enchanted, Isalla," Kanae replied, circling around a large, ox-like demon bargaining at a stall, and her voice was almost drowned out by the merchants hawking their wares.

"But... isn't the light magical?" Isalla asked in confusion, quickly following Kanae as her gaze darted back and forth. She didn't want to get separated, not here.

"Of course it is. The lampposts are foci, not enchanted. The temple of Estalia at the center of the city is built on a magical node, and it has an enchantment that causes foci on the city streets to glow if they fit certain requirements," Kanae replied absently. "The crystals inside the lampposts are simple quartz, and the posts themselves aren't very special. Plenty of people here make similar lanterns that you can carry through the city if you like, though they're not too useful since they don't work inside buildings."

"Oh. That's interesting... a better way to do it than enchanting all the lampposts, I suppose," Isalla admitted, relieved that the city wasn't as overwhelmingly wealthy as she'd feared. A moment later, she caught the scent of something that smelled absolutely wonderful, something which made her stomach growl. She glanced over to see a restaurant across the street, the windows open and showing a dining room with dozens of mortals and demons eating food that made her mouth water.

"Isalla, watch where you're going." Kanae's voice drew Isalla's attention back to the road, and Isalla blushed as she saw the demoness smile, her tail flicking lazily. "We'll eat after we have rooms, don't worry. The food here is better than what I had ingredients for."

"Oh, of course," Isalla replied, flushing in embarrassment. She hadn't thought her hunger was *that* obvious, but apparently she was wrong. "I was just noticing that something smelled good."

"I'm not surprised; the people here specialize in making visitors feel at home," Kanae said, and she waved off a handsome demon with red skin and polished golden horns, one who was wearing an open vest to show off a muscular chest and tight leather pants. Kanae told him quickly, "No, I'm not interested, and neither is she. I know my way around the city."

"As you like," the man replied, backing off with obvious disappointment, and Isalla blinked in confusion.

"Kanae? What was that about?" Isalla asked, frowning. She'd initially thought the man was a… *companion*, not a guide. He was rather handsome, she had to admit, but not really her type.

"He was going to offer to show us around the city. He's likely employed by one of the pleasure districts, and would've guided us there after a little while, to try to get us to enrich his employers," Kanae explained, shrugging as she turned a corner. "That or he works for a brothel, or even a merchant cartel. I mentioned that the people here do everything they can to squeeze your coin out, didn't I?"

"You did, but that's a different approach than I'm used to. In cities up above, the people who do things like that are street urchins or the like, not people like *that*," Isalla said, slightly stunned by the explanation as she gave the swirl of demons and mortals around her a dubious look. There were far too many pretty men and women who were dressed in clothing that was both attractive and easy to move in. That being the case, she wondered how many of them had the same sort of job.

"Yes, I seem to recall something like that. It's been a long time since I've visited the mortal world... but there aren't many street urchins in Silken Veils. There's always someplace better for them to be than on the streets," Kanae said, laughing softly. "No, tasks like this are far better performed by people who know what they're doing... at least, that's what the locals think."

"Fair, I guess. I just didn't expect something like that," Isalla said, nodding in understanding.

They passed so many buildings that looked normal that it startled Isalla, but some buildings were more like what she expected, with looming gargoyles and heavily armed guards. Still other buildings almost left her drop-jawed, though, like when she saw an elegant house that wouldn't have been out of place in the heavens, a garden of dark but beautiful flowers that glowed from within all around a small garden in front of the home, where Isalla saw demons and mortals alike taking tea with an elegantly dressed faerie the size of a human, her hair glowing like starlight and with colorful wings like those of a butterfly on her back.

"Um, I don't remember faeries being the size of a human..." Isalla said, her voice hesitant. The sheer variety of strange things she was seeing was astounding, but she also was recovering more quickly now.

"They aren't. Alteration spells can make many things possible, however," Kanae said briskly, turning a corner and smiling. "Ah, good. It's still here... I *was* a touch concerned that it might not be. Bell has talked about moving to the capital before."

"Oh?" Isalla asked, trying to peer past Kanae... and she promptly blushed.

She'd heard of pleasure quarters before, though most of the nations influenced by the heavens didn't allow them to form, at least officially they didn't. That wasn't to say they didn't exist, though, and Isalla had seen one in one of the border kingdoms where she'd been stationed before. That quarter hadn't been nearly as clean and open as this one was, and neither had the men and woman who worked in the quarter been quite as open... or as exotic as the demons in front of her were. Just as an example, a pair of succubus twins were naked in the middle of the street, and she saw a human man wavering as he spoke to the pair.

"Um, Kanae? What are we doing *here*?" Isalla asked, any sense of comfort she had quickly vanishing as the heat rose in her cheeks. Saying she was embarrassed would be like saying that lava was warm.

"I have an old friend who runs one of the more profitable establishments here. She offers me lodging for free whenever I visit, as well as privacy. I very much appreciate that," Kanae explained, glancing back and smiling as she saw Isalla's face, and then continued as the angel's cheeks heated even more. "We *may* have to pay for your stay, but we'll have to see what Bell says."

"Oh, alright. I guess that would work…" Isalla said, her tension easing slightly… right up until a handsome, winged incubus with silver skin, black hair, and who wore little more than a pair of skintight black and gold pants that hid almost nothing approached her.

"Hello, my lady," he said melodiously, giving her a smile that could melt stone. "Welcome to the Boulevard of Exotic Flowers. Would you be interested in a tour?"

"Um…" Isalla began, taken aback and blushing. She *saw* the glint in the man's eyes, but before he could say anything, Kanae interjected calmly, much to Isalla's relief.

"I'm afraid that your attempt will avail you little, good sir. The two of us are together and will be staying at Bell's Imaginarium. Unless she's changed significantly in the last decade, I don't believe that you're one of her employees," Kanae said, looking at him calmly, and Isalla blinked as she saw the man take a step back, instantly cowed.

"Ah, my apologies. I didn't realize that," he said, giving a deep bow. "Still, should you wish to have a tour, I'm your man."

"No offense taken. You had no way of knowing." Kanae inclined her head and smiled as she spoke. "I wish you luck with others."

With that, Kanae reached out and took Isalla's hand, drawing her forward as she continued down the street, explaining. "You're off-balance, and that encourages them to try harder. I'll keep them from trying to pressure you, but that will only help while I'm around."

"R-right. I'll keep that in mind," Isalla said, letting out a deep breath as they continued down the street. Kanae's hand in her own was incredibly reassuring, even if she was still wearing her gauntlets.

"Good. Now, Bell's Imaginarium is an unusual place, and those who work there are all exotic, and the type to be unusual even here. The faerie we saw would qualify to work there, but not many others would," Kanae said, glancing back as she added, "She even had an angel working for her the last time I visited, so don't be surprised."

"That... well, it's a little surprising, but not completely unheard of. I know there are demons in the northern lands of the mortal world, though not many," Isalla said, carefully avoiding talking about whether there were any in the heavens themselves. She didn't know of any, but in part that was because it was so much harder for anyone to reach the heavens. Even mortals were rare beyond reckoning there.

"Yes, but I'd rather you knew before we walked through the doors," Kanae said, circling a cluster of people on the street as she continued onward. "Don't be surprised if Bell misinterprets why you're with me, too. I haven't had a close friend in a while, and she's tried to set me up with lovers or recruit me for about as long as we've known one another. I don't care for the idea of working there, but I've brought a couple of people to her who were interested before."

"Ah. I hope she's not too forward, then. I don't like thinking myself as..." Isalla began, then blushed as she saw that not *everyone* was interested in privacy on the street and quickly looked away, fixing her gaze on Kanae's back. She cleared her throat and added unsteadily, "I just come from an area which is far more... reserved. I've never seen someplace like *this* before."

"Well, now you have. And... we're here," Kanae said, stopping in front of a gate, and Isalla looked inside the gates with surprise.

The wrought iron gate and walls were ornate and easy to see through, showing elaborate gardens much like the one she'd seen the faerie in, along with trees that would have been more at home in the mortal world and brightly colored flowers. She couldn't imagine how they were cultivated here. The building beyond was large, at least two stories tall and more of a mansion than any of the other buildings in the area, to the point that it dwarfed all but two other buildings on the entire street, and the pillars at its corners were beautifully carved to appear as women in flowing gowns, their features indistinct but beautiful. In front of the gates stood a stone statue that was eight feet tall and with a massive two-handed sword at her back. The figure was distinctly female and made of carved green-hued stone, and wore clothing over a shapely, athletic figure, and stared at Kanae with glowing rubies for eyes.

"Opira, it's a pleasure to see you again," Kanae said, giving a respectful bow. "I'm here to see Bell and take a night's respite from my travels. With me is Isalla, a friend of mine who needs rest as well."

"Kanae, it's been quite some time," the statue replied with a nod of her head, her voice startlingly delicate to Isalla, causing her to stare at the statue as she turned her head to examine Isalla for a moment, then continued. "I see. She doesn't appear to be a threat, and you're always welcome here, of course. I hope to speak with you later."

"And I with you. Perhaps when your brother goes on duty? I'd love to hear about some of your insights," Kanae said, her smile widening.

"That would be pleasant," Opira agreed, and she reached back to swing the gate open.

"Thank you. Come along, Isalla," Kanae said, heading for the door into the mansion.

Isalla belatedly nodded and followed Kanae. Once they were a few steps away, Isalla asked curiously, "Um, Kanae? Is Opira one of the stonekith?"

"Oh, you've heard of them?" Kanae asked, looking back with a hint of surprise on her face. "I run into a lot of people who haven't."

"Yes... I've heard about them rarely, but since they live almost exclusively deep below the ground, I don't know much about them," Isalla said, thinking back on the tales of human-like beings made of stone-like flesh that lived deep below the mortal world's surface. She couldn't think of any other species that fit Opira's description.

"I'm not surprised… but in this case you're wrong. Opira and her brother aren't stonekith," Kanae said, shaking her head as she reached the doors. "They're a pair of golems granted true life and sentience by Egor approximately four centuries ago."

Isalla's eyes went wide in shock, hesitating for a long moment. Egor was one of many mortal gods and was best known as one of the gods of earth and stone. The mantle he bore had gone through at least a dozen predecessors, and which side of the war it had been on had changed several times. Egor was a human who had fought on the side of the Fallen Kingdoms before his ascension, so she wasn't too surprised that his creations could be found here. It was just surprising that he'd made creatures which could think for themselves.

"Oh. I… didn't know he could create something like… well, *her*. I'd never even thought about the possibility," Isalla said after a moment, glancing back as Kanae opened the doors. "I…"

Isalla's train of thought was interrupted as she heard music from ahead, and took a breath of potent perfumes, ones that brought to mind spring mornings under the sun, fruit, and the heady scent of the sea. She quickly turned to look through the doors, her mouth slightly agape.

There were walls to the antechamber ahead of them, but she couldn't see a ceiling, instead seeing a sky full of countless, brilliant stars that were brighter than anything Isalla had ever seen in life. To one side of the room was a pool of shimmering water, and she saw a mermaid with glittering green scales over her lower body sitting on the stone wall of the pool, the pretty brunette rubbing a finger around the rim of her glass as she stared raptly at the demon on the other side of table, a demon who looked a lot like Deka with the numerous horns on his major joints.

At the back of the room was a bar, and behind it stood two bartenders, both in exquisite clothing. The man had unnaturally pale skin and hair so white that it almost glowed in the light, and it took Isalla a moment to realize he had six fingers on each hand, while his eyes were glowing pools of white light. The woman was tall and muscular, enough that she looked like she could break Isalla in half without trying, her skin almost the color of chocolate and her eyes a slightly lighter shade of brown. The woman had several scars on her uncovered arms, along with one on her right cheek, but all of them were tasteful, as if carefully placed. Or, having experienced what alchemy could do, Isalla thought it likely that any other scars had been deliberately healed.

There were other men and women in the room, and Isalla kept herself from staring at the angel at one table, though it was difficult. The man had bronzed skin, rugged good looks, and had the sort of physique that made her think he could hold up the sky if necessary, while his brown hair was held back by a hair tie and his blue eyes were piercing. He was warmly chatting with a dwarven woman, and the smile on her face was startling. Isalla felt out of place in the room, since all the patrons were well-dressed, but Kanae walked through the room like she belonged there, heading for the door beside the bar unerringly, ignoring both the stairwell that rose to an upper floor, where more guests were at a balcony table, and the halls that stretched to either side.

Isalla hurried after Kanae, surprised at how quickly she was moving, and saw the man with white hair look at Kanae with a furrowed brow for a moment, opening his mouth to speak, then froze as Kanae reached for the handle and opened the door. Isalla briefly wondered why he looked so surprised, but she followed Kanae through the door and into a brightly lit, warm cavern. A large pile of cushions was on one side of the room, along with some carefully folded blankets, and there were a couple of chairs in front of a desk at the back of the room, which looked and smelled like it opened to the sandy beach of an ocean.

Behind the desk was a lamia, wearing half-moon glasses and with raven black hair. She was quite attractive, and most of her body was on display due to the diaphanous black top she wore, along with a thicker belt from which dangled dozens of tiny gold bells. The woman looked up, and her snake-like hazel eyes widened, then she grinned as she exclaimed.

"Kanae, darling!" the lamia said, and she surged up and over the desk, sending a couple of documents fluttering to the ground as her lower body hissed over them. She descended on Kanae with a hug which drove Kanae to the ground, and Isalla gaped slightly as she stared, then closed the door behind her as the lamia spoke. "What a surprise this is! It's been an age since you visited, and I wasn't sure when I'd seen you next."

"Hello, Bell. It's good to see you, too," Kanae replied, a smile on her face, though her voice was labored, likely due to the weight of the woman atop her. "May I get up?"

"But of course! I was simply so excited to see you after such a long absence that I forgot myself," Bell replied, straightening and pulling Kanae to her feet with her, the lamia's lower body slithering into a coil as she looked up.

Isalla blinked as Bell looked her over, slightly unnerved by the intensity of the woman's gaze. The examination didn't take long, fortunately, and in the moment that Kanae was brushing the sand off her armor, Bell looked away, clicking her tongue.

"My, my... is this another of your lost sheep? Unlike the others, I'm not sure that she'd fit in here, Kanae. While an angel who has lost her wings *is* rather unusual, I don't believe that most of my patrons would be that intrigued. Perhaps if we were to have the temple regenerate her wings, but..." Bell shrugged slightly, and Isalla froze for an instant, startled and just a bit afraid.

"No, you misunderstand, Bell. Isalla and I are currently... *involved*. Whether that will last or not is another question entirely," Kanae said, and Isalla felt her face heating slightly as the demoness continued, leaning forward to gently kiss the lamia's cheek. "No, I came to avail myself of your hospitality once more. I'm willing to pay for the pair of us to stay, of course."

"Indeed? Why, I don't remember the last time you spent more than a day with someone, Kanae. As for payment, piffle! There's no need for that. I wouldn't have my establishment if it weren't for you, and you don't take advantage of my offer often." Bell waved the offer off with a slight sniff, then turned to Isalla with a smile, slithering forward and offering a hand. "It's a pleasure to meet you, Miss Isalla. I'd long wondered who might be able to break Kanae out of her shell, even if I'd hoped to lure her into working here with me."

"Um, thank you, Lady Bell. It's a pleasure to meet you... even if I wasn't aware you were a lamia. Kanae neglected to mention that," Isalla said with a sidelong glance of annoyance at Kanae, taking Bell's hand, only to be surprised when the lamia turned it and kissed the back of her hand. After a moment of hesitation, she asked, "May I ask how you knew I was an angel? Kanae said that it shouldn't be obvious."

"She wouldn't have told you. Kanae likes leaving people in the dark when she brings them to me... the better to see how they react to those who aren't what they expect," Bell replied, clicking her tongue chidingly. At the question, she smiled more and continued. "As for identifying you, your nature *isn't* obvious, particularly with your scent changed to seem like a native. That does nothing for how you move, though, nor the other minor signs of an angel. While many aspects of angels are similar to humans, your muscles are not among them, and your bone structure is slightly different. Your kind are also lighter than humans, if only slightly. I notice these things, unlike most others."

"Ah, I see," Isalla said, relaxing slightly. She supposed the muscles for her wings *did* radiate over a large portion of her torso, including through her shoulders. They weren't as strong as the rest of her muscles, but Kanae's vile elixir had helped them recover as well.

"I must thank you for your hospitality, Bell. While there are other places to stay in the city, I don't feel as secure in them," Kanae added, the smile on her face widening slightly.

"Oh, it isn't a bother, truly. Your aid was invaluable, and I truly *am* thankful for it. Even if I wish you'd come work here. You might not be as exotic as some of the others, but your skill at arms and manners make up for it," Bell said, her smile widening still more as she looked at Kanae, asking in a teasing tone, "Or are you still hiding from someone?"

"I'm likely to be hiding until the day I die," Kanae replied, sniffing slightly. "As to working for you, you know my answer. I've no interest in performing for the pleasure of random others, not anymore. Those I care about are a different story entirely."

"If you say so," Bell said, shaking her head in exaggerated dismay.

"Um, pardon me… but how did the two of you meet? It sounds like it was a little interesting," Isalla asked curiously, looking between the two women, and Bell looked at Kanae for a moment, and the demoness shrugged.

"It really isn't quite as interesting as you might think, though I suppose it might sound that way," the lamia said after a moment. "I used to live in Redflow, and I had a lesser form of my current business there. Unfortunately, the local lord of Redflow wasn't quite as… protective of businesses like my own, and after a few dozen incidents where violence broke out, I'd had enough. I decided to leave for someplace that would appreciate my business, so I looked for someone to guide me to Estalia."

"I was in Redflow to get some rare herbs for an elixir," Kanae said, shrugging. "One of the people in town had a particularly virulent disease, and I wanted to head it off before the town slowly withered away and died. I ran into Bell when I was preparing to return and decided that earning a little coin on the return trip wouldn't be amiss."

"It would have been easy for both of us, if it weren't for Wolfheim's ardent admirer, too," Bell continued, sighing sadly as she shook her head. "The man decided that an all-out assault on our caravan was necessary to claim Wolfheim, even if he wasn't interested. The battle was… much closer than I like to think about. If we hadn't had Kanae's blade, we'd have all fallen. As it was, she managed to deal so much damage to the attackers that we were able to continue onward, and she even helped heal our injuries along the way. I owe her a great debt, since the attackers would have let her go quite readily."

"I dislike bullies and those who think that, just because they're stronger, that entitles them to take whatever they want,"

Kanae added with a calm smile, leaning on the desk. "Besides, they were overconfident. That helped a lot."

"I see. That does sound a lot like Kanae, doesn't it?" Isalla said, slowly smiling as her mood improved. "I haven't been able to push her far enough to see just how good she is, yet. I'm not strong enough."

"You likely need more training as well. Kanae is a master swordswoman," Bell quickly advised. "There's a reason I'd love to have her here, after all. Not because of danger, but because some of my patrons want the exceedingly competent to attend to them."

"Which they aren't getting from me," Kanae interjected dryly. "May I get the room, please? I'd like to wash off the dust and grime, since we've been on the road for several days."

"Oh, of course. Your usual style, I assume?" Bell asked, moving with startling speed back around the desk, and collecting the scattered papers as she moved.

"That would be lovely," Kanae agreed.

"What about you, Isalla? Are you staying with Kanae, or would you prefer your own room?" Bell asked, pulling out a key from a drawer.

"I'll stay with Kanae. I don't think there's any need for us to take up two rooms," Isalla said, flushing slightly as she did so. While she liked staying with Kanae, it was embarrassing to express that aloud.

"As you like. Here you are, Kanae," Bell said, tossing the demoness the key as she smiled warmly. "I look forward to seeing you at dinner."

"I'll see you then… and thank you once again," Kanae said, giving a surprisingly graceful bow, considering her armor and the pack she was wearing.

"Think nothing of it," Bell replied airily, waving them off.

Kanae led the way out of the room, and Isalla did a double take as the sand that had adhered to her pack and armor vanished when she stepped through the door. She also noticed that some of the guests and employees were watching them more closely, now. Ignoring the attention, Kanae headed to their left, past the pool and toward the hall next to it.

BENJAMIN MEDRANO

"Kanae, why did the sand vanish off your back?" Isalla asked, frowning as she kept pace.

"Bell is an incredibly skilled enchantress and illusionist. She's woven enchantments like what you see on the ceiling, and each room is mutable, allowing her to change the scenery and feel of it," Kanae explained, slowing down slightly. "The form of illusion is unusual in that it's quasi-real, allowing you to touch and interact with it, though unless it would injure you or you actively attempt to see through the illusion you won't notice it's nature."

"Oh. That means that your room is like that, then?" Isalla asked, her curiosity roused. She'd heard of similar illusions before, but she'd never experienced any. There wasn't much call for them.

"That's right. Bell set up an appearance specifically for me years ago," Kanae confirmed, a note of amusement in her voice.

Isalla followed a bit more eagerly, now. She was curious to see what sort of room Kanae liked staying in.

# CHAPTER 33

*K*anae's room wasn't what Isalla expected. The door opened into a large gazebo with a glass roof and low walls that allowed them to look out across intricate gardens filled with flowers, some of them glowing under the starlight. The sky was a sort of idealized form of the sky of the hells, not as gloomy as it normally was, and the scent of the flowers filled the air with a gentle, soothing smell. A large bed with white sheets was near one end of the gazebo opposite the door, to their right was a wardrobe, while to the left was a large tub of steaming water that glowed like opalescent pearls as steam rose from its surface.

"This is amazing," Isalla said, smiling warmly as she looked around. Kanae approached the wardrobe and started stripping off her armor and pack. Isalla loved how restful the scene was, and it was better than most of the hells that she'd seen "I wasn't sure what you'd like, honestly."

"I like gardens. They remind me of happy times in my life," Kanae replied, and glanced up, smiling as she added, "Just don't try to go out into the gardens, hm? The edges of the gazebo are walls, and we can't go through those, no matter what it looks like."

"Ah, good to know. Bell really *has* mastered illusion magic, hasn't she?" Isalla said, following after a moment. The ground below her felt like smooth, tiled stone, and she couldn't see any flaws to the scenery.

"She certainly has. I think it's why she coined this her imaginarium. She can weave illusions of other places that can enrapture people. If she wanted to, I think she could be incredibly dangerous," Kanae admitted, finishing putting her armor on a convenient rack inside the large wardrobe. Isalla saw there was clothing hanging inside, somewhat to her surprise, though most of it looked more like what the courtesans outside had been wearing. Kanae continued calmly, starting to strip entirely. "Fortunately, she doesn't seem to be interested in that."

"True," Isalla said, pausing as she watched Kanae strip naked, fascinated despite having seen her naked before. She blushed a little, but not as much as she had at various points in the city.

Kanae wasn't trying to put on a show, Isalla knew that much, yet she may as well have been. The demoness was beautiful, with her pale skin and dark eyes and hair, and Isalla still couldn't believe that the full-figured woman didn't have any scars, yet she didn't. The demoness finished disrobing, then walked over to slide into the tub with a sigh, visibly relaxing as the tip of her tail bobbed to the surface.

"Do you mind if I join you?" Isalla asked after a moment, firmly shoving several quiet worries aside. She didn't need to wonder how safe they'd be on their journey, not now.

Kanae looked over and smiled gently as she nodded. "Of course you may, Isalla. I wasn't sure if you'd want to, anymore. Considering what you've said about your relationship with Roselynn... I wondered if you were going to break things off entirely."

"I'm not sure about it, either. I'm confused, but I also... well, Roselynn didn't contact me after we separated. I trust her, but I'm afraid she didn't reply because she didn't want to make her position even more precarious," Isalla admitted nervously, starting to disrobe as well. She was worried about Roselynn's reaction as well as Kanae's, and she couldn't honestly say who she liked more anymore. "At the same time, I don't want to lose what I have simply because of something I might obtain. I like you, Kanae."

"Be that as it may, you do know that the chances of us having any sort of lasting relationship aren't good, yes?" Kanae asked, arching an eyebrow as she gestured around herself. "You've seen what the hells are really like, now, or at least a tiny fragment of them, and I don't think you'd be happy here in the long term. I like you, Isalla... I really do. But I also don't want you to start living somewhere you hate just because you feel a sense of obligation to me."

Isalla paused, blinking at Kanae, then smiled, a hint of relief washing through her. She pulled off her underthings, then teased, "You could always come to the mortal world, you know."

"Possibly," Kanae admitted, watching Isalla through lidded eyes. "That could be complicated. Still, it's possible."

Isalla paused as she was about to slip into the water, blinking. Then she asked cautiously, "Are you serious? I was mostly joking."

"I know you were. That said, if I tell you what I promised to... I might have to leave anyway. I don't know where I'd go in that case, not right now," Kanae said, shrugging and smiling at Isalla. "I'm considering what I want to do. Unfortunately, a lot will depend on what state your friend is in, assuming we can get to her. It's possible she'll be gone by the time we get there, you know."

The thought sobered Isalla somewhat, and she felt her shoulders droop slightly as she finished slipping into the luminescent water. Part of Isalla was fascinated by how it glowed, though it felt no different than simple, warm water. A part of her mind wondered if the water might also be one of the quasi-real illusions, but she wasn't going to worry about it much now. Instead, she ran her fingers through the water as she thought.

"You're right. I'm hoping you aren't, but it's a possibility, considering how long it'll take us to get there," Isalla finally admitted, looking up worriedly. "Is there any way to get there faster?"

"A few ways, but they're far more likely to draw people onto our trail. The land between here and the spire is incredibly rugged, and we're going to have to circle the worst of a set of badlands," Kanae said, shrugging unhappily. "Two weeks is a long time, I know. Estalia is bigger than a lot of its neighbors, which doesn't help matters, and it's almost impossible to build bridges across particularly large lava flows. That limits things more than they would above."

"Ah, and without a way to fly... that would cause problems, wouldn't it?" Isalla said, sighing again. Even so, her mood improved a little. "There's nothing to be done about that, though. We'll just deal with what comes, right? And there's no guarantee that Roselynn will even care about me anymore if we rescue her."

"You know her better than I do, but unless things have changed..." Kanae paused for a long moment, then smiled gently. "If things are like they were when I was there, if she *had* feelings for you, I can say with confidence that they wouldn't have tried to destroy them. It isn't how they work, since they want the person who comes to them to feel loved."

"Oh. Well, that's reassuring," Isalla said, flushing slightly, and slowly her gaze lowered. She couldn't see much through the water, but what she did see caused her pulse to quicken. Kanae's beauty had that effect on her... and when she thought about it, Bell might have had a point about the demoness's confidence being attractive. After all, Roselynn had always been incredibly confident as well.

As Isalla began to drift toward her, Kanae's eyebrows rose, and the demoness smiled as she spoke. "I *thought* we were going to bathe, Isalla. Or perhaps you had something else in mind?"

Isalla wrapped her arms around Kanae and kissed her, enjoying the faintly sweet taste of the demoness and the warmth of her body against Isalla's own. Kanae returned the kiss passionately, her arms wrapping around Isalla, and for several long moments they held the kiss. Finally, Isalla pulled away, her breathing coming more quickly now, and she smiled, licking her lips as she murmured, "That *was* the plan... but plans change."

"Very well," Kanae replied, and then she pulled Isalla back into another kiss, her hands starting to explore.

Isalla, for her part, just enjoyed the attention, allowing her mind to drift to more pleasant thoughts.

～

THE VISIT WAS fascinating for Isalla, when they finally got out of the room. Not everyone in the building came to dinner, but enough arrived at one point or another that it was truly eye-opening for her.

Beyond the handful of men and women she'd seen before, she met a beautiful lady cyclops, a rare male dryad, a nymph, two medusas, and a minotaur. The group was eclectic, but all of them were surprisingly intelligent, and nearly half of them knew Kanae from previous visits, while the others seemed to have heard of her at some point during their time here. Isalla had also learned that Bell was the adoptive mother of seven young dragons who'd recently struck out on their own. From what she could tell, Bell had purchased their eggs from some hunters who'd killed a dragon and raised the dragons herself.

Opira had come in about halfway through dinner, and she'd found a seat next to Kanae, though she'd replaced the chair there with one that looked heavier and sturdier. The ensuing conversation had been eye-opening, as Opira started talking to Kanae about what the meaning of being alive truly was.

The woman was interesting, and Isalla had found herself oddly fascinated by the conversation, as Kanae revealed that she thought that anyone or anything that could think for themselves was alive, while those who deliberately chose not to make decisions for themselves were somewhat wasting their lives.

Opira didn't seem to disagree, at least not on the broad scale of things, but she did think that many people considered her and her brother not to be alive, since they weren't flesh and blood. Not much came of the conversation, as it was more of philosophizing, but it *was* fascinating. Eventually they'd finished dinner, and after a good deal of chatting, during which many of

Bell's employees had teased Isalla into blushing frequently, they'd headed for bed.

"Kanae?" Isalla asked, pulling back the covers to slip into bed. She was thinking about the conversation from before, trying to decide why Opira had wanted to talk about it.

"Yes?" Kanae asked, finishing brushing out her hair and looking up at Isalla curiously, a faint smile on her face.

"Why is Opira so curious about the meaning of being alive? It didn't feel like she was trying to actually *learn* anything from you," Isalla said, pulling the sheet up over her. She had to admit, the silk sheets were nicer than most she'd had throughout her life.

"Ah, an interesting question. I'm not entirely certain, but I *think* she's trying to figure out a new form of life magic," Kanae mused, tilting her head as she set the brush aside.

"Really? Isn't creating a new form of magic incredibly difficult?" Isalla asked, her eyes widening in shock.

"Yes, but she *has* time. Even if you and I are immortal, we're far more fragile than she is. I doubt we'd have the time to create a new type of magic properly, but if she's patient enough…" Kanae replied with a shrug. Then she slid into bed beside Isalla and embraced her.

"True, I guess. I really ought to learn some magic…" Isalla murmured, rolling into Kanae and letting her eyes drift most of the way shut. The smell of flowers and Kanae was comforting, as was the presence of her being so nearby. After a moment, she murmured, "We're leaving tomorrow, right?"

"That's right. Rest well, Isalla," Kanae murmured, and gave her a gentle kiss.

Ever so slowly, Isalla drifted off. Even if she was slightly warm, it was too comfortable for her to think of pulling away.

# CHAPTER 34

*T*he journey after Silken Veils was just as torturously circuitous as Kanae had said it would be, and the trip was incredible. While much of the hells was rocky, and metal tools were abundant, there were still forests and rivers, and even farmland here and there, though that was often guarded as heavily as important passes were in the mortal world.

They were mostly attacked by wildlife, often twice a day or more, but they were also occasionally attacked by bandits or other demons. Isalla had been startled and anxious the first few times, but slowly she began to settle down, feeling like she was getting used to what was happening around her. Even better, the exercise of their journey coupled with practicing with Kanae allowed her to recover her strength far faster than she'd been recovering in Kanae's home.

That wasn't to say the journey was pleasant, though. The nearest she'd come to death was when an ogre had burst out of the woods and hit her with its club, fortunately lightly since it'd been bellowing something about wanting women. Kanae had managed to attack while it'd been distracted and quickly cut the creature down before coming to Isalla's aid. They kept their distance from the lava rivers, since Isalla didn't have the resistance to their fumes that many of the natives possessed.

They passed through two more cities as well, each of them

different, though generally calmer than Silken Veils had been. That hadn't stopped one noblewoman, a statuesque demoness with a ridged forehead, long black horns, and four arms that ended in almost needle-like fingernails from asking if Isalla was for sale. Isalla had been about to retort angrily, but Kanae had silenced her with a look, then politely told the noblewoman that Isalla was a free woman, and as such could make her own decisions.

The woman had then turned her attention on Isalla, promising her a life of luxury and pleasure if she entered the noble's service. Taking her cues from Kanae, Isalla had calmed herself and politely declined, falling back on the same sort of training she'd used to speak to mortal lords she particularly disliked. The demoness had been disappointed, but she'd also accepted the result and gone on her way. Afterward, Kanae had explained that the laws of Estalia required such, and if the woman had tried to force the issue, she'd likely lose her nobility and all her wealth. That didn't mean they should be rude, since a noble could easily make their lives difficult, but it gave a measure of safety to travelers.

Isalla had hoped to meet more friends of Kanae's along the way, but she'd been disappointed. While friends would help shed some light on Kanae's odd attitudes, she hadn't spoken of any others or met any after leaving Silken Veils, and Isalla had noticed how, in some of the towns, Kanae didn't allow her sword to be more than a pace away, even when in a private room.

At last they were getting close to their goal, though, and Isalla knew she was growing more worried with every passing day.

$\sim$

"AND THERE IT IS. The Spire of Confession, retreat of Estalia's faithful," Kanae said, pausing atop the ridgeline, and with an uncharacteristic note of tension in her voice.

Isalla stopped atop the hill as well and looked in the direction Kanae indicated, breathing deeply. She was much more fit than she had been, but even so, she couldn't seem to quite match

Kanae's pace easily, even though the other woman was wearing armor.

At the top of another ridge in the distance was a structure, so distant that the haze of smoke-like fog almost hid it. While it *was* distant, Isalla's sight was good enough to pick out a few details, and what she could see startled her. The spire was enormous, with multiple wider sections to it, and she'd consider it more of a castle or citadel in most places, yet it truly *was* a spire. The massive structure extended upward and upward, and she had to wonder how tall it was. She doubted that it had more than thirty floors, but even that was staggering to her. The problem was that it was so hard to judge the building's scale.

"That is much bigger than I expected," Isalla said after a moment, frowning. "I think we'd have trouble even *finding* her if we were to somehow get inside."

"It is. I'm not entirely sure why it's so big... possibly to be a major fortress in the case of an invasion, but I don't know. I just know that it's one of the most dangerous places in Estalia," Kanae replied, shaking her head slowly. "I'd prefer to try delving down to the sixth or seventh tier of the Fungal Abyss over trying to go in there again. My chances would be better of getting out intact."

Isalla winced, looking at Kanae in some worry. After a moment, she asked, hiding her concern about moving forward on her own, "Are you sure you want to be here, Kanae? If you're that worried about everything that's going on..."

"You aren't getting rid of me that easily, Isalla. If I leave this to you, we'll be in even more trouble," Kanae said, her hesitation vanishing as she smiled at Isalla warmly. "No, we're not going anywhere near the spire itself. There's a town that ships them supplies regularly, and that's where we're going. If anyone goes to the capital, they'll go through there, and they hear all the rumors. We can gather information there and wait if necessary."

"Isn't that dangerous? If we're staying in the area, I'd think that people might get suspicious of us," Isalla said, growing more worried despite Kanae's assurances.

Kanae startled Isalla by laughing and shaking her head. "Suspicious? No, no... they won't even blink. See, some

247

residents of the spire regularly visit the town, and are rather promiscuous. Still other people who've attended the spire end up... interested in employment. Considering that, they almost constantly have visitors who're waiting in the hopes of finding someone from the spire to take with them."

"Oh." Isalla's eyes went wide, and she hesitated for a long moment, then asked, "I... is that *common*? Considering Roselynn..."

"I don't know exactly how common it is, but I know it happens. Some of the nobility do hope that the people who visit the spire end up... malleable. And some of them are," Kanae said, continuing down the path slowly. "If they want your friend, though... they're going to be fighting an uphill battle at best. Her lineage is legendary in the hells, and I sincerely doubt that Queen Estalia would give her up to any of her nobles unless that was what she truly wished for. I believe that's unlikely."

"She's legendary?" Isalla asked, her eyes going wide in shock as she followed the rocky path, choosing her steps carefully. "I knew her family was famous, but..."

"Wielders of Ember have been at the forefront of the war against the hells for millennia, and the sword has powerful magical flames that can burn demons who normally don't fear fire and has served as a rallying beacon on the battlefield," Kanae explained, her voice soft. "I've seen it myself before, twice, though I never was near Ember myself. Perhaps it... well, in any case, often they could turn the tide of the battle merely by their presence, even if the individual wielding Ember wasn't particularly strong. Someone like that always turns into a legend, Isalla... though perhaps as an object of fear on our side of the battlefield. The Flame of Ember may not be as renowned as the mortal gods or archangels, but that doesn't change the fact that her captivity will cause a lot of consternation among the hells, and spark many to wish to acquire her if they can."

"I didn't think of her from that perspective. We don't know how we're regarded on the other side, I suppose..." Isalla said hesitantly, considering the idea with a little surprise, though it slowly faded. She'd heard some legends of Roselynn's ancestors, but her lover had tried not to talk about them. Probably because of the weight of their reputation and how it led to heightened expectations for Roselynn. After a minute, Isalla nodded. "I suppose that makes sense, though. I knew she came from a famous family, and that they were important, but it didn't make much of a difference to me. So, it'll be a big deal down here?"

"Quite. That's why, if we succeed, things are going to be... interesting," Kanae said and smiled thinly. "Fortunately, I have a few ways to help her pass unnoticed. *If* we succeed."

"I really don't want to think about failing, but you're right," Isalla admitted, her heartbeat quickening slightly from nervousness. It did make her feel better that Kanae was thinking about what to do if they succeeded.

"Indeed. Come on, just another day and we'll be to the town... or we can try to push for a couple more hours tonight if you'd prefer," Kanae said, smiling warmly at Isalla. "I'm more concerned about your endurance than my own."

"In that case, let's push onward. I'd feel happier in a town, and I think I can handle pushing it. My endurance has been recovering pretty quickly after all this hiking," Isalla replied with a smile of her own, one fueled by relief that the end of their journey was so close. Or at least this leg of it.

"I'm glad to hear that. In that case, let's pick up the pace. The quicker we cover ground, the sooner we'll be there," Kanae said, turning back to the path.

~

ROSE SURFACED from the water quickly, letting out the breath she'd been holding, then inhaled deeply. She ran her fingers through her hair, pushing it back from her face so she could see more easily. The bathing pool was deeper than it needed to be, and was large enough for someone to swim laps, if short ones. She'd taken advantage of that to stay in shape over the past weeks, and she was feeling better than she had in years.

The angel still missed Queen Estalia and dreamed of her, but the ache wasn't quite as bad as it'd been in the immediate aftermath of the succubus queen's departure. Fortunately, Anna, Coral, and Tina had helped her get over the sense of loss, and things had slowly come into balance once more. It also helped that Rose loved her newfound sense of freedom. Certainly, she was being kept in the spire for the time being, but that would come to an end soon, and she'd be able to choose her own path.

"Rose? Are you done, or would you like a little more time?" Coral asked, and Rose looked over at the succubus and smiled as she stood up.

Coral was thinner than Tina, with slightly more angular features, but her soft pastel blue hair and lips helped soften her appearance, and her skin was darker than the others, causing an interesting contrast. Unlike Anna and Tina, Coral wore close-fitting, simple clothing, and she wore a holy symbol of Estalia instead of bearing a tattoo.

"I think I'm done for now," Rose replied, smiling as she extended her wings, beating them gently to remove some of the water as she walked toward the steps leading out of the pool. "While I enjoy swimming, if I'm to leave for the capital soon, I'd like to enjoy the company of each of you while I have it."

"It eases my heart to hear that. You've been a lovely guest, Rose, and it's been wonderful seeing you truly bloom," Coral replied with a warm smile, picking up a large towel and extending it for Rose. "I do hope that Her Majesty will have news of your beloved when you reach the capital."

"We shall see. Whatever is fated to be, will be," Rose said, her smile fading slightly, then it brightened as she stepped into the towel and Coral began drying her off. "Still, she said she'll search for Isalla, so I'm sure she will. For now... I'll do as she asked and try to improve myself."

"As you say," Coral said, leaning in to steal a quick kiss, her tail almost flirtatiously stroking Rose's side. "Now, let's get you dry, hm?"

Rose laughed and nodded, taking part of the towel to get to work. She was going to miss the spire when she left, as well as everyone in it, but she also looked forward to seeing just what Queen Estalia's palace was like.

Chances were she was going to be living there in the queen's service, after all. It would be so much more fulfilling than her life had been before being captured, truthfully.

# CHAPTER 35

$\mathcal{H}$aral looked at the report and frowned, tapping her desk slowly. When she'd first arranged to deal with Isalla, things had gone so well that she could hardly believe it. The complication of First Sword Roselynn's involvement had been unpleasant, but Haral had managed to intercept the woman's inquiries in time and to arrange for her to be dealt with as well. She hadn't been pleased about the angel's fate, but Haral had believed that they could arrange for Roselynn to be killed at a later time.

Then, in a bit of paranoia, Haral had performed a divination to determine whether or not Isalla had truly perished. The results had made her exceedingly unhappy since they indicated that not only was Isalla alive, but she was also in a relatively secure place near where Roselynn had been taken. She'd taken measures to try to have the woman killed, but thus far they hadn't been successful.

"I shouldn't have had her dropped so far from our territory," Haral murmured, folding her arms and frowning. "It seemed like a good idea at the time, but it makes things… difficult."

She'd at least received word of where Isalla had been spotted from the assassin's guild in Hragon, which gave Haral some options. In fact, it gave her a couple of options that were… possibly dangerous, but the last thing she wanted was for Isalla to find someone who'd listen to her wild tales about Haral and her associates. Her superiors would be most displeased if that happened.

Making a decision, Haral stood and moved to the door, opening it to look into the next room. Sorm looked up from his equipment, raising an eyebrow in surprise. A moment later he asked, the brown-haired angel's voice a gentle baritone, "Is there something you need, Haral? You look upset."

"Yes, I'm afraid so. It seems that Isalla is as hardy as a cockroach, even after being stripped of her wings and dropped in the hells. She's even managed to kill one of the assassins, which doubtlessly put her on her guard. We need to deal with her, permanently," Haral said, leaning against the door frame.

"That will be difficult," Sorm replied, frowning as he rubbed his chin. "It isn't easy to get into the hells, most of the time, and getting a group that could get in and deal with her... it would be hard to avoid notice."

"That's why I'm thinking we go for two birds with a single stone. Possibly three. We know where Roselynn is, and we were planning to eliminate her to begin with," Haral said, her gaze hardening slightly. "Put together a group of our people who are willing to *volunteer* to rescue Roselynn. They can go to Firewatch and pull together information, then kill Isalla and Roselynn at the same time. It would be shocking if the demons managed to convert her, but considering what we know of Estalia, not unheard of. If they can retrieve Ember, so much the better. There are plenty of others in her family who could wield the sword, and I'm sure there's one we could suborn easily enough."

Sorm's eyes lit up, though she also saw his caution as he set down his sword. He considered for a long moment before speaking. "That is possible, yes. I know of enough members of our cause who'd be willing, but there *is* a problem I see."

"What's that?" Haral asked, curious if it was the same problem she was thinking of.

"The demon queen," Sorm said bluntly. "She's not going to want to lose her prize, and she could destroy our chances of eliminating Roselynn."

"Yes, that's true. However, I heard something fascinating just the other day. It seems that one of Yrinna's projects has finally borne fruit," Haral said, smiling thinly, a sense of anticipation rising in her. "It's expensive, but she has an arrow which should be able to pierce most magical defenses, and which will remove even a demon lord from the equation for the time being. I believe it's designed to teleport the one shot into a mortal god's defenses, in fact. It'll take her a long time to make another batch, but I believe we can requisition one easily enough. Even better, it should do a good job of distracting everyone from our aims, if a demon lord breaks the unofficial truce by attacking a mortal god."

Sorm blinked, then smiled. "Yes, that would change things, wouldn't it? It would be a clever way to avoid needing to enchant an arrow to be able to *kill* a demon lord, too. That's notoriously difficult. In any case, it would likely put her mantle out of reach as well. If we have that, I think the task is doable. They should even be able to get out relatively easily, if we can communicate with them to open the portal."

"Precisely," Haral said, her smile widening. "You're willing to make the arrangements, then?"

"Of course," Sorm agreed. "I'll start on it this evening. Putting together a group should take no more than a day or two. However… what if someone who isn't one of our own joins the group?"

Haral paused, then shrugged. "In that case, the hells *are* a dangerous place. Casualties are almost inevitable."

"True enough," Sorm said, chuckling darkly.

Haral smiled, then stepped back into her room and closed the door. She was happy that arrangements were being made. It wasn't the perfect solution, but it'd do for now. In the meantime, she needed to make other arrangements that didn't involve a single, annoyingly resilient angel.

# CHAPTER 36

*I*salla settled into the chair, feeling a little relieved that Kanae let her have the corner where no one could sneak up on her. Kanae took the chair to her left, settling down at the table without batting an eyelash. That was more than Isalla could do, even if she wasn't staring the way she would've a few months prior. Or even a few weeks, for that matter.

The town they'd reached wasn't large, and Kanae hadn't mentioned what its name was. It was larger than Kanae's hometown, but that didn't take a lot of work to manage. More impressive was how much finer the buildings were, along with the stone wall around the community.

Even more impressive was the variety of demons that were staying in the oversized inn. It was startling to see everything from a large horned demon nearly ten feet tall next to smaller demons like succubi, bone demons, and one of the fireborn, which were vaguely humanoid, but with more bone ridges and glowing orange veins. Most of them were startlingly well-dressed from Isalla's perspective, and while she might think that cotton and linen were common where she was from, she'd learned that such cloth was rare in the hells, and many of the other people in the room had clothing made of those materials. Considering that, it made Isalla a little nervous, since many of them were watching her and Kanae.

A shorter demon quickly approached their table, his insectile eyes slightly unnerving, though at least his four arms didn't have any weapons, and he was clothed drably in comparison to everyone else in the room. He smiled as he stopped at their table, speaking in a slightly buzzing voice.

"Hello, ladies! How might I serve you? We have an excellent cook, and a rock drake was recently brought down in the area. We also have a few stews on hand, and..." The demon began, but his voice trailed off as Kanae raised a finger.

"Is any Revian scarlet available? Along with roast deathstalker?" Kanae asked, and when she did so, the server went still, as did at least one patron who was nearby. Isalla frowned, curious why they seemed so startled.

"Ah, I'm afraid not, my lady," the server said in a slightly more formal tone, bowing his head slightly.

"Indeed? May I ask why not?" Kanae asked, her left index finger slowly tapping the table.

"I'm afraid that Master Nare chose to move on to new employment some two centuries past, and he was the only one here with the skill to properly prepare deathstalker, and the reserve of Revian scarlet he bottled has long since been depleted," he explained apologetically. "If we could bring it out, I'd readily do so, but I'm afraid I can't."

"I see. I suppose I shouldn't have expected him to still be working here after all this time, but I rather enjoyed his food. Ah, well." Kanae sighed and waved dismissively, which seemed odd when compared to her usual attitude. "In that case, a bottle of deepwater wine, only lightly aged, two glasses, thinly sliced rock drake with a honey glaze, and the appropriate vegetables for the season."

"Of course, my lady, right away!" the server replied, and quickly scurried off.

"Kanae?" Isalla murmured, slightly confused by the looks they were getting, as if people were reassessing them.

"I just showed knowledge and wealth, which marks us as wealthy and dangerous, rather than easy marks. It should deal with some of the problems we might have encountered, while creating others. It isn't perfect, but better than nothing," Kanae replied quietly, returning the looks they were receiving levelly. "You're here looking for a friend named Orla, who went missing in Estalia. A blonde with striking green eyes, but who was rather plain."

"I… oh, of course," Isalla said, realization dawning on her after a few moments. She paused a moment, then shrugged. "You think she might be here?"

"It's the best lead we have; the problem will be finding out if she's here," Kanae said, her voice just a hair louder now.

The room was filled with soft conversation, some people louder than others. The staff was well-garbed, and it was a much more comfortable inn than they'd stayed in during their trip thus far. Isalla had to wonder how much the trip had cost, and a moment later regretted wondering. More than that, she felt suddenly guilty about how much of a burden she'd been on Kanae.

At that moment, a woman nearby stood, one with long, swept-back horns, reddish-brown skin, and cloven hooves, though the last were surprisingly dainty. She also had a tail which was shorter and more muscular looking than Kanae's, and she was wearing an elaborately embroidered black halter top and a pair of blue trousers. The woman's eyes were a striking shade of orange, and she held a glass as she approached, another demoness quickly following, this one garbed in much less striking clothing.

"Pardon my intrusion, but may I sit with you?" the demoness asked, pausing with a hand on a chair. She obviously expected to be given permission, but Isalla was surprised that she was waiting, considering the ornate gold jewelry that adorned her neck, wrists, and even a couple of horn rings set with garnets or rubies.

"Go right ahead," Kanae said, smiling slightly as she glanced around. "I see that there's a much more interesting crowd here than last time I visited. Have things simply changed that much, or is it because of the rumors that the Flame of Ember was taken to the spire?"

The woman laughed, taking a seat and smiling, the other woman standing just behind her. "Ah, you've heard those rumors, have you? I had almost thought you might be here about them yourself... but yes, that's a good part of why many of us are here, in the hopes that she'll be inclined to go with someone aside from Her Majesty. I am Wysterith Sorrowlight. May I ask your name?"

"Kanae Darkshade," Kanae replied, smiling slightly. "I've heard of you, Lady Sorrowlight. Your family forges excellent armor, from all that I've seen."

"Thank you for the compliment. And Kanae, really? I've heard of you, you've traveled an enormous part of the hells, and some journals of your travels are almost legendary at this point," Wysterith said, her eyebrows rising. "Is there truly an entire mountain range of iron to the far west?"

Isalla looked at Kanae in a little shock, blinking as her mouth half-opened to speak, then paused and closed it again. She hadn't heard that Kanae was famous before, and yet her companion simply smiled.

"There is, though I wouldn't call it pure iron. Iron-rich ore, and quite a bit of ash, though," Kanae said, nodding.

"Fascinating. It's unfortunate that it's too far away to make use of. We have a lot of iron here, after all," Wysterith said, sighing slightly. She glanced at Isalla and raised an eyebrow. "I hadn't heard of you having any traveling companions, though, let alone a human."

"Yes, well, Myra's friend went missing the last time she came to Estalia, and she came to me for help finding her friend. Unlike you, she didn't know anything about my travels, she just knew I knew a lot more about the region," Kanae said, smiling warmly as she glanced over at Isalla, who belatedly realized that she was the Myra being spoken of. "The clues were... unfortunately faint, but the best lead so far has led us here, to the spire. We think her friend may have joined the priesthood of Estalia, and thought we'd try to investigate. Unfortunately, getting information out of the spire is... difficult."

"That would be putting it mildly," Wysterith agreed, sighing heavily. "We don't even have confirmation that the Flame of Ember is inside the spire, despite multiple inquiries. On the other hand, Her Majesty *did* visit a few weeks ago, so I have high hopes for our chances. Not that any of us will likely *get* her, mind you, but at least there's a chance."

"Mm, I do understand. Not precisely the sort of opportunity I'd be interested in, since there isn't much guarantee of success, but I wish you the best," Kanae replied politely.

"Ah, pardon me, Lady Sorrowlight, but I have to ask... do you know if I'll be able to get in touch with my friend if she *is* in the spire?" Isalla asked, leaning forward. "I *think* she went willingly, from what I've heard, but I'm not sure."

"That is the question... and most likely. They won't tell you if she's there, but if she joined them, she'll be able to come out and visit once her initiation is complete," Wysterith said, examining Isalla closely, then smiled. "I suspect that they'll try to recruit *you* if given half a chance. Are you looking for employment, perchance?"

Isalla saw Kanae glancing at her, and she also saw the server returning with a tray piled with food. She couldn't help flushing as she shook her head and replied quickly, wishing people wouldn't keep making her offers. "I'm not. At the moment I'm just trying to find Orla and ensure that she's well before starting the journey home. I may not agree with her if she decided to join Estalia's faith, but it's her choice."

"Here you are, ladies," the server said, holding the tray with his two lower arms as the upper ones deposited the two crystalline glasses in front of them. He set down a polished bottle of wine next, then utensils, napkins, and at last a pair of platters piled with thinly cut meat and a variety of purple vegetables that Isalla couldn't quite identify. There seemed to be two types, and at a guess she thought one was similar to a cucumber, while the other was more like a potato. All of the food smelled quite good, causing Isalla's stomach to rumble softly.

"Would you like me to open—" the server began, but stopped as Kanae picked up the bottle, tapped it once, listening closely to it, then pulled out a knife. She popped the cork with an adroit twist of her wrist, with more ease than Isalla had expected, then took a sniff and nodded.

"An excellent vintage, my thanks," Kanae said, smiling at the server before carefully pouring herself a glass of midnight-black wine, then pouring one for Isalla. "Now, as interesting as the conversation has been, Lady Sorrowlight, I'm afraid it has been a long day for Myra and I. Might we have a bit of privacy to eat and rest? We can always speak on the morrow."

"Certainly. It was a pleasure meeting you, Kanae, and I hope to speak with you in the coming days," Wysterith said, sliding her chair back as she stood, and she looked at Isalla and smiled as the server silently left. "It was interesting to meet you as well, Myra. Do let me know if you reconsider."

"I'll keep that in mind," Isalla said, her heartbeat quickening with nervousness. At last the woman went back to her previous table, and Isalla picked up the utensils to eat. The meat looked excellent, and there was an odd but enticing smell to the wine.

"I hadn't realized my reputation was still well-known. It's been centuries since I published any journals of my travels," Kanae murmured, taking a bite of meat and chewing thoughtfully. "I suppose it might be good, in some ways. It'll certainly help keep others from being too forward with us, which is helpful."

"I didn't realize you had that kind of reputation," Isalla said, feeling a little chagrined.

"Not many people travel as much as I did. It was a decent way to make some money at the time, and it worked out for the best. I would've thought everyone forgot about me by this point, but apparently not quite," Kanae said, shrugging. "In any case, we may as well eat and rest. We can make inquiries about Orla tomorrow."

"Alright," Isalla agreed and focused on her food. It really *was* quite good, and among the best food she'd had since coming to the hells.

THEIR VISIT around town the next day was quickly productive.

While their inquiries into the fake Orla didn't get any answers, they did hear quite a bit about the rumors of Roselynn, which helped Isalla relax slightly, since her friend must still be in the spire. On the other hand, she also was growing concerned, because Kanae was as tense as a tightly wound spring. She didn't show it much, but Isalla had never seen the demoness look quite so poised and ready to strike. It worried her and made Isalla wonder just how dangerous the spire was. Most of the people in the town barely seemed to care, but Isalla trusted Kanae.

Kanae was also interesting to others, though, which led to an interesting development of people coming to them with information. Most others approached Kanae, and Isalla could see that at least four of the demons who approached were tentative suitors, though Kanae didn't appear interested in the slightest. She was asked many things, and after a while she began to tell stories of her time traveling the hells, and the stories were enough to fascinate Isalla as well as the locals.

Sea serpents pulling ships across ink-black oceans where titanic, predatory fish dwelled, strange jungles atop volcanic islands, and realms where no demon lords made their homes, places where the demons believed angels and mortals to be nothing more than figures of myth and legend. Kanae spoke of a city grown of coral, other gleaming cities of rubies and sapphires in a land where they were common, and another where there was virtually no water, and the handful of inhabitants lived around a few rare springs in the midst of a vast desert. It was spellbinding, and many answered virtually any question Kanae had in order to hear more.

A few of the demons also approached Isalla, trying to learn more about Kanae, and it was somewhat difficult for her to avoid answering their questions, though she managed. She didn't have permission to tell them about what Kanae was doing, and she wasn't going to tell them in Kanae's place. A couple were interested in Isalla herself, but she fended them off relatively easily.

After two days, things settled down a little, but despite that, Isalla was nervous. She didn't dare talk too much with Kanae, as they worried that the others in the inn would be eavesdropping. The question was how long it would take before Roselynn left the spire, and then she worried that they might have difficulties getting to her. She knew that Kanae had a plan, but Isalla couldn't help but wonder if it'd work.

Still, there wasn't much Isalla could do but wait and fret.

# CHAPTER 37

"I'm going to miss you, Anna," Rose said, giving the angel a quick hug and kiss. Anna hugged her in return, laughing softly as she smiled.

"I'm glad you enjoyed your time here, Rose. I like you as well, but there's a time when too *much* comfort is just as bad for you as not having enough," Anna said, her voice gentle as she looked Rose in the eyes. "I think it's time for you to go out into the world and make your decisions. I'm told that Her Majesty had your armor refitted, so it's waiting for you along with Ember."

"I suppose you're right," Rose admitted, looking down at the sword hanging at her side, still feeling a little uncertain about it. She kept mulling over Estalia's advice, but couldn't decide what she wanted to do yet. "I'm not sure I want to take up the sword again, honestly. Her Majesty made a few excellent points, but even so… In any case, may I ask why you felt the need to give me one for the trip?"

Anna's smile faded as she followed Rose's gaze, replying quietly. "I understand, whatever you choose is up to you. But as for why I gave you a sword, Rose… while you are going to have skilled escorts for the trip to the capital, I don't want you to be without recourse. Some people have attempted to kidnap those who've left the spire before, and they might do so with you."

"Truly?" Rose asked, blinking in surprise, and feeling slightly confused. "But... *why*? I'm not anyone important."

"Ah, but are you really? Your line is well-known in the hells, for the wielder of Ember has been one that many speak of when facing the Order of the Phoenix. For millennia, your line has been often at the forefront... and to many, that would make you someone they wish to possess," Anna said, shaking her head sadly. "While I've done my best to show you that most demons aren't as bad as they're made out, some are as bad or worse than you can imagine. Additionally, some are so filled with rage from those they've lost that they'd lash out at any angel they could find, let alone someone of your renown. I don't wish for you to be hurt, Rose."

"Oh," Rose said, frowning and mulling Anna's words over. It made her a little sad, yet at the same time she wasn't really surprised.

A part of her had known that already, Rose realized. The weight of her family's expectations had been something she'd dealt with her entire life, even if she'd managed to mostly discard it while she was here in the Spire of Confession. Anna, Coral, and Tina hadn't seemed to care about it, and that was... comfortable. It had made her feel better about herself, generally. Yet as she considered it now, Rose realized that she was comfortable with herself, in a way she'd never felt before. She was at peace, and if even demons had their views of her... what did it matter? Rose was who she was.

The pieces fell into place, and Rose took a deep breath, then smiled. She looked at Anna and nodded slightly as she spoke. "I think I understand, now. While I might wish that they didn't view me that way, I can deal with it. And if I must defend myself, so be it."

"Good. I'm glad to hear that," Anna replied, her smile reappearing once more. "Now, here's your cloak. It isn't perfect, but at least it'll keep the rain and ash off you."

Anna offered a dark brown cloak, one which looked like it'd been woven of silk. Rose looked at it skeptically, then asked. "Will it even fit? My wings..."

"It's enchanted, so it'll fit, I promise," Anna explained, smiling even more.

"That would certainly do it," Rose admitted, her mood improving as she took the cloak and swirled it around her back to put on. As Anna had indicated, the fabric stretched effortlessly to accommodate her wings while still covering her properly, and the angel smiled as she secured it around her neck and looked at Anna. "Thank you, Anna. You've been lovely from the first time I met you, even when I… wasn't."

"Oh, don't give me that," Anna scolded, shaking her head quickly as she reached up to adjust the cloak slightly. "You were *always* lovely, Rose. It's just that you needed to believe that you were beautiful, and we helped you find it. Now, why don't we get you going? The sooner you go, the sooner you reach the palace."

"True, true. I hope to see you again relatively soon," Rose said, and she gave the other angel a quick hug and another kiss.

Anna returned the hug and kiss, then broke away with a laugh, her eyes almost dancing as she spoke. "I know, Rose! Now go on, get moving before the day is over."

Rose laughed, smiling as she turned to leave. She wasn't entirely happy to be leaving the spire, but another part of her was looking forward to it.

Soon she'd see Queen Estalia again, and if that weren't enough, the thought of meeting Isalla made her even happier. So she laid her hand on the door and slowly pushed it open.

## CHAPTER 38

anae looked up as she saw a man rush into the inn's common room, and when she saw the expression on his face, her eyes narrowed. He looked far too excited as he ran to his employer, an augur demon with an extra eye set into his forehead. She'd already learned that the demon in question was here in an attempt to lure the Flame of Ember to his stronghold, and *that* gave her a very good idea of what was going on.

She sat back, lifting her glass to sip at the liquid in it as she saw more servants start rushing into the inn. Then she glanced over at Isalla and murmured, "It appears that the sought-after Flame of Ember has appeared at last, Myra."

"Oh? Is that why all of them are rushing?" Isalla asked, looking around with comprehension dawning on her face. There was also a little worry, but the angel hid it admirably, in Kanae's opinion. That was good, since Kanae's stomach had felt like it was tied in knots since they'd arrived. It wasn't just because they were so near the spire, either.

The other patrons were hastily preparing to leave, Kanae noticed, many of them settling their bills quickly as other servants ran to pack their things. It wouldn't be long until the building was mostly empty at this rate.

"That's my guess. I don't see any *other* reason for them to be vacating the premises this quickly," Kanae said, and she shook her head. "That being the case, it's likely best that we go."

"What?" Isalla asked, obviously startled as she looked at Kanae. "But… well, what about Orla?"

"If we haven't heard anything more about her by this point, we're unlikely to find out in the near future, especially with so many visitors having left," Kanae said, shaking her head. "That being the case, I'm thinking our best bet is to go to the capital and inquire about her at the High Temple. If we can learn about her anywhere, it'd be there."

"I suppose so. Should I go pack, then?" Isalla asked, frowning.

"I'll settle the bill, then we can get going," Kanae said, nodding and standing. As she headed for the counter, her stomach tightened still more. This was going to be the most dangerous part of their trip, and she wasn't looking forward to the results.

~

Isalla glanced back as they left town, heading back the direction that they'd originally entered from. Kanae was leading the way, and since she could see most of the other patrons heading the other direction, including Wysterith, she had to wonder what Kanae was thinking. Still, she didn't say anything yet, instead following Kanae closely.

They passed several rocky outcroppings, and a couple of farmhouses, then they were climbing a trail in the hills. In short order they reached a fork, and Kanae promptly turned left, taking a different route than they'd originally come down.

"Where are we going?" Isalla asked at last, glancing back in concern. "Everyone else is going the other way…"

"I know they are. They aren't going to have any luck, though," Kanae said, her voice quiet. "Roselynn will have escorts, and the chances of her agreeing to any of their propositions… well, I wouldn't expect that to happen in this century."

Isalla fell silent for a long moment. She was slightly

reassured, but it still didn't explain why they were going this direction. It made little sense to her, but she knew that Kanae wouldn't be this route for no reason.

"What if they attack the guards and try to kidnap her?" Isalla asked softly, voicing one of her fears. "You said that could happen, right?"

"It could, but any attempt like that…" Kanae's voice trailed off, then she laughed and shook her head. "It's a quick form of suicide, Isalla. The one who is in charge of the spire is powerful. Incredibly powerful, in fact, to the point that I'm not sure just how strong she might be. Attempting to kidnap one of those who've attended the spire is sure to bring down her wrath if it's done nearby."

"Oh. That's why we're going somewhere else, then?" Isalla asked, blanching slightly at the thought of someone that powerful being in the spire. She did wonder why this was the first she'd heard of it.

"Exactly. I'm fairly certain that she wouldn't kill either of *us*, but I prefer living free to undergoing her tender ministrations again," Kanae said, nodding as she glanced over her shoulder. "That's why I'm heading for where the escorts usually stop for the evening. I remember being taken through a hidden cave, one that leads to a teleportation circle. We should be able to use it to get a good part of the way back to Hellmount in an instant, and to throw them off our trail."

A sense of relief flooded through Isalla at the explanation. She half-wished that Kanae had explained earlier, but she understood why the other woman hadn't said anything in town. The other demons hadn't felt trustworthy to Isalla, even those who were relatively friendly.

"That sounds like a wonderful plan to me!" Isalla said, smiling suddenly, then asked, "How do you plan to deal with the guards? It sounds like you think they're quite skilled, right?"

"I'm sure they are, but I have my ways," Kanae replied, glancing over her shoulder and smiling. "There are a few fungi in the Fungal Abyss that can force others into a hypnotic state. I know how to make a cure, so I brought a sample of the fungus with me, along with several doses of the cure. I'm going to plant it where they'll come too close, and if any fight it off, we'll be able to knock them out before they can fully recover. I'll destroy the fungus before we leave, but it'll take them out of the picture until after we've made our escape."

"Alright. It sounds like that would let us convince Roselynn to come along with us, too," Isalla said, letting out a breath of relief. She nearly tripped due to her distraction, but she caught herself in time. At least the only thing injured was her pride, and Isalla focused on picking a stable path.

"At least long enough to get out of the area," Kanae agreed, and her voice grew grim. "Then we get to figure out just how much she changed, and if she's recoverable."

It was like a bucket of cold water had been dumped on Isalla, and she swallowed hard. Then she nodded and spoke softly. "You're right. I hope she isn't *too* changed."

"As do I. As do I," Kanae murmured.

~

Rose dodged as the spiny demon lunged toward her, but she shouldn't have bothered. Before it could get close enough to be a threat, the nearest of the guards had spun and cut the demon down with his axe, grunting as he did so.

Around her were the bodies of nearly twenty demons, most of them dead or dying, and she was stunned by the variety of them, or that they'd attacked so fearlessly. Even more startling were the skills of Rose's guards, and she looked at them in admiration. Any one of the five would have been an opponent to be wary of on the battlefield, though she was confident she'd have had decent odds of defeating them.

There were five guards in total, three men and two women. One was an elven man who wielded a pair of short, wickedly sharp swords, while all the others were demons or part-demons. The greataxe wielder was big, had scaled skin and claws, along with an inhuman head with a pair of large horns that curved out and upward. He wore heavier armor, as did one of the women who wielded a sword and shield, her demonic features as pronounced as his were.

The bone demon was startling, as the woman wielded a rapier with skill and speed, often holding back and moving to support her companions, and Rose found it surprising how beautiful her movements were. But last was an incubus, and the handsome man wore light armor while wielding predominantly fire magic to support the others. He also had used some enhancement spells to make the others still more dangerous, which had intrigued Rose, but in all the five worked together like a well-oiled machine.

That didn't mean she wasn't disappointed by the attack, though. The number of well-dressed demons that had approached her with offers of employment, a new home, or even a position leading a small army had been shocking, especially as they appeared not long after she'd emerged from the immense Spire of Confession. She hadn't been interested by any of them, as she was far more focused on the darkness of the hells, as well as the sheer size of the spire. She must never have seen more than a fraction of the rooms on a single floor, which stunned her.

After rejecting most of the offers, the demons had backed off somewhat and allowed them to continue on their way, at least for a little while. Just as they'd left easy line of sight of the spire, the ambushers had lunged out of the rocks and bushes that were on either side of the road, to the current, gory results.

"Well, it looks like that's the last of them," the incubus said, shaking his head and sighing. His name was Ithik, and the dark-haired man glanced at Rose and smiled sadly. "Unfortunately, this was at least somewhat expected this time around. I wish we hadn't been attacked, but there's nothing to be done for it."

"They knew the risks when they chose to attack here," Ethan said, the elf's voice heavy as he cleaned off his weapons and sheathed them. "We may as well get going."

That made Rose blink in surprise, then she asked. "We're leaving already? Aren't some of them still alive, though?"

She gestured toward the battlefield, where she could see at least four of the fallen demons were moving. Rose doubted much more than half of them were dead, though she didn't think most of them would recover on their own. Simply leaving them would be quite cruel, from her point of view.

"They are, yes. Lady Anna will be sending a group to collect the survivors shortly, to grant them succor and find out who attacked, as well as why," the man with the greataxe explained, his voice deep and resonant as he slung his weapon. He'd introduced himself as Ataron, and had been a gentleman so far, something quite at odds with his appearance. "I wouldn't stand for leaving them like this, otherwise. If aid couldn't be granted, the merciful thing would be to grant them quick deaths. Too many creatures in the hells are willing to eat the fallen."

"Oh, I didn't realize," Rose said, her discomfort easing, then she frowned and asked. "Anna already knows, then?"

"Most certainly. We have access to magical wards across the region which allowed us to signal that we were under attack as soon as the battle began," Zeera said, the bone demon's voice almost clinical, and she was certainly the least friendly of Rose's guards. "As none of us fell in battle, she'll know that we're fine, and won't be leading a force to our rescue."

"Which is why I suggested we get going," Ethan explained. "I hope there aren't more attacks like this, but the more time we give them to prepare, the worse it might go for us."

"As you say. Hopefully there aren't attacks, but it's good to know how skilled all of you are," Rose said, giving them a slight smile as she nodded. "You're a skilled team, and one that would certainly daunt me if I was up against you."

That prompted a smile from Ithik, and chuckles from the others as he spoke. "Thank you for the compliment, Lady Rose. I think I can speak for all of us when I say that we'd be wary of running into you on a battlefield."

The others obviously agreed, and after a moment, Rose smiled more and shrugged as she replied, feeling more amused. "Well, fortunately I don't see *that* happening anytime soon."

They chuckled, then Dathael, the last, almost silent demoness, nodded and started leading the way. If she hadn't introduced herself to begin with, Roselynn might have thought the woman was mute.

# CHAPTER 39

*I*salla held up the vial of blue liquid, examining it nervously. It didn't look like much, but she also wasn't exactly thrilled by the idea of a fungus which could make her stand still in a daze, even if it would make it easier to rescue Roselynn.

She looked away from the vial and over at Kanae, who was standing over near the shallow cave. The demoness was crouching down with the ceramic jar she'd pulled out of her pack, and she was carefully pulling out what looked like one of the mushrooms that attached to trees, almost looking like a shelf or ribbon. Kanae pressed it against the wall, her other hand sprinkling some liquid on it, and as Isalla watched, it adhered to the wall. Kanae quickly picked up the jar and moved away, looking visibly relieved.

"There we are. I was half-afraid it might have died on the trip, but hypnis are able to go dormant for quite a while," Kanae said, stepping closer to Isalla as she looked back. "It only takes a couple of minutes before it starts releasing its spores, and the hypnotism lasts for as long as someone is near, or about ten minutes after the person leaves the area or the fungus is destroyed."

"Will that be enough time?" Isalla asked, feeling slightly worried about their chances. "You said the back of the cave is an illusion, so it should get us to the teleportation node quickly, but what if they recognize the fungus and destroy it?"

"I sincerely doubt any of the guards have the experience to recognize hypnis. It's reasonably rare, even in the Fungal Abyss, so only those who delve into it frequently would know what it is," Kanae explained confidently. "Even if it is destroyed, I'm sure we can get out of here before any guards that succumb can recover."

Isalla nodded, then followed Kanae as she began moving farther away to where they'd have more cover and a good vantage point. They were well off the road, and the area had a little more vegetation than a lot of the hells did, which gave them some advantages, though they *had* run into a nest of nasty avians that they'd had to deal with. They settled into their hiding spot, and Isalla considered before finally asking the question she'd had for a while.

"Why *are* you putting so much work into not hurting the guards? From what you said, it would be pretty easy to eliminate them, or just leave them under the effect of the hypnosis. I know that could lead to them dying, though, but… I've just wondered," Isalla said, fidgeting slightly. She didn't like the idea of killing people who couldn't defend themselves, but if it allowed her to rescue Roselynn, she'd probably do it.

Kanae looked at Isalla, then smiled fondly as she shook her head. Her voice was quiet as she replied. "We're going to be stealing someone who Queen Estalia views as a major prize, Isalla, and that's going to annoy her enough as it is. If we kill trusted soldiers as well, there's no telling how much effort she'll put into tracking us down. Beyond that, we don't have any idea what Roselynn's mindset will be like. If we hurt people she views as friends, how likely is it that she'll trust us? I'd rather take a path that's less likely to cause problems all around."

"Ah, true enough. I don't like the idea of trying to escape with her upset *and* a demon queen after us," Isalla said, shivering at the thought. Once more, she was thankful that Kanae was with her. There was no way in all the heavens she could have done any of this on her own. She'd likely have ended up dead or enslaved before she reached Silken Veils.

"Exactly. So now, all we need to do is wait," Kanae murmured, and she settled down still more.

Isalla followed her example, though she didn't find it easy. They were so close to rescuing Roselynn at last.

❧

ROSE FOLLOWED THE OTHERS, feeling far better than she had earlier, though she *was* a little more exhausted than she should have been. It was good that she'd tried to exercise in the spire, because if she hadn't, her condition would have left Rose embarrassed. At least their trip for the day was coming close to its end, though. Ithik had explained that they'd be going through a hidden teleportation circle that would get them close to one of Estalia's army outposts much deeper in the domain. At least they hadn't been attacked again, since Rose doubted that any attackers would have been able to do much more than die.

"There it is," Ataron rumbled, his voice betraying the barest hint of relief. "I wish it was closer to the spire."

"If it was closer, it's possible that enemies could use it in an attack. Her Majesty had the spire built there for a reason," Zeera replied. A moment later, she added, "Don't let your guard down, though. Last time I was through here, a bloodvine had decided to take up residence in the cave."

"Bloodvine?" Rose asked. It sounded a little like some of the vines she'd heard of that killed people, though the name was a little different.

"A vine that disables people to drink their blood. It paralyzes them, and lets them starve to death, though most die of blood loss," Ethan explained, his lips thinning. "I hate the things, since it's such an unpleasant end."

"I agree," Rose said, shivering slightly. She had some fire magic, which should help against plants, but she didn't like the idea of dying like *that*.

"Well, we'll find out soon enough," Ithik said, following the others toward the cave. It certainly didn't look deep, but that was the entire point of the illusion, so Rose wasn't too concerned.

"Looks safe," Dathael said softly, poking her head through the wall, which was an eerie sight. "I..."

The woman paused, and as she did so, Rose felt herself growing slightly dizzy. All the others paused as well. Rose had a moment to wonder what was happening, and then her mind slowly went almost blank. She should've been more worried, but... she just didn't want to move. At all.

So Rose stopped in place and waited with her eyes half-closed, a smile on her face. She didn't even mind that her guards had stopped moving as well.

～

"IT WORKED." Isalla's voice was filled with relief, and Kanae entirely agreed with the sentiment. She'd been afraid the spores wouldn't do their job, especially on the bone demon, but they had.

The guards were slightly more numerous than Kanae had anticipated, as she'd expected only three or four of them, and these guards looked more skilled than she'd expected. They weren't Estalia's personal guard, which was a relief, but the insignia on their deep blue armor indicated they were among the elite guard of the kingdom. Kanae wouldn't have liked her odds against them, even with Isalla helping.

At the center of their formation was the woman who must be Roselynn, though Kanae couldn't be certain about that. She was shrouded in a brown cloak that bulged upward where a pair of wings were, and Kanae could only see a few wisps of red hair that poked out of her hood and the sword she wore. Isalla looked excited, though, which made her more confident. The chances of them pulling this off twice were practically nonexistent.

"Time to drink the antidote, Isalla," Kanae said, keeping her voice calm as she pulled out her vial and drank it. No matter how dangerous their situation might be, she had come too far to back out now. The liquid tasted surprisingly good, even to Kanae, like some of the berries she'd tried when she'd lived outside the hells. Of course, it might also be Kanae's memory playing tricks on her.

"Alright," Isalla agreed, pulling out her own vial and sniffing it, then drinking it. She looked startled after swallowing, then looked at the vial for a moment before putting the stopper back in and offering it to Kanae as she said, "It tastes like blueberries."

"Does it? I thought it might, but I couldn't quite remember... it's been too long since I had them," Kanae replied, not moving yet, except to put the vial away. "We'll give it a couple of minutes, then head forward. The antidote *should* work within a few seconds, but I'd rather give it more time."

"That's reasonable," Isalla agreed, settling back down from where she'd almost looked like she was going to bolt over the log toward the group.

"You think that's Roselynn? I've never seen her, so I can't say," Kanae said, nodding toward the winged woman. "As far as I'm concerned, she could be any angel, or even an ashborn."

"It's her. She's the right height, and while there's something slightly odd about it, that's how she walks," Isalla said confidently, then swallowed. "You said they... *change* the people who go there?"

"No, they convince them that they *want* to change, Isalla," Kanae corrected, remembering her own visit to the spire with a shiver. She didn't want to return there, yet at the same time she longed to go back. If Anna was still there... it took a moment for Kanae to focus on the conversation instead. "If that's Roselynn, you might barely recognize her due to any changes she's made. She'll likely have made herself look like a tiny part of her has always dreamed she could be like."

"I'll brace myself, then," Isalla said, nodding quickly as she took a deep breath, then let it out. After a few seconds, she admitted softly, "I have no idea what to say to her, once we have her away from them."

"We'll figure it out when we get there, Isalla," Kanae assured her with a smile. Deciding that enough time had passed, she stood up, trying not to think about how her relationship with Isalla was likely about to end. "That should be plenty of time. Let's go rescue Roselynn, hm?"

BENJAMIN MEDRANO

"Right!" Isalla said, standing quickly, and the two of them headed for the group.

It was a short walk, and Kanae felt her tension growing as she looked at the guards. It was fortunate that she didn't recognize any of them, or else she might have been tempted to risk giving them orders to forget her. The hypnotism wouldn't be guaranteed to work with an order like that, though, and it might wake them up. Not that they couldn't see or remember her while hypnotized, they just wouldn't be able to act.

Seeing Isalla open her mouth, Kanae spoke first, her voice soft. "Don't yell. We don't want to risk breaking the trance. Only speak softly to Roselynn and ask her to follow you. I'll check the cave again, then you can lead her to the teleportation circle."

"Okay," Isalla agreed, swallowing her words with obvious disappointment.

Kanae let Isalla approach the angel and instead moved to the illusionary wall and looked through it, glancing around the chamber. The cave was much deeper than it looked, and dim red light at the far end illuminated the teleportation circle, an elaborate enchantment that was twenty feet across and in perfect condition. It did look different than she remembered, but that was probably because it'd been replaced, not because it had been altered. The cave was large enough to make things easy to transport, at least.

Behind her, Kanae barely heard Isalla's voice, the woman sounding stunned. "What happened...? Never mind. Please follow me, Roselynn."

Turning back, Kanae gestured Isalla forward, then paused as she caught a glimpse of Roselynn's face. The woman's face was breathtakingly beautiful, yet at the same time, even in the midst of the hypnotism, there was a sense of peace to her, and her ruby lips were slightly curved in a smile. Her hair was a deep red, deeper than Isalla had described it, and she wore several pieces of glittering golden jewelry. It was obvious to Kanae that Roselynn had changed herself in the spire, but at the same time, it looked almost natural for her, even with her narrow waist and the sword at her hip.

Isalla took Roselynn's hand and led her toward Kanae, and

the demoness could see the worry in Isalla's eyes. At the same time, the look of pure relief and delight on Isalla's face caused Kanae's heart to clench slightly. Regardless, Kanae raised a finger to her lips and gestured for Isalla to enter the cave. Isalla nodded and quickly did so, though she hesitated slightly before pushing through the illusion. They were fortunate that it wasn't one of those illusions that was real until someone saw through the magic.

Once they were past her, Kanae looked at the guards warily. They'd almost certainly remember her and Isalla, but she wasn't willing to go too far. While Kanae had an unusual appearance, it'd take time for them to track down where she lived. That should give enough time for Isalla and Roselynn to escape, at the least. Even so, she hated to get the guards into trouble with the queen.

So Kanae put a hand to her chest and bowed slightly, speaking softly. "My apologies, but Roselynn is an old friend of hers. I promise that she'll come to no harm."

She held the bow for a moment, then straightened and pulled out another vial, this one filled with clear liquid. Stepping over to the fungus, Kanae undid the stopper and carefully poured the liquid onto it. The liquid hissed and bubbled on hitting the fungus, and where it touched, the pale blue flesh turned dark and pitted. It would take less than a minute for the fungus to die, and then they'd be truly short on time. Giving the guards another polite nod, Kanae stowed her vial and darted into the cave.

Isalla and Roselynn were standing next to the circle, and Kanae gestured toward the center as she approached, still not speaking. Isalla blinked, then stepped into the center of the circle, still holding Roselynn's hand, and the angel followed obediently. As they did so, Kanae rushed forward and quickly examined the circle. Her worries eased as she saw that it truly *was* the same as the previous one. That would make her task easier. She pulled out an amulet, the pendant made of glittering adamantine alloy set with several tiny diamonds, each shimmering with internal light.

Kanae held the amulet in her right hand and pressed it

against the circle as she reached within herself, breathing deep as she accessed her magic again for the first time in a couple of months. The rush of mana out through her body made her shiver happily, and Kanae smiled as she channeled it through the amulet and into the circle. The words to activate the circle were simple, and fell from her lips quickly, echoing in the cavern despite her attempt to keep them as quiet as possible. Then it was a matter of continuing to channel mana into the circle until it activated.

A minute passed, then two… and then the sound of a foot against the ground brought Kanae's attention snapping upward as one of the guards lunged through the illusion. The bone demon had her rapier drawn, and Kanae could see her anger in her stance and how tightly her lips were pressed together.

"Surrender now and I'll have mercy on you," the demoness said, but she didn't stop her charge.

Kanae considered replying, but instead she simply smiled, murmuring the words of a second spell as she channeled more mana into her left hand, weaving a spell with a couple of flicks of her fingers. Purple magic wreathed her hand just as the bone demon was about to reach her, then surged outward in a wave of purple light that knocked the woman backward a dozen paces. It didn't hurt her, and despite being almost thrown through the air, the woman landed on her feet, though she *did* look surprised.

"No need, I'm afraid. I must say, managing all this without hurting any of you *was* a bit tricky," Kanae said, and she smiled at the bone demon with a hint of admiration at the woman's quick recovery. "Goodbye."

She could hear the other guards moving, but it was just a bit too late. With a popping sound and the stomach-wrenching lurch of a teleportation, they were gone.

# CHAPTER 40

"What do you mean, they didn't come out here?" Ataron demanded incredulously. "This is the only place the circle connects to!"

"I'm well aware of that," Ithik replied, scowling in return. "All I can tell you is that no one has emerged from a teleportation *here* but us in the last day or so."

"That's not good," Ethan murmured, frowning deeply and looking quite displeased. "Bad enough that someone managed to disable all of us and kidnap Lady Rose, but they also managed to get away cleanly?"

"It looks that way," Ithik said, frowning. "Zeera? You're the only one who got a good look at them before they were gone; was there anything specific you noticed?"

"Other than the woman who spoke to us being a skilled enough mage to charge the teleportation circle *and* knock me back with telekinesis simultaneously?" Zeera asked rhetorically, then shook her head and sighed. "Sorry, that just... I came so *close*."

"We don't blame you, Zeera," Ataron said, taking a deep breath. "From what we've seen, the demoness must be quite powerful, enough to make me concerned. She *could* have hurt all of us, or even killed us. She didn't have to kill that thing that was disabling us, either."

"I know. As to what I saw... she was crouched down, on one knee, and was holding something against part of the circle," Zeera said, frowning. "I couldn't see what it was, since her hand was wrapped around it, but it couldn't have been large, and was on a necklace or chain."

"Hm, I can't say for sure what it was, but she must have had a keystone linked to another node," Ithik said unhappily, frowning. "That's quite troubling, since it has to have been one that's connected to the other end of the teleporter. That means that she *knew* it was there, and that we'd be using it to get Lady Rose here."

The group fell silent for a long moment, then Ethan sighed. "She had to have known that, to set up that trap. I've never heard of that fungus before, but it was nasty."

"I think we should make haste to the capital," Dathael said, her voice soft, but prompting everyone to look at her. "We can't follow her, so the sooner we report to Her Majesty, the better."

There was a moment of silence, then Ithik nodded. "Agreed. We don't have the things we'd need to give chase, or even to determine where they went. Her Majesty can make a decision and has the resources to do what's necessary."

The others agreed, and they quickly headed for the cavern exit. As they did so, Ethan asked, "Did anyone recognize either of them?"

A murmur of denial came back, but Ataron spoke a moment later. "While I didn't, I *do* know that she moved well. I suspect she'd have been a difficult foe even if we hadn't been disabled by her."

"Really?" Ithik asked, his eyebrows rising. "That's high praise. I wasn't in a good position to look at her, unfortunately."

"There was no fear in her eyes as I approached," Zeera said, her voice soft. "I may not know who she was, but she is dangerous."

"All the more reason to get to Her Majesty. We don't know if her word can be trusted," Ataron added, and with that they picked up their pace.

∾

Rose felt her senses drift back into focus and blinked, slightly disoriented. Her stomach was still churning from the teleportation, and they'd arrived in the middle of a clearing among scrub-like bushes. Then she focused, and her breath caught in her throat.

Rose had thought she might be dreaming that she'd seen Isalla, but it wasn't a dream. Standing there, holding her hand tightly, was Isalla. Her old lover wasn't nearly the same, with her missing wings, longer hair that desperately needed a trim, and slightly dusty clothing with forest detritus on it instead of armor, but Isalla still had that same hesitant smile, her eyes were still bright, and she somehow felt even more beautiful than Rose had remembered her being.

"Isalla!" Rose exclaimed, and she enveloped Isalla in a sudden hug, squeezing tight as she resisted the urge to pick her friend up and swirl her around. "I was afraid you were dead!"

"Oof. Roselynn, you remember me? I'd heard some stories about the Spire of Confession, and I was afraid that you wouldn't..." Isalla began, then swallowed hard and finished, smiling again shyly. "Well, wouldn't be the same. You *feel* different, too."

"That's because I'm not the same, Isalla," Rose replied, smiling and letting go, a hint of sorrow rippling through her at the same time as she saw her friend's wings were missing once more. Isalla had possessed the loveliest wings. She also saw Isalla's companion, but she wasn't interfering, so Rose focused on her friend. "They helped me realize just how unfulfilled I was. How the army had choked so much pleasure from my life... and led me to lose *you*. I was afraid I'd lost you for good, even when Queen Estalia promised that she'd search for you."

"You've *met* her?" Isalla asked, her eyes going wide. "A-and... you look really different. I almost didn't recognize you."

"I wanted to feel more beautiful, and to be pretty for when I met you again," Rose explained, smiling at Isalla's blush, happiness spreading through her with every passing moment. "As for the queen, I did meet her. There's no way to describe her... and she was one of the kindest women I've ever met."

"She always is," the other woman said, her voice soft. "It's what makes her so incredibly dangerous."

Rose stiffened, then looked at the woman more closely, her eyes narrowing. Her brief displeasure at the woman's comment faded slightly as she looked at the demoness, as it didn't look like she'd meant her words to be spiteful. The woman was pretty, with pale skin and deep purple hair that was almost black. She looked quite competent in her dark armor, and there was something... intriguing about her, something that Rose couldn't place.

"Who is this, Isalla?" Rose asked at last, studying the woman's purple eyes as the demoness looked back calmly.

"Oh! This is Kanae, she saved my life when Haral threw me off the Evergardens," Isalla said, and Rose stiffened, her eyes going wide in disbelief.

"What? Haral... isn't she the one who you said was giving you information?" Rose demanded, her gaze focusing on Isalla.

"Yes, that's right. She cut off my wings with her followers, then threw me down into the hells. If Kanae hadn't caught me, I'd have died when I hit the ground," Isalla said, flinching slightly. "Kanae's also the one who brought me to rescue you. I couldn't have done it without her."

"I see," Rose said, her voice icy with anger as she thought about Haral. If she ever had the chance, she was going to make the woman pay for what she'd done to Isalla. Suddenly, Queen Estalia's suggestion that she not abandon the sword seemed far more reasonable. After a moment, Rose looked at Kanae and relaxed slightly, nodding her head. "I think I'll return the favor to Haral if I ever meet her. Thank you for saving Isalla, Kanae. She means a lot to me, even if I'm not sure I needed rescuing."

"You're welcome, Roselynn. I do understand, since I've come to be fond of Isalla myself," Kanae replied, smiling thinly. "As for your rescue... I think it was necessary. You need some time away from Estalia to learn to breathe again."

"What?" Rose asked, bristling internally. She wasn't sure if it was the implication that Kanae was interested in Isalla or that she needed to be away from Queen Estalia that offended her more.

"I'm speaking from experience, Roselynn," Kanae said, her voice cutting off Isalla, who'd opened her mouth to speak. "Tell me, is Anna well?"

Rose froze for an instant, startled. Then her eyes narrowed as she asked cautiously, "You know Anna?"

"Yes. Unless she's changed, she's the ruler of the Spire of Confession. Blonde hair, blue eyes, a lovely disposition, and gently convincing," Kanae said, smiling gently, her gaze softening. "She's the one who taught me to wield the sword. I never came close to beating her in a fight."

"That... sounds like Anna, yes. She's well, or was this morning," Rose said, feeling off-balance. "Why are you so convinced I need time away, then? If you've been to the spire..."

"The Spire of Confession, somewhat intentionally, is meant to enrapture those who come there with Queen Estalia. I'm not sure if it's quite brainwashing, but it's close, and it's effective because they use your own hopes and desires to do it," Kanae explained, her voice calm as she met Rose's gaze steadily. "They never lie to you, they don't force you into anything... but they manipulate you anyway. If you go to Queen Estalia right now, you'll *never* leave her side, except at her command. I've seen it happen before."

Rose was about to speak sharply in return, but Isalla spoke first. "Um, Kanae? I thought that you said you'd only seen her once. The queen, I mean. How do you know that?"

"I... dare not say yet. Once we've reached my home, perhaps, and the two of you have decided whether or not to make your escape," Kanae said, shaking her head. "I also haven't lied to you, Isalla, but I've also not spoken the full truth. I met Queen Estalia once while I was in the army, yes, but I've met her more times than I can count before that. If I tell you everything, merely speaking of it will likely bring attention that we can ill afford at present."

Watching the demoness, Rose's eyes narrowed as she began to think. Despite her anger at the woman accusing Anna and the others of *brainwashing* her, Rose also felt like the woman wasn't lying to her. Like she might be telling the truth, and that made her… uncertain. She *had* rescued Isalla, which was a point in her favor, but…

"What do you mean?" Isalla asked, looking even more confused.

"Queen Estalia will search for Roselynn when she learns she's gone missing. She'll send word to her temples, have magi scry for her, and deploy others to try to find her. I've taken precautions that will make that difficult for the scrying, and even sending out descriptions of us will give us time," Kanae said, then looked at Rose as she smiled thinly. "If I reveal myself, I fear that she will act *herself*. If she acts like I expect she would, our chances of doing anything would be essentially nonexistent."

The explanation made everything suddenly fall into place for Rose, and she felt her eyes widen. Queen Estalia had said that her daughter was missing, and that she missed her terribly. Could Kanae possibly be her daughter? They didn't look much alike, but there was that tiny sense of her presence that felt so familiar. Despite her suspicions, Rose didn't say anything for a long moment. Then she finally asked, "What do you intend, then?"

"We're perhaps four days from my home. It will take at least two days for your guards to report in to Her Majesty. That means they will have only two days to begin the search before we reach the house, and that isn't enough. If you decide what you want quickly, you'll have time to begin ascending Hellmount to escape before all hope of such is cut off," Kanae said, looking back at Rose. "Or you can return to Queen Estalia, if that's what you choose."

"Four days from home? It took us *weeks* to get to the spire, though!" Isalla said, her eyes widening.

"I had a focus to allow us to teleport *to* this site, Isalla, but there isn't a teleportation platform here, and I don't know how to build one," Kanae said, glancing away to look at Isalla patiently, and the look that flickered across her face made up Rose's mind for the moment. She decided to play along for now and listened as Kanae continued. "We had to take the long way to get there but getting back was simple."

"Oh," Isalla said, then looked pleadingly at Rose. "In that case, would you *please* come with us, Roselynn? I don't know what you went through, but—"

Rose raised a finger and placed it over Isalla's lips, shaking her head in amusement as she spoke. "Call me Rose, both of you. I've decided I like it better."

"As you like," Kanae said, looking unsurprised.

"Now, considering things… I'll come along for now. I'm not sure I entirely believe you, Kanae, but you haven't harmed Isalla, and there's no reason that you would have known we'd be acquainted when you first encountered her." Rose continued, smiling thinly. "I'll come with and judge your intentions and words for myself, *then* decide."

"Thank heavens!" Isalla said, tension visibly leaving her shoulders as she abruptly hugged Rose again, which caused Rose to smile. "I was so afraid you'd have changed entirely! Come on, let's go!"

"Now, now, Isalla… not so fast. Things *have* changed, and it's been a long day for me. Why don't we make camp, and you tell me all about your time since coming to the hells?" Rose asked, smiling gently at Isalla.

"That sounds like a good idea," Kanae agreed, then nodded to the side. "There's a good camp site that direction, though I'll need to ensure it's still secure before we can settle down."

"Right," Isalla agreed, letting go and straightening.

They began to follow Kanae, but Rose noticed that Isalla hadn't let go of her hand. That made her smile even more.

LATER THAT EVENING, Rose waited until Isalla had gone to bed. She was sitting by the low fire and watching Kanae thoughtfully. The discussion of what they'd each been doing since they'd been captured had been illuminating, and Isalla hadn't believed what Rose had chosen to do to herself, since the changes were quite extensive, at least from her point of view. By the same token, Rose had found herself intrigued by everything that Isalla had gone through, as well as what the hells were like outside the spire.

There was a stark contrast between the pristine interior of the spire and the small town that Isalla had described, or even between it and the cities she'd visited with Kanae. The talk about the different villagers, including even a bone demon store manager, were fascinating. It was amazing how differently the two of them had experienced the hells, and what Kanae had done for Isalla... it dispelled much of her suspicion of the woman, though not all of it. The strangest thing was how attracted she was to Kanae despite herself, like a lodestone to metal.

So she waited until she was sure that Isalla was asleep before deciding to speak any further, as she didn't want to upset her friend.

"Queen Estalia would have her wings regenerated if we went to her," Rose said, her voice soft.

"Doubtlessly," Kanae agreed, gently setting a branch on the fire and glancing up as the coals softly popped. "All the harm that was dealt to her would be undone within a day... but at what price? She'd be ensnared by the queen's beauty, much as you are. That's her power, after all. She bears the Mantle of Desire."

Rose blinked, somewhat startled by Kanae's agreement. It wasn't what she'd expected, and she frowned slightly. The sound of her power... it *did* make some sense of how she'd reacted to the first sight of Queen Estalia, and yet she didn't really care about that. Instead, she looked at Kanae with narrowed eyes. "And? Why should that matter?"

"Why should it matter? What matters to me is how, all too often, I've seen that power used as a weapon," Kanae replied, looking over to meet Rose's eyes. "Those who she meets can't help but be enthralled by her, unless they're strong of will and prepared. Even then, the mightiest bulwarks can crumble with a single moment of weakness. Oh, most of the time she doesn't use her power that way, but when she does... it can strike home more powerfully than Serian's Hammer itself. I fear few things in this world, Rose, but I fear falling under Queen

Estalia's sway again. I don't hate or fear her. I *can't* hate or fear her."

Rose blinked in surprise, then sat back. The idea of Queen Estalia using her beauty as a weapon had never occurred to her. It might make a little sense, but part of her bristled at the thought. Another quiet part of her accepted it, though, and she thought for a long minute, trying to make sense of her thoughts.

"You're her daughter, aren't you?" Rose asked, her voice quiet.

"I'm not going to answer that question," Kanae said, her gaze dropping to the fire again, but her response confirmed what Rose had thought.

"She said that her daughter was missing, and that she missed her terribly," Rose began, then froze as Kanae looked up, a flash of utter fear going through the woman's eyes.

"Missing?" Kanae breathed out, her voice barely audible. "Are you certain that she said missing? Not dead?"

"Yes... I'm quite sure," Rose said, swallowing hard as she saw how Kanae's breathing had grown sharper and faster.

"Right, that means I need to run away, as far and as fast as I can, when we reach the house," Kanae said, lowering her head and taking a deep breath. The demoness calmed herself quickly, but her momentary near-panic had been obvious.

Rose resisted the urge to say anything for a moment, that same attraction growing stronger as she saw Kanae's distress. She wondered if it was something about Queen Estalia that had been passed on to her daughter that drew her to Kanae, but it truly didn't matter. Instead, Rose decided to change the subject, glancing over to Isalla.

"On a different matter... what about you and Isalla? I can tell that the two of you have been involved with one another," Rose said, a hint of jealousy welling up inside her. Whether it was for Isalla's experiences or that she'd accepted Kanae's company was another question entirely.

"Yes, we have been. She took solace in my company, but... I'm not sure how deep her feelings might run. I'm fond of Isalla, but..." Kanae paused for a long moment, looking at Isalla, then back to Rose, somehow looking like she'd aged in the last minute. "As soon as she heard about you, she wanted to do everything possible to rescue you. At that moment, I realized that chances were that it was the end of any relationship between us, even if she tried to keep the spark alive as we traveled to find you. Then, the look on her face when she found you…"

Rose couldn't help blushing as she glanced at Isalla, startled by her friend's bravery. It was unexpected, considering how things had ended between them before. Even more unexpected was that Kanae had helped Isalla, considering how worried she was about Queen Estalia knowing about her.

"Then why did you help her?" Rose asked, almost startling herself as she spoke. "It was an immense risk, from what you've told me, and if you thought she was gone anyway…"

"Why? Because it was the right thing to do," Kanae said, smiling bitterly. "Angels in the hells… they can't truly *live* here. If you try to go into public without guards or overwhelming power, you'll be mobbed and captured, so you have to be trapped in gilded cages, like Anna is in the Spire of Confession, or other angels who live in pampered luxury. It isn't right, to be forced to live like that. The war between the heavens and hells… it's consumed enough lives as it is. I'd rather try to help those I can find freedom."

Her words were startling, and Rose stared in shock. Even if Coral and Tina had been kind to her, and if Queen Estalia had been beautiful and accepting beyond words, none of them had said anything like Kanae had. They'd never suggested that they wanted Rose to be free, despite encouraging her to make her own choices. And as she stared at Kanae more, Rose found herself smiling as interest turned into attraction.

Kanae looked back at her and raised her eyebrows, speaking in an almost challenging tone. "What? Do you not like my reasons?"

"Not like them? Hardly that… in fact, I daresay you've piqued my interest," Rose replied, grinning as she sat back slightly. "Before, I just found you slightly attractive. Now, though… I see why Isalla likes you. *I* certainly think you're worth getting to know at this point."

Kanae blinked, looking slightly taken aback. She opened her mouth, then shut it, taking a moment to gather herself before replying dryly. "Thank you. Now, I might suggest getting your rest. I need far less sleep than either of you, and I have some problems to consider."

"As you like," Rose replied, a bit disappointed by the cool response, and she walked over to the blankets next to Isalla. She considered her old lover for a moment, then smiled, noting her shallow breathing.

Once she'd slipped into the blankets next to Isalla, Rose considered before rolling over to embrace her friend. Then she whispered softly, "You *did* decide to choose someone interesting, didn't you?"

Isalla shifted slightly, and her eyes cracked open, a sheepish look on her face. She licked her lips, then replied, her voice barely audible. "Um… I'm sorry…"

"Sorry about what? I don't blame you, not after I pushed you away. I really regret doing that," Rose replied, keeping her voice low enough that Kanae shouldn't hear. She hated what she'd done to Isalla.

"Okay," Isalla replied, blushing.

"So… what were you thinking? Are you planning to leave her?" Rose asked, smiling as Isalla's blush deepened.

"I'm… not sure. I didn't think much beyond your rescue," Isalla admitted, looking down. "I like her, but… but you're here now. You were always my anchor, Rose… even if you're different now, you're still similar enough for me to recognize. I don't know what to do."

"Well, we'll have to work things out, then," Rose said, and smiled as she added, her tone turning teasing, "Though I have to admit… I *do* think she's kind of cute, myself."

"You what?" Isalla gasped, her eyes widening. "I thought you were joking, to tease her!"

"No, I wasn't. We'll see how things go, but… I suppose I should tell you that I've found myself far less concerned about only sharing a bed with one person of late," Rose said, a smile playing over her lips. "I hope that doesn't make you unhappy."

Isalla didn't reply, instead blushing and hiding her head

beneath the blankets. Rose laughed softly, then settled in to rest. As she did so, she considered what Kanae had said earlier. At last she decided that Kanae might have had a point about taking some time to see the world and clear her head.

She could always go back to Queen Estalia later.

# CHAPTER 41

Queen Estalia sat back in her throne, frowning as she considered the guards kneeling before her. Saying that she wasn't upset would be lying, but at the same time, saying she *was* upset would be overstating her feelings. She was more irritated that they'd managed to lose Rose, but even that irritation was minor compared to her surprise.

"I don't blame you for not recognizing the danger, as I don't believe I've heard of such a hazard before either. From what you said, even my personal guard might have succumbed to it, which is a troubling thought," Estalia said at last and saw them relax slightly. She continued, her tone gentle, almost measured. "Neither could you have known that the attackers would have a way to teleport to another node. Most curious that they didn't harm any of you… you said the demoness who spoke to you was accompanied by a human woman, didn't you?"

"To be more accurate, she *looked* human, Your Majesty. All of us believed she smelled like she was native to the hells, or all but Ethan," Ataron said, his head still lowered.

"Well, of course he wouldn't. He doesn't have the keen sense of smell that you do," Estalia said, smiling at Ethan to lessen any blow to his pride. "What did this human look like?"

They looked at one another, and after a moment, Zeera spoke. "She was tall for a human, though not as tall as some, with fair skin and a thinner, more delicate bone structure. She had blonde hair, blue eyes, and wore simple silk clothing and a pack, as well as having a sword and shield at her side. She moved like a warrior, and approached Lady Rose as if she knew her."

"Indeed? But that would mean—" Estalia paused, then smiled as she murmured. "Isalla found Rose, rather than me finding her? And even managed to garner help to recover her? How startling."

She fell silent for a long moment, considering her options, then looked up and asked, "This other demoness who spoke to you... what did *she* look and act like? You said she used magic as though she was skilled, but not much more."

"Well, she was surprisingly polite. If it weren't for what she did, and the lack of an accent, I'd say she was nobility of some type. Her diction was excellent," Ithik said, frowning. "I didn't get a good look at her, unfortunately."

"I did," Ethan said, straightening. "I think she was a half-blood, if I'm being honest. She had pale skin, with just a hint of purple to it, short purple horns, and purple-black hair. Her armor looked like dull black scales, likely from a dragon or made of finely crafted steel, and it was well-used but in good repair. Purple eyes and dark purple lips, and her armor covered a tail that—"

Ethan fell silent suddenly, and Estalia realized she was smiling broadly as all of the guards stared at her. She laughed and shook her head, speaking warmly as delight surged through her. "Oh, my apologies, Ethan, but I know *precisely* who that is. Or if it isn't her, there's a doppelganger of her that I wasn't aware of. Veldoran!"

They all blinked at her exclamation, and a moment later a door opened in the side of her throne room, revealing her handsome, fit archmagus. He was a blood demon, with their typical scarlet skin, but with dark hair and bright amber eyes, and his trousers and shirt fit him well. She admired him as he spoke.

"You called for me, Your Majesty?" Veldoran asked, bowing his head respectfully, a smile playing across his lips.

"I did. Please bring a scrying orb. I need you to look in on my wayward daughter again." Estalia said, and her smile widened still more at the shock on the faces of the guards. Veldoran barely reacted, raising an eyebrow slightly, but nodded, disappearing into his room to find an orb.

"Your… daughter, Your Majesty?" Dathael asked, her voice filled with a hint of trepidation.

"Yes, that's right. Assuming it's her, of course, but that matches her description," Estalia said, sitting back and smiling. At their looks of worry, she laughed, shaking her head. "Oh, don't worry about what might have happened. She's powerful enough that you would have had a hard time doing much damage, and she wouldn't have wanted to hurt you. She's been hiding from me for the better part of a millennium, after all."

They didn't seem reassured, but Veldoran reappeared at that moment, holding a large scrying orb and its stand. He walked forward and set it up, explaining, "I must remind you, your daughter creates such potent wards that I'm not guaranteed to garner much detail, Your Majesty."

"I remember, Veldoran. She's practiced immensely to try to keep anyone from finding her, and if it weren't for your skill, I'd still be ignorant of her survival," Estalia said, nodding and sitting forward eagerly, curious if her daughter had actually been involved.

"My thanks, Your Majesty," Veldoran said, smiling in pleasure at her compliment.

The archmage ran his hands over the orb and took a deep breath, then began his incantation. Veldoran truly was powerful, the most powerful diviner that Estalia had been able to employ in her court to date. Lines of mana extended from his fingers to create sigils in the air around the orb, and in only a handful of seconds a smoky mist appeared in the orb. Estalia watched it closely, her breath catching. Fortunately, her daughter's wards didn't look like they were quite as strong as they usually were, and the mists cleared as Veldoran completed his spell.

Within the orb, a scene appeared of a location on a trail somewhere. Within was Rose, still wearing the cloak Anna had given her, along with the other two individuals that the guards had described. Estalia smiled warmly at the sight of Kitania, leaning forward as she asked, "Veldoran? Can you tell approximately where they are?"

"It's difficult, but I believe near the border of Hellmount, and somewhat to its southeast." Veldoran said, frowning slightly.

"I see. That would line up with the node closest to where she's been hiding... you may release the spell. Thank you very much," Estalia said, looking at Veldoran happily. She turned her attention to the guards and gave them a gentler smile as she added, watching the scene vanish. "Also, you're dismissed. I hold you blameless for this matter. In fact, I'm rather pleased."

"Ah, thank you, Your Majesty," Ithik said, looking taken aback as he stood.

"You are most welcome. Now, Veldoran? Would you mind letting the royal guard know that I'm taking a trip, and I'd like a full escort and a half?" Estalia asked, turning to him and smiling sunnily. The guards quickly left, though she knew they'd heard enough to be curious.

"Of course, Your Majesty. Will you need me as well?" Veldoran asked, his eyebrows rising.

"Yes, I believe I will," Estalia said, glancing back at the empty orb again. "I need to teleport if I'm to visit my daughter before she goes racing off to find a new hole."

"As you say, Your Majesty," Veldoran said, bowing deeply. "I'll have the teleportation chamber primed as well."

"Thank you," Estalia said, and sat back in her throne again, humming happily to herself.

She *so* looked forward to seeing Kitania again... or whatever name she was going by this century.

# CHAPTER 42

*S*eidrel frowned as he looked at the orders he'd received. They were terse and practically dripped with the disappointment of his superiors. Even though he hadn't been in command when First Sword Roselynn had been captured, Seidrel had been second-in-command, and for a short time he'd been worried that he'd be demoted to an even more remote, worthless post. Losing Ember and its wielder hadn't done anything good for his reputation.

The orders he'd received worried him still more, though, as the group of angels who'd volunteered to rescue Roselynn were an odd group who were quite insular. More importantly, Seidrel had never heard of any of them, which made him question their chances of succeeding. That was why he'd asked his superiors whether he might send a couple of the more skilled members of the garrison with them. The response had been brusque in its denial, which made Seidrel even more concerned. Still, there was nothing he could do about it, so he set the orders aside with a sigh.

Thinking for a moment more, Seidrel finally reached out and rang the bell on his desk. A few moments later, his current assistant opened the door, her dark hair done up in braids. Alanah tilted her head as she asked, "Yes, First Sword?"

"When were our guests going to set out?" Seidrel asked calmly, resisting the urge to drum his fingers on the desk.

"According to the quartermaster, the day after tomorrow," Alanah replied quickly. "They believe they've learned First Sword Roselynn's approximate location and intend to move as quickly as possible."

"I see. Well, instruct the quartermaster to give them all the support he can. We've been ordered to do so, and to ensure that Firewatch is here when they return," Seidrel explained, glancing down at the orders again. "Alas, my request that volunteers from our garrison be allowed to accompany them was denied."

"As you say, First Sword. I believe some of the soldiers will be unhappy, but they'll obey," Alanah said, bowing her head. "Will there be anything else?"

"No, that will be all. Thank you, Alanah," Seidrel replied calmly.

"You're welcome, sir," Alanah said, then she withdrew. Staring after her, Seidrel sighed. Alanah had been rather distant ever since Roselynn was captured, which made him even more uncomfortable. He probably should replace her with someone else.

Once the door had closed behind her, Seidrel waited a moment before standing up and moving to the window. He'd moved to a larger office for his new position, one with a much better view of the surrounding countryside, yet despite the view, Seidrel couldn't help his depression. Nothing had been going right since Roselynn had vanished, and all the things he'd thought would improve the outpost hadn't produced the results he wanted yet.

Looking at the cleared ground around the walls, Seidrel murmured, "Well, here's to hoping they manage to rescue you, First Sword. I supposed there's some truth to the phrase 'be careful what you wish for'."

～

KANAE CUT down her fifth fanged howler, dodging the claws of a sixth as the small, monkey-like creature lunged at her while shrieking. The problem with the monsters was that they came in massive swarms, and she hadn't heard that a pack of them had moved into the area before.

A gout of flame ripped across the trail, causing screams as a cluster of the scaled creatures were scorched, and Kanae pursed her lips as she followed the line back to Rose. The choker Kanae had given her hid the angel wings by melding them into her body until they were needed, but Kanae was impressed by the beautiful woman's skill and poise. Rose was quick and precise with her sword, and she had a surprising amount of strength, as well as the fire magic she could unleash with a swing of her sword.

Isalla was lacking by comparison, but saying that the younger angel wasn't skilled would be a disservice to her. Isalla was solidly competent, using her shield to block attacks and bat away her attackers while she cut them down one at a time, guarding Rose's back stubbornly. Between the two of them, they were an excellent team, and Kanae felt somewhat reassured when she saw them fight. Even if it *was* a little depressing to see Isalla almost glued to Rose's side.

Turning her attention to her own assailants, Kanae continued dodging any attacks that looked like they might pierce her armor while not bothering with the ones that weren't a threat, and her sword kept flashing out to kill a fanged howler with each strike. More flashes of fire ripped across the clearing as they fought, but Kanae ignored them, sure that Rose wouldn't hit her by mistake.

It took several minutes before the waves of attackers began to ebb, the bodies of the fallen howlers starting to make it difficult to dodge as easily as before. Kanae's armor managed to block the handful of heavier attacks, if only just, until the last of the creatures fell.

"What… were *those*?" Isalla gasped out, her breathing coming hard, and Kanae looked over to see the angel was bleeding from several fang and claw marks along her arms, legs, and even a cut on her cheek. Rose hadn't been hit as much, but she had a couple of injuries as well.

"Those were fanged howlers. They're a particularly aggressive species native to the hells, and as you can see, they travel in packs and rarely retreat unless a creature is particularly large," Kanae explained, cleaning off her sword as she grimaced. "They often strip all sources of food from an area before moving on, so they're rather hated. We probably wiped out the entire infestation in the area, but I'd far rather we hadn't run into them just now."

"I'll agree with that. Those were exceedingly unpleasant," Rose agreed, wrinkling her nose as she added, "I must admit that this makes me miss my armor."

"Agreed. If the armor the one assassin had would've fit..." Isalla said, her tone longing.

"Well, we're almost back to the house, and we'll be able to get your armor there. If you go back to the mortal world, you might even be able to wear it," Kanae said, sheathing her sword as she ignored the unhappiness lurking in the back of her mind. She really didn't need a relationship, not now. "Now, let's attend to your injuries, shall we? I know that angels are resistant to diseases, but I'd rather not take chances."

"Very well," Rose said, a smile playing across her lips, and she hesitated, then nodded down the path. "Over there, perhaps? It doesn't have any bodies to get in our way."

Kanae nodded in approval and followed the two over to the log Rose had pointed out. While they settled down, she unslung her pack and pulled out her kit of healer's tools. None of the injuries the two had looked like they'd need stitches, fortunately, but they still needed treatment. Kanae hated how bad infections could be. She'd lost a few patients over the years to infections, mostly when she was still learning.

As she began working, Isalla spoke quietly. "We'll be at the house later today, then? I think that you said we'd arrive today."

"That's right. I'm going to try to keep your presence from the locals... after you were attacked, I really don't want to risk more assassins coming after you. Even worse would be if the authorities caught wind of your presence," Kanae said, mixing a salve quickly, grateful to have something to focus on. Some of the ingredients tended to separate if given too much time. "You'll have to figure out what you want to do quickly, though. I'm still trying to decide what *I* want to do, considering things."

"Of course. If what Rose suspects is true..." Isalla let her voice trail off, and Kanae didn't reply, though a thrill of mingled anticipation and terror ran through her.

Rose had guessed perfectly, and that made Kanae more than a little concerned. She'd thought that her mother believed her dead for a long time, but if Estalia knew she was alive, the question was what she was doing. Kanae had thought she'd be dragged in again as soon as her mother knew she still lived, which made her situation still more precarious. Estalia almost never did things for only one purpose, after all. The problem was trying to guess what she'd do next, especially if Estalia knew that Kanae had kidnapped Rose. Or rescued her, depending on the point of view.

"I believe that I'm going to be leaving within a few days, just to be safe. A week at the outside," Kanae said at last, spreading salve on several of Isalla's nicks. At least her hands were still steady, and she continued quietly. "I'll probably go south, as far from Estalia as I can. Chances are that I'm not going to get far, though."

"Why are you so concerned about being found?" Rose asked curiously, her blue eyes piercing despite her mild tone. "From what I heard, she cares about you."

"She likely does. The difference is... cultural, I suppose," Kanae said, finally tacitly admitting that Rose was correct, which made her even more nervous. A tiny part of her was almost angry with the angel for causing the feelings she had. "There are desires for me that I don't agree with. You'd likely be even less comfortable with some aspects of what is considered acceptable down here, so I won't try to make you uncomfortable. Suffice to say that while Queen Estalia has desires that I find... understandable, her methods are not something I'm comfortable with."

Rose looked at Kanae with just a hint of confusion in her gaze, but she didn't say anything, instead just pursing her lips. On the other hand, Isalla paused, then asked, "Why don't you seem interested in going to the mortal world with us? You seemed to be considering the idea before, and if you're that worried about being found..."

"If I'm right, going with you would bring her down on you two. That wouldn't be right," Kanae said simply, shaking her head slightly, but being careful not to let it interfere with her work. "No, making pursuers split their attention seems like a better idea to me."

As did not getting between the two angels' relationship, but Kanae wasn't going to say *that* aloud.

"Ah. That... does make some sense. We just have to figure out what we're going to do, I guess," Isalla said, looking at the other angel as she asked. "Rose?"

"I'm still not sure. While I understand your opinion, a large part of me is still inclined to return to Queen Estalia. However... what you've said makes a lot of sense," Rose admitted, adjusting her position to allow Kanae to treat her more easily. "At the same time, I truly don't like the idea of you going off on your own to simply draw attention away from us. It feels too much like sacrificing your freedom for that of others."

Kanae blinked, then smiled slightly. "Indeed? Well, I'm glad you don't like the idea. I'm trying to figure out what to do, and I don't know. Not yet, at least. For now, all we have to do is reach my home, and we'll have a chance to discuss further. Or more likely, you and Isalla can discuss things in depth."

"Very well," Rose said, then fell silent. The forest around them was quiet as Kanae continued to treat their wounds, bandaging the handful that needed it. Finally, she sighed and nodded.

"There we are. It doesn't repair your clothing, but there's not much to be done for that. I don't know any spells to repair clothing, and I wouldn't dare take it into town, not with as fine as your clothing is, Rose," Kanae said, pulling away at last.

"That's fine. I have enough other clothing that it isn't much of a loss, and I'm sure I can get them repaired eventually," Rose replied, standing up. A moment later, she smiled and added, "Thank you for the treatment, Kanae. I really *do* appreciate it."

"You're welcome," Kanae replied, packing things up and putting them away. She finished and put her pack on, then looked up to see Isalla offering her a hand to help her up. Kanae smiled and took her hand, standing as she said, "Thank you."

"I'm the one who should be thanking you," Isalla said, smiling slightly. "You've helped me more than anyone could reasonably ask for. This is the least I can do for you."

"I only did what I thought was right," Kanae murmured, a faint sense of loss taking hold of her. Isalla's words felt like a goodbye. "In any case, let's get moving. The sooner we're back to the house, the sooner we can get a proper bath."

"A proper bath?" Rose asked, perking up a little. "What do you mean?"

"Oh, I didn't tell you about that, did I? Kanae's house has a bathing room in it, one with a bath fed by a hot spring," Isalla said, her expression brightening. "It smells a little like sulfur, but it's absolutely *lovely*."

"That does sound like it'd be pleasant after the last couple of days. I'm afraid I got used to how nice the baths in the spire were," Rose said, blushing slightly as she cleared her throat. "If it's as nice as you say, I suspect I'd like to lounge in it for longer than I probably should."

"Only if you want to roast yourself. Staying in the pool for too long is a good way to get burned, or at least to overheat," Kanae said, amusement beginning to overcome her anxiety and melancholy. The obvious attraction Rose had for the idea of a bath was something she could sympathize with, as well as her experience in the spire. The problem with the latter was that Kanae had known what was happening beforehand, and Rose wasn't quite convinced.

"Is that so? Well, I'll keep it in mind," Rose said, smiling at Kanae. "Shall we continue, then? I find that more encouraging than most of the other things we've discussed, frankly."

Kanae laughed and shook her head. Then she started down the trail again, since if she delayed too much, she might have a rebellion on her hands.

Unfortunately, it also gave her plenty of time to think about what was coming, which wasn't nearly as pleasant.

# CHAPTER 43

anae's home looked a little different as they approached it, though not much. Isalla looked around for a moment before realizing what it was. She was used to there being smoke trailing upward from the main chimneys of the house, as well as the alchemy lab. There was steam rising from the bathing room's vent, but that wasn't nearly as obvious as all the others would have been. The ground also looked a touch more overgrown than before, though it wasn't much different.

Unlike Isalla, Kanae moved toward the house with a purposeful stride. The demoness didn't look concerned by how abandoned the area looked, and Isalla started forward after a moment, feeling a bit chagrined. The dying light didn't help how the area looked, but it wasn't any reason to get depressed.

"You built the house under a hill?" Rose asked, sounding a bit surprised.

"That's right. While simple dirt isn't necessarily the *best* defense in the world, it can do the job quite admirably, especially when coupled with both enchantments and herbs that most pests don't like," Kanae replied, glancing over and smiling as she added, "Besides, I find that the roof doesn't require nearly as much work to maintain. Some, yes, but not quite as much. My worst problem was when a tree tried to put its roots through the ceiling."

"I don't think that would be pleasant," Isalla ventured, hurrying to keep up. There was something off about Kanae's smile that she couldn't quite place.

"It wasn't too horrible. I caught it early, and while it took some hard work to get rid of the tree, I learned a valuable lesson," Kanae said, then paused and admitted. "I'm going to miss the house. I've been here for a long time."

"How long?" Isalla asked, wondering if it was as long as she'd been in the area.

"Um, about four and a half centuries? I spent a few decades in town, but I was interrupted a little too much, and gathering herbs took more work. Then I built the house here, and I haven't really moved since," Kanae said, slowing down and looking around. "I lost seven alchemy labs... more than I like to think about. None in the past fifty years, though. I've put a lot of work into my home, but... it's just a place. Not something I'm truly attached to."

Isalla looked at Rose, who raised an eyebrow skeptically. It was strange seeing her friend looking so incredibly different, but the way she'd relaxed was oddly comforting to Isalla. Even so, she had to agree with Rose's skepticism. Four and a half centuries was longer than either of them had been alive by a good margin. It might not be more than both of them put together, but that was a long, long time to live in one place.

"I think you're being a little unfair. Considering how long you've lived here, it'd be strange if you didn't have something of an attachment," Rose said, approaching the door as she followed Kanae.

The demoness paused, then nodded slightly. "Quite possibly. However... for now I need to air out the house and clean up. I'm certain it's somewhat musty within."

Isalla frowned but didn't say anything as Kanae pulled out a key and murmured the words to unseal her home, then unlocked the door. It creaked open slowly, and the smell from inside hit them. The air was a little stale, thick with dust, and as musty as Kanae had suggested. Kanae stepped inside, and with a murmured word, Isalla saw the fire in the kitchen area ignite. She knew the fireplace had to be started normally, but at least the kitchen provided some illumination.

"Come in. Isalla, if you'll show Rose into the bedroom, and set things down? I'll let the pair of you bathe first while I take care of cleaning up," Kanae said, pulling off her backpack and setting it on the table.

"Are you sure?" Isalla asked, frowning. "I'm more than willing to help."

"She doesn't know where everything is, while you do. You can even keep her from using my cleaning supplies, so off with you," Kanae said, smiling as she spoke, adding, "Don't forget another towel for her wings. I find they pick up quite a bit of water."

"Alright, and I know," Isalla said, unable to help a grin at Kanae's admonishment. "I *did* have wings myself, after all. Unlike you."

"Very true," Kanae said agreeably, pulling out a dusting rag and making sure the broom was in the corner as she did so.

Isalla nodded to Rose and led the way to Kanae's room, slightly surprised that Kanae had directed her to take Rose there. She opened the door and glanced back, explaining, "This is Kanae's room. While there are other bedrooms, I'm not sure that you'd be comfortable in them. They're pretty small."

"Ah. I can't say I see, but... this seems like a nice room," Rose said, looking around the bedroom curiously as she unslung her pack. "I can tell it's been lived in, too."

"Agreed. I was relieved when I came in here the first time, because the rest of the house was always so clean and... sterile, maybe? This felt more like the place that a *person* lived to me," Isalla said, quickly shedding her pack and cloak, then considered before blushing and continuing to undress. "Before coming to the hells, I never thought of demons as people."

"Nor had I," Rose admitted, then hesitated before beginning to disrobe herself, her wings reappearing as she removed the choker. "That said... I think that Kanae is going to be harder hit by leaving here than she claims. If we're going to be gone within a few days, why would she bother going through the effort of dusting properly? Or sweeping everything out, for that matter? Don't get me wrong, I like living in a clean space as much as anyone else, but it strikes me as odd."

"That… is a good point," Isalla admitted, and her mood dimmed slightly. She hesitated as she saw Rose was wearing a corset beneath her clothing, a little surprised. It *did* explain why Rose had been consistently standing so straight, as well as how narrow her waist was… or maybe not, as she saw Rose remove the corset and reveal that it fit her waist perfectly. Isalla shook off her surprise and continued, slipping entirely out of her clothing as she blushed at Rose's beauty. She hesitated before taking out the bathrobe that Kanae had gotten for her and offering it to Rose. "Here, use this. It's mine, so it shouldn't be a problem."

"Thank you," Rose said, taking it, and watched as Isalla pulled out several towels. There were more, fortunately, though Isalla knew that Kanae kept them on hand for injuries. Five of them still put a significant dent into the number waiting for her, though. Rose hesitated, then put the choker back on so she'd fit into the robe, which made Isalla blush in embarrassment. She'd forgotten the robe didn't have wing slits.

While Isalla didn't like the idea of parading through the house naked, she was willing to since it was necessary. A moment later, she led the way out through the common room and quickly darted toward the bathing room, since the outside door was still open. As she did so, she saw Kanae was briskly cleaning the mantle over the fireplace, and it looked like she was preparing to start a fire as well. Leading the way into the bathing room, Isalla gasped as the wave of warm air hit her, and she was startled at just how much she'd missed it.

"This is rather nice. When I saw the house was underground, I was expecting more dirt, not for it to be so well-made," Rose murmured, closing the door behind her. "I shouldn't have thought that, but I did."

"I don't blame you. I was afraid that it was all dark on purpose for a little while, then I realized that all the trees in the area have black wood," Isalla said, setting the towels down and opening the cabinet to pull out her bathing supplies. "I'm more surprised that this room isn't covered with a layer of mold, since we were gone for so long."

"I'm sensing magic around us. Since I'm not seeing any runes, I'm guessing they're on the other side of the panels." Rose said, stripping again, without the modesty that Isalla had half-expected, then slipped into the pool with a sigh. The angel's eyes half closed as she murmured, "Oh, that's very nice. I see why she said you could cook yourself if you stayed too long, though."

"Yeah," Isalla said, sliding into the pool after Rose. After the last few days, the warm water was welcome, and so much better than any bath she'd had since Silken Veils. She felt her muscles unknotting, and she smiled happily. For the moment, she was able to forget most of her worries. "Heavens... I almost forgot what this was like. I understand why she'll miss it."

"Mmhm," Rose said, adjusting her position so her wings could dip into the pool more comfortably.

For a long minute, the room was silent except for the burbling of water, each of them relaxing quietly. Isalla made a few halfhearted attempts to wash herself, but she wasn't really trying yet. For the moment, she just wanted to soak.

"What do you *want* to do, Isalla?" Rose asked softly, startling Isalla when she did so.

"Hm?" Isalla murmured, looking over at Rose in surprise. The other angel was looking at her thoughtfully, which made Isalla's pulse quicken slightly.

"This is the closest thing to true privacy that we're going to get, I think. Perhaps we'll get a little more if Kanae goes into town, but for the moment this is the best time to talk," Rose explained, settling back. "You've heard her; we only have a couple of days to make decisions about our lives. What do you *want* to do?"

"That's the question, isn't it?" Isalla said, frowning and pulling her legs in close. She didn't like having this conversation in the bath, but Rose had a point. After a few moments, she admitted, "I don't think I'd be accepted back into the Order, even if Haral didn't try to arrange for my death. Queen Estalia... the stories about her scare me. It's not that I think she'd be frightening or mean, but how much you've changed... having

that happen scares me, too. At the same time, I like Kanae, and...
I just don't know."

"Mm... Her Majesty isn't nearly as bad as you're thinking
she is, but I can see your point, and Kanae's, for that matter,"
Rose said, then her smile faded as her gaze hardened. "As for
Haral... letting her get away with what she did to you is almost
intolerable to me. From what you've said about what they were
talking about... I'm concerned about what their goals might be.
To throw you off the continent and have you fall into the hells,
along with the rumors you were hearing..."

"That was a concern of mine. They might be *trying* to restart
the war in truth," Isalla admitted, shivering slightly as her sense
of worry grew stronger. "If they're trying to do something like
that, there's no telling what lengths they'll go to in order to
achieve their goals."

"Indeed," Rose agreed, then fell silent. Isalla didn't say
anything, mulling over the situation unhappily.

A minute later, Rose sighed and said, "I think we need to try
to reach Firewatch, Isalla. We can try to find out what's
happened, then determine what to do from there. I don't *want* to
rejoin the Order, I might add, but simply abandoning all those
who depended on me... that seems wrong. So does allowing
someone to potentially frame Queen Estalia for your murder, or
murder attempt."

"That seems like a reasonable plan. I'm not happy about your
armor being missing, or Ember, but it's at least doable. Especially
with that choker," Isalla agreed, relaxing a little more. She
paused for a moment, then admitted one of her other concerns.
"I'm worried about Kanae, though."

"For good reason, I think. I'm a little surprised at just how
terrified she seems of Her Majesty, but... it's her choice," Rose
said, shaking her head, then smiling. "Even if she *is* rather
attractive."

Isalla blushed brightly at the suggestive tone to Rose's voice,
giggling before replying. "You really *have* changed, haven't you?
I saw her first, you know."

"I know you did," Rose replied and splashed water at Isalla
as she smiled. "What does that matter?"

"It… it just *does*, alright?" Isalla said, blushing even more as she squirmed. "I'm not even sure how things are going between us, you know."

"Oh, Isalla…" Rose paused for a moment, then smiled as she stood up, walking across the pool's bottom toward Isalla. Isalla's heartbeat quickened as Rose leaned down until her nose was only an inch away, and then murmured, "What you *want* is up to you. As for me… I've simply learned to be true to my feelings, instead of hiding them away."

And with that, Rose leaned in and kissed Isalla, firmly and passionately. Isalla stiffened with surprise for a moment, then slowly melted into the kiss, reaching out to embrace Rose passionately, relief rushing through her.

As Rose kissed her, Isalla felt most of her worry and tension simply melt away. She truly loved Rose, and was delighted to have her back.

KANAE FINISHED RINSING out her hair, sighing softly as she did so. Her two guests had spent rather more time in the bath than she'd expected them to, almost enough time that she was worried they might hurt themselves, but they'd emerged without any injuries. At least it'd given her enough time to clean up the main room of the house. The floor didn't gleam the way Kanae liked it to, but it'd suffice for the time being.

She'd put a pot of soup on to cook, nothing too impressive but nice enough as it was. Coupled with some of the root vegetables from the garden that'd survived her absence, it had turned into a nice enough dinner for the three of them, even if Kanae was sure that it hadn't been enough to impress Rose. She knew what the meals in the Spire of Confession were like, after all.

"They've pretty much reconciled," Kanae murmured, certain that neither angel was close enough to hear her. They'd have to be pressing an ear against the inner door to overhear her, and she'd have heard them approach. She'd noticed enough to tell that Isalla's red face hadn't been entirely from the warm water.

Knowing that the two women were on good terms *did* make Kanae happier, but at the same time she felt her sense of loss growing stronger. If Isalla and Rose had made up, that was pretty much it for her.

"Oh, quit feeling sorry for yourself," Kanae suddenly scolded herself, shaking her head firmly as she stepped on her emotions. "You knew it wouldn't last from the start. The chances of Isalla choosing to stay here were minimal, and now… either they'll go to Her Majesty, or they'll go to the mortal world. As for me… I'm going somewhere else."

The thought *did* hurt, but Kanae was used to that. She'd lost enough people over the years that it was more like a dull ache rather than a sharp pain anymore. People moved on or died, and she was left behind, over and over again. Kanae never liked thinking about it, but it was just how things worked out for her. She should have learned not to get close to people, but… it was hard.

Letting out a sigh, Kanae washed herself off calmly, taking her time to do the job right. As nervous as she might be, there was no reason to rush. Either they'd get out of the area in time or they wouldn't, and she needed to make her peace with that.

It took a bit longer to finish than she liked, but at last Kanae finished the bath and dried off. She had moved some of her things into the rooms she had for patients, since she'd be far more comfortable in the beds there than Rose would be with her wings. How Isalla and Rose chose to figure out their sleeping arrangements was entirely up to them.

Slipping into her bathrobe, Kanae started out into the main room, using the towel to dry off a stray bit of water from her hair, then paused as she saw Rose. The angel was in a flowing green gown that accentuated her hair and eyes, and Kanae admired her for a moment. No matter what Anna and the others in the Spire of Confession did, while they could guide those who came there into wiser choices, it didn't help when the person who they were taking care of had poor taste. Rose obviously wasn't one of those, which made her even more… wistful, possibly. Rose was examining the books on the shelf and glanced toward Kanae after a moment.

"You've done quite a bit of studying, I can tell. Did you teach yourself?" Rose asked, nodding toward the books.

"Not entirely," Kanae said, looking at the books and considering them for a moment, wondering what she was going to do with them. She couldn't take them all with her. "I learned some of the basics of alchemy growing up, though I only touched on the peripheral parts of healing salves and the like. I first began to take an interest in healing when I was in the army, as there were so many injuries. I learned a few things there, but I didn't have time to properly learn, and many thought I was strange for asking about anything more than first aid.

"Once I left the army, though... I was on my own and traveling to many different places, realms far beyond what is commonly known in the hells," Kanae said, stepping forward slowly and reaching out to touch a couple of volumes, running a finger down their spines. "Not all those places developed the same, and I learned some from the people there. Others didn't have healers at all, so I passed on what I could. It was an evolution, really... but I taught myself much of what I've learned since I settled down here."

"Ah, I see. What are you going to do with everything, if you're leaving? I doubt that you can take more than a tithe of your things with you," Rose said, turning to face Kanae, looking a little concerned. "To have stayed here for so long... I can't believe it will be as simple to leave as you implied."

Kanae laughed and shook her head, smiling in return. "While I appreciate the sentiment, that's where you're wrong. Leaving will be easy. How I feel about it... less so. Most of my things I'll give to the locals. I'll have them sell off my alchemy lab, I suppose... no one in town is an alchemist. I'll take some things with me, but not too much, just the things that are important to me. I'd guess a little more than a backpack worth."

"That doesn't seem like a lot, after five centuries here," Rose said, frowning slightly. "I'm nowhere near as old as you are, obviously, but while I never considered myself one to focus on minor items, even I had more things that I valued after a century in the army."

Kanae paused, blinking at Rose, then her smile turned sad.

"Perhaps I would have more things that were important to me, but... I've lost many things that were precious to me, Rose. I heard Isalla tell you that I was involved in the siege of Rosken. I was there at the end, in fact. I lost almost everything that day... compared to the trinkets I valued, I lost so many friends... after that, I've never dared place too much value on items. I've lost enough over the years since, that I believe it's a good decision."

Shock was obvious in Rose's gaze, and Kanae could see the angel hesitate for a long moment. It wasn't that surprising, since Kanae knew that many people didn't think about it. The longer she lived, the more opportunities for loss she encountered.

"I hadn't realized that. I'm sorry," Rose said, averting her gaze at last. "What about people, then? Do you care about them?"

"Of course I do. If I didn't care about people, I'd never have become a healer. I may not be able to do much, but I try to help people. But I don't think that's what you're asking about, is it?" Kanae asked, her gaze sharpening slightly as she folded her arms as best she could with the towel in one hand, anger beginning to ignite within. "You wonder if I was just toying with Isalla."

Rose paused, then nodded slightly, her voice quiet as she said, "Approximately, though not in quite those terms. You don't strike me as the type to *toy* with someone. I'm more wondering how deeply you care about her."

Kanae let out a soft sigh and shook her head, keeping the anger under control as she murmured, "I thought so. Well, let me put it this way. I *try* not to care. I try to keep my distance. Isalla was... so incredibly vulnerable. If I said I wasn't tempted early on, I'd be lying. Even so, I tried to keep my distance, emotionally and physically. She was the one who approached me in the end, even if I told her I was interested initially, Rose... and I let her. I knew any relationship was temporary and likely doomed from the start, yet I let her grow close. Now... now she has you again. When the two of you leave, one way or another, it will hurt. It won't be as painful as it could be, simply because I *have* understood that she would leave eventually, but it's going to hurt. On the other hand, I've been expecting this since we set out to rescue you."

"Oh. I… well, that isn't quite what I meant," Rose said, and took a breath to continue, but Kanae let out a sigh and shook her head, interrupting as she felt the familiar flickers of tired grief washing over her. She'd felt this so many times.

"I'm sorry, Rose, but… I can't do this right now. I'll speak with the two of you on the morrow, and tell you more," Kanae said, letting out a breath in frustration, tears prickling at her eyes. "I hope the two of you rest well."

As Kanae turned and headed toward the room she'd claimed for the night, Rose spoke, her voice growing a little more concerned. "Wait—"

Kanae firmly closed the door behind her, cutting off the angel. And then she closed her eyes and shook her head as the tears welled up in her eyes. It'd been so *long* since she cried, and she didn't want to now. Above all, she didn't want someone to see or hear her cry.

So instead, she wept silently, listening to be sure Rose was on her way to bed before she dared slip into her own.

"THAT DIDN'T GO how I wanted it to," Rose said softly, closing the door to the room she and Isalla were sharing. There was the faint scent that she'd associated with Kanae throughout the room, though it was faded from time.

Isalla looked up from the bed, blinking for a moment, then asking, "Oh? You just said that you wanted to talk to her, and since you dressed up, I was wondering what you had in mind. I saw less… ornate clothing in your pack, you know. I'm not sure how you fit all that into it, anyway."

"I wasn't entirely sure what I had in mind myself, not until I went out there. I was planning to ask a little about you and her, to help ease her mood," Rose said, pausing and shaking her head as she moved toward the bed, reaching up to slip the loop holding her dress up over her head. She felt her fingers trembling as she did so, to Rose's shock, but at least her voice was steady. "It appeared to have the opposite effect. I wasn't trying to make her distraught, but... even if she hid it in her voice, I could *see* the pain in her eyes, Isalla. I didn't mean to hurt her, yet I did."

"What?" Isalla almost yelped, sitting up quickly. "I... it hurt her? I've never seen her do more than roll her eyes, really."

"Yes, sadly," Rose said, shaking her head as she dropped the silken material of the dress on her pack. She'd take care of it properly in the morning. "I wish I hadn't taken that approach."

"I... maybe I should go talk to her," Isalla said, reaching down to throw the covers back, but Rose quickly shook her head to forestall her.

"No, I think she wanted to be alone. She wouldn't let me talk to her when she decided to leave," Rose explained, pulling back the covers on the other side of the bed, then admitted, "I regret it, honestly."

Isalla chewed her lip for a moment, then drew the blanket back up as she spoke slowly. "If you say so... I'm just worried. What did you want, anyway, that you were trying to get her to relax?"

"I... was going to invite her to share the bed with us if she'd like," Rose said, glancing away and trying to keep her tone level instead of slightly embarrassed. "While it'd be somewhat tight for the three of us, there's more room here than there is for her on one of those cots."

"You..." Isalla began, but her voice trailed off in disbelief as she stared at Rose, then a blush rose in her cheeks. "You *what*?"

"You've shared a bed with her before, so I thought... what did it matter? I wouldn't mind, and if it was more comfortable, so be it," Rose said, then sighed regretfully. "Alas, it seems I made a mistake. Perhaps I can make it up to her tomorrow."

"Rose, you're incorrigible. I thought Kanae was embarrassing enough when I first met her, but you..." Isalla announced, shaking her head in obvious shock. "Heavens, I don't even know what to say!"

"Well, *I'm* saying good night," Rose replied with mock severity. "I hope you rest well, Isalla."

"Fine," Isalla huffed, then spoke a word to extinguish the

light next to the bed, settling down again herself. A moment later, Rose heard her mutter, "How did I end up in a situation like this, anyway?"

At least *that* made Rose smile. She'd wondered the same thing over the past few weeks. Still, she couldn't say that her previous life had made her happier. Before she started to drift off, though, her smile faded slightly. She'd have to apologize to Kanae the next morning. She hadn't meant to hurt her.

# CHAPTER 44

Kanae started her morning as she always did, even if she didn't begin in her own room. The other two weren't up, so she got up and prepared a pot to start water heating. While it went against her habits, she was planning to make nicer food in the morning since she wouldn't be able to bring the stores she had with her when she left. Then she went outside to chop wood, just as she always did.

A striped monitor attempted to eat her while she was cutting wood, but it wasn't a match for her axe, fortunately enough. After cleaning off the blood, she continued cutting wood for a little while, then dressed the giant lizard. While many animals in the hells weren't safe to eat, at least monitors were decent, and it gave her something more filling for dinner as well.

Eventually she returned to the house and saw that Isalla was awake already, yawning slightly as she waved at Kanae, then spoke tiredly. "Morning, Kanae. What are you doing for breakfast?"

"Oatmeal, I think. Would you mind putting it in for me? I need to rinse off." Kanae asked, pausing for a moment before adding, a hint of wariness rushing through her. "Unless Rose is in the bath."

"Oh no, she's just getting up," Isalla said, blushing slightly. "I'll put in the oats, then."

"Thank you," Kanae said, and she dropped by the room to grab her towel before heading for the bath. At least her emotions were under control again, so she wasn't in danger of crying in front of Isalla or Roselynn. Truthfully, she felt emotionally wrung out.

Keeping her bath short was a bit difficult for Kanae, but she managed by reminding herself that food would be done soon, and she had plenty of things to do that day. She'd have to take care of things quickly.

~

"YOUR MAJESTY, it's clear to me now why it was so difficult to scry on your daughter," Veldoran said, a hint of respect in his voice as he looked around. "She may not be a grandmaster, but she is an artist. I've never seen such subtle, intricate wards over such a large area before."

Queen Estalia and her escort had given the town a wide berth, as Estalia didn't want to draw too much attention to the area. Now they were in the woods near Kitania's home, and the look of surprise on Veldoran's face had caused Estalia to smile. She wasn't surprised that Kitania had managed to build wards that impressed him, not after this long, but it *did* please her.

"Indeed? Are we in danger of being detected by the wards?" Estalia asked, tilting her head slightly. "My daughter never specialized in detection spells, but that could have changed in the intervening years."

"No, no... these spells aren't *that* sort, Your Majesty. What she did here was an incredibly complex web of wards to misdirect divination spells focused on a specific individual. Likely herself, but I couldn't tell you for certain without examining one of the anchors," Veldoran explained quickly, smiling broadly in return. "They're also designed to be almost undetectable, which is difficult for wards of this power. If I weren't so skilled at divinations, I might have missed them, and *that* takes a skilled mage to manage. I'm curious exactly how she did it."

"I see. Well, why don't we get closer and take a look? I'm not going to want to be spotted yet, though. I want to make an approach on my own terms," Estalia said, and looked to her guards, quickly spotting the man she wanted. "Ah, Sir Qorr, would you mind helping with that, once we're close?"

"Of course, Your Majesty," the black-skinned man said, bowing deeply. She did like the skilled illusionist and smiled warmly at him.

"Thank you. Now then..." Estalia said, gesturing for the guards who'd been taking the lead to move onward.

They took the lead readily, watching for traps, and Estalia smiled a little more. It really had been too long since she'd seen her daughter in person. While she'd left Kitania alone for a long time, that had been before her daughter had abducted Rose. Estalia certainly couldn't let *that* slide, not without at least demanding an explanation in person.

"THERE WE ARE," Kanae said, finishing drying the dishes and setting the bowl in the cabinet, then hanging up the drying cloth. The meal had been good, and they'd gone through a bit more of her honey in the process. Even with splurging on meals, Kanae wasn't sure they'd get through all her better food stores before it was time to leave.

"Right. So... now what?" Isalla asked, wiping off her hands. She'd been nice enough to wash the dishes, and while Rose had offered, there hadn't been enough space for her to help.

"Now we're going to have the explanation I promised," Kanae said calmly, glancing over at Rose at the table, then added, "You can sit however you'll be comfortable. For myself, I'm taking a seat by the fire."

"Alright," Isalla agreed, taking one of the chairs from the table and moving it near the fireplace, while Kanae headed for the stuffed chair. She was going to miss that chair, too. Even if Kanae *had* replaced the stuffing and leather more times than she cared to think about.

Rose hesitated, then got up and moved her chair next to

Isalla's, her eyes following Kanae and a pensive, almost thoughtful, look on her face. Kanae strove to ignore it, especially since she didn't especially *want* to talk about what she was going to.

Once they'd settled down, Kanae paused for a long minute, then sighed and spoke softly. "I've kept this secret because my relationship with my mother is… fraught. I fear what would happen to me if I fall under her sway again, so I've hidden from her."

"Um…" Isalla began, only to be quieted by Rose laying a hand on her arm and shaking her head. Kanae smiled slightly at that, amused despite herself.

"To be clear, you're right, Rose. My mother is Estalia, Demon Queen of Desire and monarch of this nation," Kanae said, smiling thinly, feeling a little like she was walking on broken glass. "My birth name isn't Kanae, and this isn't what I looked like growing up. I've had changes made in order to hide more easily. My father… well, I don't know. Mother always smiled and changed the subject, but rumors around the palace claimed that my sire was my long-dead uncle, who passed within a decade of my birth. Considering my own mutations, and a culture that isn't as… critical of incest as that of angels or mortals, I suspect it's likely true."

"Ick!" Isalla gasped out, blanching. "I mean, I knew you were probably her daughter, but going that far…"

"Believe me, you don't *want* to know some of the things that I do," Kanae interrupted, her amusement growing a little more. If Isalla was discomfited by just the mention of that possibility, she probably would die of mortification if she knew the rest.

"Be that as it may, I don't think that's all you were going to say. Otherwise, this conversation would have taken place long ago," Rose said, watching Kanae closely as she held Isalla's hand. "It makes little sense to me that the daughter of a powerful demon queen would be out *here*, of all places."

"You're right. You're *exactly* right, Rose," Kanae agreed, her impulse to smile fading as she did so, and after a moment of hesitation she pulled her feet up into her chair and sighed before continuing. "My relationship with my mother was difficult. I grew rebellious, and while I'm certain that she loved me, I don't think she knew how to deal with a teenage daughter. So instead, when she decided to calm me down and teach me discipline, she sent me to the Spire of Confession."

The other two gasped, though Rose didn't seem quite as surprised as Isalla, instead looking more confused as her brow furrowed, and Kanae smiled mirthlessly at her. "I knew what happened there, Rose, unlike you. I thought I would get through it just fine, but I wasn't prepared the way I thought I was, and when she wants to be, my mother can be ruthless. Consider how much you changed in a few months, Rose… and now consider that she left me there for two *decades*. I was pampered, given excellent schooling and everything else, but I never saw the outdoors for all that time. I didn't change as much as other people would have, in part because my mother didn't *want* to have me changed too much. She just… didn't want a rebellious daughter who didn't listen. And she got exactly what she wanted, for the most part. I became an obedient, perfect daughter for quite some time… though that seemed to frustrate her even more than my previous rebellion."

"Oh. Oh dear," Rose murmured, paling slightly. "I… didn't consider that she might do that. She was so incredibly nice to me that… well, I don't know what to say."

Isalla was just looking at Kanae in horror, and Kanae smiled a little more as she shook her head. She weighed her words for a few moments, trying to decide how to say what she needed to tell them.

"I don't blame you. Neither did she, and she didn't seem to know what to do, either. So we had an unsteady peace between us for a few decades that stretched into centuries, but she never seemed to know what to do about me. Until the War of Decimation began. It was bad enough that even my mother was forced to commit some soldiers, and I responded with excitement, finally relieved to have something I could do to show my skill, how much I'd grown," Kanae said, smiling thinly as she saw their looks of horror grow. "I *saw* her hesitate, though

I didn't understand it at the time. Then she let me go. She knew how bad it was going to be, I think. The war... if nothing else could break some of my then-absolute faith in her, that could and did. I saw so many people killed, so much destruction wreaked, that I just... lost faith in her. At last was the siege of Rosken, and I barely survived it. Most of those I knew didn't, so I just... faked my death. I pretended that I *had* perished and got the aid of a transmuter to change my body. I chose to move on, because I knew that if she found me, she'd bring me back. She'd make me into the pretty, beautiful tool she wanted me to be. And I... I couldn't stand for that anymore."

"Heavens... if you're that afraid of her, then why did you help me? Why did you stay in Estalia at all?" Isalla asked, looking horrified as she fidgeted.

"I'm not afraid of her. I'm afraid of what would be done to me. I helped because you deserved it. To not help you would have been..." Kanae paused, then sighed. "Cowardice, I suppose. I wasn't going to value preserving the minimal life I've had over the happiness and freedom of someone else."

"I... appreciate that, Kanae," Rose said, her voice soft. She was looking at Kanae closely, and she spoke again. "That doesn't answer Isalla's question about why you're *here*, though. If you fear what she'd do to you so much, why would you stay so close?"

"Because I can't help myself," Kanae said softly, looking down at her legs, and feeling her tail flicking nervously. "I tried to stay away. I was drawn back, almost as if by a lodestone. This is as far away as I've been able to stay comfortably, though... well, I suspect I *could* go further, but no matter what I do, some of my... conditioning from the spire still is there. I love my mother. I just hate what she does to me."

"I'm... I'm sorry. I wish I could help, Kanae. I really wish I could," Isalla said, looking down guiltily. "I didn't realize that you were in that sort of situation."

"How could you?" Kanae asked, shrugging. "I hid it as best I could. I've lived my life here in a way that I was sure wouldn't draw my mother's attention, and which was as comfortable as I could manage. In the end... it is what it is. Since she knew I was alive, that means it's only a matter of time until she comes after me. It could be tomorrow, it could be a decade from now. I have no way of knowing for certain. The only thing I know is that if I don't leave soon, I'm going to have her show up, and from there... I don't know what will happen."

Rose considered Kanae for a long moment, her lips pursed. Isalla's mouth opened and shut, obviously uncertain of what to say at this point. Kanae wasn't surprised, considering what she'd said.

"What would you have us do?" Rose finally asked, tilting her head curiously. "I have to assume you told us all of this for a reason."

"Ah, but *that* is where you're wrong, Rose. I don't care what you do, now that you know," Kanae said, smiling in amusement at last, letting her feet slip down to the floor again. "I didn't tell *you* anything for a particular reason. What happened is in the past. No... I promised to tell Isalla the truth. You learned the truth because she trusts you, no more and no less."

"Well... thank you, Kanae," Isalla said, looking up at her, still seeming distraught. "I didn't know, and I... well, I'm sorry I got you into all this."

"Don't be, Isalla. You're not at fault for any of this, except maybe for inciting the hornet's nest of some conspiracy that tried to kill you. Mere chance sent you in my direction, and I *chose* to save you," Kanae replied, shaking her head as she stood. "Regardless, the two of you have a decision to make on your future. I need to go into town to take care of a few things, like collecting some of my funds from the trade house. That should give you some privacy to discuss things, which I think is necessary."

"That... will be appreciated. We have a good deal to consider, after what you've told us. I certainly do," Rose said, then smiled unhappily as she admitted, "What you've said *does* carry a little more weight about what happened to me, though. I'm going to have to think on it for a while."

"I... I don't want to force you out of the house, Kanae. It isn't just because of us that you're going into town, is it?" Isalla asked, looking rather anxious.

"No, no... I need to go into town, Isalla. If nothing else, I need to break to people that I'm going to be leaving permanently soon," Kanae assured her, stepping over to get her sword. Keeping moving helped her focus, rather than breaking down. "It's going to be a bit hard on them, but I've tried to spread some training through the townsfolk over the years, just in case."

Isalla's tension seemed to ease a little, and she nodded after a moment, smiling hesitantly. "Alright, then. I'm just... I worry, alright? I'll see you when you get back."

"Of course," Kanae said, smiling gently at Isalla, though it hurt a little. Then she headed for the door. She thought the angels needed some time to themselves.

∽

"Ah, there she goes... leaving the angels in her house alone? Isn't that a surprise?" Estalia murmured, but her lips slowly curved into a smile. "Well, she *is* my daughter, even if she has a different approach than I do."

"Your Majesty?" Veldoran asked, tilting his head curiously.

They could see the home Kitania had been staying in, but despite herself, Estalia found herself amused as she watched the strange figure of her daughter walking down the path toward town. Kitania wasn't armed the way she'd always been before vanishing, her appearance was markedly different, and she even walked different, but Estalia would have known there was something familiar about her even with the changes. Estalia also liked what Kitania had made of her life in hiding, as the house was both interesting and practical.

"Oh, just that I'd wondered if she'd grown selfish and decided to abduct the two for herself. It appears that she wasn't doing that, though I *could* be wrong. If I'm wrong, she's likely trying to ease them around to adoring her. Probably not, though," Estalia said, waving a hand dismissively as she watched her daughter. "Still, she doesn't look like much, does she?"

"I'm not sure that I'd say that, Your Majesty," Gregory said. The current head of her guards, he was a burly demon with a spiked tail, and Estalia could just see his purple eyes watching her daughter warily. "She doesn't possess your beauty, but she moves like a warrior, and from the way she wears the sword, I'd not take her lightly. You've also said she's a mage, which means that physical appearances may be misleading."

"True, true... I didn't mean to belittle her. I simply meant that she's managed to blend in well. She's hidden her true beauty, wields a weapon that was always her second or third choice, and likely hasn't truly *practiced* her magic in ages. It's a shame, really," Estalia said, sighing as her daughter slowly vanished from sight. "I so mishandled her when she was young. I should've known that my mother's approach wouldn't work."

"As you say, Your Majesty," Veldoran said doubtfully. Then he asked, "What now, though?"

"What now? Now I go have a chat with Rose and her lovely friend before I decide what to do. You're not to start a conflict with Kitania when she returns, but if *she* starts it, feel free to do what you feel is necessary," Estalia replied. Pausing, she tilted her head for a moment before adding, feeling a bit amused, "Oh, and don't feel the need to hold back against her under those circumstances. I'll be honestly startled if you manage to kill her."

Estalia saw the doubtful look on Captain Gregory's face, but she ignored it, simply smiling as she started down toward the house. She doubted that Kitania would start a fight, but if she did, he'd learn why Estalia had said that.

"I DIDN'T KNOW Kanae had been through anything like that," Isalla said, feeling terrible about her decisions. As much as she had wanted to rescue Rose, she hadn't meant to put Kanae into a situation where she might return to what sounded like little more than slavery.

"As she said, how could you?" Rose asked, shrugging helplessly. "I didn't, either. She's the one who chose to help you, Isalla, not you. I wish that she was easier for me to understand, though. Every time we've spoken, it feels like my attempts have

BENJAMIN MEDRANO

come across wrong. I don't *want* to upset her, and yet I keep doing so."

"I'm sorry, Rose," Isalla said, feeling even guiltier as she shifted in her chair. "I didn't mean to make light of your situation, either. I... well, I thought I was rescuing you from a fate worse than death. Instead, you seem like you were *happy* there."

"I was, but I'm also happy here, with you," Rose replied, reaching out to squeeze Isalla's leg reassuringly. "I told you that Queen Estalia promised to find you, even if you'd been killed, didn't I? As for my happiness... I do wonder what would have happened if I'd reached the palace. Kanae's description of what happened to her was a bit chilling, though it's possible that such only occurred because she *was* Her Majesty's daughter. I've seen enough parents that can't relate to their children that it seems likely to me."

"True enough. I had enough problems with my parents that —" Isalla began, only to be interrupted by an insistent knock at the door. She looked over and blinked, frowning. "I wonder who that is? It can't be Kanae... she barely left."

"How about you check the door?" Rose suggested. "I'll go to the bedroom."

"Alright," Isalla agreed, standing up and waiting for Rose to reach the bedroom before starting toward the front door. She supposed that someone might have seen Kanae working out that morning, but how they'd have missed her going into town was another question. Just to be safe she made certain her sword was at her side as she reached the door. Reaching for the latch, she started to speak. "Yes? Kanae is in town, so you're going to have to wait if you're looking for—"

The door opened and the words froze in Isalla's throat, her mind staggering to a stop as she saw the woman on the other side. The descriptions of Queen Estalia she'd received before left no doubt in her mind as to who it was, though she did differ slightly from the tales. Instead of wearing a flowing gown, the demon queen wore blue and silver full plate with softly glowing blue sigils etched into it, shaped to accentuate her figure without sacrificing much protection. The queen was smiling gently at Isalla, and the sight completely turned Isalla's mind to mush.

"Kanae? So that's what my lovely Kitania has been calling herself, is it?" Estalia asked, smiling even more. "Ah, but you must be Isalla. Are you going to invite me in? I'd dearly love to speak with you and Rose."

"Oh, um, of course," Isalla said in a daze, and she quickly took a step back to let the stunning woman into the house.

# CHAPTER 45

$\mathcal{I}$t didn't surprise Kanae that her visit to town was chaotic. She'd have been more surprised if the townsfolk had taken her sudden return well, and when Kanae had told Rekkal that she was leaving, that's when things had fallen apart. Even if he had a large portion of her investment on hand, Kanae knew that the second he got word to everyone else in town, she was going to be all but under siege. Unfortunately, she quickly realized that she'd underestimated the reaction her departure induced.

Manog was the first to arrive, but only the first. Before the shopkeep had been able to get out more than a dozen words, Cyr had arrived, the pink-haired lamia tearfully asking where she was supposed to get her scale oils if Kanae left. Then Enkax, Qirress, and the petite demoness's squirming son had arrived.

Those had only been the start, and one by one, Kanae had managed to either calm down the people who came to her or send them on their way. She wasn't going to change her mind, though she *did* feel somewhat bad about some of the panic her departure was causing.

Eventually she managed to chivy off all but Manog, and Kanae looked at him, then sighed and said, "Why don't we go to your shop? I need to pick up some supplies anyway."

"Very well," Manog said unhappily, turning to lead the way

back to his shop. Only once they were inside did he speak again, his dismay somewhat uncharacteristic. "May I at least ask why you're leaving, Kanae? You're lovely, and everyone in town adores you. I know that at least half the young men and women have spoken of trying to court you over the years. Even setting aside your medical expertise, you've been a fixture here for longer than I've lived here."

Kanae didn't say anything for a long moment, simply perusing the shelves and considering what she'd need for the road. Not much, to be perfectly honest. Some additional crossbow bolts, more food, and a new cloak would suffice. Finally, she asked, "Manog, how many people specifically inquired after Isalla or a woman by Isalla's description while I was gone?"

"About three that I can think of? There might have been more that didn't talk to me," Manog said, frowning. "I know word spread not to talk about her or you to outsiders that we didn't personally know, but that doesn't mean that everyone told me when someone asked about one of you."

"That's what I thought. Assassins came for her, Manog. People who wanted her *dead*, and I defended her. That means they're after me as well at this point," Kanae explained patiently, glancing over at the bone demon. "If it were only that, I wouldn't be too concerned. I live outside of town, and I can handle myself for the most part. No, my concern is that I've been living a reclusive, quiet life for a *reason*. Once upon a time, I was in the army, and after the War of Decimation, I chose to go into hiding. I didn't want to get involved in it anymore. Still, others aren't willing to let me go, so the attention is more than I can risk. Worse, I don't want to bring that attention down on the town, Manog."

The bone demon paused, tilting his head slightly. Then he spoke softly. "That explains a few things. Your mannerisms, and how you tended to avoid groups of soldiers over the years. If that's the case, I suppose... did you know that there were soldiers from the capital on the road this morning?"

"There were *what*?" Kanae demanded, spinning to face him as the blood drained from her face. She hesitated only a moment at the startled look on Manog's face, then came to a decision. She didn't have anything in hand, so she all but ran for the door.

"Kanae!" Manog exclaimed just as she was out the door, but he was too late, as she jogged for the gate leaving town, ignoring the startled looks she got as she moved.

"How in all the fires of the magma sea did they come here so *fast*?" Kanae muttered under her breath, fear surging still higher. "I checked her for tracking spells, so that can't be it. Could they have figured out that Isalla was here?"

She quickly left the town, and once she was on clear ground Kanae broke into a run. A tiny part of her wanted to believe that it was just a coincidence, that it wasn't actually someone after her or any of her guests, but Kanae couldn't bring herself to believe that. Her instincts were screaming that something had gone terribly wrong. That feeling was born out as she turned the last corner leading back to her house and she came to a halt, swearing under her breath.

Thirteen men and women were arrayed around her house, and the sight of them completely destroyed her mood. Twelve of them were in the midnight blue and silver of Queen Estalia's royal guard, while one demon was in finely made maroon clothing, complete with a wool trench coat, all of his clothing stitched with arcane runes. Two-thirds of the guards were in heavier armor, more like warriors, while the other four had light or no armor, striking her as magi. They all tensed at the sight of Kanae, watching her warily.

"Of all the things I expected, this had to be damn near last on the list," Kanae muttered, scowling at the guards. At least most of them didn't have weapons out, and as she watched the one in a trench coat, she tensed as she looked over his clothing. The runes she saw were of protection, and they were disconcertingly powerful. She could create more powerful spells than what was imbued into his clothing, but making something like that was incredibly difficult or expensive. Which *probably* meant that he was her mother's current court magister.

"I must compliment your skill with wards. It was somewhat difficult to pierce them, which is rare when it comes to individuals of your power," the man said, a slight smile on his face as he studied Kanae. She really wished she'd been paying more attention to who the powerful magi were in Estalia, as Kanae hated not knowing who she was dealing with.

"I probably should be flattered but pardon me if I find that difficult at the moment. I was trying to remain missing, if you please," Kanae said, her voice tight as she glanced between the man and the guards. "I don't recognize any of you, but that's unsurprising. It's been more than a millennium since I interacted with the royal guard. Am I going to have to fight, and likely lose, wait, or do I get to go into my house and find out what's been done to my guests?"

Kanae was ready to fight at a moment's notice, but she knew better than to think she could win under these circumstances. With the armor she'd had during the war, and a different weapon, maybe, but not in her current condition.

The mage laughed softly, grinning at her response, but a couple of guards glanced toward the man with captain's insignia along the collar of his armor. The man studied Kanae for a moment, then spoke. "Her Majesty indicated that we were not to start any conflict with you, and she did not forbid you from approaching. However, I will not allow you to enter with a weapon in hand."

"It wouldn't be in my *hand*, it'd be on my belt," Kanae griped sarcastically, but she approached, unbuckling her belt as she did so. "What do you expect me to do, scratch her? Unless I'm terribly mistaken, *Her Majesty* keeps in practice with her own sword, and the day I beat her is the day the mortal world falls into the hells."

"Be that as it may, I'm not going to risk her safety more than I must. Even with her own flesh and blood," the captain replied, though he betrayed a slight smile at her comments. "Perhaps I should say *especially* with her own flesh and blood."

"I'd argue, but I've heard enough of succession wars that that seems wise," Kanae said, scowling as she offered her sheathed sword to the nearest guard. "I'd *also* say to take good care of it, but I know that the sword isn't up to your standards. The day you steal it is the day the royal guard lost a dozen armories."

The woman she'd handed it to blinked with all four eyes,

then slid the sword an inch out of its sheath to study it for a moment before looking up at Kanae and replying mildly. "It isn't *that* bad. Not my first choice, but decent enough."

Kanae relaxed ever so marginally as she buckled her belt again, looking at the captain. She tried to keep her tone from growing caustic, but it was hard, considering what she knew was coming. "Can I go in now? I'm rather certain I'm going to be upset about whatever mother dearest has been up to."

"Very well. If you try to hurt her, though…" the captain warned, and Kanae snorted in derision.

"If I try to hurt her, she'll laugh and pin me to the wall so she can lecture me on how a young lady is supposed to behave," Kanae retorted. "Pin me with a sword, or maybe a few knives, that is."

They gave her a few odd looks at that, but Kanae stalked past them, her tail lashing due to her unhappiness. The chances of a few townsfolk coming over and spotting the guards was all too likely, but that was nothing compared to the unmitigated *disaster* she had waiting for her.

The door opened readily at her touch, showing that Isalla hadn't had the presence of mind to lock it. Unsurprisingly, considering how Kanae felt when she looked toward her stuffed chair and saw her mother. Kanae had braced herself for Estalia's presence, but even with that, her mind reeled at the sight. A thread of utter longing welled up inside Kanae, a thread which she tried to smother as she inhaled and almost choked at the scent pervading the house.

Estalia wasn't wearing her armor, that was sitting on the table alongside a pair of large sacks, while the monarch's sword leaned against the side of her chair. Neither Isalla or Rose were in sight, which told Kanae everything she needed to know, and she glared at Estalia as anger surged up inside her, then said, "I hate you, Mother."

"Oh, Kitty… that's not true. You know it as well as I do," Estalia said warmly, her smile almost lighting up the room the way her skin did. "I'm pleased to see you're doing well, even if I *am* somewhat disappointed by the lengths you went to in order to avoid me."

"Ah, but for once I *do* hate you, if only a little," Kanae retorted, her eyes narrowing. "And my name is Kanae."

"You may be going by Kanae, but it isn't your name. You can change what you are called, but you cannot change who you *are*, Kitania," Estalia corrected ever so gently, but she looked surprised as she tilted her head. "Truly, you're angry? Why?"

"What have you done to Isalla and Rose?" Kanae asked, glancing toward the bedroom with a baleful eye, ignoring Estalia's claim about her name as she closed the door and leaned against it. She didn't need an audience for this.

"Ah, so *that's* how it is, is it?" Estalia asked, a smile slowly growing on her face. "You're afraid that I've bedded the two lovely angels who're staying with you."

"Mother..." Kanae said, her voice a soft growl at this point, practically seething inside.

"Ah... well, I do not blame you. They're a lovely pair of women, aren't they? Even if poor Isalla lost her wings," Estalia said, her eyes dimming with obvious regret, and she raised a hand to put it on her chest. "That said, *this time* you're doing me an injustice, Kitania. Despite the immense temptation that it posed me, I managed to resist their advances once I realized both were attracted to you. So I'm afraid you're doing me quite the injustice. No, they decided to work off their frustration together, leaving me to wait for you."

"What?" Kanae asked, put off-balance by the explanation. The idea that both women liked her distracted Kanae for a moment, then she shook her head, trying to regain her focus.

"I said I didn't do what you're accusing me of, dear," Estalia said gently, slowly standing up. "Now then, let's have a look at you, shall we?"

"That's beside the point. Why does my appearance matter, anyway?" Kanae demanded, taking a step to the side, feeling like she was a mouse in front of a cat at this point. "What are you even doing here?"

"I'm curious because I thought transmutations didn't last more than a few hours for you. You tried changing your appearance often enough, growing up," Estalia replied, watching Kanae closely, her lips pursed. "I don't mind the taller look, but did you have to destroy your face? You had such refined features, and your skin…"

"I wanted to make sure you couldn't recognize me," Kanae said shortly, crossing her arms defensively. "Now what do you *want*, Mother?"

"I've left you alone ever since I figured out where you were a couple of centuries ago, darling," Estalia said, taking a couple of delicate steps forward and reaching up to run a finger down Kanae's cheek, causing her to shiver at the gentle, intimate touch. Estalia's eyes were a deep blue that could swallow almost anyone, and it took everything Kanae had not to let them overwhelm her, too. After a moment, Estalia ran a hand down Kanae's arm, tracing the muscles as she continued. "I knew you were upset, and I wanted to give you time and distance. I made poor choices when you were growing up, and I don't blame you for your reaction. However, you made it *far* more difficult to keep your distance with this little stunt, hm? Kidnapping Rose after her training was complete… that was going just a *touch* too far, wasn't it?"

"Isalla wanted to rescue her friend," Kanae replied, her heart racing as she resisted the impulse to relax or run away. Neither would result in a reaction she wanted. "Besides, you stole her life."

"That's where you're wrong, Kitania," Estalia said, suddenly pulling away and frowning at her. "I *saved* her life. For now, at least."

"How do you figure that?" Kanae asked, her eyes narrowing slightly. "You stole her away from an angelic redoubt and dragged her into the hells, then sent her to the Spire of Confession. If that isn't stealing her life, what is?"

"My people didn't capture her. A group of mercenaries approached me," Estalia said, moving halfway across the room, folding her hands behind her as she almost danced over to the fireplace, studying the flames. "They'd been hired by a group of angels to question and dispose of First Sword Roselynn Emberborn, wielder of Ember. They came to us because they knew that we could get the most information for them, and when I asked for Rose and all her things, they agreed to the price. If I had refused, she would have been brutally questioned by some other group and then either broken or slain. What I did left Rose with a life, and one she's happier with than what she had before."

Kanae's eyes went wide at the information, and her blood suddenly chilled. Estalia glanced over and smiled gently, her eyes glittering as she spoke in an approving tone. "Ah, I see you had the same sort of thought that I had. After speaking with dear little Isalla, I believe that whoever tried to kill her also wished to eliminate Rose as well. Is that what you were thinking?"

"Yes. That's exactly what I was thinking," Kanae admitted, her heart almost feeling like lead. "If they would go to such an extent to eliminate threats to their secrecy... what are they plotting?"

"That *is* the question, isn't it? I'm not certain myself, but I don't wish for them to succeed," Estalia said, her smile fading slowly. "No matter what they choose, they are planning to disrupt the current uneasy peace. Dropping Isalla into Hellmount couldn't have been an accident, since they'd have to deliberately open a portal from the heavens to do so. That means they were likely trying to implicate the hells to start another war, at least in my opinion."

"Oh? And what you want is any better?" Kanae asked, another flicker of indignant anger flaring up inside her. Estalia looked over at Kanae and sighed, shaking her head.

"Oh, Kitania... I truly wish we could understand each other more easily. You and I are too much alike, alas," Estalia said, shaking her head sorrowfully. "While we have similar goals, we simply have different ideas of how to go about it."

"I'm just not willing to manipulate people into your worship to convince them to serve you," Kanae retorted, turning to enter the kitchen. "You really think that's a proper solution, rather than trying for a lasting peace? The current truce has lasted for a millennium!"

"The truce has been frequently broken by raids, minor clashes, and wars between empires," Estalia corrected, her voice gaining a hint of steel to it. "Unless every archangel, demon lord, and mortal god who'd participated in the wars dropped dead tomorrow, *and* the history books of virtually every library were erased, there's no chance that any *peace* would last more than a few centuries, Kanae. After millennia of bad blood, there's no chance of people truly choosing to leave the war behind. Perhaps my solution won't work either, but if I can convince a few people to worship me, and they convince a few more, who in turn convince more… uniting enough people under a single figure is at least a faint hope. I'm unwilling to let that possibility slip away simply because you disagree with it."

Kanae gritted her teeth, mostly because she'd heard the explanation before, though it hadn't had the truce to point to. She wished that the truce *had* held for all this time, because then it would have been easier to counter Estalia's claim. Instead, it had bolstered her mother's plans, which didn't make her any happier. She took a deep breath, then let it out as she shook her head.

"We aren't going to agree about this," Kanae said, frowning. "It's been a thousand years, and we're *still* disagreeing on the approach."

"Indeed. You'll note I've never insisted that you help me with my path, either," Estalia told Kanae as her frown faded.

"Perhaps, but it doesn't change the fact I found your presence stifling," Kanae replied, frowning in turn as she leaned on the counter. "Anyway… I understand you wanted to visit. *Now* what?"

"That is the question, alas. Before I came out here, I was going to examine things and unless you'd gone off in the deep end, wanting to enslave poor Rose, I would've let you stay here without too much argument. Unfortunately, the word about the assassins and plots in the heavens has me… concerned," Estalia said, sighing and shaking her head sadly. "I *cannot* let them succeed in silencing Isalla and Rose, since they're the only clues I have so far. Your involvement complicates things, but at least I don't have to worry about you dying. That means there are only two options I'm willing to entertain."

"And what, pray tell, are those?" Kanae asked, eyeing her mother warily. She knew that tone and attitude, and Kanae didn't like the implications.

BENJAMIN MEDRANO

"The three of you can stay in the palace. I will house them as guests of honor and protect them while my agents work to find out who the deplorable individuals behind all this are, and what they're doing," Estalia said, and her statement made Kanae's stomach tighten more. "Another option is that they could decide to go investigate themselves, trying to find those in the angelic legions who aren't corrupted or involved to deal with this. I'd send a few agents along with them to aid in keeping them safe, of course, and you could involve yourself. I suppose a third option is that you could abandon them entirely and go scurrying off to whatever hiding place you had in mind next... I'd be disappointed in you, but it *is* an option."

"Really? Those are the only options?" Kanae asked, annoyed but mostly arguing for the sake of arguing. "I'm pretty sure I could come up with a few more."

"You could, but after talking with the girls, I'm fairly certain that those are the two solutions they'd ended up at. Like it or not, Kitania, that's what they're going to do. Even without me interfering. Well, except for my assistance if they go investigating," Estalia replied, smiling warmly. "The only question is whether you're going to try to help them or not. I would, but you're not me."

"Oh, really?" Kanae said, glowering at her mother. She hated these discussions, since it rarely felt like she had a choice. At least she was growing used to Estalia's presence... or was falling under her sway. Either way, it didn't much matter. "So, how long are you going to be here? Are we going to have to deal with you constantly interfering, or will they have the chance to decide without you entrancing them?"

"Mm, I think a few days will be enough. I can't stay out here for that time, though. If nothing else, my presence will be a problem if anyone is watching, and rumors travel faster than I care to consider," Estalia said, shaking her head. "No, I intend to head back to the palace within an hour or two, darling. I'm going to leave a quartet of guards to keep an eye on you and your lovely guests. They'll be ordered to keep Isalla and Rose safe, and to be your escorts once you've made your decision."

"Just guarding *them*?" Kanae asked, growing slightly

annoyed despite herself. She'd wanted Estalia to leave, yet at the same time she found herself frustrated that her mother wasn't worried about her. For her part, Estalia simply sighed.

"Kitty... you know exactly why I'm giving those orders. You're more survivable than either Isalla or Rose are," Estalia scolded gently, then paused and tilted her head. "Have you told them?"

"No," Kanae replied shortly, her arms tightening around herself as she did so. A faint sense of guilt rushed through her, and she shook her head. "Some secrets are just... I don't want to talk about it."

"Very well," Estalia said, bowing her head slightly. She was silent for a long moment, then Kanae blinked, startled as she saw a single, shimmering tear track down her mother's cheek. It was the first tear Kanae had seen her shed in all her memory, and Estalia spoke softly, her voice trembling in a way that made Kanae's heart lurch. "I... thought I'd lost you, after Rosken. I seriously considered trying to hunt down those who were involved in the battle, darling. I would have, if it wouldn't have destroyed all that I'd been working toward, and if I hadn't known it wouldn't make you happy."

"I..." Kanae began, then fell silent. After a moment, she sighed and shook her head, almost whispering through her guilt. "I'm sorry. I just... wanted to get away."

They were both silent, Estalia wiping away her tear with a careful gesture. Kanae couldn't remember her mother showing vulnerability before, and it silenced her. A minute passed, then two. Finally, Kanae nodded toward the table and the bags on it.

"What are those?" she asked, her voice soft.

"Oh, that? I brought armor I made for Rose, and let her pick between her old armor or the new set. She chose the new one," Estalia said, smiling again at last, almost shyly. "I think she liked it. As for the other bag, it holds Ember. It belongs to her, after all."

"I see. That's just like you, Mother," Kanae said, letting out a soft sigh and unfolding her arms. "I'm not sure what I want to do."

"Well, that's something you're going to have to figure out,

Kitty," Estalia said, approaching slowly. She'd used the name so often when Kanae was a child. She reached up to cradle Kanae's face, smiling slightly as she teased gently. "You being tall causes all sorts of problems, you know? Come down here."

"Is it really so wrong that I wanted a little extra height?" Kanae asked, a smile flitting over her lips, but leaned down obediently.

Estalia stroked Kanae's face gently, then leaned forward and gave her a gentle, chaste kiss. Then she pulled back and spoke, her voice soft. "Please don't disappear on me again? I know I've made my mistakes, Kitty, and I'm trying not to make them again. I'm not going to pen you up or make you into *my* vision of what you should be. I want you to be yourself. And when you need to talk… I'll be here, waiting."

Kanae felt her hesitations begin melting away, and while a part of her wanted to distrust her mother, another part of her was just happy to not have the weight of having to hide hanging over her head. Finally, she nodded and murmured. "As you like, Mother. As long as I have the freedom to do as I will… I'm not going to hide anymore."

"Good." Estalia said, smiling brilliantly as she let go of Kanae's face. "Now, I just have to ask… how *did* you get the transmutations to last? We had trouble making even permanent ones last more than a few hours, as I recall."

"Well…" Kanae squirmed a bit, hesitating, then looked away as she cleared her throat. "I… had the enchantments carved into my bones. It's an enchantment that's powered by my mana."

Estalia winced sympathetically, looking at Kanae in fascinated horror. "Really? You had them carve enchantments into your *bones*, darling? That… I can't imagine the pain it must have caused."

"It worked," Kanae countered, grimacing as she remembered the pain she'd gone through. "Not something I'd care to go through again… but it worked."

"I suppose it did, at that," Estalia said, then walked back over to her chair and plopped into it. "Now, why don't you tell me about your life as *Kanae*, darling. I want to know what you've been up to."

"Are you going to talk about my father?" Kanae asked, settling into a chair as she watched her mother, unable to keep her lips from curving into a smile.

"Not right now. Maybe next time we get together… I suppose it's been long enough that I can talk about what happened," Estalia replied, smirking. "You kept your survival a secret, I can keep a few more under wraps until I'm satisfied."

"Fine, fine," Kanae said, then sat back and took a deep breath. It was going to be a long conversation. Even if it *was* going better than she had expected it to.

# CHAPTER 46

*R*ose came out of her daze slowly, a smile still on her face. Estalia's visit was almost a blur in her mind, at least compared to the last while with Isalla. The warm glow permeating her was one of the most pleasant feelings she could remember, and she didn't want to move.

That was why she opened her eyes, blinking as Isalla pushed the sheets back and began squirming toward the edge of the bed, her skin glistening where light touched her. Rose half pushed herself upright as she protested. "Isalla? What're you doing?"

"Sorry, sorry… I just thought I heard Estalia and Kanae… and it *sounded* like Estalia was getting ready to leave," Isalla explained, pausing and flushing in the dim light. "I didn't want her to go without at least saying farewell, especially since we kind of… abandoned her."

"She's leaving?" Rose exclaimed, sitting up abruptly. A sense of shame washed over her, because she knew Isalla was right. They'd left Estalia rather abruptly, and that hadn't been polite. After Estalia had come all the way out to see them, it made Rose feel quite guilty. She shouldn't have left with Isalla, even if Estalia *had* encouraged them to.

"I'm not sure; I just thought that was what I heard," Isalla replied, relaxing visibly as she began searching for her clothing again.

"Well, we'd better check," Rose said, looking around and quickly starting to get dressed. It wasn't too hard, thankfully, since her clothing stood out against the dark floor. "I'd be mortified if she left while we were in bed."

"I don't blame you," Isalla said, flushing even more as she slipped into her clothing. "I'm a *little* more concerned about Kanae, if I'm being honest. After what she explained…"

"True enough. I didn't really figure out how things were from Her Majesty's perspective, but if they aren't agreeing, or if she's planning to drag Kanae back with her…" Rose began, letting her voice trail off after a moment. Her feelings were tangled on the subject, as she both liked Estalia, and thought that Kanae deserved the chance to have freedom.

"Exactly. I don't *think* they're arguing, but I have to check," Isalla said, then quickly ran her fingers through her hair, and Rose saw her wince as she undid a few tangles. "There, ready."

"I'm almost there," Rose replied, slipping on her gown again. At least it went on almost as easily as it came off. She was thankful that one of the changes she'd made at the spire had made her hair far less prone to tangling as she ran her fingers through it. Then she nodded. "I believe I am as well."

"Right, then let's go see what's happening," Isalla said, and Rose's lover approached the door and opened it. She froze for a moment, and Rose blinked, then smiled at the sight.

In the main room, Estalia was standing still as Kanae helped her put on her armor. Estalia was speaking as the door opened. "…really isn't *that* complicated, you know."

"I can't remember the last time I had occasion to help someone put on plate, Mother," Kanae retorted, adjusting a strap. "Taking it off, certainly, but putting it on? That hasn't been one of my duties since I was in the army. I'm sure I've helped a few people since then, but it's been a rare thing."

"I suppose that I should be thankful that you remember how to do it at all, then," Estalia replied, her smile somehow warmer than Rose remembered it being. She was utterly enchanting, Rose realized dreamily. Yet at the same time, Estalia didn't quite take away from Kanae's presence. It was odd, considering how Rose felt that most of the time Estalia simply overwhelmed everyone else in the area. The queen glanced over and smiled. "Ah, I see that your guests decided to join us before I left, Kitty."

"That they have," Kanae murmured, and Rose blinked at the nickname, somehow amused.

"Kitty?" Isalla asked, sounding slightly stunned. Rose nudged her, and Isalla stepped out of the way, allowing Rose to enter the room.

"Oh, that's just what I call Kitania sometimes," Estalia said, glancing over her shoulder with a smile. "She was rambunctious and willful as a child, just like a cat."

"Mostly you call me that in private, though. You must be in a rare mood, to share it in front of others," Kanae murmured, moving on to another strap.

"Perhaps so. I'm just happy to have finally at least *somewhat* reconciled with my wayward daughter," Estalia said, letting out a soft laugh.

"You're leaving?" Rose asked, feeling a little unhappy at the thought.

"Yes, I am," Estalia replied gently, looking over at Rose kindly. "While it would be quite pleasant to stay here for a while, we *are* on the edge of my domain, and I'm likely to attract unwanted attention."

"Your guards have likely already managed that," Kanae interjected quietly. "The townsfolk saw you heading this direction on the road this morning. It's why I came back in such a rush."

"Indeed? Still more reason to vacate the area while I can. Knowing that unusual guards were in the area is far different from knowing the queen herself visited," Estalia said, letting out a soft breath of annoyance. "You have enough things to discuss and arrange without all the problems my presence will cause."

"You mean we won't see you again?" Isalla asked, her voice almost tiny. Her question caused Estalia to turn, putting her hands on her hips, and Kanae stood back, shaking her head slowly.

"Now when did I say that?" Estalia asked, looking at Isalla chidingly, her tone prompting Rose to smile. "I have to return to the capital, Isalla. You're a darling young lady, but have you already forgotten what we discussed before? I'm willing to *help* you, and it seems likely that Kitania will help you as well. You need to decide what you want to do, then you can come to the palace and I'll help you. So you *will* see me again, Isalla."

"Ah, yes, we *did* discuss that, didn't we?" Rose said, flushing slightly in embarrassment. "I'd almost forgotten about that…"

"That's another reason she needs to go. My mother's very presence has a tendency to distract or cause all thought to fly out of people's heads," Kanae added, her tone dry as she eyed Estalia. "Even if I'm happy that you *weren't* reacting the way I expected, you're still an incredible distraction, Mother."

"I know," Estalia replied, not a hint of shame in her smile. "Now then… I'm going to get going, so come down here, Kitania."

"You aren't going to let me forget that I'm taller now, are you?" Kanae asked, but leaned down to hug Estalia, somewhat to Rose's surprise. The lack of tension through Kanae's body was remarkable, compared to pretty much every other time Rose had seen the demoness. It was just another thing that made her respect Estalia more.

"Of course not, at least not until you decide to get a sane height again," Estalia retorted, hugging Kanae firmly. "I hope to see you soon, Kitty."

"We'll see, Mother," Kanae said, then let go.

Estalia turned to Rose and smiled as she extended her arms. "Now then, you didn't think I was going to forget you, did you? Come on, Rose."

"I just wasn't sure, after last time," Rose said happily, coming over and leaning down to embrace Estalia. She was just as comfortable to hug as last time, at least aside from the armor. After a lingering moment, she added, "Thank you for bringing Ember and the armor. No matter what choice we make, I'm glad to have it. You had a definite point about defending myself."

"I'd far rather you had it and didn't need it than the reverse," Estalia said, hugging Rose tightly, then letting go and looking at Isalla. "Now, are you someone who likes hugs, Isalla? It was a pleasure to meet you, even if you and Kitty *did* lead me on a bit of a chase."

"Um, sure," Isalla said, blushing yet again as she took a few hesitant steps forward. "I thought it was the best idea at the time. Sorry about it, though…"

"It's fine," Estalia said, giving Isalla a hug as well. "I just have to tease, hm? Now, I'm going to go. I'll have a few guards hiding out in the area, so when you're ready to come see me, they'll escort you to Silken Veils, and the teleporter there."

"Alright," Isalla said, seeming to relax a little as Estalia pulled away. "Thank you."

"Oh, don't mention it," Estalia said, pulling away and smiling broadly. She waved at them, then headed for the door.

Then she was gone, and Rose blinked, then looked at Kanae. The other woman let out a sigh, then murmured, "Well, that changed things, didn't it? Let's see what we can decide."

"Agreed," Rose said, then paused as Kanae looked at the two of them.

"However, I think the two of you need to take a bath first," Kanae said, a thin smile flickering across her face. "Otherwise you'll be *quite* distracting."

Rose blushed at the demoness's teasing tone, and looked over to see that Isalla was blushing brightly as well. After a moment, she nodded, replying as calmly as she could manage. "Ah, you have a point. We'll be back in a bit."

Isalla took the chance to flee, but Rose chose to follow at a more sedate pace. She had to have *some* dignity, even if she was privately mildly mortified.

# CHAPTER 47

$\mathcal{K}$anae sat back, watching as Rose pulled out the armor. While many people didn't see items like the armor often, Kanae had known that Estalia would have made it valuable. No matter what her mother might say, someone like Rose was a prize worth preserving. That was why she wasn't startled at the sight of it.

Isalla was gawking as the armor plates came out one at a time. The plate was multiple shades of red that gave it a flame pattern, though large parts of it were a deep maroon. Glittering against it were the gold runes of the armor's enchantments, along with a large ruby over the chest, another on the forehead of the helm, and one set into each vambrace. There were even long, thin sections to protect the upper edge of Rose's wings, and Kanae smiled at the sight of them. Estalia always had been cautious about her wings. Still, from the looks of things, the armor had been shaped to fit Rose's figure without losing much protection, though with the magic imbued into the armor, even that was a minor sacrifice at most.

"I didn't say anything when she showed it to me, but how could she possibly have had this made in the time she had?" Rose asked, holding up the breastplate and admiring it. "This was obviously made for me, and if I'm not mistaken it's made of mithral. The armor alone would have taken weeks to make, let alone the enchantments."

"Never underestimate what the right connections and what a well-trained group of artificers can manage," Kanae said calmly, taking a sip of water as she smiled sardonically. "Mother always kept a group of trained artificers on hand, ones who were so used to working together that they could split the workload. I don't know what the group is like *now*, but that has all the hallmarks of one of their projects. Artistic, practical, and strong."

"What do you mean?" Isalla asked, looking up quickly. "I don't know what the enchantments are."

"She didn't tell you?" Kanae asked, her eyebrows rising. She looked at Rose, and the angel shook her head.

"No, she didn't. She just said that the armor was heavily enchanted," Rose confirmed, frowning. "I suppose I should have asked, but it didn't occur to me at the time. I was just happy to get it and Ember."

"I'm not surprised. Bring the breastplate and vambraces over, and I'll take a look," Kanae said, sighing softly. "Hopefully she hasn't come up with something new."

Rose quickly retrieved each piece and brought them over, her curiosity obvious. She spoke after a moment. "I did notice that some of the runes had something to do with fire... I've some skill with fire magic, since I was tutored in it growing up."

"Ah, quite understandable. I don't know how the wielder of Ember is chosen, but it makes sense that they'd want anyone who used it to understand fire magic. It'd make your attacks more effective," Kanae said, setting aside her mug before taking the armor and setting it in her lap. She examined it closely, her fingers running over the runes of the breastplate. It was oddly nice to touch such impressive armor again. Almost like being back home, in its own way.

"Oh? I didn't realize that," Isalla said, her voice musing. "You never talked about it."

"Ember was more powerful than my spells, so I mostly didn't bother using my magic," Rose explained. "I practiced a little, but all of us were drilled in fire magic growing up. I wasn't the best with it, though after Ember chose me, my talent strengthened."

"Oh," Isalla said, frowning. "I don't think I was ever tested for magical talent. They just asked if I had any training when I joined the Order."

"I wish they'd standardize testing, but the authorities never bothered. Magical techniques were as far as they were willing to go," Rose murmured, obviously annoyed.

"No military wants the expense of raising large numbers of magi," Kanae said absently, shaking her head as she pieced together what the armor did. Fortunately, none of the functions she could see were too unusual. "Training a mage takes a lot of time and effort, and even for angels and demons, trying to raise them from nothing is an enormous expense. It's far easier to recruit those who've already been trained, or improve those of high standing or who have known talents with useful magic."

"Much is explained," Rose said, scowling. "I hadn't thought about it that way, but you're likely right."

"Maybe I should get tested, then? Could either of you test me for talents?" Isalla asked hopefully.

"I'm afraid I wouldn't be the best for that, Isalla. I'm skilled with protection magic, including anti-scrying wards, and with midrange telekinesis. Primarily protection," Kanae said, looking up at Isalla regretfully. "My talents were limited, so I chose to heavily focus on a narrow variety of magic, with a related type for offense."

"I might be able to test you for fire magic, but it wouldn't do much good," Rose added, shaking her head. "If you have a talent, I wouldn't be a good teacher."

"Of course," Isalla said, sighing. After a few moments, she asked, "Do you know what the armor does, Kanae?"

"Yes, approximately," Kanae said, tapping the armor and smiling thinly. "Like most armor, it possesses enchantments to strengthen and harden the metal, while it contains magic that helps turn aside blows. It's quite a powerful enchantment, too. More unusually, there's an enchantment that effectively lightens the armor to make it easier to fly in without losing maneuverability. Based on what I'm seeing, I suspect the helm will help protect you from mental attacks, Rose.

"Another major benefit is that the armor accelerates your

healing and protects from poisons," Kanae added, tapping the central gem as she continued, a note of admiration in her voice. "This contains mana which neutralizes poisons and heals you. It naturally recovers, but in an emergency, you could recharge it as well. The armor further strengthens your body, making you stronger, faster, and tougher. As for the vambraces, each of them contains magic which amplifies fire magic, which is also charged over time by the gems. The suit as a whole mitigates any cold or fire attacks as well... it's an impressive set of enchantments, I must say."

"I suppose you could say that," Isalla said, her jaw almost hanging open. "I've never heard of anyone wearing armor like that before, outside legends."

"I have, but not for someone who isn't a general or even more powerful than that," Rose said, staring at the armor in obvious surprise. "I knew it was powerful from the beginning, but..."

"Mother wanted to ensure you were safe. To almost any demon lord, you'd be an incredible prize, and she wouldn't want you to be defenseless." Kanae said, then offered the armor back. "Here you are. What of Ember? Is it in good condition?"

"It is, thank you," Rose said, smiling as she took the armor and set it on the table again. She pulled the sword out of the sack, and Kanae studied it for a moment. The sword was a little longer than her own, and was in a lacquered red and gold sheath reminiscent of flames, and the hilt was red leather, with a gold pommel and cross-guard each set with a ruby. Ember didn't radiate as much magic as she expected it to, but she knew better, since the blade was dyed red and runes along its blade would light up with inner fire when drawn by its wielder.

"Good. Now, then... let's get some of this conversation out of the way. I give it half an hour before the locals come to investigate," Kanae said, letting out a soft sigh. "And that's if we're lucky."

"Oh. Oh, I didn't even *think* of that," Isalla said, blanching. "You think they know that something happened out here?"

"I heard there were soldiers on the road this morning, and all but ran home to check on you," Kanae explained dryly, amused by the angel's response. "So yes, they know. Most likely someone came out to check on what happened, then saw Mother's guards and retreated. With any luck they won't recognize that they were the royal guard, but we're *going* to have visitors."

"Lovely," Rose said, sighing softly. "I'd hoped to avoid that."

"You aren't the only one, but… rural towns," Isalla said, shaking her head slowly. "You know how it is."

"True enough. News travels through them like lightning," Rose agreed, her worry seeming to ease slightly. She considered the armor on the table for a moment, then left it and Ember as she took a seat. "Alright, if we don't have much time… what are we going to do?"

"That *is* the question. From what my mother said, linking together events, it sounds like a faction of the angelic legions is trying to restart the war," Kanae said bluntly, frowning as she tapped her foot slowly, nervousness rushing through her. "Between throwing Isalla into the hells and having Rose kidnapped, it seems likely. It *could* just be their way of disposing of problems, but I think they could have come up with more efficient ways of doing that which didn't involve the hells."

"They had me kidnapped?" Rose asked incredulously, just as Isalla inhaled.

"According to Mother, the group of mercenaries that captured you were hired by angels," Kanae explained shortly, focusing on the discussion rather than her guests. "They wanted all the information you had, then for you to be disposed of. She asked Anna to coax all the information she could out of you, figuring that in your… *illuminated* state, it'd suffice for their request for disposal."

Rose scowled at that, murmuring, "Oh, those evil… well, it explains the conversations with Anna. I told her practically anything she wanted to know. I'd be annoyed, but at least I'm alive."

"It also explains what you meant, about people trying to start a war. I'd wondered why Rose got captured so soon after I was attacked, it seemed just too unlikely of a coincidence," Isalla said unhappily. "Adding in the assassination attempt on me, and it starts leading places that I *really* don't like."

"I don't like them either. I don't want the war to flare up again, even the skirmishes I hear about are quite bad enough," Kanae agreed, shivering slightly as she folded her arms. "From what Mother said, you'd pretty much settled on two options. Going to investigate and finding allies among the angelic legions to break open the conspiracy, or taking Mother's protection and letting her agents investigate."

"I do remember discussing that somewhat. Without Ember, I'd be hesitant, but... no, what do you think, Isalla?" Rose asked, looking over at her friend. "I don't want to decide for you, not after everything you've been through."

"We've both been through a lot," Isalla retorted, then fell silent, obviously considering the question. Kanae felt just a hint of surprise as she watched Isalla. She seemed much more focused than Kanae had seen before, and the sight was interesting. At last, Isalla spoke softly. "I can't just sit back and watch someone else deal with this, Rose. Even if the command staff all but threw us out, the heavens are our homeland. The number of innocents who'd die if the war reignites in truth... I can't imagine how bad it would become."

"I agree. While I'm not happy about the idea, we also have at least one thread of hope," Rose said, nodding in approval. "Firewatch should still be there, and there had to be a good reason for me being ambushed while I was outside. I know there are people there who I can trust, and they should be able to point us in the right direction."

"Assuming they haven't been replaced by people who're more likely to do the bidding of whoever wanted you eliminated," Kanae interjected softly, still sitting back.

"Yeah," Isalla agreed, then fell silent, looking at Kanae for a moment. Then she asked, "What about you, Kanae? What are you going to do?"

"That *is* the question, isn't it?" Kanae murmured, smiling thinly. "I'd like to help you, to be honest, but... you have each other, and having a demon in tow wouldn't help your case. I would likely hurt it, in fact."

"Why would you *hurt* our case?" Rose asked, frowning.

"Because she's a demon. They'd probably think that she was controlling us," Isalla said, frowning heavily. "I… is there some way you could change your shape, or look like you were human? From what you've said, you changed to look like you do now, and Estalia *said* you were taller."

"I'm afraid not. The method I used to change my appearance isn't something done easily or in a short period of time. My unique mutations cause any shapechanging or other transmutation to wear off extraordinarily quickly," Kanae replied, shaking her head. "Even permanent transmutations are undone within an hour or three. I had an unpleasant encounter with a medusa once, and that *very* much startled her."

"Well, drat," Isalla said, looking even more unhappy.

"Either way… we'll have to figure out exactly what you want to do, and what *I'll* do," Kanae said, unfolding her arms and slowly standing. "At least I have a little more time to deal with the house and get my things situated. It appears that I've been rather unfair to my mother for all these years."

"Based on what you've told us, I don't think I blame you," Rose said, standing up more quickly. She was studying Kanae closely, far more closely than Kanae was entirely comfortable with. Finally, having taken entirely too long for someone of her background to notice, Kanae realized what she was seeing. Rose took a deep breath, then spoke. "Kanae, I wanted to apologize if I've offended you over the past few days. I kept seeming to make mistakes, when what I really wanted was—"

"Rose… please don't," Kanae interrupted softly, shaking her head as her stomach clenched again, her emotions swirling into turmoil. "I should have realized last night, but I wasn't paying enough attention. I was too absorbed by my hopes and fears to realize that you were attracted to me. Mother mentioned it, but then she distracted me with the rest of the conversation we had. However… I feel the need to keep my distance for now."

Isalla was watching them, keeping quiet as she tilted her head. Kanae could practically see how she wanted to interrupt, but was thankful that Isalla didn't. This would be hard enough without multiple people interjecting. For her part, Rose looked somewhat disappointed and confused, with just a hint of annoyance in her eyes.

"May I at least ask why? You didn't seem to object to getting close to Isalla," Rose asked finally.

"Of course. With Isalla, I didn't know how long she was going to stay for. It took a fair amount of time before she approached me, and we'd had plenty of time to get to know one another. Despite my heritage, I don't *casually* develop relationships anymore. I shouldn't have told her I was interested at all, in fact," Kanae explained, a hand reaching up to unconsciously rub her throat. "Now... you might note that I've left you and Isalla together ever since your rescue. I've deliberately avoided doing anything more because I knew that you were likely to leave soon."

"Kanae..." Isalla began, only to be silenced when Kanae looked at her.

"No, Isalla," Kanae said softly, shaking her head. "I don't want to hurt you. I truly don't, but at the same time, I also don't want to hurt *myself*."

Rose blinked in surprise, then slowly frowned, looking quite unhappy, though about what was another question. After a moment, she spoke softly. "I don't understand you, Kanae. You've gone through all this effort, and for what?"

"That *is* the question, isn't it? If you figure it out, please let me know," Kanae said, then blinked as she heard what sounded like footsteps. "Ah, it appears that visitors are approaching, so we need to wrap all this up."

"We'd better take your things into the bedroom," Isalla told Rose, quickly standing up. As she started moving to help Rose pick up the armor, Isalla suddenly paused and added, "I just have to ask... Kitty?"

"I don't know why she likes the name so much," Kanae replied, sighing. "As she said, my original name is Kitania. Use the one you like. Now, I need to deal with our guests, preferably without letting them catch sight of Rose."

"Alright. Good luck," Isalla said, the worry on her face easing slightly, and she quickly picked up several pieces of armor.

Moments later, there was a hesitant knock at the door, and

Kanae waited until the other two had moved into the bedroom with Ember and the armor before opening the door. On the other side were Deka and Manog, both of whom looked nervous. Deka relaxed slightly at the sight of Kanae, while Manog was just looking at her in concern.

"Kanae, you're alright! After we saw that group of soldiers around your house, we were concerned you might have been taken away or something," Deka said, lowering his club as he reached up to run a hand over his leather helm, smiling in relief.

"No, I'm here for the moment. That was just my past catching up with me, unfortunately. I thought I had more time to run, but I'm afraid not," Kanae told them, deliberately not inviting them inside. She was sure there were signs of visitors, and she didn't want them to think people were still inside. "Instead, I have a few days to deal with all my things, then I'm going to be taking an escort to Silken Veils."

"Oh. That doesn't sound good," Deka said, his smile fading.

"Kanae... what is going *on*? Those weren't normal soldiers. I didn't recognize the armor, but I've seen expensive gear before," Manog said, looking around nervously. "They had to be important."

"Well..." Kanae paused, pursing her lips for a long moment, then sighed and shrugged. "Suffice to say, I was not of low birth. After the War of Decimation, I faked my death for freedom, and it seems that my family wants me back. While I have *some* choice in the matter, there isn't much I can do, not safely."

"What?" Deka yelped, his eyes going huge. "You're a *noble*?"

For his part, Manog blinked, then sighed and shook his head, his voice annoyed, but finally regaining just a bit of his usual, charming manners. "Ahh, I see why you were always so insistent on me learning how to assist you, Kanae. Might I at least hope that once you're safely ensconced in the upper class that you'll not forget us? Our town *is* ignored much of the time."

Kanae smiled and laughed, shaking her head as she did so. "Oh, I think you can safely assume that I'm not going to forget you. Now, whether or not I'll be able to do anything to *help* is another question entirely. I'm not entirely sure what sort of situation I'm going to end up in."

"Ah, I see. Well, I do hope you end up in a position that's appropriate for such a lovely lady." Manog said, smiling and straightening. "May I ask what you plan to do with everything out here?"

"At the moment, I was planning to give you the medical texts and what herbs and other supplies I have on hand. The alchemy equipment you can choose to sell, or you can try to find an alchemist who'll move into town," Kanae said, then paused and shrugged. "Beyond that? I intend to leave behind the key and command words for the door wards, and anyone who wants to move in, or split up what I leave behind is welcome to it."

"That's kind of sad. I mean... you've lived here for years, and you're just going to leave?" Deka asked, looking rather unhappy.

"I have little choice, Deka," Kanae replied gently, taking a deep breath, then letting it out as she looked at Manog. "That said, I need to start figuring out what to pack. I'll come into town with some of my things tomorrow, alright?"

"Very well. While I'd deeply prefer to discuss your situation more, I suppose I can wait for you to come into town," Manog said, then he bowed. "Good day, Lady Kanae."

"And to both of you," Kanae replied, then shut the door and locked it, letting out a soft sigh.

Looking around, Kanae eyed the door to her bedroom and muttered, "It's going to be a long couple of days."

Sighing again, Kanae went ahead and decided to get to work before Isalla and Rose could interfere. Much.

# CHAPTER 48

*E*ziel glanced around, making certain she couldn't see any of her companions. Despite the powerful winds around the hellhole in the middle of Hragon, she found flying quite easy. It was made still easier by the powerful thermal the portal to the hells created. Still, she couldn't see any of her companions, which meant that everything was going as planned.

Reaching up to her earring, Eziel channeled mana into it and murmured softly, "Descend through the portal, then head south."

None of the others replied, as they weren't supposed to. While the chances of demons seeing through their invisibility or eavesdropping on their conversations were miniscule, it was still more than they were willing to entertain. Sorm had made it clear that their mission couldn't be allowed to fail.

Eziel's feathers rustled in the wind as she began to descend toward the hells. She hated that she was going into the hells at all, as the horrific monsters that came from it weren't worthy of living, but for their purpose she was willing to take any risk. Besides, the Assassin's Guild had sent enough information for her to be fairly sure of where their targets were, coupled with a few divinations. If it turned out that Roselynn was as far from the palace as they'd heard, she'd even be able to send back most of the items they'd brought with them.

As she approached the yawning abyss before her, Eziel murmured. "May the Lord of Light bless us, that we may purge all evil from the world."

~

"THERE YOU GO," Kanae said, nodding as she set the last crate in the cart. It clinked slightly from the glass inside, but she'd padded the vials enough that they wouldn't break unless someone dropped the crate.

She'd taken a full day to sort through her things and decide what she was keeping, which wasn't nearly as much as Kanae would like. Lots of things simply lacked portability, like her bed or the spring, so she'd had to make some hard choices. Losing the mirror was going to be frustrating, but she rarely used it anyway. In fact, Kanae couldn't remember the last time she'd had reason to use the mirror, which was why she'd reluctantly handed it over to Manog as well. It should help him in diagnosing injuries.

"That's it, then?" Madiel asked, the big man's voice rumbling deeply. He had four arms and had been an enormous help in clearing out the alchemy shed. He also looked a little unhappy about Kanae leaving, but that was hardly unusual around town at the moment. Kanae was mostly relieved that no one had spotted the guards Estalia had left behind. They'd certainly been keeping a lot of distance between them and the house, though.

"Yes, that's everything, at least for now," Kanae said, dusting her hands off. "Thank you, Madiel. It would've taken a long time to get that to town if it weren't for your help."

"I just wish you weren't leaving," Madiel replied, sighing as he grabbed the handles of the cart. "It's going to make the Abyss a lot more interesting to visit."

"I know it will. I'd suggest telling everyone to take it easy and be careful," Kanae told him, shaking her head. "I know I've helped pull people out of there when necessary, but I'm not going to be around for that anymore."

"True enough," Madiel replied, then smiled, obviously trying to keep his spirits up. "At least we have a little more time before you leave. I'll get this to Manog's shop safely, don't you worry."

"I'm glad to hear it. Unfortunately, I still have plenty to do inside," Kanae said, glancing toward the house. "I'll see you before I go."

"As you say, Kanae," Madiel agreed, then started trudging forward, pushing the cart as he went. Kanae watched him go for a minute, then headed for the house.

She opened the door and paused, seeing that Isalla had her armor on the table and was going over it closely, probably to make sure that it was in good shape after being in storage for a few months. Isalla looked up and blinked before asking, "Yes, Kanae?"

"I was just thinking that if I'd had someone else with me, this would have been a *very* awkward sight," Kanae replied, gesturing at the armor and closing the door behind her. Isalla's decision startled her a little, but it didn't surprise her much.

"Perhaps so, but we noticed that you've been taking pains not to let anyone get a good look inside the house, lately," Rose said, setting a box near the wall with a thump. "Isalla needs to refamiliarize herself with her armor and see if there's anything to be done about the gaps for her wings."

"That's a point," Kanae agreed, frowning as she thought about the problem. "I hadn't thought of that, and I don't know that I have a good solution."

"Neither do I," Isalla admitting, sitting back. "They're large enough to be problematic."

"True. We could try to fill them in, but it's very likely that Mother will offer to regenerate your wings in the capital," Kanae pointed out. "You really shouldn't need to worry about it, since I'm fairly sure getting to Silken Veils will be safe."

"Maybe so," Isalla said, sighing again.

"True enough," Rose agreed with a smile. "Based on what I've seen of her, she's almost certain to offer."

Kanae was about to say more, but then she stiffened as a mental alarm went off. After the surprise visit by her mother and the guards, she'd put up new wards that helped keep an eye on anyone who approached other than from the town. They were a

BENJAMIN MEDRANO

good way out, but even so, she wanted to be cautious. Especially since they hadn't heard anything more from the assassins yet.

"Someone set off my wards. I'm going to get my armor and investigate," Kanae said, heading for her current bedroom. She'd moved her armor rack into it for the moment.

"Do you want help?" Isalla asked, and Rose laughed.

"What, and let everyone know we're here? Let her go, Isalla," Rose said, shaking her head. Kanae couldn't help smiling as well.

"Right, right…" Isalla said, slumping back in her chair.

"Hopefully it's just one of Mother's guards, or maybe a bigger monster," Kanae said, starting to put on her armor. "Either way, I'd say to be ready for an attack, just in case. We've had enough surprises lately."

"Very true," Isalla agreed, watching Kanae with a worried expression. "Let us know if something's gone wrong?"

"Of course I will," Kanae said, smiling as she got to work. It wouldn't take her long to get her armor on, and then it would be a question of finding the intruder. That they'd come from the north made her feel… anxious.

# CHAPTER 49

*K*anae paused as she took another step to the north. Something felt wrong, and the forest was quiet. Too quiet for what it normally was like, and that meant that there was something dangerous nearby. That was normal enough in the hells, but even so, she recognized the sensation of being watched.

Glancing around casually, Kanae looked at the usual spots for predators that were native to the area and frowned slightly as she realized she couldn't see any. Her gaze rose slightly, and she resisted the urge to tense or let her gaze linger on the tree branches. Instead, she turned and meandered away, yet as she walked, her body was as tense as a coiled spring.

The branches of the trees to the north didn't bow like that naturally. After living here this long, she knew about how much weight the branches could hold, and the sight of them bowing that much made her lips thin. There were at *least* six branches with people on them, yet she hadn't seen anyone, which meant they were invisible somehow. Considering the open area above the branches, she suspected they had wings, and that meant either angels or demons, which—

The hissing sound was nearly silent, but Kanae reacted instantly, sidestepping and spinning around. An arrow glanced off her left shoulder with a sharp sound, and Kanae's sword cleared its sheath as she looked up and winced.

"You idiot!" a woman exclaimed in angelic, her voice filled with irritation. "If you're going to attack, *kill the damned hellspawn!*"

On one of the branches that she'd seen was an angel. He was in close-fitting armor which was darker than most armor angels favored, the breastplate dark brown, and he wielded a bow. As she watched, he nocked another arrow. The air shimmered, and Kanae cursed as fourteen *more* angels appeared all around him, all of them armed.

"Shit," Kanae murmured, and dove behind a particularly large tree as magic began to gather around the hands of three of the angels, and she internally was thankful that she didn't need to hide her magic anymore.

Gathering her own magic, Kanae prepared to strike back. Then she could start on her defenses properly. More than a dozen angels was a bit much with her current equipment. 

~

THE CRASHING SOUND echoed even inside the house, and Isalla froze for a moment, looking up from her armor at Rose. She swallowed and said, "That... didn't sound good."

"No, it didn't. And it came from the north," Rose said, her lips pressing together. "I don't think Kanae's magic could've made that sound."

"She said she used defensive magic and telekinesis, so probably not," Isalla said, scowling. "Help me into my armor? I'll help with yours."

"Right," Rose said, standing quickly and moving quickly to help. As she did so, Isalla flinched as she heard a cracking sound like thunder.

She hoped Kanae was okay. They hadn't managed to work out what was going on between them yet.

~

SIR QORR SWORE as he saw the lightning bolt lash across the sky. He glanced back at the other guards impatiently. "Come on, finish getting ready!"

"What's it matter if we're a little slow? We're just supposed to keep the two angels alive, not protect Her Majesty's daughter," Omna said, the woman pulling on her armor at a more relaxed pace than Qorr would prefer.

"Yes, but we're pretty far away so no one would spot us," Qorr replied sharply, looking across the rest of their team. "If she goes down too quickly, we can't get there fast enough to help."

"Isn't that a little paranoid, Qorr?" Kordon asked, picking up his two-handed sword in one pair of arms, and his shield with another arm. "We all saw the wards on the house. It'll take a *lot* to punch through them."

"You're assuming that Isalla and Lady Rose *stay inside*," Qorr retorted and saw all his companions pause at that.

"That... is a very good point," Marian said, the human woman frowning and quickening her pace. "I'd best hurry."

"Yeah," Omna agreed, looking distinctly unhappy at the thought.

Qorr didn't say anything more, satisfied that the others were at least taking it seriously now. He wasn't happy with how many of his fellow guards had decided that Her Majesty's daughter was expendable due to the queen's orders and their jealousy.

Besides, he'd been telling the truth, and was keeping an eye on the door of the house nervously.

"HOW IS SHE STILL ALIVE?" Eziel demanded to herself, firing another arrow at the woman, still angry about the injuries that several of her soldiers had sustained.

A shimmering field of purple light surrounded the demon, and the way Eziel's enchanted arrow bounced off made the angel still angrier. Despite being surrounded by six angels in melee, the demoness was holding her own and casting spells at the same time, which was simply shocking. Every spell seemed to layer yet another defensive barrier over the demoness, which was what was so ridiculous.

The woman had started with a telekinetic blast that shattered every tree within ten feet of her, sending wooden shrapnel everywhere and slightly injuring most of Eziel's company. Eziel's magi had lashed out with their own magic, but the demoness had dodged two of the attacks and blocked the lightning bolt with her barrier. Now she was as persistent as a damnable cockroach.

One of Eziel's magi lashed out with a spell to rip apart magic, and the purple barrier flickered. Eziel's eyes glittered with delight at the sight, and her soldiers down below attacked eagerly at the same time that she and the archers loosed their arrows at the woman.

The demoness's smile caused a hint of alarm to rush through Eziel, though, and the woman quirked a finger with one hand, her lips moving as she dodged two strikes, blocked a pair with her armor, and slipped her sword under the guard of one of her attackers, stabbing him in the gut and causing the man to fall with a cry of pain. One man was about to slam his sword home into her, but magic shimmered outward from the woman's grasp as purple tendrils took hold of Eziel's arrow and deflected it. Her eyes went wide in horror as the enchanted arrow slammed into the man's shoulder, and the sword fell from his suddenly nerveless grasp.

The other arrows didn't care about the betrayal of one of their number, though. One missed, three bounced off the woman's armor, leaving deep gashes in the metal scales... and one punched through, penetrating into the woman's side. She gasped, then laughed.

"Ah, fifteen heroic angels against a single, lone demoness... doesn't this bring back memories? How very valorous of you," the woman mocked, dodging and taking advantage of the confusion of combat to stab the man who'd been hit by Eziel's arrow in the leg, dropping him to the ground. "What next, another group of assassins?"

"That blasphemous... kill her already!" Eziel demanded, looking at the magi angrily.

One of them nodded and began weaving a spell, but a wave of heat caused Eziel to look up and she flinched, yelling. "Dodge!"

The woman in red armor was unfamiliar, but the blazing ruby-bladed sword in her hand was unmistakable, as were the wings on her back. Eziel almost missed the figure on the ground, wingless but wearing the armor of the Order of the Phoenix as she raced forward with a sword and shield in hand. Most important was how a column of fire was extending from the upraised ruby blade, and then it came *down*.

Eziel and the other angels quickly dodged to the side as a blade of fire ripped through the forest and through the trees where the magi had been standing, incinerating wood and setting the trees alight where it passed.

"Stand down and you will not be harmed!" the woman in red armor called out, her voice clear across the battlefield, magic seething within her sword. "Continue, and I will have no mercy on you!"

"Death to traitors!" Eziel cried out, gesturing forward one of her magi and hesitating herself as the demoness on the ground restored her shield, despite the arrow sticking out of her.

This wasn't going as planned, and even if the mage was skilled in countering fire magic, she needed to ensure that Roselynn and the other woman *died*.

"No demon queen, but I don't have time for this," Eziel muttered angrily, rage almost overwhelming her. So she reached into her quiver and found a different arrow, this one made entirely of mithral and with glittering gold feathers for fletching, the entire length marked with runes.

Taking aim at the demoness, Eziel muttered, "Block *this*, hellspawn."

And then she loosed the arrow.

Isalla rushed forward, then dodged to the side as an archer fired an arrow at her. She didn't quite get far enough, but raised her shield in time to block it. The enchanted tip bit through the steel face of the shield and partially out of the back, but it did its job.

A mage threw a spell at Rose, causing Isalla's heart to lurch in her chest, but Rose dodged, instead extending Ember and snapping out a quick incantation, launching a ray of fire at one of the archers and knocking her out of the sky.

Isalla focused on rushing to Kanae's assistance, wincing as she saw the damage done to the demon's armor and the arrow protruding from her side. Multiple scales of Kanae's armor were missing, and enchanted blades had cut deep into the pauldrons and vambraces. Kanae wasn't moving quite as adroitly as she usually did, and she was under attack by three warriors.

"Kanae, this way!" Isalla called out, and she smiled as Kanae began shifting in Isalla's direction, still dancing about, holding off her attackers, while multiple layers of enchantments enveloped her. Isalla had seen some magi use similar magic before, reinforcing their skin or armor with spells, but she'd never seen someone do both at the same time as well as a shield around them, though the barrier seemed mostly focused on spells or the like, since the swords of the nearby opponents cut through it.

As Kanae retreated, a glimpse of movement drew Isalla's gaze, and she paled as she saw the raven-haired angel's bow drawn and an arrow glowing on it that was far brighter than the others. Isalla spoke just as the woman let go of the bowstring. "Dodge!"

The arrow leapt from the bow like a thunderbolt, a crack exploding through the air loudly as multiple silver shockwaves exploded outward from the arrow's wake. Kanae started to dodge, but it was too late as Isalla watched in shock, then horror.

The arrow hit the barrier and didn't even slow as the spell shattered. A few fragments of the breastplate exploded outward as it hit Kanae's chest, and then it was through. Kanae only barely began to stagger, her lips parting as if to say something... and golden light erupted from the arrow.

An explosion of gold erupted across the clearing, along with a sound almost like a heavenly chorus. Isalla staggered under the reverberation, then looked up.

There was no one where Kanae had been standing, just an empty spot on the ground. The fragments of armor tinked as they hit a rock, and Isalla froze for a moment, disbelief rushing through her... and whispered softly, tears welling up in her eyes as grief tried to overwhelm her. "No..."

# CHAPTER 50

*K*anae's breath left in a rush as the arrow punched through all her defensive spells and armor effortlessly. How *mild* the pain was surprised her, considering the power it had to pierce everything else, and it didn't hurt nearly as badly as the other arrow that'd lodged in her side.

She opened her lips to tell Isalla she was okay, but that was when the arrow surged with immense magical power and golden light. Kanae didn't have time to resist as the magic rushed in and took hold of her, and with a flash of golden light, the world moved.

The teleportation was far more violent than any Kanae had experienced before, and she felt her stomach lurch hard, roiling painfully as she was ripped through space violently. Kanae came out the other side gagging, almost unable to hold down her nausea. Then, with pain rippling through her, she looked around and blinked in confusion.

Kanae was in the middle of what looked like a courtyard, with perfectly fitted white stones beneath her feet, and elegant fountains set into walls around the broad courtyard. Beyond the walls to either side she could see the upper branches of trees, their bark brown and leaves green, and above *them* was a brilliant, blue sky, a yellow sun, and white clouds.

More important was the temple-like building behind her, and what looked like a gleaming palace ahead of her, most of it white and with gleaming silver roofs to the buildings. Guards stood atop the gate to the palace and Kanae blinked. She knew she was in the mortal world now, but why had the arrow brought her *here*?

Magic rippled through the area, and all around the courtyard Kanae saw spells begin to form, just as an alarm sounded in the palace ahead of her. Kanae tensed, gasping out the words of a defensive spell, reforming the shield around her body, but as the spells around her took form, Kanae's heart sank.

"Oh, brimstone," Kanae muttered, despair overwhelming her.

Dozens, no, hundreds or thousands of arrows formed of pure magical energy took shape all around her, forming not only a line around the courtyard, but a full *dome* above her head. There were more than she could count, and the magic hadn't finished yet.

"This is going to hurt," Kanae said, tensing to try to dodge.

The arrows all launched forward at the same time, and no matter what she did, Kanae didn't see a way through them. Her barrier lasted less than an instant under the torrent and shattered. Her armor didn't last even that long.

At least the pain was over quickly, and everything went black as Kanae hoped that the guards would reach Isalla and Rose in time.

∼

ROSE HISSED ANGRILY as she blocked an attack, then used her attacker's stomach as a springboard to launch herself at the other. The woman in front of her looked startled, but she prepared to block, obviously not expecting just how ruthless Rose was feeling.

Ember sheared through the angel's wing effortlessly, setting multiple feathers on fire as it cut through them, and the woman screamed as she fell from the sky.

"You monster! You've betrayed your people and the heavens

themselves! Lay down and die!" A woman cried out, loosing another arrow at Rose, but it was all too easy to dodge with the enhancements the new armor gave her.

"Betrayed? Isalla was betrayed by those she trusted. Someone paid for me to be ambushed, another angel. Then *you* came here and killed someone who only offered us succor!" Rose retorted, lashing out with Ember, surging her mana through the blade, which amplified the power and turned it into a wave of fire that lashed out at her attackers.

The mage behind the woman hurriedly cast a spell and quenched the flames before they could reach the woman, and Rose's lips pressed together tightly. While she'd managed to take down two attackers so far, she wasn't sure how much longer she could last, especially with four tying down Isalla. Her friend was fighting frantically against one woman on the ground, her shield battered and with several arrows embedded in it.

A lightning bolt lanced toward Rose as she thought that, and she only partially managed to dodge, gasping as part of it discharged through her body, causing her muscles to spasm and her to go a little off course. At least it threw off the aim of the archers aiming at her, and Rose stabilized, feeling a wave of warmth rush through her body from her chest, easing the pain.

"Only as is appropriate, from what I've seen!" the woman cried out, nocking yet another arrow. "You deserve to fall here!"

Rose blinked as the man who she'd launched off suddenly descended from above, his sword held in both hands as he brought it down toward her, and she braced to block it, hoping her armor was strong enough to handle any arrows.

The next instant, a huge axe swirled through the air and hit the man in the side, knocking him away as he choked, the blade leaving a huge gash in his side that bled profusely. The axe kept swirling through the air until it was caught by a demon on the ground, the man in heavy armor and with four arms, two of them holding the axe, while one of the lower pair held a shield. He was accompanied by three others, all of them in midnight blue and silver.

Another man's hand flicked through the air, and a swirl of amber light flashed outward, sweeping aside the arrows that had just been loosed at Isalla. The black-skinned man grinned, and a hooded woman with abnormally thin fingers spoke. "By My Lady's Grace, may Her enemies have leaden wings!"

A cloud of darkness rippled across the field of battle, and all the angels Rose could see cried out as they were dragged to the ground, their wings stained black by magic. Rose had heard of such magic before, though she'd rarely seen it used by demonic forces. There just weren't any conflicts large enough to require it that she'd been involved in.

The last woman was vaguely draconic, and she launched toward one of the angels, snarling savagely as her claws extended. The man's eyes widened, having just gained his balance on the ground, then the mage was taken down by the woman's brutal assault.

"Who are you?" Rose demanded, her sword at the ready. The four-armed man was already charging toward the angels around Isalla, but she wasn't going to drop her guard yet.

"Queen Estalia left us to keep an eye on you and guard you during your trip back to the palace," the woman said, extending her staff and speaking a word. A length of glowing red light lashed out at the woman who'd been speaking to Rose, then turned into gleaming bonds that restrained the woman. Painfully, from the way the woman screamed, at least until it gagged her.

"Where were you when they shot Kanae?" Rose demanded, dodging as an attacker loosed an arrow at her, only for the angel to be promptly blown into a tree by the black-skinned demon's magic.

"Too far away," the demon replied, his voice about as deep as she'd thought it'd be. "We stayed out of Kanae's wards, but with preparing for combat and getting over here, that just took longer than we'd have liked."

"No time to talk, Qorr!" the staff-wielding woman said, and the woman and man both raised a magical shield as the last angel mage launched a beam of blazing light at Rose. Their shield blocked it, and Rose's fury reached a peak at last.

"That is *it*. Ember, may your fire consume all it touches!"

Rose cried out, raising the sword high as she poured her mana into it with reckless abandon.

The blade ignited, glowing even more brightly than it had at any point in the battle. Fire surged out of it, bombarding the area with heat as it rippled with her anger and rage. Only when it was blazing like the sun did Rose fix her gaze on the mage, and she saw his face pale with fear. She didn't let that stop her, though, and she brought Ember down with all her strength, releasing the hilt as the blade pointed at the man.

Ember shot across the landscape like a meteor, its fires burning all in its path. The angel let out a scream in the moment before Ember impaled him, but the scream didn't last more than an instant as the blade incinerated him and slammed through a dozen trees and into the hillside, burning a hole all the way. Rose extended her hand angrily and beckoned, and after a moment, the sword ripped out of the glowing hole in the hillside, spinning through the air as it returned to her hand.

"Hellfire, why didn't you do that *before*?" Qorr asked, looking stunned, but he cast a spell that caused one of the angels to stagger, looking confused before the man fell unconscious.

"It takes a lot of mana, and I can hardly control it," Rose spat, glaring at the demon. She wanted to take out her frustration on someone else, especially as she was upset about what had happened to Kanae, but all of the angels were pretty much dealt with. She growled under her breath, then quickly flew toward Isalla.

Her friend was frantically looking around the area where Kanae had vanished, and as Rose landed, Isalla looked up, tears leaving tracks down her face.

"Rose, she's *gone*!" Isalla cried out, her voice trembling. "One second she was here, and the next she was… she was…"

"I know, Isalla. I saw it happen, too," Rose said, hesitating before sheathing her sword, her rage starting to subside as she looked at the empty spot. There wasn't any sign of Kanae, and as she thought about how the demoness had fought fearlessly, despite being surrounded by over a dozen opponents, tears welled up in Rose's eyes.

Rose spread her arms, and Isalla rushed into them, sobbing

as her armor clanged against Rose's own. Hugging Isalla, Rose lowered her head and wept. She hated that she couldn't have stopped the woman who'd shot Kanae.

Why couldn't the guards have arrived just a couple minutes sooner?

# CHAPTER 51

Queen Estalia's guards had left Isalla and Rose to their tears, instead quietly moving about the former battlefield as they gathered the fallen angels together and put out the forest fire. Isalla wasn't sure why they were gathering the angels together, and was even more unsure as to why they'd stabilized those who'd lived. A third of the angels had died during the battle, but that still left ten of them, all of them injured to one extent or another. Isalla was a bit surprised that one of them wasn't dead, but she also didn't much care. They'd killed Kanae, and even now Isalla's eyes burned with grief, her tears only barely held back.

One of the demons, his skin black as pitch and with a pair of horns that protruded from his helmet, came closer and cleared his throat. He paused for a moment, then spoke, his glowing amber eyes bright against the darkness of the rest of his body. "Pardon me, ladies, but… while I must admit it's unlikely, it *is* possible that your companion is alive."

"What?" Isalla demanded, looking up at him suddenly, a little incredulous. "I saw that arrow engulf her in light!"

"Yes, but there was nothing left. That's unusual, Lady Isalla," he replied, his voice respectful. "As it *was* so unusual, and considering she's Her Majesty's daughter, I investigated and I found something else was unusual. What you saw was a *teleportation* effect, one so powerful it could ignore the ley lines to reach its destination."

"Are you certain?" Rose asked, standing suddenly, just as hope surged through Isalla, but the man raised his hands, as if to caution them.

"Calmly, ladies, please. Yes, I'm certain. Her Majesty has a few items capable of such, but they're expensive, and ours take a good deal of time to set up. One was left with us for emergencies, to return you to the palace quickly, but knowing how it works allowed me to see the similarities," the demon explained, his tone soothing, and his expression darkened. "That being said, if she *is* alive, I doubt she's in a good situation. I can't imagine someone using a weapon like that to teleport an opponent someplace nice."

"That sounds accurate to me. And if she *is* alive, Isalla, we can find her," Rose said, looking at Isalla with growing hope in her eyes.

Isalla felt her grief lessen, and she swallowed hard before nodding, speaking softly. "R-right. If there's a possibility, however slim, we have to check. The question is, how would we *find* her?"

"Her Majesty has an archmage who specializes in divinations in her employ. If you asked, I'm certain she would look for your Kanae. She *is* her daughter," the man offered.

"Very true. Rose? What do you think, after everything else we've gone through…" Isalla said, swallowing hard. "I really don't want to delay, not if we're to have a chance of finding Kanae."

"You're right. We've spent enough time here, and we drew down these… *things* on Kanae," Rose said, scowling at the angels angrily, and Isalla tensed. "Why did you even leave them alive?"

"Her Majesty will wish to question them and learn what they know," the man said, straightening slightly. "While killing them would have been easy, it's far more important to learn what we can from them."

"True," Isalla said, relaxing slightly, then took a deep breath and looked at Rose. "Let's grab what we can of the things that Kanae was going to bring with, alright? Then we can go."

"Sure," Rose agreed, still frowning at the angels. Then she looked at the man and asked, "I don't think we asked your name. How are you planning to get all of them back to the palace, anyway? There are only four of you."

"My name is Qorr the Shimmering," the man replied with a bow, then smiled. "As for transport, I believe this qualifies as an emergency, and we do have that teleporter. As soon as you're prepared, I think we'll vacate the area and take you to Her Majesty."

"Alright. Let's go get what we can, then we can go," Rose said, her expression hardening. "And if *anything* could make me even more determined to rip open this conspiracy you stumbled on and drag it into the open, Isalla, *this* did it."

"Agreed. Now I'm even more upset than I was," Isalla said, standing up and taking a deep breath, then headed for the house. Behind them, Qorr turned to his fellow soldiers, and Isalla took a mental note to thank him later.

For now, she just wanted to get together as much of Kanae's things as she could, then go meet Queen Estalia. She wasn't going to give up on Kanae, not yet.

ROSE DIDN'T HAVE MUCH of a chance to look around the palace, though at least peripherally she realized that the building was gorgeous, constructed to both awe and be defensible from sky or ground. The teleportation had been brutal, leaving everyone almost heaving, and some people did throw up, including several of the angels, to the point that the guards had to quickly keep them from choking on their own bile.

Even so, the guards quickly rushed Isalla and Rose through the palace, down wide halls that she half-wished she could tour more slowly. In short order, they'd been led to a sitting room with plush chairs, fine tables, and delicate-looking porcelain on display. Each of them took seats, and Rose was uncomfortable in her armor, considering the circumstances.

A maid bowed and spoke softly, her green scales slightly at odds with her delicate voice. "Her Majesty has been informed of your presence and will arrive as soon as she is able to. Would you like refreshments while you wait?"

"No," Isalla said shortly, and Rose nodded in agreement. She was in no mood to eat, not now.

"Very well, if you change your mind, simply ring the bell," the maid said, nodding toward the table and a bell sitting on it.

"Thank you," Rose said, then fell silent as the woman left the room.

For a long minute, they were silent. Then Isalla spoke softly. "I hate myself."

"Why?" Rose asked, blinking in surprise at Isalla's sudden comment.

"If I hadn't asked her for help *rescuing* you, she wouldn't have ended up like this," Isalla said softly, her voice filled with loathing. "We were taking our time deciding, too. Sure, she encouraged us, but they came for *us*. They were talking about how we were traitors, and... and I hate that I might have gotten her killed."

Rose swallowed, opening her mouth, then closing it again. She didn't know what to say, so she took some time to think. It took a minute, then she murmured, "You aren't the one at fault, Isalla. If anything, we both share some blame for what happened. I... didn't think we would encounter danger like as that. I never thought a group of such power would be dispatched after *us*. If Kanae is dead... I'm never going to forgive myself, even if I manage to avenge her."

"Well, fortunately for you, you won't *have* to forgive yourself," Queen Estalia said, her voice echoing through the room, and for the first time Rose didn't quite lose herself at the sight of the incredible woman. Estalia stepped into the room and waved off her guard, closing the door behind her firmly.

"You already found her?" Isalla asked, her voice eager as she stood abruptly, excitement on her face.

"One moment," Estalia said, shaking her head. She pulled out a tuning fork and gently rapped it against the bell on the table, filling the room with a soft, persistent tone. She examined it for a moment, then smiled. "There we are, no eavesdropping, hm?"

"Your Majesty?" Rose asked, blinking in surprise. She didn't think that this was a subject which needed to avoid eavesdropping.

"Ah, you're wondering about my caution? I'm always careful regarding this, but I believe that it's worth the risk of telling you in this specific case," Estalia said, smiling brilliantly at them. "I asked Kitania if she'd told you, but she said she hadn't. She's always so... *reticent*."

"What are you talking about? Didn't you have your archmage scry for her?" Isalla asked, looking as confused as Rose felt.

"No, I haven't. Unfortunately, Veldoran is out of the palace for a few days, on a trip to gather some rare reagents," Estalia said, her smile fading slightly. "Unfortunate timing, since I never expected something like this to occur. At least not now."

"Then why are you so sure that Kanae... no, *Kitania* is alive?" Rose asked, correcting herself carefully. "If you haven't performed divinations, isn't that a little too much to guarantee?"

"If it were anyone else in the world, whether the heavens, mortal world, or hells, I'd agree with you. But Kitania..." Estalia let her voice trail off, then shook her head, smiling sadly. "No, my little girl is alive. She's immortal, you see."

"What? But... all angels are immortal. So are the vast majority of demons," Isalla said, sounding even more confused.

"Ah, but you misunderstand. Yes, most demons are immortal... but Kitania is special, even among demons. She told you she survived the siege of Rosken, yes?" Estalia asked, raising an eyebrow curiously.

"Um, yes?" Rose confirmed, frowning. "I recall her saying it was a terrible battle, and that she lost a lot of friends there..."

"Yes, she did. There's a reason why I thought she died there," Estalia said, her smile fading again. "See, she was stationed on the central wall of Rosken. The epicenter of where the battle between the archangels, demon princes, and mortal gods fought. She was stationed in a place that, to this very *day,* rages with the wrath they unleashed, destroying the fortress and all the people inside it... all but Kitania."

"What? But... but *how*?" Rose asked, her eyes widening enormously.

"That is the question, isn't it? I don't know. We learned of her gift fairly early on, though we didn't know the extent of it. Kitania can heal from any injury, and even shrugs off transmutations in minutes or hours. Once, when she was terribly depressed, she threw herself into the gullet of a hellfire worm," Estalia said, and she scowled. "That was a bad day. She regenerated after we cut it open, much to my shock, considering how little of her was left. Afterward, we tested her regeneration power, and it proved resilient to every form of damage we could come up with. She even attempted to test it a few more times, to my horror, and *nothing* seemed capable of killing her, not even being turned to stone and shattered. Rosken... if anything could kill her, I thought that could do it. Yet it didn't. Some tiny fragment of her survived and came back."

"Heavens..." Isalla said, blanching, yet she let out a breath of relief. "You mean she's alive? For certain?"

"Nothing is certain in life, but I would bet my own life on her being alive," Estalia assured them, and her eyes hardened as she added, "That said, I don't intend to forgive the people who attempted to kill my daughter. I will have them tell me *everything* they know, and nothing will stop me from finding out."

"That sounds perfect to me," Rose agreed, taking a deep breath, then asked, "What about when your archmage returns?"

"When he returns, we'll find out where they sent Kitania, and then we'll figure out what to do from there. If she was sent to the heavens, we're going to have a problem. Anywhere else, though..." Estalia paused, then smiled. "We'll just have to retrieve her, won't we?"

"Agreed!" Isalla said, her eyes shining with hope at last.

"Very much so," Rose added, relaxing a little. The tangle of her emotions needed to be sorted out, and for that, she needed time with Kitania.

"In the meantime, I believe that we need to get the two of you settled into the palace," Estalia said, silencing the tuning fork with a touch, then looked at Isalla as she added, "And we really *do* need to discuss getting you your wings back, Isalla. Your armor doesn't fit quite right."

"Thank you," Isalla said, smiling with palpable relief.

Rose suddenly realized she was smiling too, and she murmured, "We're going to get her back."

# EPILOGUE

*A*t least she wasn't in pain when she woke this time, Kanae reflected, approaching consciousness at last. The last time she'd regenerated fully had been after being caught in a rockslide, and it had *not* been pleasant to have half her body still crushed in the rocks when she woke up.

This time she wasn't in pain at all, and Kanae kept her breathing slow and level as she took stock of her body. It wasn't just a lack of pain that had her alert. The temperature was comfortable, if slightly on the cool side, and she was laying on a bed or cot, from the feel of the thin pad beneath her. A cool pair of metal rings were around each wrist, and her hands were raised on the pillow, which gave her an idea of what sort of position she was in, especially with how it felt like her mana was being restricted.

Thinking back on her arrival in the plaza, Kanae winced internally and murmured, "That… really hurt."

"Most people who went through what you did wouldn't be in any position to say that," a woman replied, and Kanae tensed. She hadn't realized someone else was nearby.

Opening her eyes, Kanae looked around and blanched, blinking tears from her eyes at the light. It wasn't incredibly bright, but her eyes weren't used to it. She was inside what looked like a jail cell of smooth gray stone, a narrow window with bars on the wall behind her head. Toward her feet was a wall of bars, giving her no privacy at all, though the door was on the opposite side of the small cell, which made sense when she realized that the chains around her wrists were secured to the opposite corner from it. What made Kanae so nervous was how she could see magical runes carved into every stone brick and all the bars, meaning that an immense amount of power had been expended on the cell.

Outside the cell was a hallway that was mostly normal sized, and on the other side of it was an elven woman sitting in a chair. She had straw-blonde hair, brown eyes, and was wearing light chain that gave a good idea of her thin, athletic physique. She had a sword and horn at her belt and was otherwise surprisingly normal looking to Kanae.

"I don't suppose they would. Alas, I've always been a bit unusual, and—" Kanae began, moving her hands downward to sit up, and then suddenly paused, looking down at herself, and flinched as she murmured. "Oh. Oh, hellfire... the damage must have been worse than I thought."

Kanae was naked beneath the thin blanket, but that wasn't what prompted her comment. Instead, it was what she looked like that concerned her. Gone was the pale, faintly purple-tinged skin she'd possessed when she was last awake, instead she had a soft pink skin more suited to a flower than a demon or mortal. Her chest was larger again, and at a guess, she'd lost at least three or four inches of height.

"Oh? You seem to have recovered just fine. Despite traumatizing a goodly number of the housekeeping staff," the elven guard said, a hard edge to her voice.

"Yes, well, it wasn't exactly by choice. I haven't found a way to overcome my regeneration yet," Kanae replied, running a hand down her left arm. "I had a hard enough time keeping the transmutation spells carved into my bones from healing as it was. Alas, it appears that those didn't survive my... *experience*. I suppose I'll have to get used to my original body again."

The woman blinked, obviously startled, then pursed her lips as she looked at Kanae. She seemed to debate for a moment, then asked, "Those were transmutation spells? Someone thought they might be why you kept growing back, so decided to destroy your bones. Obviously, that didn't work."

"Yes. I *liked* being taller, thank you," Kanae said, then sighed. "So, where did I end up, anyway? I got shot with an arrow that teleported me. One second I was in the hells, and now I can tell we're in the mortal world."

"I'm not telling you," the guard said promptly. "Milady ordered you imprisoned, and she intends to question you in person."

"Oh, just lovely," Kanae replied, closing her eyes and inhaling deeply, trying to firmly step on her worries. "That means… likely in one of the border regions or in the Kingdoms of Light. Just lovely."

The woman didn't reply, but that was enough of an answer for Kanae. After a few moments, the woman asked, "What's your name?"

"If I tell you, will you return the favor?" Kanae asked, opening her eyes to look at the woman.

The elf considered for a moment, then nodded. "I don't see any harm there. I'm named Maura Eldwood."

"Nice to meet you, Maura, or as nice as it can be under the circumstances," Kanae said, and then she made a decision. If she had her old body, she may as well use her original name, or most of it. "My name is Kitania. I've taken several surnames over the years, but… Kitania works well enough."

"Indeed? Well, I'm sure Milady will be interested to hear that," Maura replied, smiling thinly. "It isn't every day that a demon intrudes into the home of a goddess."

Kitania winced, then murmured, "Well, that explains all the arrows. Do you have any idea when she's going to question me?"

"Not a clue. When she's ready to, I presume," Maura replied, looking amused.

"Well, that being the case… I suppose I may as well rest," Kitania replied, sitting back again and pulling up the blanket.

"You've been resting for three days!" Maura protested incredulously.

"No, I've been *regenerating* for three days," Kitania corrected, rolling over to face the wall. "There's a difference between being unconscious and rest."

Closing her eyes, Kitania dearly hoped that Isalla and Rose were safe. That was far more worrying than her captivity, at least to her.

~

"STILL NOTHING. Heavens help them if they're fooling around," Haral muttered, clenching her fists and breathing in deeply.

She hadn't gotten word from the strike team into Hragon yet, which was making her anxious. Her superiors wouldn't be pleased if they'd failed yet again, and she deeply wished to avoid their wrath. Considering for a moment, she came to a decision.

"If they failed, I'll deal with the problem *myself*, as soon as I figure out what happened," Haral said, truly annoyed. "I should've killed them both personally, despite the possibility of someone tracking their deaths to me."

Haral let out a breath and forced herself to relax. Despite her frustration, otherwise, things were going well. All they needed was time.

Then the heavens could return to the glory they truly deserved.

# AUTHOR'S NOTE

I'm a little surprised with how *Heaven's Fallen* turned out. Many characters surprised me, and the plot is only starting to truly get moving at this point, yet it's the best break in the story I could think of for the first volume of *Mantles of Power*. I can't guarantee how soon the second book will be out, titled *Mortal Gods,* but it's on my short list of projects.

To me, the story is fascinating because of how different so many characters are when compared to classic tropes, even when I intended things to turn out differently. How it will end... who knows for sure? Certainly not me, though I have a rough idea of where I want the story to go. I'm more than happy to allow Isalla, Kitania, and Rose to make their choices and see where it takes me.

I hope you enjoyed *Heaven's Fallen,* and would deeply appreciate it if you left a review. After all, reviews are the lifeblood of self-published authors.